THE
TREASONOUS

Rachael Ritchey

RR PUBLISHING

For Grammy

Love does not delight in evil
but rejoices with the truth.
It always protects, always trusts,
always hopes, always perseveres.
1 Corinthians 13:6-7

CHRONICLES OF THE TWELVE REALMS

The Beauty Thief (Book 1)
Captive Hope (Book 2)

TABLE OF CONTENTS

Crescent Cave Nation
Emlyn
Landon
Berne
Dark Lands
Taisce
Wyeth
Gonleth
Solfen River
Bear River
Parlan
Nashua
High Castle
Nevin
Larue
Desert Regions of Ahka
Tappen
Marodan
N
W
E
Opal Sea
Map of the Twelve Realms

CHAPTER ONE
EIGHTEEN MONTHS AGO

UNDER THE MURKY GUIDANCE OF predawn light, he half-dragged, half-hobbled up the loose rock crumbling from the side of Ophira's Peak. The clatter of tumbling debris echoed off the cliff face, but moving any other way proved impossible in his mangled state. With time not on his side, it was crucial he get out of sight before the morning sun made its appearance and revealed his location to the enemy.

If not for the remaining power of the life he'd already stolen, Nox would have died in that fall, but fate remained his steady companion. Still, the searing pain of broken ribs, clavicle and arms, as well as hundreds of cuts, deep bruises, and gashes made him almost wish he were dead. Almost. The thought of revenge kept him going. The royals would pay dearly for stealing away his fresh infusion of beauty's life-giving force.

It would be three years before another total lunar eclipse visited the realms, and they'd taken his amulet. He couldn't resist reaching for the empty space on his chest where it had hung. He cringed from the horror of its loss as much as the pain of moving his arm, but he vowed he would get back what they stole.

His wavering certainty whispered that they couldn't have pierced the amulet with the ruby arrow without also having killed princess Caityn. Surely she was as much dead by the hand of her beloved as Nox had been damaged so extensively in the fall without the restorative power of her stolen beauty. The thought of successfully undoing the curse remained inconceivable, but amid his agonizing crawl his scant hope rested wholly in their inevitable failure at shattering his precious amulet.

The curved halo of sunshine assaulted him from the right but afforded the exact balance of light and shadow to reveal the entrance to a small cave hidden among the slide of rock and rubble. He inched his way closer, growing more wary of exposure with each passing minute, but soon found himself within the welcoming darkness of the entrance.

Now hidden in the covert hollow, he had little concern over being apprehended. With a groan, Nox lowered himself to the floor and let unconsciousness overtake the throbbing aches of his aging, battered body.

The entire day slipped by as Nox let the power of time and stolen life force begin his healing while he slept. The essence of its magic gradually flowed away, and the need to repair bones and flesh used up more residual power than time alone, but Nox lacked control over it.

The power of life could be harnessed within the amulet, but once absorbed he could not direct it. This mattered not at all, since he desperately needed the assistance to heal if he were to make it back to the cave, to the locked room where his most-prized possessions were stored.

He woke and rolled his shoulders. The aches and pains still ravaged his body, but the bones mended little by little, which was all he wanted for his trek. Ignoring the tightness of his muscles, he worked his way to a standing position and crept toward the mouth of the cave.

The night sky glowed, awash in the waning light of the moon, perfect for him to sneak through the woods to the entrance nestled under the dead tree. Nox gauged the time to be midnight, which gave him several hours to slink his way through the heavy growth of trees and underbrush.

Consumed by the need to retaliate and recover the stolen amulet, Nox limped down the rockslide with practiced stealth and into the welcoming cover of the thick forest. Before the next midnight, he believed he could gain everything he needed to make his plan for revenge complete. No one would stand in his way.

Hours later, the healing effects of the remaining power continued coursing through his veins and aided his forward momentum, but it wasn't enough. Slicing, agonizing stabs bit into his ribs with each lift of a leg and every labored breath, but he dragged himself up the last steps and into the opalescent room of his hidden cave where he collapsed on the smooth rock floor. The moonlight reflecting off the walls offered a dim outline of the space and the dark presence of the stone seat at its center. It proved to be the last thing he beheld before consciousness faded from his eyes.

* * *

"I think he's coming to," a young man spoke from nearby, his voice hesitant.

Nox wanted to crack open his lids, but even that basic movement subsisted near the impossible. Instead, he stifled a groan and attuned his ears to the sounds of men now accosting his sacred room. He had no idea how long he'd been unconscious, but it must have been the rest of the night and most of the following morning. Or had it been longer? The quality of light filtering through his eyelids gave the impression daylight seeped into the massive den through the expansive opening of the south wall.

"He doesn't appear to be awake, Kelor."

"I swear he made a noise, and I saw his hand move."

One of them kicked at his leg, which Nox let flop lifelessly.

"He's still out cold. Is the captain almost here?" the second of the strangers asked, his voice already fading as he walked away.

"Hern said he arrives tonight," the first replied.

At least now he knew these men were soldiers. The prince must have sent them. Nox learned, when listening to the men he'd sneaked past in the forest, that Prince Theiandar had been successful in undoing all Nox's hard work. *May he suffer by my hands!* Centuries of successes wiped out by an overzealous young scoundrel. A furious rage simmered in the depths of Nox's dark soul at that news.

If true, why bother sending these men to Nox's lair?

As if it weren't bad enough that the young rogue prince had nearly killed him with that fall, Theiandar had also stopped the final, irreversible draw of Caityn's beauty from the amulet to Nox's body and *then* successfully stolen it back to her person. Nox desperately needed that refreshment before his near-death fall. Now! Now he'd be forced to journey a thousand leagues in his wretchedly aged state to obtain the elements necessary to remake the shattered amulet.

Revenge would not be enough. No.

Nox would not live in secret anymore. Once he regained his youth and vigor, the prince would regret the day he ever interfered in Nox's simple, unassuming life. He only wanted to live. Couldn't anyone understand an all-consuming need drove him? It was not want but need—pure need—which required stealing the beauty of innocents…but only just enough. Never too much.

A reluctant admiration settled within the hatred in his heart. No one had ever done what Prince Theiandar had done, and now Nox vowed to rob the prince of so much more than beauty.

He would destroy everything the prince had ever loved.

Everything.

"Sir, he's definitely awake. What d' you want me to do?"

"Truss him up, Kelor. Why haven't you done it yet?"

"Well, sir, he's all bruised and old. It didn't seem right."

"I don't care how old he is," the other man said from somewhere nearby. "If he's in here, he's probably dangerous. Or for all we know he's one of the Crescents sent to steal and spy. King Orn will want a report about him right away. Here."

Nox heard something *whoosh* through the air and the distinct *thwap* of loose rope slapping on rope as the nearer man caught the item. The soldier's firm grasp clapped on his wrist, yanking it down to meet his other one behind his back. Nox's eyes shot open as he jerked his hand out of the still-loose rope before the loop tightened.

"Woah! He's awake!" the greasy-haired Kelor shouted.

Two more guards ran over and gripped Nox's arms. He stopped fighting as lack of food and still-healing injuries reminded him of his weakness and that he needed to live in order to exact his revenge.

The realmsmen were quick about their work, trussing him up like an animal. The raven-haired, thin man dressed in black who'd first spoken to Kelor squatted down next to Nox's face and tilted his head to look eye to eye. "What have we here? Are you spy? Traitor? What have y' locked up in that room yonder?"

"You'll never know."

Nox watched the man's eyebrows rise in challenge at his soft-spoken pronouncement and an uncontrollable mocking grin slipped across his craggy face.

"We'll see 'bout that, old man." The black-clad man stood and kicked Nox in the stomach.

Nox gasped and sputtered as fresh pain rippled over him.

"If you won't tell me, I'm certain King Orn will extract what he wants by other, less pleasant means."

Whoever the young pup was, he would regret what he'd just done. He would regret it. In the meantime, Nox would gather as much information as possible to determine his next move. Capture hadn't been expected, but men could be bought. Nox knew this tale of greed—one stretching back through the ages—he knew it better than any man alive, for he'd lived a thousand lifetimes.

He turned to the rascal who'd been standing guard over him and said, "Lad, would you help an old, injured man to sit up? I mean you no harm."

"Suppose it couldn't hurt," Kelor said and wrapped his fingers around Nox's upper arms, lifting his fragile frame to a sitting position. He dragged him back five or six feet to lean against a wall.

"Thank you. I'm tired and parched."

Kelor looked at him sideways but soon understood the implication of the unspoken command and walked a short distance to a bucket of water placed near the stone throne at the center of the room. His wary eyes never left Nox, but he brought the water back.

"Here y' go, old man."

"Thank you," Nox said and drank from the ladle. He relished the feel of the liquid slipping down his burning throat and along the age-worn creases of his face before dripping onto his bloodstained shirt.

"What's in the locked room?"

Nox leaned his head against the wall and smiled at the boy, for to him these soldiers were nothing but children at play. "Tis nothing."

"Can't be nothing. That lock is like nothing we ever saw before. If there's a lock, it has to be something important."

"Mayhap 'tis locked to make you think there is something important within. Mayhap 'tis only a distraction."

He studied the confused look on the soldier's face and relished the knowledge that a seed of doubt had been planted. It only ever took a seed. Doubt was a powerful magic entirely its own.

CHAPTER TWO
THE PRESENT

AHMAD SPRAWLED OUT ON HIS stomach on the ground and waited for the signal. It would be any second, but he lowered his head to his forearm and took a final, deep breath to still his nerves. The pungent scent of damp earth and decomposing leaves permeated the close, hidden space, but Ahmad found that preferable to the stench of his and the other knights' days-old sweat.

The only discernible sounds were the hushed footfalls of their target who slinked through the ravine below. The Crescents knew they were being tracked, made evident by the hand motions they used in place of words to communicate. But equally clear was their lack of awareness they'd been located because they continued to move forward at a snail's pace in a compact, single-file line.

Ahmad flexed his fingers, attempting to bring warmth back into the frozen tips. The chill of the approaching winter hung fast with each passing day, but still the Crescent raiders crossed the borders of Emlyn in search of Almighty knew what. Thus far, the realmsmen knights captured none of the sneak-thieves, and when on the extremely rare occasion they came close to apprehending even one, the man would take his own life before being captured.

This time, the captain Ahmad served under had gained the help of a local man to track the Crescents, and the plan to drive them into the ravine had succeeded. Now they would cut off the Crescents' escape while keeping at least one alive. It made no sense to Ahmad why the men would take their own lives. The realmsmen were not interested in anything but discovering the truth behind why the Crescents continued to venture over the border even after they had negotiated a tenuous peace treaty between the kings.

A branch snapped, breaking the stillness of the thick forest, and the men in the ravine froze in place for half a second before changing formation, spreading out in either direction down the corridor of the foggy ravine.

The whiz of an arrow sounded next, followed by the cry of a Crescent to raise the alarm.

Ahmad jumped to his feet at that signal, sword already held tight in his grip as he slid down the embankment, using his free hand to balance against the side, stirring up rotting leaves heavy with forest dew in his mad dash to the bottom. He joined the fray with seven other knights, and more still were on the ridge above, shooting arrows in a pattern meant to spook and contain the foreigners. They fired to injure any escapees but not kill.

The voice of the guardsmen's captain rang out above the din. "Men of Crescent Cave! Cease your battle and lay down your arms. You are surrounded with no chance of escape."

Ahmad reached the bottom on hearing the last sentence and came face to face with a man with a wild look in his eye. He barely took another step before the man fell on his own sword. He looked to the next nearest man, who did it too. The same insanity happened along the ravine.

Ahmad vaulted over a log in one quick movement, sheathed his sword in the next, and tackled a Crescent from behind. He attempted to grab the man's wrist, which held a knife poised as if ready to inflict self-harm.

"Oh, no you don't," Ahmad said amid a grunt as the two toppled to the ground.

He had no difficulty wrestling the knife away from the slight man, but as soon as Ahmad had him disarmed and pinned to the ground, he discovered why it was so easy.

"You're nothing but a boy."

"I'll never speak," the boy squeaked out in a high-pitched soprano.

That voice arrested Ahmad's attention. He saw how fear shone brightly, made clear by the impossibly huge whites of the boy's eyes against the thick, dark dirt smeared across his youthful face.

"You can torture me, but you'll never learn the truth. I'd rather die."

That heavy northern accent did nothing to mask what Ahmad slowly realized: the boy was actually a girl.

He balked, sitting back, then yanked the hood from the girl's head and shook his own in consternation. Without ceremony, he snatched the hood back up over her head, effectively hiding the upper half of her face. *What is this secret that even girls barely out of nappies will die to protect? Whose secret?* He stood and pulled the young girl to her feet, his hand wrapped around both her wrists. Reluctance slowed his decision to tie her hands behind her back, but it couldn't be avoided.

While he tied them, he leaned in and whispered. "Do not let anyone see you are a girl. Tis bad enough you are a child."

She twisted her head to the side and spit at the ground by his feet in answer, but Ahmad sensed she comprehended the danger her hidden femininity might muster.

The entire attack and capture happened in the space of five minutes. He dragged his prisoner over to where the other men gathered around their captain and, in short order, decided she would be safer if no one knew she was a girl. Ahmad noticed that three of the nine in the raiding party had been taken alive. It looked as though five were dead. One had escaped.

"Good work, men," the captain said. "Six unsuccessful months of trying to capture even one of their ranks has been galling, but now we are getting somewhere. Our odds were better today with such a large group of them. Well, very good. Sir Ahmad, you get these prisoners back to camp alive. Chose six knights for your company and start back."

"What of the rest of you, sir?" Ahmad asked.

"Some will bury the dead. I'll have a unit join the tracker to follow the one who escaped."

"I could be a help to the tracker, sir," Ahmad said.

"Your skills are renowned, but the tracker knows these woods better than anyone, and I need a leader I can trust to deliver these men to camp."

Ahmad wanted to argue, feeling his tracking ability far outweighed his prisoner transporting, but it would be poor form. Besides, he'd received high praise by being entrusted with such an important duty.

"Yes, sir."

The captain nodded and shifted his attention to the tracker. Ahmad stared a moment longer before he called out to his friends from the high prince's guard who'd also volunteered to come protect the border of Emlyn against the sneaking invasions by the Crescents. Between the five of them and the men who already had custody of the other two prisoners, they would have the manpower required for the task.

They had a five-mile journey back to where they'd last made camp, and the noon hour had come and gone. With one gravely injured captive, they moved at a snail's pace. They spread the prisoners out between themselves, not willing to entertain the possibility of them doing anything underhanded that might jeopardize the mission.

Their horses had remained at camp, which meant tramping over uneven terrain through the towering forest of pines, spongy soil, and overgrowth with the chill of the oncoming winter making itself known in biting gusts throughout the the afternoon. Ahmad resisted the urge to shiver. Did one cold day more matter?

He took the lead but couldn't resist looking over his shoulder to check on the girl. His concern earned him a glare in return, but it did not sit well that the northern kingdom of Crescent Cave sent children—girls, no less—who looked to be no older than fourteen out on such deadly missions. What were the Crescents playing at? And why wouldn't they admit that these were their people?

The three prisoners appeared to range in age from fourteen to thirty. The oldest kept repeating to the others, "Never speak—never, upon you lives." Eventually the man who had custody of him jammed a fist in the bound man's face and demanded silence. Quiet accompanied them the rest of the way.

Two and a half hours later they arrived at camp. The sun had not yet descended below the horizon, but the canopy of brittle needles and rough branches blocked out most of the light, leaving them in relative darkness.

When they arrived at their destination, the camp bustled with activity as they prepared the evening meal, and men clamored to get a hot serving before the best portions of it were gone. Ahmad had to admit he longed for a proper meal. He'd been here for three months, protecting the borders, attempting to capture at least one enemy soldier. He'd just never expected it to be a child.

They led the prisoners to a small fire and tied each to separate trees near the spot. Ahmad took charge of the girl again and fought back a surge of pity. Through the thick layer of dirt covering the prisoner's face, Ahmad thought she looked both scared and defiant.

While he kneeled in front of the child and adjusted her restraints, he said, "Just tell us what we need to know, and you will be safe."

The defiance he met with doubled, but no words passed the youngster's pressed lips.

Ahmad rocked back on his heels and squeezed his temple. He ran his hand through his hair. What would it take to get information out of these people? He saw a meager chance of avoiding torture if they kept up the silent treatment.

"Listen to me. I know you're scared and you think whatever secret you're protecting is important, but no secret is worth losing your life over. Please, just tell us what it is you're doing in our lands and what you're searching for."

"Some secrets are worth dying for."

He frowned at the conviction in her low tone but had no idea what else to say to convince her otherwise. He shook his head and tried to ignore the defeated feeling.

"Sir Ahmad?" someone asked while approaching from the main camp.

He turned his attention toward the man who'd said his name and stood up to await his arrival. The other man, a guardsman of High Castle by the insignia on his tunic, laid his fist across his chest and made a slight bow. "Sir, I have just arrived from High Castle. You and the rest of unit Delphor have been summoned."

"How soon?"

"Immediately."

Ahmad's brows knit together. "Anything serious?"

"The heir to the throne was born one week ago. They will hold his dedication ceremony in three weeks' time. Delphor's presence has been ordered by High Prince Theiandar. He has sent men to replace your unit here at the border."

Idra's face flashed, unbidden, before his eyes. The fleeting glimpse twisted in his chest, but he suppressed the sudden desire to hold her in his arms again. Instead, he nodded. "Thank you for your report. We'll leave at first light."

"Unless something changes, that baby will never reign," the girl said from behind Ahmad.

He sensed a tone of melancholy in the words. Ahmad swiveled around and glared at the captive. Without thought, his hand went to the hilt of his sword.

"Are you making a threat to the crown?"

"No," she replied without malice or hesitation. "But there are powers at work of which you know nothing."

Ahmad got down to the girl's level and looked her in the eye. "What powers? Explain."

She stared back into Ahmad's eyes, but the knight saw darkness and defiance in the deep almond shapes before the young girl turned away with her lips clamped tight. She would be no help to Ahmad, and her words only caused the knight further distress as he now contemplated the safety of their future high king.

He stood but kept his eyes trained on her. She verged on womanhood, lanky but still so much a girl with the soft roundness of youth still present in her cheeks. He regretted she had to be secured this way. Ahmad's heart told him this girl should be knitting sweaters with the wool of her sheep while sitting next to a toasty Crescent Cave fire, not sitting upon the hard earth with a rope digging into her body or restraints upon her wrists. His jaw clenched at the frustration of it all. Why were the Crescents doing this? Why did they test the Realms and taunt toward war?

"If you change your mind, ask for me. I am Ahmad."

The girl glanced at him, and Ahmad thought he saw fear in her eyes before she turned away again to stare off into the distance where the horses grazed in an open field.

With a stifled huff, Ahmad walked away, ready to get some dinner and prepare the others of Delphor, High Prince Theiandar's personal guard unit, to return to High Castle. It seemed a waste of time to attempt to gain anything else from the girl. Ahmad hoped after a night in captivity she'd change her mind.

Ahmad took his bowl of thin stew and sat down on a log at one of the many fires scattered throughout the camp. There were other men gathered; some he knew, some he did not. Most of them talked and laughed together, but Ahmad's thoughts distracted him too much to heed them while he ate. The captain of his unit startled him when he called his name.

"Yes, sir?" Ahmad stood with his half-empty bowl in hand.

"Don't get up. Finish your supper. You certainly earned it today."

Ahmad nodded and sat back down. The captain lowered himself onto the log next to Ahmad with an exhausted grunt and leaned forward with his elbows resting on his knees. Ahmad waited for him to speak.

"I just returned and was informed Delphor has been called back to the high prince's side."

"Yes, sir, but they sent reinforcements to take our place. I think you'll find they're worthy replacements."

"Yes, Sir Ahmad. I am sure you are correct. I have a favor to ask. With the successful capture of these men, I am renewing the effort to capture more. If I am to do this, I can't spare the men necessary to escort these prisoners to the stronghold at Castle Emlyn. I need you and your men to take them. You will only add one day to your return trip."

"Certainly, sir. It would honor us to handle the prisoners' transport to the castle. We leave at first light. Are there extra horses available to carry the prisoners?"

The captain nodded. "Thank you. You've made my job much easier. I've come to trust you a great deal. You've proved to be a worthy asset, and I'm sorry to see you go, but if what I hear is true, it means you have much to celebrate upon your return to High Castle."

"Yes. The High Prince and Princess have given the entire kingdom a reason to celebrate." They grasped arms in friendship and respect. "Thank you, Captain, for your confidence in me and my fellow guardsmen. I pray your time here will be successful."

The captain's broad smile revealed his unspoken thanks before he strode away toward his tent. Ahmad watched him go and silently prayed for the man's protection. He'd proven himself a capable and honorable leader.

CHAPTER THREE
WHAT A SURPRISE

ONE DAY OF TRAVEL BROUGHT them to the gates of Castle Emlyn, having come disturbingly close to losing the eldest of the prisoners when he attempted to throw himself from his horse into a canyon along one particularly slim section of trail. From that point forward, they tied securely the prisoners to their mounts with shackle upon their wrists.

Ahmad hated the need for such restraint, especially after hearing Gavin relate how his cousin Lady Idra had described being shackled and carted off by that dastardly mercenary, Zaide. Thinking of that time made him regret his impulse to volunteer on the borders. It took him away from her again—not that he had a chance of securing her affections, but he longed to be near her.

If he'd been there then he wondered if he might have prevented Lady Idra's abduction and won her heart, but he couldn't change the past. He hoped for Idra's comfort and still wondered what she meant by returning her handkerchief to him. He dared not believe she'd hidden it in his satchel as a declaration of love, but it seemed possible that she gave it in friendship, though he wanted a great deal more.

"Ahmad, we're within sight of the drawbridge. Tis up. Why do you suppose that is?" Zaccur, another of High Prince Theiandar's guardsmen, asked, disrupting his musings.

Ahmad took a second to compose himself and get his thoughts under control before looking toward the castle. To see the drawbridge raised in full daylight left Ahmad with misgivings.

"Could it be repair work? Or possibly a threat of some sort?" Ahmad asked.

"Nothing looks out of place, and I see nothing in the surrounding area to imply foul play."

"That copse of trees is thick and may hide any smoke if there are intruders camped nearby. We'll approach with caution. Parker can ride ahead and announce us."

He gave the order. Parker passed off the reigns of the girl's horse to Ahmad, then rode at a fast clip toward the raised approach to the castle.

The castle of Emlyn sat on a huge section of rock jutting out of the landscape. A valley flanked two sides, a unique combination of slate and granite spires rose on another, and interspersed throughout were shadowy nooks and crannies, fertile river meadows, and forest. The only entrance into the castle followed along a natural ridge with a drop-off on either side and a wide path carved out of the hard surface and lined with short stone walls.

Ahmad found the whole of the place to be rustic and yet majestic. Emlyn's castle stronghold was the oldest of the castles in the Realms, and its ancient atmosphere drew him in. He felt it impossible to wander the castle without the ghosts of the past and histories untold seeping into his bones.

He observed the lowering drawbridge, its halting motion accentuated by the creaks and groans of ancient wood. Parker slowed upon his return and positioned his mount to face back toward the castle. Ahmad moved to ride next to him, the girl on her horse just behind them.

"All is well, Ahmad. They were quick to lower the bridge as soon as they saw us as realmsmen."

"Disconcerting," Ahmad said and looked into the distance, eyeing the forest once again for any signs out of the ordinary.

"We'll find out soon enough," Parker said, his hand held out to accept the girl's lead rope from Ahmad.

Ahmad handed it to him and urged his horse to move faster toward the drawbridge. He arrived at the castle gate fifty yards ahead of his fellow realmsmen and dismounted before the horse had come to a full stop. The gatekeeper moved out from the shadows and bowed to him.

"Why was the drawbridge raised?" Ahmad asked without preamble.

The man bowed again. "There came an attack on Queen Moira two nights ago, most worthy knight. The king is taking precautions only."

"What of the attacker?"

"The queen killed him. He was a regular merchant at the castle, but the consensus believe him to be a Crescent spy."

Ahmad studied the gatekeeper, instinctively comparing the man to his own father, the gatekeeper of Castle Nevin. While the man appeared polite and succinct, he lacked any warmth or intelligence in demeanor or mien. He delivered the attacker's fate without an ounce of feeling one way or the other, as though death were all too familiar.

"That is disturbing news, but thank you for the report, keeper. Has the king been informed of our arrival?"

"Yes. I sent the boy to give word to the steward, who will be telling the king any minute, I suspect."

Ahmad nodded and thanked the man. He walked toward the stables, the others having arrived at that moment, and handed off the reins to a stable boy. He unstrapped the girl-disguised-as-a-boy prisoner from her saddle, and she slid off to land unsteadily on her feet. She'd refused the bulk of the food offered and drank next to nothing. It gave the impression that she wasn't trying to die so much as punish herself. For what? Foolish.

Five knights of the castle approached. The one in the lead Ahmad recognized as Sir Drew. They'd met when Prince Theiandar and Delphor unit had made their regular rounds through the Realms during the last four years, but he did not know him well.

"Sir Drew," Ahmad said and lowered his head a fraction as a sign of respect. "We've come from the patrol camp to the north with prisoners, people of Crescent Cave, apprehended on our land. Captain Jericho ordered them brought to the castle at Emlyn for interrogation."

"This *is* good news you bring. How were they taken alive?"

Word had traveled throughout Emlyn of what the Crescents were doing when facing capture. Sir Drew's familiarity with the desperate acts of these men didn't surprise Ahmad.

"The Great One gave us success that day. We have captured three."

"Very good. The king will want to know right away. Come."

Sir Drew turned and his fellow knights parted to let him pass, then followed behind. Ahmad and his men did the same, escorting the prisoners. The men strode toward the keep in relative silence, but the stilled movements of the castle folk didn't go unnoticed. Ahmad had never perceived such a sense of unease in Emlyn before.

They marched toward the great hall where important meetings were held. The castle had none of the extravagance of High Castle or even the simple elegance of Taisce. Their ancestors had built it as a true outpost castle with little in the way of opulence or luxury outside what the king deemed necessary to appease the desires of his wife and six daughters.

King Ekreton stood near the far fireplace in a heated discussion with another man. Ahmad recognized him as the steward. As they approached, he picked out bits and pieces of the conversation when their voices rose and fell.

". . . imbeciles who . . . outrageous to expect we . . ."

". . . unforgivable, Sire. I apologize for bearing this unpleasant news."

"You should. Now, tell Cook we have guests."

"Yes, Sire," the steward said with a bow and strode from the hall.

King Ekreton breathed deep and released an exasperated huff. He turned toward Ahmad and the others, who waited some ten feet away for his permission to approach. Ahmad saw the tension in the king's jawline and the repetitive clenching of his right fist but had no inkling what the bits of conversation he'd heard meant.

The king finally seemed in control of his temper but spoke in clipped sentences as he moved in their direction. "Well. Unpleasant business. You have arrived from the north, I take it. You had better have good news, otherwise turn around and leave."

Sir Drew cleared his throat—covering a laugh, Ahmad thought. "They come with spies to interrogate, Sire."

"Spies you say? This is good news."

His face brightened, though Ahmad knew he didn't mean it in a sinister way. King Ekreton had been responsible for keeping peace at the borders with Crescent Cave, and over the course of the last three years the other nation complicated relations. Increasingly, the Crescents had been threatening to raid, to pillage, to plunder.

They had done it many times, but there should have been a ceasing of all quarrels, skirmishes and sneak-thievery since the time High King Dante and Prince Theiandar had traveled to Emlyn to sign a peace treaty with King Donegold of the Crescents. King Ekreton of Emlyn grew desperate to put an end to whatever underhanded deeds ensued, the happenings for which King Donegold vehemently denied being responsible.

"Yes, Sire, these . . . men are from Crescent Cave," Ahmad replied, gesturing to the three who were shackled, and hesitating over whether to reveal that one of them was a girl. "We were ordered to deliver them to you for interrogation on our way to High Castle. Unit Delphor must leave in the morning to complete our journey."

One of the king's thick eyebrows curved up in question. Ahmad stared into his expressive dark eyes and waited for his orders. King Ekreton's mustache twitched at the corner, but otherwise his expression remained unreadable. Ahmad waited.

"Take those two to the dungeon. The girl will go to the tower room," the king said with a tone of bemusement. He put his hand on Ahmad's shoulder. "I see I've taken you by surprise, but when you have six daughters, you learn to recognize that special look of defiance only a brave young woman can master. Sir Drew, escort our guest to the tower. I'll have Cook send up water for her to wash."

Ahmad's hand dropped from the girl's arm. She looked angry, defiant, and frightened in the same instant as Sir Drew pulled her toward an inner doorway. But her pleading gaze—*pleading for what?*—locked on Ahmad, who held nothing but worry over her well-being.

She disappeared out of view and the king clapped him on the back, bringing his attention around.

"Ah, Sir Ahmad, with the way these Crescents are, you may have just saved that young girl's life, and I assure you she will be treated well here. If we can discover their motives, they may be freed, if they have caused no mischief in our lands.

"Stay and rest, then you may leave at first light. Take whatever provisions will be necessary for your journey. I will have a letter for you to deliver to the king as well."

"Yes, Sire," Ahmad said and bowed.

The king walked away from the group without another word. Ahmad watched him go and considered the burden the king carried, keeping the integrity of the border with Crescent Cave while also ensuring his realm stayed healthy and well provisioned. It seemed a daunting task considering the way the Crescents were continually pushing the boundaries to the limit. In recent years no one had died due to the unstable relationship between the two nations, but bad blood haunted them still, opening the door to new feelings of suppressed anger and vengefulness.

Ahmad did not envy King Ekreton in the slightest. On that consideration, he and the other men retired to the barracks to eat and rest, but worry over the girl in the tower filled his mind. Hours later he admitted to himself with great reluctance that something about her would continue haunting his mind. To set his thoughts at ease, he decided to check on her one last time. At the landing of the winding, circular steps to her tower cell, Ahmad found a guard near the heavy wooden door and one torch burning on the wall opposite the guard. The man stood tall as Ahmad approached and nodded.

"I'd like to speak to the prisoner. Open the door."

The guard hesitated only a moment, but soon grabbed the key from his waist. "She's not eating, sir," the man explained as he unlocked the door.

Ahmad sighed at the revelation, not surprised but disappointed. "I'll see what I can do. Thank you." He stepped into the dim room, his torch the only thing lighting the open space.

The door closed and the bar dropped in place, locking him in as his eyes scanned the rounded room for the girl. He found her, now garbed in clothing befitting her fair sex and huddled on the floor against the stone wall under the barred window placed high in the wall. He smelled the damp of the room and fresh hay, which must have been used to stuff the mattress on the pallet bed secured to the wall on his right. She'd been given a blanket and pillow. Ahmad, knowing of what this girl could be capable, worried what she might choose to do with the kind offerings, but he prayed to be wrong about her will to live.

He cleared his throat and noticed the plate of food by the door. Ahmad picked it up and placed it on the edge of the bed, taking the fresh roll from it and bouncing it on his palm as he approached. She didn't move and reminded him of a scared animal hoping to disappear into its surroundings. He slid down the wall and sat next to her with the roll held out for her to take. It took a minute, but she snatched it from his hands and bit off a chunk.

"I leave at first light, but I wanted to make sure you were well."

"Why? Because I am a girl?" Her question sounded more inconvenienced than annoyed. "I can kill you just as easily as any boy." She took another, bigger, bite.

"Where I come from the women do not do the fighting. It is different in Crescent Cave?"

"Yes," she said around the bread in her mouth.

Ahmad had never heard of the women of the north being warriors, and it surprised him. The idea didn't entirely put him off after having seen the hidden champion within Lady Idra in her time of distress, a concealed strength to which he found himself further drawn, but it still felt wrong to him.

She swallowed and motioned forward. "Drink."

The way she commanded Ahmad surprised and amused him. He smiled and got up to get her the cup from the tray. After he stood, he slipped the torch into the holder fastened to the wall and came back to sit by the girl.

As she guzzled the small portion of water, he asked the same question from the day she'd been captured. "What's your name?"

She finished drinking and swiped at her mouth with her sleeve. "Sh-Sabine."

Ahmad stared at her, sure she'd just lied but relieved to realize she'd put her guard down at least a little. "Sabine?" he asked. He watched her nod once without looking up from the cup in her hand. "From where in Crescent Cave do you come, Sabine?"

She kept silent, and he wondered if she regretted having answered his question. He didn't want her to shut him out, so he asked her age instead.

"I'm not a child. I'm sixteen," she responded with a hint of rebelliousness in her voice.

"No, not a child in some ways and still so much so in others." Ahmad laid the back of his head against the stone wall and sighed. "You should not be here, Sabine."

They sat in silence before Ahmad rose and pulled Sabine to her feet, guiding her to take a seat on the bed. He set the tray of food on her lap.

"I know you think you are protecting someone or something by offering your life and keeping a secret, but I believe nothing you hide from us is worth your life, Sabine.

"Promise me you will eat and not harm yourself, no matter how long you're here. I will continue to inquire after your welfare. It will be many months, but I'm told the only thing that will set you free is for you to tell the truth regarding your ventures into our lands. If you refuse this, I fear you will never leave here."

"You might be surprised, sir," she said and dipped the spoon in the stew. Before the tepid meaty concoction passed her lips, she whispered, "I promise."

"And I swear to you, Sabine, you will be treated kindly here. The men you were with, though in the dungeon, will also see fair treatment. King Ekreton is a good man. Blame it on Almighty blessing him with six daughters, but the man is soft under that gruff exterior."

He nodded once as a sort of farewell and left the room, not fully satisfied with the outcome of their successful capture of

Crescent spies. It would drive him to distraction, wondering about this girl, but he had no other part to play here.

He went in search of Sir Drew and gained the other knight's agreement to send word of anything regarding the prisoner Sabine. Ahmad thanked him and went to rest before they left in the morning.

CHAPTER FOUR
TRAVEL HOME

THREE DAYS OF TRAVEL FROM sunup to sundown brought the five knights to the open gates of Wyeth Castle. The night grew long, darkness having settled over the land an hour earlier, but exhausted or not, they anticipated real beds and food within the castle walls. Ahmad knew they would first need to announce their presence at the keep before seeking rest.

"You men go on to the stables, and I'll meet you at the barracks," he said as he jumped down from his horse in front of the keep entrance.

He handed his reins to Parker and watched the others canter away, then knocked. He endured a long pause followed by muffled voices on the other side of the door before the steward, Wayne, cracked it open and peered out.

"Ah. Oh. Yes. Sir Ahmad, do please come in by the fire." Wayne pulled the heavy door open wider and swept his arm out to point the way to the great hall.

Ahmad looked sideways at him. He seemed his usual nervous self and yet something needled at his mind. He monitored the other man and then did a quick scan of the darkness before stepping in fully to precede Steward Wayne toward the fire. Once in the large space, it didn't surprise Ahmad to see various groups of men milling about the hall, drinking and eating the supper left out even at such a late hour. King Orn's castle never seemed to sleep.

He stood ten feet from the blazing fire and stared into the dancing flames. The welcome crackling of the burning wood soothed his overworked senses. Wayne cleared his throat and Ahmad turned his attention back to the hunched man. "Wayne, I hope I find you in good spirits. You are well?"

"Oh yes. Yes. Quite. To be sure." Wayne's face transformed with what looked to be a forced grin. "I would not be concerned . . . uh . . . for me."

Ahmad's eyes pinched in disquiet and question, but Wayne hurried on in that same perplexing and nervous way.

"Our king has been in such an ambitious mood of late. I find he . . . he seems to be a new man. He's finally been given a purpose for his life."

"Purpose?"

"What?" Wayne said and jerked as though he'd been slapped. "I-I meant he's discovered a new lease on life. That's all."

The words were pleasant enough, but something in Wayne's tone niggled at the back of Ahmad's mind. He knew men could change, but for King Orn to have miraculously changed since last they met did not ring true. Steward Wayne's overly-pleasant report had to be taken with a grain of salt because he doubted Orn would ever care for anything more than he cared for himself.

"I'm spent, Wayne, and I'd like to retire, but it seemed wise to first announce myself and four other High Castle knights to the king. Is he still awake?"

"Oh yes, Sir Ahmad, but he is busy conferring with a guest. I will tell him of your arrival when he is done, but you can be sure he will be happy to accommodate you and the other knights."

He blinked, never imagining King Orn would pass up an opportunity to demean one or more of the high prince's guardsmen. But instead of drawing attention to this, he said, "We will leave at first light, as we have been called to High Castle for the new prince's naming ceremony."

"Not to worry. King Orn does not require you to come before him. You are welcome here," Wayne said and ushered Ahmad toward the door.

Ahmad stepped out into the night and looked back at Wayne standing just inside the entry with one hand resting on the heavy door and the other gripped upon the frame. His weak smile disappeared into the shadows as he took a step back in order to close the door. Ahmad's curiosity persisted. "Who is this special guest, if I might ask?"

Wayne hesitated, the door halting its progress. "I know not. The king told the entire household that his visitor is from far off and requires rest and solitude, which His Highness has granted, ensured by a tower room guarded by his most trusted knights to keep the curious away."

Wayne's voice had certainly raised a notch. The faint note of anxiety in his speech further rankled Ahmad's mind, but there seemed to be nothing left to discuss on the subject without crossing lines which were not his to step over.

"Thank you, Wayne. Give our regards to the king. We will not likely see you come morning."

Wayne nodded and quickly closed the door in his face.

* * *

Tears shimmered in Faye's eyes as what remained of her golden-flecked, auburn hair danced about her slim shoulders.

He wrapped the severed braid over his fist and set the knife on the table by his favorite chair.

"You have nothing to fear, Lady Faye. This is merely a message for your brother, should he fail to grasp the serious tenor of the circumstances." He held out her hair and watched how the firelight danced off the unique strands. "You will be safe unless he chooses to be a fool."

"My brother is honorable, my lord, and he will not betray the high prince for my sake."

Orn raised one brow. "That is not what your uncle tells me. In fact, he even shared in particular detail how far your dear brother will go to keep you safe. If not for your uncle's intervention with you, Florian would never be in the grand position to which he's been elevated as a royal guardsman to the high prince. You would have been the ruin of his dreams and aspirations but for your uncle ensuring you insist he go."

"No matter what my uncle threatened, I would have done anything to make sure Florian escaped my uncle's heavy-handedness. He could have married me off to any wretched beast of a man, and I'd have still begged my brother to fulfill his destiny. I do not fear my uncle."

The breathless quality of her voice when paired with her steely gaze enthralled Orn. He stepped closer to the young woman and towered over her by at least a foot, but she held her ground. Even with his shadow draped over her form, he still saw her shiver of fear pass from head to foot.

"It is not your uncle whom you should fear, child, but if you have any sense, fear me."

Her lips parted, but before he garnered any satisfaction from driving the fright home, a knock sounded on the outer door. With his focus disrupted, he motioned for the man dressed in black with hair to match to come out of the shadows and take the girl to her room. Once they'd left through a second, hidden door, Orn's most favored knight Havrik opened the first one to receive Steward Wayne into the king's presence.

"Did you send him on his way?"

"Yes, Sire."

"Did he suspect anything?"

"No, Sire." Wayne's gaze darted to Havrik and back. "At least, I don't believe so. Sir Ahmad and his men only wished to stay one night. They are on their way back to High Castle, and I am certain he was too tired to care, even if he found the excuses made out of the ordinary. Please, Sire, I'm sure he will cause you no trouble."

"You had best hope you are right, Wayne, or you will find your service here coming to an abrupt and painful end."

Wayne looked meek, and Orn took pleasure in his cowering. Since his special guest arrived, King Orn had been given a new lease on life, a reason to live, and a way to fulfill his greatest wishes. He just had to make sure no bumbling stewards or meddlesome High Castle buffoons got in his way.

* * *

They'd ridden hard. Another six long days and little sleep brought them to the gates of High Castle. During that time, Ahmad thought often of Sabine, of the Crescents, of the secret for which they searched and their devotion to it. Nothing became clear to him, and soon other thoughts crowded out his time in the north.

The gates were wide and Ahmad's heart hammered in his chest as he anticipated the familiar and unknown they would encounter when behind the walls. In his most unreasonable moments, he wanted only to drink in the sight of Lady Idra before all else. No one would bother to notify her of his return, but the pressing desire for her presence persisted, as if pondering her from the depths of his soul had the power to send her a message.

As it was, their arrival proved a quiet affair; no one stood by to welcome them or throw flower petals at their feet. Still, a festive air floated about the castle city as folk prepared for the naming ceremony and dedication. Soon, kings and dignitaries would arrive from all corners of the Twelve Realms.

The familiar stables and barracks were good to see, as well as to be greeted by fellow guardsmen and smell the scents of the main market street. After leaving their horses at the stables, Ahmad and the others walked to the castle keep to report to High Prince Theiandar. Step after step, his heart rate increased notch by notch until it hammered like a crazed woodpecker upon a tree. Once finished with their duty, they would be free to rest from their travels, but Ahmad had hopes for much more.

A compulsion—a deep longing—drove him look around every corner, at every face, hoping to glimpse High Princess Caityn's lady-in-waiting, Lady Idra, but when they arrived outside the king's meeting room without having seen her, he had to suppress his irrational disappointment. Inside the room were both High King Dante and his son, Prince Theiandar, or Raz, as the elite guardsmen of Delphor affectionately referred to him.

Ahmad and the others bowed to the two royals, then took seats at the round table. Ahmad sat next to the high prince and smiled when the prince gripped his shoulder.

"I understand congratulations are in order, Your Highness."

"Tis a great boon and reason to celebrate. Thank you, Ahmad," Prince Theiandar said. "I'm eager for you to meet our new prince. Caityn is looking forward to introducing you as well. Once we finish here, you are each invited to attend an informal dinner with Princess Caityn and myself in the lesser dining chamber. Our son will make an appearance."

Ahmad smiled at the sound of contentment in High Prince Theiandar's voice. It brought a twinge of jealousy that he hadn't expected to feel and quickly snuffed out. This was a time of celebration and called for nothing except joy for his friend and for the future of Twelve Realms.

After the men had given a report of their ventures in the north, Theiandar dismissed them to prepare for the forthcoming dinner with the princess—a rare and enjoyable invitation. Ahmad had another reason to look forward to dinner; Princess Caityn's presence ensured Lady Idra would be there.

"Delphor, wait," Raz said to Ahmad and the other men who'd returned from the north.

He waited for the last of his father's men to exit after the high king, and Ahmad's neck hairs rose at the conflicted look on Raz's face. He spared a glance for Lieve, Zaccur, Jarl, and Parker to see if they detected anything out of place.

"I'm sorry to delay you further from a much-deserved rest, but there's something I must tell you before you go to the barracks," the prince said with an air of gravity. "While you were away in the north, and before my son's birth, I filled Hanif's position in Delphor." He raised his hands in an allaying gesture even though his words were followed by a palpable silence. "I know what a shock this news must be, and trust me when I say I empathize, but it is our duty to see the realms united and protected. My father reminded me of the need to see Parlan represented among my guardsmen, and I accept the wisdom in this. I do not deny the difficulty, but it is done."

The prince stopped here and took a deep breath. Ahmad, already ambiguous in his feelings about this piece of news, grew concerned about how Raz hesitated.

"This choice I have made might be difficult for you to accept, but I feel it is the right one."

"Who've you chosen, Raz?" Ahmad asked, his tone biting for some inexplicable reason.

Raz stared him down, unflinching. "Xavier of the house of Gratham." They knew the name, and the next words need not have been uttered. "Hanif's younger brother."

The pronouncement hit Ahmad like a battering ram to the chest. "Why?"

He and the prince studied each other before Theiandar said, "He is well-trained, honorable, intelligent, and Hanif always spoke highly of him. I met with him and several other young men, but when we talked I felt it right; it will honor his brother's memory. He longs for it. I have decided. It is final."

"Is he here?" Zaccur asked.

Ahmad heard a slight clip of tension in Zaccur's voice and felt a little less guilty for his own unaccountable anger over the decision.

"Yes, he's here and will be at the dinner. I warn you, he is young. Younger than any of you when you were chosen, but not unworthy. Give him a chance and welcome him."

"I can only speak for myself, but the warning is appreciated," Zaccur said. "I think we will only need time to adjust. A brother of Hanif is welcome."

Prince Theiandar's lips pressed tight as he nodded. He excused himself to prepare for dinner.

Any agreeable thoughts Ahmad had turned morose upon the revelation of Hanif's replacement. Knowing Hanif's brother would be the one to fulfill the lack in Delphor only dug at Ahmad's core. No matter how many times he told himself to let go of his guilt over his friend's demise, he struggled to distance himself from it. That he'd been responsible, even in the slightest way, for Hanif's death haunted Ahmad at every turn. His mind betrayed him with memories he'd locked away as silent regrets rose to the surface.

They walked back to the barracks in silence, each of them absorbing the news in their own way. They were greeted by the rest of Raz's guardsmen, but the sight of Xavier caught their attention. For Ahmad, it was a nightmare. The young man appeared to be a replica of his older brother Hanif — like staring into the face of a ghost.

* * *

Idra touched her hair while looking in the mirror for the thousandth time. She prepared to attend a dinner unlike any other, one to welcome back the guardsmen of Prince Theiandar who had volunteered to protect the borders with Crescent Cave . . . one where she would encounter a man who flitted into her thoughts, unbidden yet welcome. Sir Ahmad.

He'd declared his affection and intentions toward her what seemed like centuries ago, but in reality it had been just under five months since that moment. She'd been abducted by mercenaries for ransom and nearly sold into slavery soon after Ahmad's avowal. The snatching had occurred while he had been away from the castle on mission with the high king and prince, and he could have done nothing to stop it.

During that most frightful time, she'd met a broken man, a pirate, who'd fallen in love with her and then given his life to save her from the mercenary Zaide—a man bent on her destruction. She'd come to care deeply for Simon the pirate, but Sir Ahmad had captured her heart long before he'd made his declaration, though she'd only admitted it to herself once he'd made his intentions known.

At a most terrible moment, as the reformed pirate lay dying, Sir Ahmad had seen Idra and Simon together and misunderstood their deep connection forged in her captivity and escape.

The night he'd told her he would not pursue her hand, Idra had been angry with Ahmad, confused and embarrassed by his words. She'd been quick to forgive his blindness hoped her small, secret token—a particular and meaningful handkerchief hidden in his satchel before he left for the north—would convince him of how wrong he had been.

Tonight she would see him after ten weeks apart with no word, and her heart flipped about in her chest like a fish out of water. No matter how many times she checked her hair or smoothed her skirts, her nerves refused to stop shaking her from the core.

Another glance at the clock told her the time had come. Idra stood straight and strode out of the room with all her mustered courage, but the hollowness gnawing at her gut persisted.

* * *

Caityn and Idra were the first to arrive in the lesser dining chamber, which appeared small but would be the perfect intimate setting for a party such as this. Idra mentally checked off the guest list. Yes, the royal couple, herself, and the twelve guardsmen of High Prince Theiandar left space to spare.

Idra checked the settings at the table once more; the rank of each guest dictated the required arrangement of seating. Butterflies fluttered about in her stomach as she stared at Sir Ahmad's place. Dread welled up inside as reality settled in.

Rejection. She detested her fear of it at this first meeting after their misunderstanding. What if he were angry? Had he changed over the last months? Had he changed his mind about her? Met someone else? The thoughts were poisonous, eating away at her composure.

"Idra?"

"I'm sorry, Caity, my mind wandered." She'd not been attending to her cousin's last-minute instructions.

Princess Caityn motioned for the servants to leave the room and came to stand before her, placing her hands on Idra's upper arms. "All will be well. You know Ahmad, and you know what a steady character he has. His feelings were and are real."

Idra nodded once, but the beginnings of panic set her on edge. "I want to believe what you say is true, but what if he doesn't trust my word? What if he never asks again? What will I do?"

Caityn's arms encircled Idra, who returned the embrace, gaining strength and courage from her cousin, who always looked for the best in people and situations.

"No matter what, you will be well. Your heart will mend," Caityn said and released Idra.

The women looked into each other's eyes, and Idra found comfort in her cousin's fortitude. The nursery maid walked through the door, carrying the prince, and unintentionally interrupted the quiet moment of imbued strength. Caityn took the sleeping baby boy in her arms and Idra stroked his wispy, soft hair. Like Prince Theiandar, he had dark locks, but in his fine features, Idra perceived that he would resemble his mother.

A servant announced the high prince and his guardsmen, who filed into the dining room dressed in their finest garments. Idra's hands dropped to her sides, and she balled them up in the folds of her indigo dress. She squeezed her eyes shut for half a second and pasted on a smile.

Caityn rescued her from an unmerciful panic attack by passing the baby into her arms while she welcomed their guests. Idra found renewed comfort in the little person she cradled close, in the perfect turn of his pert lips and his long, dark lashes brushing against his pink baby cheeks. She kept her eyes off the men, only allowing her gaze to move from the sweet child in her arms to her cousin as Caityn greeted her husband, Prince Theiandar.

"Thank you for coming," Caityn began. "This dinner is out of the ordinary, but you men are not ordinary, and you will play an important role in our son's life. Now that you are gathered, those of you who traveled to the north having returned, I felt it an opportune time to introduce you to our precious gift and the future king. He will not only need the wisdom of his father, but our son will gain much from that of the men who will grow wise with him." Caityn reached out for the baby and held him where the men could see his face. "Though the naming ceremony is a week and a half away, we want you to meet Prince Bastien."

Upon that pronouncement, High Prince Theiandar took his son in his arms and presented him to each of his men. Idra had been successful in keeping her eyes averted, focusing only on Caityn and the baby during her speech, but as each guardsman paid his respects to the new little prince, she watched them, anticipating and dreading when she'd lay eyes on Ahmad.

When the temptation refused to be ignored, outstripping the treasonous voice of fear in her mind, she stared. Idra's heart raced and sweat slicked her palms. She grabbed the heavy material of her skirt and slid her hands down the fabric to rid herself of the evidence. But in the light-headed mess of her mind she drank in how strong, and dashing, and rugged, and . . . and perfect he looked with his hair grown long, curling at the collar of his deep green tunic, and his brown eyes fixed upon Bastien with the most tender of expressions enhancing his newly shaven face. How had he only grown more handsome? And here she stood, in a room full of handsome men, with eyes only for this noble man with a glint of sorrow in his eyes. What clouded his features? What is her? Had she hurt him so deeply?

CHAPTER FIVE
TWO HEARTS

HIS BREATH CAUGHT TRAPPED BEHIND the lump in his throat. She bloomed more beautiful than he remembered. She'd been dirty, bruised, and thinner when they'd come to her rescue at Gankobi, but time had healed her wounds. Seeing her in the flesh again confirmed Ahmad's lingering fervency, and he blinked away the unbidden moisture that built in his eyes. Almighty, how he wanted to hold her in his arms. Prince Theiandar presenting his son, Bastien, proved the only thing capable of wrestling his attention from her. Ahmad peered at the tiny bundle cradled in his father's powerful arms.

"What a beautiful son you have, Sire."

Theiandar's merry laughter brought a smile to Ahmad's face. "Yes, and I fear he will use it to his advantage when he is older."

"Not with a father and mother such as you and the princess to guide him," Ahmad said, finally able to relax somewhat after the earlier shock he'd been given combined with the anticipation of seeing Idra.

Theiandar moved down the line and Ahmad's gaze slipped back toward Idra. This time, their eyes met, but her thoughts remained indiscernible. His stomach tightened as a warmth filled his body and he swallowed, unable to place his own emotions. But as quickly as their gazes locked, she looked away, down at the floor. It left him cold.

After Bastien had been introduced to each guardsman, the maid took the child into her charge once again and removed him to the nursery. The prince and princess sat at either end of the table, and the guardsmen made their way to their chairs. Ahmad sat on Theiandar's right, while Idra took a seat halfway down the table on the opposite side. On her left sat Xavier, and the sight of him caused Ahmad's brow to furrow.

Idra chose that moment to glance his way, and the hesitant smile she wore wavered. Ahmad strove to change his expression to one of reassurance, to speak with his eyes what unutterable words he longed to share, but he thought of it too late; she'd already looked back toward Xavier who continued to speak to her with animated gestures and features that more and more reminded Ahmad of Hanif.

Idra and Xavier were clearly familiar with each other as they conversed easily, and Idra's kind smile punctuated her responses. Ahmad could not hear what they spoke of, but he'd have given his left arm to know. Throughout dinner, he kept glancing their way. Only that once had his eyes met those of Idra.

A frantic internal quest to manufacture a reason to speak with her alone dominated his thoughts. Gavin elbowed him and winked, which prodded Ahmad enough to realize he'd spent most of the meal staring down the table at Idra, and it hadn't gone unnoticed.

Theiandar explained to the guardsmen who'd just returned that day that nobility from across the realms were arriving for the naming ceremony. "As my guardsmen, you'll all be required to attend several dinners and parties hosted by various families near the castle."

"Must we, Raz?" Florian asked, sounding much like an unhappy child but voicing the general irksomeness felt among the men. "This dinner is the extent of my sociability."

Theiandar laughed. "Yes, Florian, you must attend, and you will be required to dance."

Florian glowered but did not hesitate to share a defeated smile. Ahmad grinned in amusement, knowing of Florian's nobility. But Florian had lost his parents when he was just a boy and had been raised by his uncle, who reveled in the trappings of wealth more than seemed natural. It had become a burden for Florian to associate with his father's brother, and he'd strived to distance himself from that life and take up the banner of protection over the weak. Ahmad thought he had done well in this endeavor as Florian's compassion and instinctive protection over innocents outshone them all.

"King Trygg and his son Prince Melvin arrived yesterday, which surely you'd be most interested to hear, Ahmad," Theiandar said. He stopped to take a sip from his goblet. "King Orn and his retinue are due to arrive on the morrow. King Ekreton will stay at Emlyn as expected, but the letter you delivered to my father explained that his wife and daughters would be attending. It mentioned the attack on Queen Moira and expressed concern over their well-being."

"Yes," Ahmad said, "King Ekreton seemed shaken over the event."

"He is wise to send them here while he has Crescent prisoners in his dungeons. As for the other nobility, we do not expect their arrival until the day before the tourney."

"I'm exhausted by the idea," Gavin said with a satirical smile.

The evening soon ended, and Ahmad had not contrived a single way to speak directly with Lady Idra. The outcome left him deep in disappointment when he wanted nothing else—only her soft voice and gentle smile and to stare unhindered at every sweet curve of her comely face.

The princess left before the rest when the nursery maid requested her presence, and Theiandar excused himself to be with his wife and son. As the men stood to leave, Idra took Princess Caityn's place at the door to wish each a good evening. Ahmad seized his only opportunity and put himself at the end of the line.

It seemed to take forever for the others to say their thanks. Florian queued in front of him, and for having an aversion to nobility, he certainly knew how to act like them when the time required. He bowed over Idra's hand and thanked her for a lovely evening. Ahmad tamped down unwarranted jealousy and clenched his jaw in response to the amused smile she bestowed on Florian. He gave the other guardsman a pointed, stern look and jerked his head to the side, hoping Florian would not miss the hint.

Heat crept up Ahmad's neck when Florian took the chance to tease him without mercy in front of Lady Idra.

"Oh, yes, right. I shall be going now. I have overstayed my welcome, I think," Florian said in exaggerated slowness accompanied by a teasing grin spread wide across his well-formed face, a face Ahmad wanted longed to punch at that precise second.

"Goodnight, Sir Florian," Idra said with a chuckle.

Ahmad shifted his gaze to her watching Florian leave and did his best to still the suddenly frantic beat of his heart. He did not know what he would say to her, but his fingers had reached inside his tunic, unbidden, and pulled out the handkerchief she'd given him. When she faced him, he held it out between them.

"I found this in my satchel after I left and questioned Gavin when we returned. I've no doubt he's the one who slipped it in, but why?" The words had spilled from his mouth in rapid succession without his express permission.

She didn't answer right away. Instead, she stared at the cloth with an unreadable expression before she pulled it from his cramped fingers and toyed with the edge where her initials were embroidered.

"My mother gave me this on my sixteenth birthday. She said she embroidered it and made the lace on the edges when I was only a few months old. I never understood why she waited that long to give it to me, but just knowing how she kept it safe all those years reminded me of her love. I carried it with me from then on."

He stared at her down-turned face while she spoke, sure his heart had stopped beating. Ahmad couldn't find words; he feared speaking or breaking the moment, even if he had anything worth saying.

She looked up with a shimmer of unshed tears in her eyes. "I asked Gavin to put it in your satchel because I wanted to remind you . . . to beg you to see my love as constant."

Ahmad did not believe what his ears heard. "What are you saying? Am I to understand—"

"Yes," she said.

"I thought you—"

"You thought wrong. You didn't even give me a chance to explain."

Her impassioned and anguished tone broke his heart. She spoke true. Three months ago he hadn't been ready to listen. He'd been devastated and selfishly wanted to run away from the woman he assumed would never love him back. *Fool.*

"Must you remain silent?" she asked in a tight voice.

Ahmad noticed the rigidity of her shoulders and the way she gripped the handkerchief. The need to touch her—to comfort her—overwhelmed him, but he held himself in check and lowered to one knee, bowing his head.

"My lady, I beg your forgiveness. You speak the truth and I am ashamed."

"Do not kneel. Only . . . only say you still love me."

Her soft words were punctuated by the tremor of her fingers fanning along his jawline to his chin, where with one touch she raised his head so that their eyes met. Ahmad's breath caught, and he stood to his feet—slow, deliberate—their bodies coming close enough he felt the heat of hers as she blushed. He lost himself in the sensation of nearness. Her head tilted up and lips slightly parted, their chests rising and falling in an otherworldly union.

A clatter of dishes from near the table startled them out of their distraction and silenced Ahmad with his hand raised toward Idra's face. A maid worked frantically to clean up the mess of food from the floor and another arrived to assist her, but Ahmad did not miss the sly grin passed between the two young women, assuring him there would be fresh gossip for the morrow.

He shook his head and turned his attention back to Idra, but thin, frigid air greeted him from the place where before she'd been standing only inches from him. Ahmad looked down, frustration and disappointment jarring his body, and saw the handkerchief spread out on the floor by his feet. He bent to retrieve it, held it to his nose, and placed it back in the safety of his inner pocket.

Though upset that the interruption cut their conversation short, he left with a renewed sense of hope. Idra had all but said she loved him, and that proved to be enough to wake him from his own foolishness. But now he had to find a way to demonstrate his love for her endured.

* * *

Idra stopped running once she'd dashed up the stairs and turned the corner toward her room. She fell back against the wall with her hand pressed to her thundering heart as she worked to control the rapid rise and fall of her chest. Noreeta, her lady's maid, would notice something amiss when she walked into the room if she did not rein in her emotions.

She'd learned to be bolder, but what she'd just done existed far beyond anything Idra ever imagined herself undertaking; it shocked her. When the serving girl had accidentally dropped the plate, divulging her eavesdropping, it had woken Idra from whatever dream world she'd entered when looking into Ahmad's earnest face. It sent her running from his presence like a retreating army.

She closed her eyes in the hall's darkness, hidden in the shadows between torches, and imagined the scene she'd just escaped. The intense yet tender look on his face, the smell of his freshly washed hair, the rough stubble of his square jaw, the heat radiating from his body. Why didn't she ignore the maid? The realization came too late. Why did she run away? The side of her fist hit the wall with a dull thud, and she gave up trying to answer questions for which she did not truly want answers.

But one more nagged at her. "What if he doesn't love me?" The whispered question passed her lips and dissipated into the dark night, with no answer echoing back to relieve her fear. After standing there a minute longer, she moved away from the wall and tiptoed toward her room where, when she finally lay in her bed, dreams of drowning in the sea, a redheaded pirate always running away from her, and Ahmad's lifeless eyes staring at her from the floor of the dusty slave market in Gankobi riddled her sleep.

CHAPTER SIX
FAMILY AND FIENDS

FLORIAN BENT AND SPLASHED COOL water from the basin onto his face once more. He straightened but didn't bother wiping off the excess and let it drip down onto his shirtfront. He'd received a letter from his sister Faye, which unsettled his already tense nerves. It was carried by a knight who'd arrived with his uncle and King Orn of Wyeth. Faye lived with their uncle and had just turned sixteen a few months ago. Because of that, Florian had incorrectly assumed she'd be accompanying Jeron to the festivities. After reading her letter, he couldn't get the words out of his mind.

He sat on his bunk in the quiet of early morning and read it again.

My Dear Florian,

I miss you terribly and wish you could have been here for my birthday. Uncle wasn't going to host a ball until the king mentioned it when we were in attendance at a castle supper. Do not tell anyone, but the king makes my skin crawl. He made a fuss over me that night and insisted Uncle have a party for my birthday. Of course, he said he already planned one, though we both knew that was not true. When Uncle gave the party for my birthday, it did not truly celebrate my coming of age so much as show me off before eligible men of Wyeth as potential wife, like a cow for sale. King Orn seemed to take great pleasure in it. It was awful, and I can only think that if you could have been here, it wouldn't have been nearly as insufferable.

But I do not wish to make you unhappy with this report, thus I shall tell you of other, more pleasant happenings. Uncle did let me pick a puppy from the stable master's litter for my birthday. I picked out a boy and named him Fidget. I know how you will laugh at it, but I thought it would be a reminder of you. How I miss you, Brother! Fidget is my constant companion . . .

Her letter spoke of Wyeth and the endeavors of teaching herself basic skills of varying subjects, since their uncle considered it worthless to have a tutor for a girl. She spent much of her spare time with Cook in the kitchen or caring for the chickens and pigs their uncle kept.

After reading the letter again, Florian felt worse. The awful weight of regret weighed down on him for not having asked permission from Raz to attend his sister's sixteenth birthday. It had been his original intention, but during that time Lady Idra had been kidnapped and taken to be sold as a slave in Gankobi. His sister had responded with grace and understanding—too much so—but Florian had certainly let her down when he'd sent her word he was needed at High Castle. He should have gone. There were plenty of others to care for and protect the royals. His absence would have been little sensed by them, whereas to his sister, she had no other person who cared for her as much as him.

Florian's irritation at his uncle Jeron festered. His father's brother may have taken them into his home after his parent's murder, but he'd never treated them as his own even though he and his wife remained childless. His aunt had only lived a few months after they'd taken in Florian and his sister, succumbing to a mysterious illness that had plagued her for years.

When Florian received the opportunity to join the ranks of High Prince Theiandar's guardsmen, he hadn't hesitated, but soon after that, he realized he'd be leaving Faye behind. He'd almost declined the honor, but she'd found him writing the letter to the prince and snatched it away. She'd torn it up and insisted he must not turn back from this path, that she would be well, and that he should make her proud. His sister, at only twelve, had been brave beyond her years.

Florian had become friends with one knight who served his uncle's household, and that man had delivered the letter to him when King Orn and his entourage, including Florian's uncle, had arrived the day before. The friend had implied that Faye seemed disappointed about not coming, and her letter only added to his frustration over their beholden situation to their uncle.

This same friend had mentioned King Orn's mysterious guest. While a curious thing, it didn't seem suspicious as far as Florian imagined. He assumed someone hid under the protection of King Orn or possibly the king wanted this someone hidden from society. Whatever the case, he didn't much care as long as Faye remained safe, which his friend implied she had been when he'd last seen her before their trek south to High Castle. Regardless, Florian vowed to himself that as soon as the festivities were over, he would take the time to go see Faye and, with his own two eyes ascertain her comfort.

He tucked the letter back under his mattress and pulled on his boots, then his tunic and belt. Florian and the other members of High Prince Theiandar's guardsmen, unit Delphor, were to spend the morning on the practice fields, and the others had already gone to eat breakfast in the great hall. He disliked the idea of breaking the fast at the castle since there were already a great deal of noblemen filling the palace and making themselves at home.

"Florian, we've brought you some food," Gavin said in a sing-song cadence as he and Xavier stepped into the room.

Gavin held the platter out but grabbed a biscuit from the edge and popped the whole of it in his mouth. Florian laughed and accepted the trencher.

"You are a saint, my friend."

"I sat across from your uncle while I ate, and Xavier perched near enough to attest to this; let us just say I am reminded of why you do not enjoy his presence. But don't expect to become accustomed to such extravagant gifts. Twas a once-in-a-lifetime gesture of pity."

"I will take what I can get. Thank you both."

Florian dug into the food on his plate, practically inhaling it, and when he finished, the three of them made the companionable stroll to the armory to suit up for practice.

* * *

Ahmad and the others were gathered on the practice field preparing to spar, but for reasons he refused to identify, he stayed distracted and irritable. He knew the source of his angst, but it pained him to watch as Xavier slid his sword from the sheath and tossed it back and forth between his hands as he prepared to face off against Parker. Xavier grinned at Parker in such a way that caused Ahmad's heart to constrict. He already looked too much like his dead older brother, without also having the same mannerisms and facial expressions.

Ahmad glowered and shifted his gaze to Parker. The older knight, though still not two and twenty, had a definite appearance of maturity as compared to his young sparring partner. Parker shifted to the right, crossing his feet one over the other in slow, steady steps with his weapon poised in front of him. He exuded confidence balanced with prudence.

Xavier's quicker movements and the cocky smile he wore paired with the downward tilt of his chin gave the impression of a youth not yet prepared for battle. It irritated Ahmad further as he watched the two circle for another three steps. Hanif's brother made the first strike, but Parker parried it away like the slight annoyance of a fly.

Twice more Xavier attempted to strike, and with each blow Parker made only the slightest move to ward off the attacks. Ahmad grew suspicious, and the next strike confirmed his intuition; without a second between, Xavier moved in on Parker and made two quick blows, both of which Parker barely held off as he'd been lulled into a false sense of security.

It took him less than a second to realize his mistake, and the battle grew heated as they traded off the offensive and defensive positions. Xavier's trick reminded Ahmad that they needed to be wary of such feinting in battle and life. Too easily could a man be lulled into complacency by fabricated weakness. Vigilance was not only necessary for a soldier, but it was vital to his survival and to those he served.

The fight raged on, but Parker's advanced skill and superior strength won out against the younger, less experienced knight. When Parker held his dull blade to Xavier's neck as he kneeled upon the dusty earth of the practice arena, it signaled the end of the match, but both men, breathing hard from exertion, were smiling.

"Well done," Prince Theiandar announced as Parker pulled Xavier to his feet.

"Thank you, Raz," the men said in unison and pressed a fist to their hearts.

"That's enough for today. Bathing is in order." In fine humor, Raz pinched his nose and waved his arm. "Prepare for the card party to be hosted at Hamlin House this evening."

A mixture of responses arose from the men. Some were enthused, ready to meet a young lady to woo, while others, like Florian, moaned at the prospect. Ahmad stayed neutral over the situation, since he would have no opportunity to meet with Idra that day. That thought in and of itself caused him enough displeasure. They had unfinished business.

"Raz, I'd rather not go," Florian said, voicing Ahmad's thoughts.

"You're just worried the pretty girls will run away from that beard on your chin," Zaccur remarked with a chuckle.

"Ah no. Not a one of you will escape a game of whist with Hamlin's daughter," Theiandar said. "These parties are not about you or I but are in celebration of my son's birth, and in order to avoid gossip or unrest it is important to socialize, to be seen as undivided in every respect possible. You men became more than knights or soldiers when you were chosen as my guardsmen. You know this already, but I cannot stress enough, especially at such a time as this, that you've pledged your lives to the crown, and not a day will go by that your service is not required."

They placed fists to hearts, and Florian said, "Of course, Sire. I'm sorry for speaking out of turn. I wasn't thinking."

Ahmad saw compassion flicker in Theiandar's eye as he approached the knight and rested a hand on Florian's shoulder. "There's nothing to apologize for, my friend. I'm only sorry to ask you to do something distasteful to you. But take heart. My mother once told me the best way to overcome something frightful or uncomfortable is to face it head-on and then head-on again until it's lost its power over you."

Florian nodded.

"You are dismissed."

Ahmad prepared to approach Florian to commiserate when Xavier bounced up next to him first and wrapped his arm around Florian's shoulder. Ahmad fought down startled indignation because he did not realize the others had grown close with Xavier over the month and a half that he'd been in their ranks.

As the two walked away, Xavier said something to Florian that had him smiling and laughing, but instead of giving Ahmad comfort, it incensed him. Hanif's younger brother might look like him, but Xavier had nothing else in common with the former guardsman. In Ahmad's mind, Hanif had been down-to-earth and serious though untested, while this brother of his acted like an immature jester most of the time.

It dawned on Ahmad that he should stop comparing the two, but he had no desire to and felt compelled to protect the memory of Hanif—his friend—who'd died under his command.

* * *

Florian tucked the edges of his fine white linen shirt into his pants and slid on his reddish-brown wool vest with bronze studs detailing the edges. He cinched it at the waist with a belt and tugged at each of his billowy sleeves. Though he owned a matching hat, he refused to stoop to wearing it. Florian had no doubt his uncle would say something when he arrived at the party because it symbolized his rank, but his uncle would have to be disappointed.

"You know, Florian, you'll never be able to hide your lordliness. It seeps from your pores, and that fine outfit just confirms what the world already knows."

"Stow it, Gavin," Florian replied as he rubbed his newly shaved jawline and wondered with regret if he shouldn't have left it be. "Tis not as though you have room to make jests over my mere nobility, seeing as how you are nephew to a king."

"Conversation is always a repartee with you."

The two walked out together, where Gavin kindly had both their horses saddled and ready to make the short trek outside the city to the manor of Lord Grey of Hamlin. The others waited in their saddles. Xavier exited the barracks last, still tucking his shirt into his pants as he walked.

They rode out of the city in a jovial spirit. Even Florian found himself having a good time and anticipating what he hoped would be an enjoyable evening—as long as he didn't consider the presence of his uncle or King Orn. He wanted to find out what nuance about the king of Wyeth caused his sister's distress but no memories of anything but vague contempt for the selfish monarch surfaced

When they arrived, Prince Theiandar and his twelve guardsmen entered by the massive front door. Two servants who bowed to the prince and knights held the heavy maple doors open. Florian thanked them as he passed by, remembering how his uncle had forced him to learn each chore and position at the manor house, working sometimes double what he expected of any servant. Uncle Jeron told him it would make him a better steward once he reached his majority and inherited his father's lands, which were in his uncle's care after his father's death. The labor had been undeniably difficult, but it had taught him to appreciate the many individuals who maintained the huge household, and it had indeed taught him how to be a better master than his uncle, a man he vowed never to emulate.

Even without having seen his uncle that day, the man already made the muscles tense across Florian's back. He rolled his shoulders twice to loosen the tautness, then took a deep, calming breath.

"Florian, where can a fellow find a drink to quench his thirst?" Xavier leaned in and asked.

"Follow me, my young friend. But I caution you now. Beware Hilde of Hamlin. Granted, she's not unpleasant to look upon, but if she sets her sights on your handsome face, it will doom you to a night of incessant talk and endless whist playing."

He kept his expression deadpan while staring at Xavier, but as his friend glanced about in anxiousness, his composure weakened and dissipated in laughter.

"I wouldn't worry, as the Meddling Maid of Hamlin has already attached herself to Ahmad. Look there," he said, motioning toward a table situated near the tall windows. "I'm relieved to say she hasn't set her sights on me at the varied events I've attended."

"I'm surprised anyone would seek out Sir Ahmad. I've known him two days, and he's been nothing but severe," Xavier said while frowning at the knight across the room.

"Go easy. He's his reasons, but I assure you he's a kindly older-brother type, though he has no siblings of his own." The words left Florian's mouth before he considered what he said or to whom. He looked at Xavier to gauge his reaction to the thoughtless phrasing, too easy a reminder of the older brother Xavier lost. "I'm sorry, Xavier. I didn't think."

He saw that his words affected Xavier, most likely catching him up in memories of his brother Hanif.

Xavier grabbed the back of his neck and looked down for a second. "No, Florian, don't apologize." Their eyes met and Xavier's melancholy smile struck a chord. "I could use a big brother right now. I know Hanif respected Ahmad a great deal. He's just not what I imagined."

Florian only nodded at first, his mind provoked by unpleasant memories of Hanif's death. "Ahmad hasn't been the same since your brother's death. He feels responsible because he made the decision to camp out on the trail where we were ambushed. I have to admit, looking at you is akin to looking at a younger, slightly more roguish version of Hanif. I think, without intention, your presence is a reminder."

He examined Xavier while the younger knight visibly reflected on what he'd said. Sharp as the truth stung, Xavier's presence held a physical reminder to which even Florian found it difficult to adjust.

"I hadn't thought of that. Of all my brothers, my mother often remarks on our similarity of appearance."

"Florian!" a man's stern voice interrupted further conversation.

It had taken Florian's uncle less than fifteen minutes to find him in the crowded rooms, but Florian promised himself he'd be respectful. It was the least he could do. After all, when his parents had been killed, his uncle had the power to ship him off to school or sent him and Faye to live with relatives of their mother whom they'd never known. Of course, as he thought of it, he wondered if that might not have been better. Had that occurred, the only downside would have been never becoming a royal guardsman.

Florian sent Xavier an apologetic look as the other knight stepped back. He then shifted his focus and bowed his head in due respect. "Sir, you are looking well."

Jeron's benign smile spread wider as he patted his round belly. "Life is treating me well."

"And how fares my sister, sir?"

"Faye? Oh, she is becoming an attractive thing after all. She'll do well for us. I've had at least six men approach with offers for her."

Florian's jaw clenched, but he worked to keep his tone even as he responded, unable to let the flippant remark pass. "Faye is still too young for such talk, and I should be a part of choosing her husband *when* the time comes."

The smile disappeared from Jeron's face, only to be replaced by a stern look, his brows lowering over his deep-set, dark eyes. "You have been away these four years, Florian. You have practically no say in that irksome girl's life. When I say it is time for her to wed, then she will wed, and I will decide—not you, her, or anyone else."

"Except perhaps her king," Orn said from behind Jeron, whose posture stiffened almost imperceptibly, but enough for Florian to notice.

They bowed to the lower monarch, but what Jeron had just announced and what the king of Wyeth had added left Florian preoccupied.

"Of course, Sire," Jeron said, the benign smile back in place. "You are wise, and I fully rely on your astute ability to make a perfect match for my niece as you desire to bestow us with your favor."

"Very good, Jeron. Have you told your nephew of our plans?"

"Ah, no, Sire. I only just found him, and he started off with impertinent questions."

"Tis no matter. I will explain to the young fellow to whom his true fealty shall be. You may leave us, Jeron."

Florian, already tense from speaking with his uncle, now felt his spine harden and stood alert at King Orn's cryptic pronouncement. He didn't bother to look at his uncle, who bowed once more and left them alone. The king looped his arm through Florian's and urged him out into the brisk night air of the garden, where they strolled to a bench awash in the light from a window. It appeared to be far enough away from the main partygoers that none would overhear their conversation.

King Orn sat on the bench but did not offer a seat to Florian. He spread out the opulent cream-colored doublet he wore, crossed his legs, and leaned back against the rest. Florian noted the repeated circular motion of the king's thumb over an odd green bauble hanging from his neck, but even the unhurried and relaxed posture of the king did not dampen the unease which grew within Florian with each passing second.

"Sire?" he asked, unable to wait in silence.

Orn inhaled deeply and sighed. "The smell of autumn is almost gone from the air and death of winter seems to settle in." He shifted his gaze to Florian, but his eyes hid in the shadows where the knight could not read what might lurk in their depths. "I remember you. Why is it that when Prince Theiandar and his guardsmen pass through Wyeth, I do not see you?"

The accusatory tone of Orn's voice had a strange effect on Florian, who had to fight against the constricting of his throat. He clasped his hands behind his back to hide any shaking his limbs might betray over discomfiting words that held little in them but idle complaints.

"Sire, I have been in attendance at those times, but I am not ranked at a position to be needed in court presence when we travel."

"Nonsense. Wyeth is your home, is it not? Are you not a lord of Wyethian lands?"

Florian nodded, though the hairs on the back of his neck prickled.

"You must always present yourself at court when you arrive at my castle, Sir Florian."

"Yes, Sire. I shall do so from now on. Is there anything else, Sire?"

King Orn stood with more rapidity than Florian expected, causing him to step back abruptly, almost tripping into the cascading fountain behind him. The king's laughter filled the crisp night air.

"I have the distinct impression that my presence unnerves you, Sir Florian." Orn paused, and the joviality dissipated from his demeanor. "I assure you, you have every reason to feel so."

The king paced back and forth a few steps, then pointed at the bench. "Sit," he commanded and continued to pace with his hands clasped behind his back.

Florian could do nothing but obey. He took four wary steps to the bench and lowered himself onto it, his attention focused on King Orn.

"You remember that little thief who hid himself in my mountains in Wyeth?"

Florian nodded again. *How could I forget?*

"He stole beauty, if I understand the stories correctly. Well, Sir Florian, you are a knight of Wyeth, a lord of Wyeth . . . and a devoted brother."

Florian forced himself to relax and hide his anxiety at the vague allusion to his sister. What did the king imply? His nostrils flared. He held himself rigid on the bench, not wanting to interrupt the king in whatever tale he unfolded.

"Yes, a devoted brother, a lord, and a knight. Sir Florian, I am going to share a secret with you, but you must not reveal this to anyone or risk losing your lordship and your status as brother, if you understand my implication."

"I'm not sure I do, Sire," Florian said, choking on the words as fear of what the king insinuated seeped into his core.

"Oh, I think you do. Your sister is no longer at your uncle's manor. I will now make it evident that he and I are in complete agreement. No. We've removed your sweet, delectable sister to a secret location. I offer you this token. Her life is in your hands, dear boy."

Florian stood, unable to contain the instant rage which overcame him at the king's words. "How dare you threaten the life of my sister!" he said through clenched teeth, his fists in the same state at his sides and his face mere inches from Orn's.

"Ahem," a voice echoed from the distance.

Both Florian and King Orn looked over to see Xavier standing in the doorway's light.

King Orn whispered, "Not a word if you value your sister's life."

"I'm sorry to interrupt, Your Highness. Prince Theiandar asked me to find Sir Florian."

The king's menacing smile shifted to one of kind regard as he spoke to Xavier through the darkness. "Of course, young man. He'll be along in just a moment. I have been giving Sir Florian a report of his sister and his lands, have I not, Sir Florian?"

Florian scarcely squeezed the words out of his dry throat and past stiff lips. "Yes, Sire."

Xavier hesitated a moment, then disappeared from view as he retreated inside.

"You will come see me in my private chambers at the castle tomorrow at noon, Florian. Do not be late."

Florian nodded once, too angry to do more.

"You're dismissed."

He walked away without a backward glance, but Orn's words consumed his thoughts and blackness engulfed his vision. He made his way to Prince Theiandar in a fog and couldn't recall how he'd arrived there.

"Highness?"

"Florian, deliver a message to your uncle for me. Caityn has kindly insisted we invite him to sit with us at the tourney before the naming ceremony. Apparently, my mother mentioned how nice it would be."

"Sire?"

"Immediate relatives of my guardsmen who are in attendance have been given the honor, but with your parents . . ."

"I understand," Florian said, though he could not mask the displeasure in his voice.

"Is something wrong?"

"No, Sire. Tis nothing. If you'll excuse me, I will seek my uncle this minute."

"By all means. And Florian," the prince said, laying a hand on his shoulder before he could step away, "you may leave once you've done with speaking to your uncle. You look pale."

"I'm feeling unwell. Thank you, Sire."

He bowed and ignored the deep look of concern on Raz's face. After ten minutes of searching out his uncle, a red-hot anger burning in his soul, he found the scoundrel had left the party.

"Florian!" Xavier called to him near the main entrance doors.

He halted mid-stride without turning around and wanted to pretend he hadn't heard Xavier's call. He thought to leave without waiting for the younger knight to catch up, but in two seconds his friend stopped next to him.

"I heard you were leaving, and I'm ready to make my escape as well. I'll accompany you."

"No," Florian said with a stern finality he didn't recognize in himself.

"But I—"

"I have business at the castle, and it doesn't involve you."

"I'll just ride back with you then, and you can go attend to your business."

Florian hated the quizzical and slightly hurt tenor of Xavier's voice. It had been an adjustment to have Hanif's younger brother fill his empty place in their ranks, but Xavier had quickly proved his worth and friendship. Florian's shoulders sagged with guilt over his short-tempered response, and he nodded.

They went to the stable to collect their horses. Without waiting to see if Xavier kept up, Florian charged back to the castle, but the rush of biting autumn night air did not cool his growing rage. His uncle had best pray for Faye's safety, or there would be a terrible cost to pay . . . whose cost, he could not say, but whatever King Orn and Jeron were up to would surely mete out serious consequences.

Only the waxing brilliance of the half-moon guided them on their mad dash; it, the only light Florian saw on a night dark with evil intent.

* * *

"She's not here."

Ahmad's brow furrowed. "I'm sorry, Lady Hilde?" He refused to admit he knew to whom she referred.

"Lady Idra, you absurd, lovesick pup."

"My lady, I'm at a loss."

Hilde, eldest daughter of Lord Grey Hamlin, who seemed to take more pleasure in orchestrating the love matches of other people than finding one of her own, moved ever closer to becoming an old maid. While quite skilled in the art of matchmaking, her reputation for it seemed to have built up a barrier around her that most men feared to cross. Instead, manufactured rumors by jealous women professing her to be a jabbering ninny abounded. Ahmad knew better, and when meeting at parties such as this he valued her insight and confident ways, which portrayed her as someone much older and experienced than her true age should embody.

"You are no such thing. At a loss, my foot," she said and stamped hers, emphasizing her words. "Lady Idra is all your eyes will say. This room is full of beautiful women, and you see nothing but the distant lights of the castle parapets."

Ahmad tilted his head toward her. "I cannot argue with you, my lady. You have read my mind with an unmatched and startling alacrity."

"You must go to her. Do not wait upon ceremony."

"Lady Idra detests the gossip of the castle, and if I did, it would only cause the tittering of idle mouths to crescendo."

"She's far too strong to be beaten down by the prattle of court biddies and too pretty to be ignored by the thirsting eyes of gentlemen. No, you must go to her and stop this unmanly pining."

The dire quality of her tone caused Ahmad to look twice at her to determine whether she jested. "You wound me with your piercing words."

"They pierce only because their aim is true. You must realize you cannot know if she will wait for you. Others have esteemed her loveliness and charm."

He bristled. "What? To whom do you refer?"

"I've interfered here enough for one evening, Sir Ahmad, but I caution you not to put off until tomorrow what can be done today." Lady Hilde stood and held out her hand for Ahmad to kiss, which he did once he scrambled to his feet. "Good night."

"Good night, fair lady."

Hilde's wan smile did not quite reach her hazel eyes, and Ahmad sensed a sorrow in her he hadn't recognized before. She walked away and blew a kiss to her mother before gliding up the wide staircase to the upper floor. An uncomfortable and peculiar sensation of guilt washed over him upon her departure, as if he'd done something wrong. But her words—*you are not the only one who esteems her loveliness*—wouldn't stop echoing through his mind.

CHAPTER SEVEN
WHEN TREASON RUNS IN THE FAMILY

HE MARCHED TO JERON'S SUITE of rooms. Florian pounded on the door but did not await an answer before barging in. Florian couldn't—no, he refused to—mask his infuriation or urgency, and his trepidation grew with each passing step. He slammed the heavy door closed and stood in the middle of his uncle's room.

The candles glowed, flickering waves of eerie light and shadows across the walls with the swift displacement of air from his hasty entrance. The shimmer of the shifting flames danced a sinister tempo in the reflection of Jeron's eyes.

Jeron didn't move from his seat by the fire, a goblet raised part way to his lips. "What manner of thoughtless behavior is this, Nephew?"

"I don't know, Uncle. You tell me."

Florian flexed his fingers open wide as the tension rippled through his shoulders and arms where Jeron's nonchalance added kindling to the fire burning inside him.

"Don't be ridiculous. Since you are here, you may as well sit and have a drink with me. You are man enough for it now, I suppose."

"I'll not be drinking with you, Uncle. I want answers."

Jeron moved without concern as he set his goblet on an end table to his side before uncrossing his legs and resettling his robe. He pointed to the other seat, but Florian refused to budge. He knew if he stepped closer to his uncle, it wouldn't be that much farther to grab him by the throat and choke the answers out of him. Something about this whole situation did not bode well, and he didn't understand how his uncle could put his sister—Jeron's own niece—in harm's way. When Jeron finally spoke, his annoyance seeped out with every word.

"Really, Florian. I treat you like a man, and you insist upon acting like a child. Take the blasted seat, and then we will talk."

The king's veiled threat upon Florian's sister consumed him, but he saw with all too much clarity that Orn and his uncle held the keys, that whatever his part entailed, he was nothing but a means to an end; end of what? He had no idea, but he planned to find out. He did his best to rein in the crushing anger and in stilted movements approached the chair offered him.

"That's better. I had my doubts, thinking the prince had chosen poorly in you. What royal in his right mind would choose a childish, disobedient boy as a guardsman of the first order? Oh, that's right, Prince Theiandar would. Never mind."

"Silence your disrespectful tongue, Uncle."

"Ah, the child has grown brave. Or stupid."

"I have sat, but I will have answers and no more of this useless, insolent talk. What is this you and King Orn have schemed, and where is Faye?"

Jeron's displeasure appeared genuine, but Florian, with terrible distress crushing his chest, finally realized he couldn't trust his father's brother.

"You mean to say King Orn didn't tell you? Oh, that's troubling." His fingers tapped against the armrest while he stared off into the fire's dying flames.

"Uncle. Where is Faye?" Urgency spurred Florian on—and fear, but that much he refused to admit.

"Faye. Ah, well. Faye is where she is best kept, and safe for the time being," Jeron answered without looking at Florian.

Unable to contain himself further, Florian sprang up from his seat and grabbed hold of the thick material of Jeron's robe. "Where is she?" he said through clenched teeth, his eyes boring into those of his uncle.

Jeron's response was anything but fearful. He grasped Florian's hands and pried them loose from his collar, rested his hands on the arms of the chair, and pushed himself into a standing position, his face mere inches from Florian's as they moved with one accord.

"Honestly, you continue to be an immature and stupid boy. Faye is in the care of King Orn and taken to an unknown location. I am at his mercy in this regard as much as you, though for my part I am quite relieved."

"Scoundrel! I don't believe you," Florian yelled and slapped his uncle.

He watched in stunned silence as Jeron's head snapped sideways, shocking them both. Never in a thousand years would he have thought himself capable of truly laying a hand on his uncle, his father's only living relative.

Jeron touched his lip and looked at the smear of blood sullying his fingertip. He dabbed at his lip with a handkerchief and glared.

Florian breathed hard, hot air escaping his nostrils in quick puffs and tickling his newly shaved upper lip.

"Do not ever do such a thing again, or you can be sure there will be consequences. If you choose to deny the truth of what I've said, Faye might as well already be dead. She is safe for the time being, but you will do everything—and I mean *everything*—you are told without question and without exposing the minutest detail of our plans to anyone, or I swear she will be punished. I do not care for that outcome any more than you, therefore I suggest you heed our words."

Florian could not assimilate anything his uncle said. His mind reeled with truth, deception, lies, threats, fear, in unending loops of insanity. His words came out mumbled and weak. "The king has revealed nothing except that he claims he has custody of my sister, that you are a party to some plan. That I am to speak to no one." His raging thoughts were interrupted only by a vision of punching his uncle, a man he'd never believed carried a cruelness so deep no matter how hard he had been on Florian growing up.

"Orn is intelligent. He's much smarter than most give him credit for, and there are those of us whose loyalty cannot be questioned. I'm sure when the time is right, he will tell you what you must know. Now get out before I have you thrown out."

"I'm not leaving until you tell me where Faye is."

"Insipid child. You best make yourself comfortable in one of those chairs if that's the case, because I tell you I do not know where the king has taken her. I only know she is being gently cared for, but if you do not play along, there are orders set in place to have her abused and then killed. I am unaware of the manner; I only know you and that you will not let such a thing happen to her. If you care for her at all, you will do as you are told, no questions asked. Her life is in your hands."

"That's exactly what King Orn said."

"That's exactly what he means. Now leave me or sleep in the chair. I care not which you choose," Jeron said and climbed into his bed as though he didn't have a care in the world. He blew out the nearby candles.

Florian stood helpless, his fists balled at his sides and more questions than answers filling his mind. He would gain nothing else from his uncle so he left the room, but the haze of clouded thought blocked all else from his mind and caused him to wander the streets of High Castle in aimless torture, wondering and worrying over his sweet younger sister's safety. There had to be a way to get to her, to save her from her own king. The preposterous revelation tore at his heart as he questioned his very place in the world and the purpose of loyalty when such betrayal could fall from the hands of family and leaders.

* * *

Idra looked from Bastien's precious face to the shadow of night out the window of the nursery. Caityn had insisted her dressing salon be converted into the baby's room. She knew it went against the way of royalty, of having the nursemaids care for the babies, except for feedings and special occasions, but she vowed to raise her children as her mother, Queen Ismene, had raised them.

Bimala, Princess Caityn's nursemaid while a child, had been a young woman of the castle Taisce. When Ismene had first married Othniel, she had befriended Bimala, who'd been given charge of the royal couple's children as they came. But even with Bimala in that capacity, Queen Ismene had been continually near and always mother.

Idra, gathering wool—reminiscing on the past—leaned on the cool stone of the wall by the window and swept a gentle finger along the curve of Bastien's forehead and cheek. "Precious one, you are already intensely loved," she whispered.

"You know, Idra, you were free to attend the party tonight," Caityn said from her seat where she sewed by the bright firelight.

Idra sat next to her on the settee and leaned in to let Caityn smile down at her sleeping son. "I couldn't leave you right now. That wouldn't be right."

"Nonsense. Bastien and I would be fine. Besides, the nursemaid is nearby."

"Mmm." Idra made no other reply as she imagined going to the party and what she might encounter there—who she might encounter.

"Idra, I know you better than you realize. Why are you afraid to see him?"

Bastien stirred in her arms and she stood to rock him softly from side to side. "I'm not afraid."

"What is it then?" Caityn set aside her sewing and folded her hands in her lap.

"I-I told him I loved him, and he didn't say it back." Idra laid Bastien in his cradle and touched his soft brown hair. "He's beautiful."

Caityn came and stood next to her, both staring down at his angelic face. "Yes. I could not disagree." Caityn took Idra's hand and pulled her back to the settee. "Just because he didn't say it doesn't mean he didn't want to. Did you not tell me by your own admission that you ran away just after telling him?"

"Yes," Idra conceded with some reluctance.

"You see? He didn't have a chance. If you'd gone to the party, you may have been able to speak without causing a stir."

Caityn's words, though meant kindly, irritated Idra. "I have had enough gossip whispered about me in the last two days. I couldn't stand to see the giddy eyes of courtesans at the Hamlin's, though I'm sure Hilde would have had some witty remarks."

"You two have gotten close over the last few months."

"Mmm. When she comes to the castle with her father, she always seeks me out. Tis strange, but she makes the spurious words of others seem trivial in a way that few have the ability to do. And other than you, my dear cousin, she is the only one I feel capable of being myself around."

"I'm glad you've found a friend here, Idra. I didn't realize how my marriage and now Bastien's arrival would give us less time together and leave you alone in an unfamiliar and vast place such as High Castle."

A flicker of gratitude overcame Idra. "You are good to me, Cousin. Thank you for this attempt to take my mind off my absurdity."

"Tis not absurd to wonder about Ahmad or his intentions. He has offered his love, then taken it back, most confusingly. I, for my part, have no doubt that he is entirely and deeply in love with you and will soon renew his attentions. You must be patient with him. He is no different from any man—act first, listen later."

Their eyes met in a moment of amusement.

"Men," they said in unison and giggled.

Bastien stirred in his sleep, a dreamy whimper catching their attention. Caityn moved to the cradle again and gazed down at her son. Idra watched, touched by the scene.

"Yes, my sweet Bastien, even you will grow up to be a man. But you will know the love of your mother, who will teach you how to treat a woman with respect. You will be a good man like your father, my son."

Idra hated to disrupt the moment, but the hour drew late and soon the high prince would return. She swept up next to Caityn and kissed her cousin's cheek, then left the room without another word.

On her way to her room, she turned the corner and literally ran into Sir Florian, who flew down the hall; he moved as though his own sort of tumbling storm. The knight caught her by her upper arms for a second as she staggered back due to the shock of their collision.

"My lady!" he gasped. "My sincerest apologies. I—"

"No, Sir Florian, I am well. I did not expect to meet anyone in the hall this evening. I assumed the guests near my room would be at the gathering still."

He seemed altogether in a different mental world, only half-listening to what she said. "Yes, well, most are. If you'll excuse me, my lady."

He bowed at the waist and stepped around her, his motion once again a raging storm ready to burst forth from below the surface. Idra watched him go and with great compassion wondered what had caused him such distress, wishing to be of some help in easing his mind. But she had no right to press him further. She continued on to her room, where Noreeta waited in a chair by the fire.

The lady's maid stood and curtsied when Idra entered. "My lady."

"Noreeta, I'm sorry. I didn't realize you were waiting for me. I was holding Prince Bastien and lost track of the hour."

"I can help you undress, my lady."

"Thank you. If you'll just undo the stays, I can take care of the rest, but you have already had a long day. You have thrown yourself into your work, helping me and performing the thousand other tasks you've taken on that are not your responsibility. I feel you will work yourself into an early grave if you do not rest."

Idra witnessed the heat rise in Noreeta's cheeks. It never failed that any time she spoke of the girl's diligence or good deeds, the lady's maid would balk. She denied such praise and often stammered in her speech in such moments. Idra found herself terribly curious to learn the girl's history, but Noreeta refused to open up about herself.

Noreeta went to work undoing the stays, and when she finished, she curtsied and whispered her farewell before slipping out the door. Idra watched her squeeze through the crack of the open door and vowed to uncover whatever mystery lay buried in her past.

"Good night, Noreeta," she called as the door latch tapped into place.

* * *

Florian tossed his belt onto the end of his bunk and, after ripping off his vest, yanked at the ties of his shirt. If he had any idea where the king had taken his sister, he would be on his way there right now; nothing would stop him from locating her and taking her far from the grasping, greedy hands of Jeron and Orn. He sat down on the edge of the bed and pulled his boots off, dropping them haphazardly on the floor with no concern over the amount of noise he made.

Xavier leaned upon his elbow and cleared his throat just loud enough to catch Florian's attention.

"What?" he asked and wished he hadn't. He really didn't care to know what the young knight wanted.

"Your horse is back in his stall, though he seemed almost as agitated as you do now. What's bothering you? Did your business not go well?"

"That is none of your concern." Florian leaned his forehead into his hands, his elbows resting on his knees.

"I was only being—"

"Meddlesome," Florian said, a glower screwing up his handsome features in the shadows.

"—a friend."

Xavier had said the two simple words without malice or anger. It caused Florian to reconsider his angry retort. Xavier wasn't the problem. He acted as a friend would.

Florian shook his head, and his shoulders slumped. "I'm sorry, X. I received some unpleasant news, and I'm not sure what to do about it. I'll . . . figure something out. Not to worry. Sleep well." He swung around to lie flat on his bed, his arms clasped on his stomach and his eyes unfocused on the boards of the bunk above.

Xavier didn't respond, but Florian sensed his analyzing, pondering stare. If King Orn was serious, Florian wouldn't be able to say a word to anyone or risk his sister's safety. The thought left him sick to his stomach and unable to sleep.

CHAPTER EIGHT
THE BAD NEWS GETS WORSE

THEY HAD GIVEN KING ORN a suite of chambers in the north tower, facing Solfen River and the forests of birch and pine on its opposite bank. Florian thought of it as one of his favorite views, reminding him of Wyeth, of his childhood home and his sister. But as he pondered it now, he realized Faye might be out there somewhere, and it killed him to imagine someone might hurt her.

He stopped outside Orn's private salon and glared at each man standing guard on either side of the door. As if the maddening grit in his eyes from lack of sleep weren't enough, the man closest to the latch looked at him with disdain and caused Florian's glower to deepen. He recognized him as one of the men who'd taken part in the high prince's guardsmen trials when Raz had gone to Wyeth to choose a man from among the elite of the realm.

"The king is waiting."

Florian didn't acknowledge his terse words but opened the door and ignored the intuitive warning screaming in the back of his mind. Once he walked through the doors, there would be no turning back. Inside, the salon had a nicely situated seating area and a dining table with four seats. The curved outer wall of the tower room sported three windows facing to the north and west. Warm light from the promising fall day streamed in and gave the space a serene atmosphere.

"Right on time," King Orn said from his seat at the table while he wiped at his mouth. "Come. We will discuss our venture over a meal as civilized men."

Florian hesitated only a second before he bowed and approached Orn. He recognized where he stood with the king since the monarch had not bothered to wait until Florian arrived to eat.

"Sire, I'm not particularly hungry. My sister—"

"Your sister is a precious gem, though fragile."

Florian jerked forward, a gut reaction to the king's insinuating tone. Orn obviously didn't miss it, since a dark cloud of unfettered satisfaction crossed his face.

"Unassuming, sweet Faye is safe, but it is poor form to insult your monarch by refusing to eat with him."

Florian sat, but he screamed on the inside. Dealing with a king had more pitfalls and politics than doing so with his uncle. The placement of knights around the room worked as a subtle reminder, but it didn't stop him from imagining himself shaking the middle-aged king loose of his sordid secrets. They watched each other, but Orn's face had become unreadable while he piled Florian's plate high with the choicest cuts of meat and freshest fruit.

"The weather is fine for the tourney. I will not be taking part, of course, but my best knight," Orn motioned behind him with a two-pronged fork to the knight who'd entered behind Florian, "Havrik, there, will represent Wyeth in the games. You will be in the tournament, I assume."

"Yes," Florian said, ignoring the sumptuous food while he examined the hulking man near the window.

Orn took a bite and spoke around it. "No. You will not. You will be busy guarding your prince and his family."

"Sire?" he asked, his eyes focusing back on Orn's face.

He couldn't keep the question from his voice. Might the whole business of secrecy just be Orn's way of using him to gain favor with the high prince? If that explained it, he would gladly play along. He watched Orn pick up a strange sort of trinket that dangled from a chain around his neck and rub it with his thumb, then release it again to wipe his mouth with the napkin.

"Leave us."

Orn stared at Florian but spoke to his guards. Florian kept his vision trained on Orn, but, out of the corner of his eye, watched the other men file out without a backward glance. This arrangement seemed preferable as far as Florian was concerned. He had private, personal questions for which he did not want an audience.

The door stopped scant inches from being closed and creaked open another foot before a knight's head tipped into the gap. Orn's attention shifted to the door.

"What is it?" he asked with a high level of perturbation.

"One of Sir Florian's associates is below. What should we do with him?"

Florian gripped the edge of the table and stiffened. He'd been in such a state he hadn't even noticed anyone following. Then he remembered Xavier had been expecting him at the armory before noon. They'd made plans early the previous day, but Florian had completely forgotten. He'd walked by the armory to get to the castle keep, and Xavier must have seen him. But why had he followed?

"Should I be concerned, Sir Florian?" Orn asked, interrupting his thoughts with the question implying much more than he'd said.

"No, Sire," Florian said without pause. "I've said nothing. I was supposed to meet my fellow guardsman and forgot to tell him I had a change of plans. He must have followed to inquire after my whereabouts. I swear he is no threat to you."

Orn's eyes leveled on Florian. "Send him on his way."

Florian relaxed and picked up a piece of fruit when the door clicked shut. Thus far, the king had given him no reason to suppose he might be in personal danger, and he did not want to appear fearful or anxious. Orn seemed more pleased with himself and his plans than interested in harming Florian except by his veiled threats to his sister. For now, Florian needed to stay calm and collected if he were to assure himself of his sister's welfare.

"Now, where was I? Ah yes, last night I told you the beginning of a tale. Or mayhap 'twas the end? In either case, the Beauty Thief, or Nox as he is called, did not die when pushed from the cave at Ophira's Peak."

"He was not pushed," Florian said, overcome with a need to make the distinction clear though not truly trusting Orn's words. "But it matters little. No man lives through such a fall. Has someone then claimed to be him? Why has the high prince not been informed of this? Is this why you've asked me to guard him during the tourney? Are you expecting this false Nox to attack the prince?"

Orn laughed a wretched, unnerving trill. "You cannot fathom who you are dealing with, young guardsman. This is your same Beauty Thief with powers beyond reckoning. And now he works for me. Your loyalty is not to High Prince Theiandar. It belongs to me. Nothing I am about to tell you will be repeated or spoken of by you to anyone." He rubbed the greenish talisman at his chest with his index finger. "On your sister's life, you must swear this."

Florian had a sinking sensation in his gut. Nothing good could come from something that required threats against his sister or swearing by her name.

"I cannot swear on what I do not understand," he said, unsure of how to respond and worried he might put Faye in further danger if the king did exercise control over her.

Orn threw a chicken bone onto his plate and licked his fingers. He stood and moved to stare out the window to the north. "Understand this." His words were hollow as they echoed off the window glass. "Faye will find herself the next sacrifice to the awesome and ancient power Nox will give me if you do not swear your complete fealty."

He turned to face Florian, who couldn't breathe, and in the gravest manner continued speaking while he pulled something from the pocket of his tunic. A beautiful braid of hair matching his own dangled from the king's hand, the sight of which entrapped Florian's sight. Orn's next words blistered his soul.

"Once she's been stripped of her beauty, the hag that will then be your sister shall be paraded before your very eyes where the life will then be drained from her with no escape and no chance of salvation. I will imprison you for the remainder of your life, left to rot in the dungeons and feed on your own regret. Swear you will tell no one and will submit to all I command of you, or this will be the consequence of your disobedience."

Orn's words carried a finality that Florian refused to believe, yet he could not deny the truth ringing in them as he stared at the shimmering golden braid of his sister's hair. The varied many hues of auburn, peppered with sunny flecks of blonde entwined neatly together, reminding Florian of his mother's hair—a sharp contrast against the king's vile fingers.

Orn had lost his mind and would do exactly as he threatened. The realization caused painful stabs of wrenching fear to brutalize Florian's consciousness, but no matter how he tried, he couldn't formulate a reply. He grew numb, his dry mouth bitter from the import of Orn's threat.

"Swear it," Orn snapped as he strode back to the table and rested a knife against Florian's throat, just below his Adam's apple.

Florian's wide eyes looked into those of Orn. There were no words for the depth of malice he saw there. "Take my life now, Sire."

"If I take your life now, it will only ensure Faye's own demise."

The press of cold metal on Florian's neck became his only reality. Even if the king withdrew the knife without taking his life, Florian would be a dead man, if not in body, then certainly in spirit. He must protect Faye. Many strained seconds of silent battle ticked by before a stinging sensation on his neck, followed by the fleeting warmth of blood trickling down to the hollow between his collarbones, spurred his response—not for himself, but for Faye's sake.

"I swear," he whispered and fought back tears.

"On your sister's life, swear it."

What choice had he? Agonized thoughts held him prisoner.

"I swear on Faye's life," he said, but choked on the words.

Now he could only hope Orn wasn't the dastardly sort of fellow he'd been reputed to be from whisperings back home in Wyeth. The king slid the knife away from Florian's throat and retook his seat, tossing a napkin at Florian as he did.

"You've made a wise choice, Sir Florian. Faye will be grateful of your devotion."

Orn placed a grape between his teeth and grinned wide. It made Florian sick to his stomach to watch the man speak of devotion and betrayal, wisdom and death, as if they were one and the same.

"She will despise me if I have made a vow in her name in vain." Florian said the words almost to himself and braced to hear what King Orn would require of him.

"We shall see. Business, young sir. Nox is alive and has been my prisoner, or shall we say guest, these last eighteen months.

It took him quite a while to heal from his many injuries sustained during the fall, but still less than any normal man. A shock he lived at all after his tumble, since no ordinary man would have. But once he healed enough to regain strength, the old man offered me a prize for my help in retrieving pink sands from the coral beaches of Agora. With the items he has traded to me, I will overthrow High King Dante and take his place as ruler of the Twelve Realms."

Florian shook his head. He doubted his ears. The words made little sense as it was, but the man rambled madness that would get anyone involved killed. "You could never."

"Oh, but I can and I will. With your help."

"I'll never betray the prince!" Florian shouted and half-stood, leaning forward on the table.

Orn rested his arms near the tips of Florian's splayed fingers, one on top of the other, and spoke in a low voice. "You will help and do it gladly, my fellow. Or you can be sure Faye's lifeless, haggish body will not make a pretty sight dangled from the walls of High Castle."

Faye. He caved in defeat. She had no one in the world besides Florian to protect her. Obviously, their Uncle Jeron didn't care for either of them, which meant Florian had already let her down in that regard. He sank back into the seat and gritted his teeth.

"That's better." Orn had picked up the knife, but now placed it back on the table. "Your task will be simple. I've traded Nox a good deal of gold for this blade." He reached toward another chair and held up a bejeweled, curved dagger. "But there is an enchantment upon it; it will kill whoever is stabbed by it. It must penetrate deeply. A mere scratch will only cause a sleep as deep as death to overtake its victim."

Florian listened and, in a different way, experienced his own life slipping away; as if he existed only as an apparition witnessing the scene from without. His awareness went on in torment over the notion of the Beauty Thief, the threat of his wrath sinking in, and Florian lost himself in the fear of seeing Faye exactly as he'd witnessed Princess Caityn when Nox had stolen her beauty, inside and out. Faye needed him. He could not abandon her to the mercy of Orn or Nox, and if he revealed any of this treachery, he'd do just that. But could he be an accomplice to such a treasonous act against the royal family? Against his king? Against Raz?

"Under the guise of protecting High Prince Theiandar and his family, while you are seated with them on the last day of the tourney, you will stab the high king. The knife will do the rest. I have arranged it through the unsuspecting Princess Caityn that your uncle will be present to accuse High Prince Theiandar of attempting to murder his own father. They will seize the prince. Princess Caityn and the baby will be escorted to her rooms and placed in custody, confined there. Your part will be over and your sister will be safe."

"Where is Faye?"

"Not far."

"Where?" Florian's jaw tightened as he ground the one word out.

"Safe. And that is all you will learn."

"I can't do this. Tis high treason! I cannot and would never kill the king."

"Oh, my dear Sir Florian, you can and you will, or you may prepare to say goodbye to your sweet baby sister. Poor Faye, who has never been in love or watched the moon set over the Opal Sea. She who has never seen the rolling hills of Parlan or walked the steps of High Castle to witness the elevation of her brother. And in contrast, we both know the High King of the Twelve Realms is not innocent or pure. You must understand this, Florian. Her beauty is such that I will take it . . . however I deem fit."

Florian imagined himself lunging for the king, but he endeavored to ignore the man's goading. He had to restrain himself because his actions could endanger his sister. There just had to be another way, but what? But nothing. No ideas surfaced, and desperation set in while the cruel words of one who should be an honest and brave leader stripped Florian bare of his own will.

He walked to the window where the king had stood minutes before and stared off into the distance, his eyes peering into the beyond of time and space in desperation, searching for his sister. "I will obey, Sire," he heard himself saying as though in a dream.

A single tear slid down his cheek and completed his defeat. He swiped it away and frowned at King Orn. Orn's wide grin spreading across his face turned out to be the last nail added to Florian's coffin. If anyone deserved to die, this man did, but the current moment rendered him untouchable.

"Wipe the blood from your neck," Orn demanded, and Florian obeyed reflexively. "Now leave me, and when the day approaches, I will give you this blade. It must stay hidden on your person or risk someone recognizing its intricate and fine details later."

Florian stumbled toward the door. He recognized himself moving, but had no idea how it happened. As he walked past Orn's secretive knights outside the door, he noticed the sinister grin of a man he hadn't recognized before, but even that slipped from his mind, still unable to come to grips with the terrible twist his life had taken.

CHAPTER NINE
FIGHT OR FLIGHT

FLORIAN EMERGED FROM THE RELATIVE darkness of the castle hall into the bright sunshine of what should have been a beautiful fall afternoon, but he was numb to the warmth of it on his icy-as-death skin. Somehow, the approaching winter must have frozen him from the inside out. Florian flinched, startled from his mindlessness by Xavier's searing touch upon his shoulder.

"Florian, you look as though you've seen a ghost."

He pushed Xavier's hand off with nothing but a glare in response and drifted toward the armory, having no idea what he would do once he arrived. For the first minute or two, Xavier seemed to take the silence in stride, in the same way he walked next to Florian, but the quiet didn't last.

"What happened in there? King Orn's men gave me the impression they thought I shouldn't be trusted. They detained me when I walked up the stairway in the tower, but released me without another word after that big fellow nodded. Not a word. He just nodded once and they told me to leave."

"Nothing happened, Xavier," Florian said. A thin layer of sweat beaded on his upper lip, and he wiped it away. "Leave it be."

"What happened to your neck?"

Florian reached up and brushed his finger along the fresh cut. "Nothing. I . . . cut myself shaving."

"I understand we haven't known each other long, but since yesterday you seem different. I can tell. Something is bothering you. And you didn't do that shaving. Has someone threatened you?"

"No."

"Is there anything I can do to help? Is there trouble back home with your lands? Is the king of Wyeth offering you a position in his own guard? Are you considering leaving High Prince Theiandar's service?"

The questions flew at Florian in rapid succession, but none were even close to the mark. Or were they? The rambling questions posed by the younger knight held notes of truth . . . at least in a small way. Florian scoffed and shook his head.

"You could say that."

"You can't leave, Florian. It's unheard of for a guardsman to rescind his commission as a high king's guardsman."

"I don't think it will come to that, Xavier," Florian said, trying to close the conversation. He did not need more questions. Neither did he care to risk putting Faye's life in any more danger.

"If you're not leaving, then what's bothering you?"

Florian stopped. His abrupt halt caused Xavier to stumble two steps, then turn to stare after him. He could think of nothing to say that would appease Xavier's curiosity. "Tis a private matter. Now leave off with the interrogation."

Xavier's hands went up. Florian's tone had been clipped, but the events of the last twenty-four hours continued to press down upon him like a lead weight, and he couldn't breathe under the pressure.

"I'm not meaning to pry, my friend, but you seem out of sorts, and I only want to help."

"Well, you're not," Florian said, more agitated than before but at least feeling something again.

He pressed past Xavier who now stood between him and the path to the armory. Florian used more force than necessary, but Xavier positioned himself to be the easiest target upon which to take out his frustration. The physical act of pushing Xavier away might have been considered a personal necessity; it seemed the only way to avoid imploding from fear and rage. He felt trapped and silenced, but he didn't yet know if a caged lion or a pet rabbit better described him. Only time would tell, but in the interim, he had to push everyone else away to keep them safe.

Xavier caught up to him and said not another word as they marched on to the armory, where both men outfitted for practice in leather armor and various weaponry. Florian's mind reeled again with the words King Orn had spoken, causing him to pay little heed to his surroundings as he considered the possibility that he'd become a puppet controlled by an outside force with no will or purpose of his own. The unpleasant sensation left him fighting back tears which had no place in the life of a knight of the Realms.

They took their gear to the indoor practice arena and fought, but several times Florian had to hold himself back from taking out his animosity on Xavier who lacked Florian's strength and experience. He didn't question Xavier's capability, but the new guardsman had much to learn, and Florian carried enough responsibility for his sister and her situation; he did not need to add more to his load by injuring Xavier too.

But it didn't take Florian long to lose himself. He swung his blade, blocked oncoming assaults, and ducked hefty swings of his opponent's sword, but in the heat of battle he kneeled over

Xavier, his fist planted squarely in the other man's jaw—not once, not twice, but three times before Gavin's hand stopped him. The shock came first, followed by humiliation and self-loathing as he realized what he'd just done without consideration or self-control. He stumbled to his feet and backed away.

"I-I don't know what happened," he said and walked out of the arena.

He didn't look back. He couldn't face anyone. If they only knew what he contemplated doing, what he had sworn to do in his sister's name, they would kill him on the spot. If the roles were reversed, he'd never let any of them do what he'd given his word to do. Who in their right mind would agree to kill High King Dante?

Still armor-clad and with spear in hand, Florian walked with his head down, not toward the barracks but out the castle's east gate, trekking north along the city's sprawling wall. The brooding, churning Solfen River stood between him and the northern realms. Just on the other side, Conleth's realm began, and beyond that, to the north and west, stood his home in Wyeth. He closed his eyes and pictured the simple house he'd grown up in, south of the castle. Florian pictured the nearby village close to where Rusty, the master fletcher, made his home. He remembered how his father would swing his little sister—sweet, innocent Faye—up into the air and back into the safety of his arms, and his chest ached to have his father back right at that precise moment.

"Father, I'm weak. I'm sorry I have failed you, and Mother, and Faye. I wish you were here. You would kept her safe. Oh Almighty, how can I do this thing that's been required of me? But I see no other way to save Faye."

His impromptu, whispered prayer ended without another word because the more he said, the more sickened at his own depravity he became. How could he even consider the prospect of treason against the high king? Could he live with himself if a man such as Orn were to take power? Not likely, but Faye would be spared, and he could smuggle her from the country, get her to safety. But the chaos left in their wake? He knew Faye well enough from her letters to appreciate she'd grown into a strong and confident young woman who would never forgive him for being a part of treason even if to save her. But he'd lay down his life for his sister. He had no escape and no idea how to rescue Faye without doing as Orn commanded.

* * *

Orn reclined in his chair and picked more food from between his teeth with the tip of the knife he'd held to Florian's throat. While he examined the bits of masticated meat, Jeron stepped out from behind the dressing screen where he'd been hidden throughout the exchange between his nephew and the king.

"Are you certain he won't turn on us, Jeron?"

Jeron lowered his hefty frame into the chair Florian had vacated minutes before and ate the untouched food from the plate set there. Orn waited for him to swallow, but his patience wore thin. Florian hadn't reacted to the green pendant's power at the party at Hamlin House, and he fought against it here. That Jeron didn't require its power to be persuaded had to be good news. They'd been friends and allies for far too long. Jeron coughed on the bite he chewed and downed a goblet of red wine before he spoke.

"Since the time of his parent's death, he took it upon himself to protect his sister. The only reason he agreed to join Prince Theiandar's guardsmen came about because I told Faye if she didn't convince him to go, I would betroth her to Lord Ducon of Berne and marry her off at thirteen. I implied without beating around the bush that she held her brother back from his destiny," Jeron said and laughed.

"You already told me this. I am not convinced. Set men about to keep a close watch on him and anyone he speaks to in more than cursory conversation."

"Yes, Highness."

Jeron took one last bite of chicken and pushed up from his seat, making a succinct bow before leaving the room. Orn watched the older man leave and wondered at the man's deviousness. Orn alone held knowledge of Jeron's less-than-spotless history with Florian's parents, not to mention Jeron's own wife, whom he'd killed slowly with poison. Jeron's doing and advice had led Orn on a similar path, one which would soon see him free of his virtuous wife, Nikita.

"Havrik."

"Yes, Sire?"

"You keep a close watch on Sir Florian. Take the blade with you, and use it if you see the need arise."

"My liege, I obey your command."

Havrik placed his right arm across his breast and bent forward at the waist. Orn nodded once and watched the tall, broad-shouldered Wyethian walk out the door. Havrik also need not be controlled by means beyond a man's natural ability. He'd rescued the knight as a boy and raised him in his household.

Havrik had been passed over for High Prince Theiandar's guardsmen in favor of Jeron's nephew, Florian. It had worked out in Orn's favor, of course, but it had left a sour taste in the young knight's mouth and solidified his allegiance to Orn. If it weren't for the fact that he thought of Havrik as a son, he'd have put him to the deed of murdering High King Dante, but he wouldn't risk his death when there were other means available. Orn could only hope that Florian could be bent to his will.

* * *

Idra adjusted the bow guard on her arm for the thousandth time and glared at her cousin Gavin. He grinned back and shrugged his shoulders. She assumed he found her poor aim to be far more amusing than true gallantry would allow and wanted nothing better than to shoot an arrow at his feet just to spite him, but she wouldn't. It had taken far too long to convince him to help her learn to use various weapons and defensive ways to protect herself against attackers.

After what she'd been through in the last year, she tired of feeling defenseless and had begged her cousin to teach her what skills she needed. At first, Gavin had been adamantly against her learning to use weapons or physical force, saying it didn't suit a lady of her standing, but she'd soon convinced him of the importance that she be able to protect herself and the high princess, as well as the little baby about to be born. That had been before the royal child had arrived—a son, an heir to the high throne of Twelve Realms.

Once Gavin had been thoroughly convinced of the advantage of it, after Idra had laid on enough guilt over her previous experiences of kidnapping and near slavery, he'd agreed to train her. They'd commenced with basic movements to escape someone's grasp, then progressed to knife throwing and fighting, but by comparison, on this day, the lesson in archery seemed tame.

Idra had had some experience with archery since childhood. Princess Caityn, her cousin and now the future high queen of the Twelve Realms of whom she served as lady-in-waiting, had taken lessons, but Idra had not been interested. She'd only shot a bow a handful of times.

Idra pulled back on the string and sighted her target down the shaft of the arrow. She took in a slow breath and released it. At the same time, she let go of the arrow and watched it whizz through the air, where it soon slammed into the hay target with a satisfying thud and sent a mini eruption of dry grass flittering into the air. She grinned and bit her bottom lip as she examined her hit from a distance.

"Well done, Idra. You've improved since last week. Have you been practicing in secret?" Gavin asked with one brow raised.

She didn't mind his mocking, as he meant no harm by it. "If you count the little toy bow and arrow set given to our sweet new baby cousin, then yes, I have been. Now," she said, leaning lightly on the bow limb, "can we move on to the staff? I enjoyed that last we practiced it."

She couldn't hide her smug smile at the look of distaste that flitted across Gavin's face. She'd proved herself quite adept with the long staff after the first lesson. On their last round of practice, she'd knocked Gavin to the ground, stood over him with her legs straddling his waist and the staff pressed to his upper chest. She'd been quite proud of herself, but he'd ruined the moment by knocking the staff to the side, throwing her off-balance and then trapping her in much the same position he'd been in seconds before. But the true moment of triumph had come when she'd pulled his leg out from under him, and he'd toppled to the ground in a heap of flying dust and grunts. She hadn't won, but he hadn't come away unscathed that time either. Idra wasn't sure if she wanted to prove to herself or to Gavin that her capabilities were ever improving, but the idea of a rematch gave her a jolt of excitement, one she'd have to suppress if she didn't want to appear unladylike.

"Get them," Gavin said and motioned toward the training staffs gathered in a jumble near the far wall of the armory.

With Idra being a woman—and noble—they agreed to keep their practice within the confines of the armory's interior training room to reduce the possibility of gossip. If Idra hated one thing, the tittering of idle tongues could top the short list, and since moving to High Castle with Princess Caityn, she'd already had enough of that to last a lifetime.

Idra didn't waste a second as she pulled the back of her skirt up between her thighs and tucked it into her belt in the front, grabbed two of the lighter ash wood staffs, and carried them to the center of the ring. One in each hand, she hefted them with a bounce to measure the weight and thought they were even. Of course, Gavin's greater strength, speed, and training gave him the advantage. Still, it seemed fair to her, no matter that by comparison she lacked in these areas.

She tossed her grinning cousin his staff, and he caught it without taking his eyes from hers. They moved within the circle as though hunting prey, contemplating their next meal. Idra smiled with a growing sense of confidence while she watched Gavin's movement. When first they'd begun these training exercises, she'd been timid and unsure, but the more they practiced, the more she grew to love the feeling of power she gained.

He circled to her left, she to her right, but when he pounced, she stood ready. With her arms extended and elbows bent, Idra used her newly strengthened muscles to keep the staff in place as a barrier against his oncoming blow, but it jarred through her bones upon impact. He would go easy on her, but to the onlooker it must not have appeared so, and after countless parries, swings, and thrusts of her own, Gavin took her legs out from under her with one quick swing of the staff. She landed on her back, and as the air gushed from her lungs, she heard a man's angry yell.

Before Idra knew what hit them, Gavin thundered to the floor, rolling about in a tangle of arms and fists with another man.

Ahmad? Idra questioned in her mind, not quite believing what her eyes saw.

"Ahmad!" she yelled, sitting up in shock.

He didn't seem to hear her, so she took her staff in hand and used the end to press into his ribs, pushing him to the side to get him off Gavin who appeared to be working harder to block Ahmad's blows than to fight back. It looked rather confusing to Idra, but she took some satisfaction in witnessing how her hard push had dislodged Ahmad from her cousin.

"Ahmad!" she yelled again. "What are you doing?"

He'd fallen back on his rear end, his hands splayed out on either side to keep him upright. "What am I doing?" he bellowed. "The question is, what are *you* doing?"

He spoke to them both, but for the life of her, Idra couldn't fathom why he appeared upset. Gavin spoke up before she formulated a reply.

"Tis nothing, Ahmad. Idra only wanted some training in self-defense."

"Nothing? Self-defense? That was more than self-defense, Gavin. Lady Idra is a lady. And you . . ." he said, getting to his feet and turning to face her, "you have no reason to learn any such violence. There are men to protect you."

Ahmad's reaction, though similar to Gavin's initial feelings, made her angrier than words could express. "Men to protect me? You must be in jest! In protecting me, men have died! And I stood by, unable to do anything to help myself or them. Can you not understand how weak that makes me feel, how utterly defenseless and frightened?"

She stood, arms akimbo and feet spread wide, her lightweight, thin skirts loosed and swishing about her legs, and she glared at him. Never had she spoken with such ferocity and passion, but in the heat of the moment, she didn't care. He didn't say anything, and Idra thought she might have stunned him into silence, which felt both empowering and frightening.

Her hands lowered to her sides, but impassioned anger still burned in the clench of her fists. "You have no say in this, sir. I am neither your sister nor wife for you to order about, and I'll not hear another word from you about whether I should learn such things. I refuse—absolutely refuse—to ever again fall prey to another man's evil whims with no knowledge of how to protect myself. I will not be a victim in need of rescue. I will not live in fear. I will never again be left vulnerable."

She didn't wait for him to reply, but bent to retrieve her staff from the ground. Idra stood to her full height and stared at Ahmad without really seeing him. She held the smooth wooden staff in both hands as she marched toward him and, with more force than necessary, shoved it into Ahmad's chest, where he fumbled to take it. Idra kept her eyes trained on the open vee of his tunic, because she didn't want to see the disappointment or disapproval on his face. Once he'd taken the staff from her, she stormed from the armory without a backward glance.

Idra couldn't explain what had come over her. A powerful and satisfying force trembled through her chest as though she recognized herself for the first time. Her brisk walk took her toward the castle gates, where she hoped to cool down before someone saw her in this agitated state and made up some awful story about her.

CHAPTER TEN
MISUNDERSTANDING

AHMAD WATCHED HER GO, UNABLE to fully grasp what had just happened. At first, he'd been shocked and appalled by what he'd witnessed when entering the training room, but again, Idra's words struck true. The scholar-turned-pirate Simon's face swam before his vision in a wretched reminder. She had been through too much in the last two years. Foolish, idiot, dimwitted, thoughtless imbecile all described his behavior. And he doubted he was being too hard on himself.

He looked from Gavin's appraising stare to the staff wrapped in his fingers and back up. Gavin had gotten to his feet during Idra's tirade and now stood leaning on the pole with a lopsided grin quickly spreading across his face.

"I'd say something myself if Idra hadn't already said enough."

"If you utter a word," Ahmad said with a growl, "I'll wallop you."

Gavin raised his staff and assumed a defensive stance, eyeing Ahmad in such a way he knew what would come next.

"I think you already tried that, but just to give you a fair chance at it again . . . ." Gavin attacked without warning.

A smile twitched at the corner of Ahmad's mouth, and the two sparred for several minutes before he lost interest. He gave one last quick pass with his weapon and knocked Gavin's pole from his hands. Out of breath, he asked, "How long have you been training with her?"

The thought pestered him, and he couldn't focus on the fight. Gavin's stance relaxed, and he shrugged before bending to retrieve his staff.

"I don't know exactly. Just a little over two months, I believe. Right after you and the others left for Emlyn, she approached me with the idea. But don't even for a second think I came up with this harebrained idea. I understand what you're doing. You're trying to decide whether to be angry at me, but in my defense, I refused. She kept asking me every day for nearly a week, then threatened to ask someone else. I can imagine there are plenty of knights willing enough to spend time . . . training a lady. And because she persisted, I thought it best that I be the one to do it since I'm her cousin. I must say, I find it interesting that as much as she detests gossip, she would even consider asking me, let alone someone else. And as hard as it is to admit, she's a quick study. I think we've underestimated her pluck and mettle."

Ahmad absorbed the words, but he continued to struggle over the idea. "You put the handkerchief in my saddlebag that morning."

"Yes," Gavin said, even though it hadn't been a question. He'd already admitted as much days ago. "She asked me to do it, and I didn't see the harm in it, especially as it is clear how much you care for her. And she loves you, but you were willing to just throw that away."

Ahmad's eyebrows scrunched together as he frowned. He hadn't considered his gesture of returning the handkerchief, thus releasing her from any promise to consider a courtship with him, as a destructive or reckless move. But here fell more truth he couldn't quite swallow. When had he started allowing his emotions to dictate his actions? He would need to rectify that problem.

"I'm sorry to interrupt, Sir Ahmad, but I hoped I might speak with you."

He turned to see who spoke, since the voice was only vaguely familiar. Xavier stood in the doorway of the armory practice room with one hand resting on the hilt of his sword and the other relaxed at his side. Each encounter, unexpected or not, sent a jolt through Ahmad as if he were seeing a ghost.

"What is it?" Irritability tinged his tone.

"If now is not a good time . . ."

"You've already disrupted us; you may as well be out with it."

Ahmad saw the faintest twinge flit across Xavier's face, but his irritation over the convoluted situation with Idra distracted him, and he didn't care how his response made the other man feel.

Gavin cleared his throat, pulled the staff from Ahmad's clenched fingers, and put it away with his own. "I'll just leave you two to discuss what needs discussing," he said and squeezed past Xavier who partially blocked the doorway.

Ahmad watched Gavin lay his hand on Xavier's shoulder in some friendly gesture as he passed by. He looked at Xavier for a second but didn't linger, because even after days of forced interaction with the young replica of Hanif, he couldn't abolish the deep sense of regret that swept over him. It irritated him and left a foul taste in his mouth.

He'd decided the day before that if he just ignored Xavier, maybe he'd not be constantly reminded of the past, but it seemed like the other knight kept showing up out of nowhere.

Ahmad's guilt gradually morphed into dislike and might have well been on its way to hatred, but for the fact that deep down Ahmad knew Xavier wasn't Hanif. Deeper still, he knew Xavier resented him for Hanif's death, but this would never be said aloud.

He took a deep, calming breath and went to the wall of knives, where he picked out two of medium length. He faced the target and sensed Xavier standing a few feet behind him, off to the left. He stared at the thick wooden target wall, covered in myriad dents and pockmarks. After giving careful aim, Ahmad threw the blade, but Xavier chose that moment to speak and his aim faltered at the last second, sending the knife flailing off course.

"Sir—"

Ahmad watched the knife flick off the wood and land in the dust on the hard-packed dirt floor. Turning only his head, he glared over his shoulder at Xavier before taking careful aim and lobbing the other knife at the board, hitting it dead center on the bull's-eye.

"Uh, Sir Ahmad, I didn't know who else I should speak with as High Prince Theiandar is preoccupied with—"

"He's engaged by important matters of state regarding the birth of his son. He's not preoccupied," Ahmad said, still eyeing his knife planted firmly in the target and irritated at the impudence of this stranger-boy.

"Forgive me. I meant nothing disrespectful. I only meant I didn't want to disrupt him when he was obviously busy, but there was something that's bothering me about one of the other guardsmen, and I needed to ask advice about it. Hanif once told me you . . . that he'd come to you when he needed help."

Ahmad closed his eyes and bowed his chin to his chest for a second. Of course, Hanif would have told his brother such a thing. He couldn't count the times he'd been a teacher and mentor to Hanif before his untimely death.

"What is it?" he asked in a soft, resolved tone after a span of immeasurable time in silence.

"It's about Florian. Something happened last night that upset him, and then he went to King Orn's suite of rooms in the northwest tower today. I met him just outside the keep. He went white as a sheet, and when I asked him what troubled him, he said nothing, but—"

"If Florian said nothing troubled him, nothing did. He doesn't care to meet with his uncle, who likes to be in attendance with King Orn. That is likely what rankles him."

"But 'tis more than that, sir."

Ahmad's eyebrows raised in displeasure at the argumentative yet forthright response. "I think I know Florian better than you. Two months is not long enough to truly know a person."

One side of Xavier's mouth quirked up, but Ahmad noticed how he seemed to stand a little taller.

"I mean no disrespect again, Sir Ahmad, but I have a feeling, an intuition, about this. Something is seriously wrong."

Ahmad crossed his arms over his chest. He stood only an inch or two above Xavier and used his height to his advantage. Xavier didn't seem to be impressed as he matched Ahmad's stance, even wearing the same sort of grim expression. They stood there, face to face, arms crossed over their puffed-out chests for several seconds before Ahmad decided how he would respond.

"I appreciate you are concerned, but you needn't be. Florian is one of us, and if he has a problem, he will come to us first. You, I do not know. Leave Florian be and find something more productive to do with your time than spy on your fellow guardsmen."

He watched Xavier's lips part and surprise color his cheeks. It shouldn't have felt satisfying to put the new guardsman in his place like that, but it did, which added to his niggling sense of guilt, a guilt he now chose to fully ignore as he would this young, immature boy who stood before him.

Xavier glared, and without a word, left Ahmad standing alone just inside the doorway to the training room, looking out into the main armory. There, four knights were gathering equipment, their heads ducked down and eyes averted, which only added to Ahmad's irritation because it meant they'd heard at least the last part of the conversation and were likely to be repeating it. Idra was right; gossip ran rampant through High Castle like a disease.

* * *

Idra headed north across the field and took the foot trail meandering along the edge of the woods. She kept near the walls of High Castle and, as Princess Caityn had ordered, any time she left the confines of the castle walls, she had to be escorted. She couldn't walk out the gates without someone following her, and this hadn't changed. It didn't seem to matter that the entrance to High Castle bustled with activity; the gatekeepers still knew when she came.

There were days when it amused her, but today she wanted to be alone. Still, she found some comfort in knowing she had company. Without looking, she assumed her companion to be the same guardsman who escorted her most days. They'd rarely said a word to each other.

He kept a respectable distance until they moved into the shadows, but the next thing she knew, he rushed up right behind her. She stopped and swung around to stare him down, not willing to deal with impudence or untoward behavior. To her surprise, it was not who she expected to see.

"Sir Xavier! Your face. What happened? Wait. What are you doing following me?" Her hands went to her hips, and she fought the temptation to send him back to the castle and leave her in peace.

"I apologize, my lady." He touched his cheek and winced. "Tis nothing. Just a bit of practice. I made my way out of the castle in search of Sir Florian, but I saw you at the gate and offered to keep you safe since—"

"Sir Xavier, how can you keep me safe and search out Sir Florian at the same time?"

She watched a blush crawl up his neck, then across his cheeks, and she pinched her lips together to hide her smile.

"I-you make a good point, but there is a reason. When I saw you, I had just come from speaking with Sir Ahmad. You are close with him, are you not?"

"What an impertinent question."

"I only heard—"

"You only heard rumors, sir, but I shall forget any mention of it because, in this case, there is some small truth. It's much more complicated than the gossip would imply. But, um, what is the reason it should matter to you?"

She shifted uncomfortably from one foot to the other and attempted to discern what her relationship with Ahmad, or lack thereof, had to do with anything Xavier might need. But with her curiosity piqued, she smiled to encourage him to speak on.

He cleared his throat. "It's actually about Sir Florian, my lady. I have a suspicion that all is not well, though I have no evidence to the fact other than a negligible cut to his neck and his stark shift in mood."

Idra noticed him shuffle his feet but took no pleasure in his discomfort, even while she grew more and more confused with each word he spoke.

"I asked Sir Ahmad for advice and he . . . he told me to leave it be, but I can't. Florian has been my closest friend since arriving here, and he's been instrumental in helping me to adjust. He is usually smiling, and he doesn't lie or yell. He's rarely an angry man, but he behaved so last night, and then today he walked about like the living dead."

He paused for a second and let this unpleasant folktale image sink in. Idra waited for him to continue, because he obviously had more to explain. Why would Ahmad dismiss Sir Xavier's concerns without consideration? He treated the guardsmen of Delphor like brothers, and he'd be concerned if something proved askew with one of them. Something must be distracting him. She knew what, or who, that might be but refused to admit she'd rattled him with her desire to learn battle techniques.

"My lady, I hoped you could speak with him on Sir Florian's behalf. I am confident he would listen to you, and in that way you would help Sir Florian who, as it has been clearly pointed out to me, is 'one of them' and would tell his fellow guardsmen if something were wrong."

She heard a touch of anger in his words. No, it resembled resentment, and she realized Ahmad must have made him feel like an outsider. She frowned. Ahmad was a man of action, but he could also be caring, wise. Strange. Why would he be unkind to Xavier, the brother of a man he'd called friend?

"I'm sorry there is a concern for Sir Florian's well-being. Did you say he's wandering about out here?"

"Uh, yes. He stormed off earlier, and I followed him to the gate, but realized he probably needed time to cool off. I went in search of Sir Ahmad to little effect and decided to try once more with Sir Florian myself, but maybe you could help me."

He sounded hopeful and the youthful, imploring expression on his face melted away her lingering uncertainty.

"Of course I will try to help, but I cannot guarantee any success. I've angered Sir Ahmad, and I'm not sure he'll be receptive to my interference. Let us first search for Sir Florian, and I'll see if I can find out anything of what is bothering him."

"You would do that?"

"Of course. Sir Florian is my friend, as are all High Prince Theiandar's men. Now, where might he have wandered?"

Idra scanned the golden waving grass of the field, looking back toward the castle wall.

"I couldn't say, my lady. I wasn't exactly thinking when I decided to search for him," he said with a sheepish, lopsided grin.

She smiled back. It seemed thoughtless wandering was the prerequisite for exiting the castle walls that day. She considered what she knew of Sir Florian and decided northward made the most sense. Idra walked out from the edge of the forest and into the openness of field. The rustling of the dry grass as it slipped along the silky, light material of her skirts soothed her agitated senses, and she ran her palms over the fuzzy tops of the seedpods. The calm tickling of them on her fingertips held her attention for several minutes.

She heard Xavier walking behind her by several feet. It reminded her of her position in society and the fact that they walked within sight from the wall of the castle. Xavier had grown up in a wealthy though untitled family in Parlan, and he'd been well-educated in the rules of propriety. While she appreciated his sensibility would protect her reputation, she hated she could not walk out with a gentleman without arousing suspicions.

"How long ago did he leave the gates?" she asked over her shoulder.

"It's been over an hour, my lady."

"Do you suppose he's already gone back into the city?"

"I asked at the gate, and they said he hadn't returned yet."

She nodded and kept walking but picked up the pace, and Xavier kept in step behind her. Idra raised a hand to her brow and shaded her eyes to look into the distance. The castle wall stood clear of any trees or bushes for a distance, which made easy viewing along the wall until it turned, which it did over and over. The wall had been erected around the existing town located outside the original castle where the royal family resided. High Castle functioned more like a bustling city within a city within a wall, when Idra thought about it.

She didn't see the guardsman, but unless he'd gone out into the forest, she thought it unlikely he'd have wandered any other direction, since no other villages or manors besides Hamlin House were within two miles of High Castle except for the occasional cottage or farmhouse. The nearest village lay five miles out. That he might have gone there wasn't inconceivable, but it seemed improbable.

They searched for twenty minutes before Xavier spoke up. "My lady, I cannot ask you to wander out here any longer. Our light is diminishing, and it is not safe to continue. Please, let me escort you back to the keep."

Idra rested her hands on her hips and worked to calm her elevated breathing from their quickened pace. She nodded and looked around, hoping to catch sight of Sir Florian, but to no avail.

"Yes, you are right. I'm sorry, Sir Xavier. Let us return, but I promise to help you however I can. I know Sir Ahmad, and I am sure he is just preoccupied with other troubling thoughts."

Xavier's light laughter distracted her.

"What is so humorous?"

The guardsman's sheepish smile returned. "Tis nothing, my lady. Your choice of words just reminded me of an earlier conversation."

Her face scrunched up in confusion, but his mysterious response stirred up her amusement more than anything. "I shall ask nothing further on the subject then."

"Thank you, Lady Idra. Your help is most valued."

She smiled and nodded. His easy smile and friendly ways made her self-conscious and caused a rare stir of fluttering around her heart, so seldom had she been complimented by anyone but her mother or cousin . . . or Sir Ahmad.

Xavier stepped back to allow her to pass back the way they'd come, which she did without making eye contact, turning her face slightly away to hide the flush of her cheeks. She hoped if he noticed, he'd mistake it for the exertion of their marching over the hilly trail next to the castle wall.

When they arrived at the gates, Sir Xavier asked after Florian.

"Haven't seen hide nor hair of him, sir," the gatekeeper's young son told them. The intelligent and highly observant boy of ten had a special reputation throughout the entire city for his ability to recall impressive amounts of details.

"Thank you," Xavier said.

He and Idra left the gate and made their way toward the keep, where he bowed low and left her to enter on her own. She watched him walk away and appreciated his high level of respectfulness for such a young man. Ahmad's aversion to him remained incomprehensible. No one who knew him well could mistake how he slighted Xavier, and she wanted to understand why.

CHAPTER ELEVEN
THE BLIND LEADING THE BLIND

AHMAD STEPPED AROUND THE CORNER into the courtyard but stopped short to lean against the wall. He watched from a distance as Idra and Xavier progressed toward the keep's entrance. Jealousy won out over guilt now, and he thought it wouldn't be hard to hate Xavier after all. His jaw clenched tight, but he rolled it to loosen the straining muscles. Idra's countenance betrayed no heightened feelings toward the younger knight. She only looked peaceful and easy with her generous smile. When he stayed focused on her, it chipped away at the negativity clouding his judgment.

Idra was a sweet breeze, a precious pearl. His gaze shifted from her diminishing facial profile to her shoulders and back, covered in the leather armor used for practice but modified to fit her more feminine curves. The fabric of her shirt sleeves peeked out from under the leather, and the lightweight material of her dark green skirt billowed about in the gentle breeze stirred by her forward motion. Her soft suede boots peeked out from beneath the hem with each graceful step. He had to admit that he found the ensemble rather attractive on her. It certainly highlighted her posture and strength. Seeing her like this recalled the image of her standing in the practice room, wielding the staff as though second nature, and stirred feelings of admiration for her strength in him he didn't realize were possible.

He shook his head to clear his thoughts and realized he'd been openly staring. Ahmad looked around to see who might be watching him watching her, but, thankfully, found that none of the people wandering the courtyard had noticed his inquisitive pining.

Relieved, he slipped into the shadows and took a different route back to the barracks. He did not want to run into Xavier at that moment.

* * *

Florian slunk back into the city by the open gate just as the sun set over the horizon. The lamps were already lit, and the streets had died down of activity. Now there were few people to come in contact with but the various man or woman on their way home from a hard day of labor—none who'd be interested in his presence lurking about.

He had to find out where Orn kept his sister secreted away. He needed to find out who might be privy to the insane man's plans and who had joined him. Florian reasoned that in order for King Orn to move forward with such an insane plan as to overthrow High King Dante he'd have to garner the backing of other nobility from Wyeth and across the Realms, but he couldn't imagine who would do such a thing. Orn had a terrible reputation. Why would anyone want him for high king?

The only way to find answers to these questions would be to spy on King Orn and his uncle, to see who they were in contact with and where they went when not attending the requisite dinners and balls held in honor of the newly born high prince. If only he had help! It was too much of a risk to tell anyone, and he had less than a week to rescue Faye and stop Orn's sedition.

While on his walk outside the castle walls he had come to the terrible conclusion that if he failed to kill King Dante, his uncle would make sure both of them died, and that meant Faye would be left at the mercy of Orn. And beyond this, he realized Orn might not keep his word to him about her safety once the treason against the crown had been accomplished. What would stop him from using Nox's power to steal away Faye's beauty and leave her to rot, haggard and soulless?

Florian returned to the armory, removed his training gear, and trudged his way to the barracks. He arrived in time to see that most of the others were prepared for the evening ball to be held as an opening ceremony for the tournament that would take place over the next week in honor of High Prince Theiandar's new son and heir. He shed his dirty clothes and slipped on his nicer undergarments before freshening up at the water basin. With his face still over the bowl of water, he looked at his dim reflection as it danced in the light of the torches burning along the wall and wondered at the stranger staring back at him.

"Florian, you best hurry. We're going to make our way to the castle together," Gavin said while giving him a thwack on the back.

He stood up straight and shook his head. "No, I'll be a few minutes. You go on ahead, and I'll catch up." He wanted to pack a few extra weapons into his clothes without being noticed and couldn't accomplish that with eleven of his fellow guardsmen staring at him, questioning his reasons for such covert necessity.

Gavin shrugged and called to the others. "Florian needs to pretty himself up before he can attend the ball. Who knows, he might meet his princess charming!"

The others laughed and offered more friendly jibes at Florian, whose awkward smile, though feigned, assisted to cover up his ulterior motives. Gavin patted his shoulder and followed the others who left Delphor's shared room in the barracks. Once alone, he set straight to work adding knives, long wood and metal darts, and other inconspicuous weapons to his person. He put on his thicker tunic to cover the slight bulges the items added to his chest and waist, then cinched his sword belt tight. He would not forego this one thing for show tonight. He pulled the shining metal blade from the scabbard and inspected it in the torchlight before letting it plummet back in with a dull *whoosh* of blade on soft wood lining.

It took him just a few minutes to arrive at the castle keep, where he took a deep breath and walked up the steps. Whatever half-formed plan he had would have to serve, because he swore not to let this week pass without doing his utmost to save his sister and avoid killing King Dante. If he failed . . . . He had no other choice; he couldn't lose hope. From this moment forward, his life would never be the same.

* * *

Idra stood beside Princess Caityn's throne and watched the people milling about, visiting and waiting for the ball to begin in earnest. The orchestra prepared on the balcony above, where the beautiful sounds of their combined instruments would drift down upon the dancers. The great hall of High Castle overflowed with nobility from across Twelve Realms—knights and honored ladies, rich merchants, and anyone of standing who had made the effort to attend the naming ceremony for High Prince Theiandar and High Princess Caityn's baby son.

She searched for one person in particular, but he hadn't arrived yet. Idra's mind taunted her with thoughts of how she'd yelled at him and stormed out of the training room earlier in the day. It had been unseemly, and she wanted to apologize. She wanted any excuse to speak with him, to see his face and hear his voice. Idra worried the reason for his short-tempered treatment of Sir Xavier had somehow been exacerbated by her brazen choice to learn to fight, and she wanted to speak on his behalf. She did not see Ahmad as a man who would intentionally take out his emotions on poor Xavier—or anyone else, for that matter.

"Idra, I see him," Caityn said in a loud whisper after pulling Idra down to speak near her ear.

Idra smiled at the sound of excitement in her cousin's voice. Caityn had been doing her best to bring Idra and Ahmad together since she discovered there had been a budding relationship between the two. She straightened from her bent position and nodded in response, since words failed her upon seeing him dressed in his finest tunic, his broad shoulders accentuated by the diagonal arc of his sword belt across his chest. He faced away as he looked over his shoulder at another of the guardsmen, who'd entered at the same time.

When he turned back, with his profile in full view, her eyes were drawn to his smiling lips. Her mind jarred to a halt, traveling back in time to his impassioned and all-too-short kiss on the streets of Gankobi, and sending a warm heat through her abdomen and into her cheeks. That moment felt like an age ago now, and she feared she'd missed her chance with him. Caityn assured her Ahmad's heart still belonged to her, that her husband who had the knight's confidence could corroborate the truth of it, and that she must be patient for events happen in Almighty's time.

Her fingers slipped from their grip on the carved finial of the throne, and she floated down the steps toward Ahmad in a daze, uncaring of what anyone in the room might be assuming or saying about her. She lost herself in the reminiscence of his kiss and waking to his presence on Captain Scott's ship, and for once in her life, she didn't care what anyone thought. She refused to let this moment escape her. Uncertainty ruled life, and she did not know if there would ever be another chance. Idra tired of wasting chances.

The soft rhythms of music wafted through the air around her and added to the moment in some romantic way to which only Idra was privy. Her inner resolve and the relaxed appearance of Ahmad's countenance dashed away the last bits of fear she harbored over the possibility of rejection, and a genuine smile spread across her face.

"My lady," Sir Xavier said, stepping in front of her, halting her forward momentum and shaking her loose from her daydream-like state.

She frowned at him but he kept right on, even as she leaned around him to look at Ahmad who hadn't seen her and walked in the opposite direction.

"My lady, I must speak with you. May I have this first dance?"

She blinked twice and let his question sink in. "I . . . yes, Sir Xavier." Idra put on a kindhearted smile and laid her hand on top of his to be escorted to the dance floor. She couldn't help but glance over her shoulder to see where Ahmad had gone, but she hadn't expected to see him staring back and with a brooding, angry look, no less. Her heartbeat crept into her throat, and she feared his anger over her learning to fight continued. Hopefully, he hadn't been too hard on Gavin after she'd run off.

Her dance partner pulled her attention back as he took her hands in his in a crisscross pattern and stood facing her. They raised their right hands over the center and pressed their palms together before releasing their left hands and turning in a slow circle.

"Thank you again, Lady Idra. Florian will be here soon, and I hope we can together understand his angst. He did not return until near the time to leave for the ball, and I've not spoken with him."

Idra listened and nodded where appropriate, but said nothing. She followed Sir Xavier through the steps of the dance, in and out, around and through the other dancers. When they were once again facing each other, she said, "I will dance with him at some point this evening and will make full effort to gain his confidence."

"I ask for nothing more," he said with a slight bow of his head.

They continued through the dance with little conversation outside the standard pleasantries passed between partners. At the conclusion, Sir Xavier bowed over her hand and led her from the floor straight into the ominous face of Ahmad — or his chest, since its broad expanse hit closer to her line of sight. He stood in front of them like a solid wall.

"Sir Ahmad, Lady Idra mentioned to me how she loves the Concordian. I believe they are playing it next."

Idra dared to look up into Ahmad's face, shy and irresolute after how sure she'd been half an hour previous. To care this desperately about someone else and also fret over how he felt in return grew irksome. She hated thinking he had fallen out of love with her, if that were even a possibility. For her part, she didn't believe the turn of phrase meant anything more than a poetic way to say one never truly loved to begin with, but seeing what appeared to be disapproval on his face made her doubt even herself.

"Lady Idra, I came this way to ask for the next dance," Ahmad said, his voice gruff, effectively ignoring Sir Xavier in the process.

Idra noticed his disregard. She'd assumed his animosity had been aimed at her in some way, but in truth, she now saw that his resentment pointed at Sir Xavier. In a sudden rush of sisterly affection, she wiped the besotted look from her face and frowned at him.

"Sir Ahmad, while I would love to dance, I am not sure if the Concordian is appropriate for me to take with you, as I feel our minds are not in agreement. I will offer you the Dispassia Grand," she said with finality and curtsied low before grasping Sir Xavier's arm and pressing him to walk on around Ahmad.

Idra's internal critic screamed a barrage of cruel thoughts. She'd lost her mind instantly and without notice. Her refusal, subtle or not, to dance with Ahmad, acted like a battering ram to her gut as she railed upon herself for stupidly turning him down. All she'd wanted for months was to be near him, to feel even the briefest touch of his skin, to smell him, to hear the breath of his words pass his smiling lips. When she'd been a prisoner on that pirate ship, bound for a life of slavery, she'd hardened her heart to the love of him. The threat of it happening again, of losing him, stabbed deeper than before. At that precise moment, she wanted to cry, but she bit her lip and pressed her eyes closed for a second to contain her emotions to avoid adding one more bit of gossip to the halls of High Castle.

"Lady Idra, I'm sorry. I didn't realize . . . I didn't think I would make trouble for you by searching you out for the dance. I have obviously stirred up a rather awkward situation."

Sir Xavier's hand pressed atop Idra's in a comforting gesture, and his words were low, meant only for her as they moved away from the dance floor toward the front of the ballroom. A sigh escaped her, and Idra shook her head. Gratefulness for his forthright disruption of her internal chastisement soothed her.

"Tis not your fault. I'm sure you are aware I've been learning defensive tactics and weapons from my cousin Gavin." She watched him nod. "Sir Ahmad didn't know about it and came upon us while we trained this afternoon. He—no, I became angry and said some things before storming off. Not exemplary behavior on my part."

"And now I've made things more awkward," Sir Xavier said, his face askew with consternation.

They stopped near the steps to the thrones and Idra looked up at him. "How do you come to that conclusion?"

Sir Xavier took a turn to cock his head in confused surprise. "You mean you don't know?"

"Know what?"

"Sir Ahmad is jealous, my lady."

"Jealous?" She laughed, but doubt sneaked past the armor protecting her heart. "Don't be ridiculous. Sir Ahmad knows how I feel about him. I made it quite clear. He . . . he's no reason to be jealous."

"Be that as it may, he is jealous. He also hates me, which means he is doubly jealous."

"You are speaking nonsense, Sir Xavier. He most certainly doesn't hate you. Ahmad would never hate you, the brother of his friend and fellow guardsman. You must just give him time, and he'll adjust. He took your brother's death like a terrible blow. In fact, I'd say his damaged arm has healed better than his heart, where your family is concerned."

"So you say, but I have yet to see."

"There's no need to be pessimistic, young knight. Ahmad is not a man to hold grudges or follow the path of hatred. He is the most levelheaded among Prince Theiandar's knights, and though it may take him time, he will come 'round. Be patient."

Sir Xavier's accepting smile brought one to Idra's face, though her heart still ached with concern for Ahmad. If Sir Xavier's perception were accurate, it meant that Ahmad did care for her, that he may even still love her, and the thought quickened the thumping beat within her breast. She chanced to look for Ahmad once again but did not see him, and her heart plummeted into her stomach.

"My lady, there's Florian. I didn't see him enter. May I tell him you'd like this next dance?"

"Of course. Please send my warm wishes to Sir Florian. I'll find out what I can."

Xavier pressed his hand to his chest and bowed before he made a beeline for Sir Florian some thirty yards away. He leaned in and spoke to the other knight, then they both turned and looked her way. She smiled and bowed her head in acknowledgment. Sir Florian turned to Xavier and said something, but soon he approached with a kind, though strained, smile on his face.

CHAPTER TWELVE
DANCING AROUND THE ISSUE

"MY LADY IDRA, MAY I say you look exquisite this evening? I understand I might be honored to have this next dance with you," Sir Florian said with a flourishing bow.

Idra smiled, warmed by his genuine chivalry. "It would be my honor to walk the dance with you, Sir Florian," she said and placed her palm upon the top of his hand in the same way she'd done with Sir Xavier as he'd led her out into the dance.

The music had grown louder and the talking incessant. In the midst of her tumultuous emotions, for Idra, the celebration lost its luster, proving to be a cacophony of noise and chaos. She now wished she had not been asked to pry into Sir Florian's private affairs. It really was none of her business, yet the curiosity to know what could possibly be bothering him held fast. If she were able to help, it would certainly distract her from her own troubles.

The dance moved in close quarters, spent solely between the two partners rather than weaving amongst the other dancers. Idra knew it would give ample opportunity to discover whatever may be at issue.

"Sir Florian, I see your uncle has come, but what of your sister? She is now old enough to attend such festivities, and I hoped he'd bring her to the celebration."

She monitored his face, not wanting to miss any minute detail of his reactions in case it would reveal what ailed him. When she mentioned his sister, a hint of something flashed, but it passed with such haste she could not discern its merit.

"Uncle Jeron has little interest in escorting young maids to such frivolities. He barely endures to be put upon to celebrate her sixteenth birthday." His voice was tight and he sighed. "I should have been there for that."

Idra heard his deep regret and wondered if it signified what bothered him. She imagined his sister might be angry with him for missing her coming-out in society. Sixteen was a special age, a time of entering adulthood, one might say. She still remembered her own sixteenth birthday and the celebration her parents had made of it. Idra hadn't experienced a formal coming-out, because as lady-in-waiting to her younger cousin she did not have the freedom to be courted without the permission of her princess.

While not a pledge to chastity, her position meant she had different rules. Besides, with Caityn four years her junior and only twelve then, she had not been prepared for Idra to leave. And Idra would never have done so, her sense of loyalty and obligation already strong. Instead, she'd been celebrated without the same pomp and circumstance as girls preparing to look for a future match. It had become a double-edged sword for her as she grew older and realized she would soon be considered an old maid, past the age considered desirable for marriage. The uncomfortable consideration caused her to wonder if Sir Florian worried his sister would end up old and alone. That could explain his subtle misery.

"Your sister will find a match, I am sure. You have nothing to worry about, Sir Florian. She is young yet, and there are many years before you need worry after her comfort in such matters."

"Oh, that doesn't worry me, Lady Idra, though I appreciate your concern. What does worry me is my uncle forcing her into a detestable marriage, playing with her life like she was a pawn in a chess match. I must protect her—from such an occurrence, that is."

"Can she not come live here with you or other family?"

"As a bachelor and living in the barracks, I cannot accommodate her here, and the rest of our family is far removed, people we've never met from my mother's side."

"I see. That does present a problem."

"But Faye was . . . has been content with our uncle in Wyeth. She—" He stopped abruptly and frowned.

"What is it, Sir Florian?"

Something caused his eyes to cloud with hatred, and Idra read it with unmistakable clarity. It unnerved her, but her curiosity had her so far gone she couldn't stop now.

"Tis nothing, my lady. I . . . my sister is . . . is well. I cannot speak further of her. I feel I must stop or—"

"Or break your heart, surely. You are a good brother to her, Sir Florian," King Orn said from behind Idra.

She jumped at the sound of his voice less than a foot from her.

"I must cut in on your dance and make away with the beautiful Lady Idra. You will excuse us, Sir Florian," Orn said with a wave of his hand.

Florian bowed to them and backed away, Orn stepping into his place. Idra looked on with surprise. Rare were the occasions anyone cut into another's dance, and this would draw the sort of attention she sought to avoid.

"It has been over three years since I last laid eyes on your beautiful face, Lady Idra. On our High Princess's sixteenth birthday. May I say that you've only grown lovelier with each passing day?"

King Orn's steady gaze made her uncomfortable, and something in the touch of his hand caused unease to ripple through her. She had to say something, but every reply seemed wrong. She settled on the standard answer to a compliment.

"I'm flattered, Sire. Thank you."

"What were you and Sir Florian so deep in conversation about, my lady?"

For the life of her, she had no clue why the king would be interested in her conversation with the knight, but the question pricked at her subconscious and made her aware that Sir Xavier might really be onto something, though she didn't discern her own awareness of it right away.

"Sir Florian and I were discussing his sister, Faye, and her coming out. He is upset that he neglected to attend the celebration."

"Is that all?"

The way he said it implied two things to Idra's sensibilities. The tone of his voice carried relief, while the look in his eye held suspicion. Idra did her best to not appear guilty, and, as far as she knew, she had no reason to feel that way except for the niggling sensation at the back of her mind.

"Yes. I told him that if he were worried about not being there for her, he should see about bringing her closer. They are siblings, after all, and she is a young woman, on the cusp of adulthood and marriage proposals. I'm sure he would like to take full responsibility for her now that he is well of age."

"The young Faye has been placed in the charge of her uncle. He will be her guardian until she is wed. Sir Florian has nothing to fear on that account."

Idra shrunk back in surprise as King Orn's fingers wrapped possessively around her wrist in a way not fully congruent with the dance. He pulled her arm high and held it aloft, their entwined arms between them as he leaned in and peered into her eyes as if searching for something. The proximity of his face and the pressure of his hand on her wrist left her breathless as the dance ended. His grip relaxed and his fingers slid down the soft inner part of her wrist and arm before his touch left her skin. She shivered. Something undefinable, but resembling fear, had been left as an uncomfortable abrasion on her composure.

King Orn escorted Idra to the edge of the dance floor and kissed her hand before leaving her there, alone.

* * *

Orn strode away from Idra with purpose masked in nonchalance. The woman had changed since last they'd met. The once aloof lady no longer demurred in that timid, easily swayed innocence of youth. She carried herself with grace and quiet dignity; that had always been something hidden within her, but unmistakable in the subtle force of her gaze. While he found her new strength of body and will alluring, he also saw the danger in it and knew she could be trouble, especially with her vicinity to the high royals.

He caught Havrik's eye and motioned him over. The knight had been wooing a silly, coy little thing, but he came to his king without a second thought. Once the obedient knight stood by his side, Orn sipped at the goblet of wine he'd taken from a passing servant and nodded toward where Lady Idra had been joined by another of High Prince Theiandar's guardsmen.

"Get one of the others to follow her. She's putting her nose in places it doesn't belong, and I don't want any trouble on her account."

"Yes, my liege, as you command, I obey."

"Wait until after the ball. If you leave now that we've spoken, it could draw unwanted attention."

"You are wise, Highness."

"Enjoy the night, Havrik. You deserve it."

"Thank you," he said and moved away from Orn, back toward the ladies, who giggled and fanned themselves as he drew near.

Orn smiled, remembering a time when he'd had the same effect on women. If he so desired, he could still draw them in like moths to the flame.

* * *

Xavier didn't leave Idra alone for long as he practically bounded up next to her in a youthful state of excitement.

"What did you find, my lady? Is Florian leaving Raz's ranks? Is he being offered a position with King Orn's guard? A wife back home? What?"

"Slow down," Idra said and attempted a laugh, but the discomfiture of her encounter with King Orn persisted. Whatever intrigue she had stumbled upon went deeper than Sir Florian's sister's coming-of-age, but she had no idea what it could possibly be. The Wyethian king's level of concern, no matter how nonchalant he attempted to be, over what she and Sir Florian had spoken of during the dance had been unreasonable. Free of King Orn's scrutiny, she scanned the crowds for a sight of Sir Florian but couldn't find the knight anywhere.

"My apologies, my lady. Did Sir Florian share what troubles him?"

"No, I don't believe so, but I think there is something bothering him. He shared his melancholy, speaking only of his sister. I've never known him to seem quite that hopeless. Then King Orn interrupted our dance and asked about what Sir Florian and I had spoken of. I'm more curious than before."

Idra peered at Sir Xavier. He searched the crowds, probably looking for Sir Florian.

"I think he's left," Xavier said. "He looked none too pleased to see the king."

She followed his gaze and noticed Ahmad leaning in toward Lady Hilde as though sharing some secret. He smiled as he spoke, and Hilde laughed, accepting his hand as he led her to the dance floor. An unfamiliar, disagreeable sinking sensation landed in Idra's gut, and she couldn't stop scrutinizing them. Xavier touched her shoulder.

"Dance with me again, my lady?"

Idra saw a hint of compassion in his eyes, a sure sign he'd seen her staring at Ahmad and noticed her less-than-pleasant reaction to the sight. She placed a smile on her lips, though no pleasure reached her heart.

"Ah, no, Sir Xavier. While I appreciate your thoughtful offer, it would do more to stir up the gossips than anything else, and I believe I'm tired. I've had a great deal of excitement for the evening already, but I am feeling overheated. Mayhap you would walk with me on the veranda overlooking the garden? They've placed beautiful lighting throughout. It's quite spectacular this evening."

"I'd be honored to walk with you," he said and offered his arm, which Idra took without hesitation.

It felt much like being rescued from a dark pit as they walked out into the night air. Not one castle existed in the Twelve Realms as magnificent as High Castle, for no others had the grandeur or luxury afforded here. Idra had explored the vast keep, in awe of the spaces she encountered such as the ballroom, used only for these celebrations and parties, and the garden that stood between it, and the exotic conservatory — one of Idra's favorite places to visit when she needed solitude.

"Lady Idra?"

"Hmm?" she asked, her mind still making the effort to focus on the beauty of the night as opposed to the obvious familiarity between Ahmad and Lady Hilde. She refused to let wild imaginings take over.

"Sirs Gavin and Florian have become my good friends since I've come, and the stories have circulated throughout the realms of what Princess Caityn and even you have endured in the past two years. My lady, I heard of your courageous escape from the henchmen of the Beauty Thief and how you fought off pirates and the seer of Gankobi.

"When I first arrived, my interest led me to question why some of Prince Theiandar's men were not present, and Gavin told me how Sir Ahmad had gone north to protect the border, causing some others to join him. But he said something about it that caught my attention. He said Sir Ahmad left to escape and regroup. I'm a naturally curious fellow, though this is not something I brag about, for my father has warned me over and over that it will get me in trouble someday. But I had to know what Gavin meant by that, and he explained how Sir Ahmad lost his senses when you were taken down seas to be sold as a slave. He also mentioned how you'd met someone and —"

"Say no more," she said as the quickening of her heart filled her ears. Breathlessness pinched her lungs as she thought of Simon who'd been a lost soul but in love with her and willing to die to save her. He'd done just that. She thought of Ahmad and how that must have looked to him. It broke her heart that she'd caused him pain. "Sir Ahmad is a good man. A fool in some matters, yes, but a sweet man who must now be convinced my deep affection for him is sincere."

She didn't know why she spoke openly to Sir Xavier. She barely knew him, but he asked such candid questions, and it made her want to answer.

CHAPTER THIRTEEN
UNPLEASANT SURPRISES

"SIR AHMAD, YOU MUST STOP this at once."

"Lady Hilde," he said, stepping to her right, then her left as they danced, "you have this way of speaking to me in some strange language I cannot decipher. What must I stop? Dancing?"

Her light laughter matched the amused gleam in her eye. "Silly fool. You continue to play the oblivious, but we both know what you must do, and tonight. Tonight you must speak in earnest to her."

"You saw her. She is angry with me. She's happier with other . . . pursuits."

"I can hear the petulant little boy in your voice, sir. You really are quite blind. She is only angry—"

She paused mid-sentence as the dance moved them far apart. Ahmad grew restless to hear what she would say. Lady Hilde always had such interesting insights into the ways of men and women. He found her predictions to be accurate and often uncomfortable, yet he wanted to know more.

"She is only angry, sir, because she cares. If she did not, she would not be so. That is all you need know. You must make amends for embarrassing her. And while you are at it, ask if there is a knight who might also teach me to fight."

Ahmad's eyes bored into Lady Hilde's until he recognized the unmistakable mirth in her eyes. For some reason, he wouldn't be surprised if the lady did, in fact, want just what she'd said, but didn't want to appear brazen. He smiled and shook his head.

"You are an exotic bird among women, Lady Hilde. Why is it you have not been caged?"

Her chin rose, and her lips formed a pert smile. "I have yet to meet a man who can tame me, sir."

A short, surprised laugh escaped Ahmad. "While I am curious to see it, I hate the thought of anyone taming you, my lady."

The music ended and he bowed. Lady Hilde curtsied and motioned with her head toward the veranda doors. Ahmad didn't understand how her mouth could smile but her eyes, full of merriment only moments before, could now look empty, but she'd been right; it was now or never.

"Thank you for the dance," he said and left her at the edge of the crowd. Outside the door, he would confront his fears; he would confess his heart and hope Idra wouldn't trample it to bits. This time, he would listen.

"My lady, I have come for my dance," Ahmad said from five feet behind her.

The burning torches along the balcony left Idra and Sir Xavier appearing as silhouettes in the dark, but he made out her nod to Xavier, who bowed and moved away without a word. That brought him a measure of relief, since Ahmad had nothing kind to say to the other man.

"Sir Ahmad, I'm pleased. The Dispassia Grand is my second favorite dance."

"What does that mean for me?" He asked, intending to sound lighthearted, but even he heard the tension in his voice.

"It means nothing except that I've saved the best for you for next time."

"I'm sorry for the way I acted earlier, Idra," he said, his tone and use of her given name alone a silent plea to return to the past intimacy they'd shared. "Please, forgive me."

"You know I do, but Sir Xavier seems to be under the impression that you were jealous, though I assured him you have no reason to be so."

His eyebrows pinched together at being read with such ease by the young knight. Idra didn't hide her smile. It must have pleased her that Sir Xavier had been accurate in his estimation of Sir Ahmad's feelings, something of which even he himself was not fully cognizant.

"I am not jealous."

"Oh?"

"No," he huffed. "I-I was merely preoccupied by other thoughts."

"That is not very flattering to me, I must say," she said, teasing him and simultaneously putting him at ease, until the tone of her voice dampened with her next words. "You and Lady Hilde seem close."

He had to pause and consider what she'd just said. "Yes, I've known Lady Hilde for almost seven years. As long as I've been a royal guardsman. We met at the first ball I ever attended here in celebration of Raz's majority." For some reason, he felt like this conversation would cause him trouble.

"Lady Hilde is wonderful kind. I wonder why she's never married. Do you not? She's almost the same age as me, you know."

Where were her questions leading? Ahmad shifted and cleared his throat. "I . . . well, I do not know. But as much as I appreciate Lady Hilde, there are other things I'd like to discuss with you."

"The Dispassia isn't a song conducive to speaking. Would you mind terribly if we sat it out? I'm actually rather tired of dancing tonight," Idra said apologetically.

"Of course," he said and thought how he'd much prefer to speak with her at that moment, to attempt once more to expose his heart before he lost the nerve, which dissipated with each passing second.

They had just passed over the threshold and reentered the ballroom, but instead of heading to dance, they veered off toward the thrones and tables arranged near the other end of the room. Ahmad walked next to Idra without touching her, but the longing to take hold of her hand raged from the depths of him. The vanilla scent of her skin wafted past his nose and drew him in, irresistible and tempting. If it were possible, he'd stop there, pull her into his arms, and kiss her until she couldn't breathe. She was a siren, and he, her ensnared sailor.

He bit his tongue to bring his drifting mind under control. Ahmad could not let this opportunity escape. He couldn't let himself be distracted, but had to speak his heart and expose himself in the most vulnerable way, even against his mind's rationale for avoiding the pain it might cause. Had he not already endured the worst of it?

Idra sat and offered him a seat angled toward hers. They were close enough their knees almost touched. Ahmad ignored the other people sitting nearby, most of whom were nobles from across the Realms. He told himself he hoped to give the gossips something celebratory to spread about.

"Idra, there's something I need to say to you."

He leaned forward and filled the frame of his vision with Idra, shutting out the surrounding distractions. His lips parted to confess the entirety, but a commotion sent a multitude of gasps reverberating around the ballroom. Ahmad cringed, desperate to forge ahead with this confession. But the thrones where Princess Caityn and Prince Theiandar sat with High King Dante drew Idra's attention away. Feeling slightly defeated, Ahmad followed her gaze, but he recoiled at what he saw there; a young woman with ragged dress, tumultuous hair, and dirt-smudged face grappling with two knights arrested his attention. Ahmad had to look twice.

He jumped to his feet. "Sabine?"

"You know that girl?" Idra asked, full of incredulity.

"Yes, but—"

"But what, Ahmad?"

What unsettled her tone? Anger? Concern? Annoyance? Jealousy? Fear? Unease? Ahmad struggled with coming to grips with what his eyes saw, and couldn't ascertain the meaning behind Idra's reaction. He shook himself loose of his shock and jogged over to the guards who hauled the girl away from Princess Caityn. "Wait, I know this girl," he said with his hand stretched out in front of him.

Princess Caityn stepped around Prince Theiandar and motioned for the guards to stop and bring the girl back. "Sir Ahmad, how do you know her?" Caityn asked. "Who is she?"

Idra came to stand near him, and suddenly Ahmad became the center of attention in the room, the squirming girl only second to him now.

"Your Highness, I'm unsure what to say, but this is the Crescent girl who we captured and escorted to Emlyn Castle to be questioned, then returned to her people."

"Your son is not safe," Sabine cried out. "I warn you. Skotos lives!"

Theiandar and Caityn stepped forward as one, and the prince said, "What threats do you speak of?"

"Idra," Caityn said with sober urgency, "go to Bastien now."

"Yes, my lady," she said and dashed out of the ballroom, leaving the space next to Ahmad cold in her wake.

Sabine stopped her struggle and stood clasped at the upper arms by both guards. "I-I do not know the threat; I only know the outcome. Your son will never rule unless you listen to me."

"Take her away," High King Dante said.

"No. Wait!" Ahmad spoke out, unsure why he had. But after seeing the young girl again, and in such a state, he felt responsible for her somehow. Maybe it had to do with him being the one who'd captured her. "I'll take charge of young Sabine, Your Highnesses. I swear she's no threat to you or your son." He directed his last statement at Raz.

High King Dante spoke before Prince. "Do you have some knowledge of this girl that can prove such a statement, Sir Ahmad?"

He had nothing to offer but his gut feeling. He looked from the royals to Sabine and back. "No, Sire. I have nothing but my word as a guardsman of High Castle and Twelve Realms."

"Take her to the dungeon, for we have no proof she is not an assassin sent by Crescent Cave," the high king pronounced with finality.

"I'll take her, Highness," Ahmad offered and sighed inwardly when the king nodded in reply.

The other guards handed her off to Ahmad, who gingerly wrapped his fingers around her upper arm and escorted her from the room. She didn't fight or protest, for which he was relieved. He heard the king call for the return to festivities, and the orchestra resumed their melodies.

The farther they moved from the ball, the softer the voices and music got. Neither of them said a word. After five minutes of this, Ahmad discerned the steady tap of footfalls behind them and looked to see Prince Theiandar making long strides to catch up.

"Ahmad, this is the girl you captured at the border?"

"Yes, Raz. She goes by the name Sabine. I'd honestly thought I'd seen the last of her, and I know not how she ended up here. King Ekreton made it clear he'd return her home once he'd gleaned any information he could from her."

"I escaped to warn your wife," Sabine said to Prince Theiandar. "She, her family, your son, they are all in danger because Skotos won't stop until they are all dead."

Theiandar stopped them outside the door leading to the dungeons below. "What mischief do you threaten by this unsolicited warning? Why Princess Caityn?"

"What I know, Sire, cannot be explained in terms men understand. Only one who's been touched by his power will believe the truth of it."

"By who?"

"The thief who defies time."

"You speak in riddles, child." Theiandar's frustrated words echoed down the hall.

"I'm no child."

"Sabine, please, we want to understand," Ahmad implored.

Her frowning face shifted from one man to the other. "Let me see the baby. At least the princess."

"No. Absolutely not," Theiandar said.

"Then I've wasted my time. Your child's life might be in danger, but for certain, his future is. And the future of your kingdom hinges on his."

"You'll go nowhere near my son."

"I mean him no harm."

Prince Theiandar took a step back. "I cannot trust your word."

Sabine, her arm still gripped in Ahmad's hand, stepped toward the prince. "I cannot prove my word except by giving you what you need."

He leaned down and spoke with his face directly in front of hers. "You have nothing to offer us."

Ahmad, dumbstruck by the quick repartee, saw Sabine in a whole new light. It reminded him that appearances could be deceiving.

"It's late, Sire. Instead of the dungeon, may I place Sabine under guard in the inner tower's upper room? King Trygg and Prince Melvyn can be trusted. I'll make sure there is a guard present at the door at all times, and she'll be shackled within, I swear."

"I give you leave, Ahmad. Take care of it. Now I must go attend to my wife and son. Caityn is distraught. And you," he said to Sabine, "we will have an explanation from you in the morning."

The prince strode back the way he'd come, and Ahmad closed the door to the dungeons. Palpable relief overtook him at not having to take her down into that dank pit of cells. He hoped she realized her fortune at avoiding the dungeon as he pulled Sabine farther down the hall and out a side door into a courtyard.

"I don't know what else I can tell you without first seeing the princess and her son."

The sorrow and frustration mingling in her voice sounded genuine to his ears.

"Sabine, I realize we are strangers to you," Ahmad said, "but we mean you no harm, as you have said to us. Please think on it this night and reconsider. If there is a threat to the new prince, you might be our only hope."

He kept observing her, not sure the reality of her presence or this situation had quite sunk in yet. Her arrival did not constitute the sort of gossip he'd hoped to give the castle folk. What must Idra be thinking now? He could only imagine.

"How did you escape King Ekreton's castle, Sabine?"

She delayed, tipping her head back and sighing. "I didn't. Not exactly. He decided I am insane and charged three of his soldiers to escort me to the border with Crescent Cave to hand me over to my people, but before we arrived, I slipped away unnoticed and came here. But understand, I could have gone home and continued my mission. Instead, I have come here to help your people, and that is against my king's wishes."

"Why? What does it matter to you?"

"I-I can't explain it to you. I cannot. I must see your Princess Caityn and her babe. I-I thought I could do this on my own, but I can't."

"Do what? Please, I can help," he said as he walked her up the winding steps of the tower past the rooms of kings and princes, their ladies and servants, to the top of the inner tower.

"You cannot help me, but I will help you and your princess if I am able."

She stepped into the little room and he right behind her. There were already shackles hanging on the wall just outside the door to the chamber, which he picked up on the way in. He put them on her outstretched wrists. "Can I get you anything? Water?"

"No," she said without a trace of self-pity, and she lay upon the thin bed, not saying another word or attempting to flee. She reached down to the end of the bed to retrieve the simple woolen blanket to cover herself.

"Good night, Sir Ahmad," she said and rolled to face the wall, the echo of cold chains clinking louder than her words in Ahmad's ears.

Her calm and matter-of-fact demeanor left him dumbstruck once again, and he couldn't wrap his mind around what had transpired in the last twenty minutes. There were many questions. How had she gotten into the keep? How could she, in her current state of disarray, have sneaked past the guards stationed at every door to the ballroom? How had she made it through the crowded room to the thrones without catching the attention of courtiers? It seemed entirely impossible that anyone could infiltrate the security of that room without someone noticing.

But instead of asking, exhaustion hit him like a battering ram, and he bid her good night as he closed the door, barring it. He couldn't bring himself to leave, still held in the grip of a sense of responsibility for the insane child. There would be time enough for answers tomorrow. He sat in the lone chair at the table and didn't bother to light the candle collecting dust there in the center. Enough moonlight shone in through the high window that he could make out the entire space.

He stared out the arrow slit in the tower wall and tried to imagine the untold possibilities for the warning Sabine had given. Nothing came clear to him, and the surfeit of ways the baby prince could be in danger was overwhelming. Anyone hungry for power could prey on the innocence of children in countless ways. The thought of someone hurting their new prince angered him, but there had been no other hint of treason in the realms, no secret plots to overthrow or harm the high royals. It made Ahmad wary, but did not give him answers.

Ahmad heard faint voices from below, followed by the steady and familiar clatter of weaponed bodies ascending the stairs. He assumed it to be King Trygg of Nevin and his consort, but the rhythms of movement grew closer until he knew someone else approached. He stood and, as a precaution, pulled his dagger from its sheath. The light of torches rounded the bend before the people, and to his relief, it turned out to be Gavin, followed by Xavier, whose presence Ahmad ignored.

"It seems you left out some of the more interesting details of your time at the borders. You didn't say you captured a *pretty girl*," Gavin said with a lopsided grin.

"That's neither here nor there. But in my defense, she was dressed as a boy and covered in more layers of dirt than a warthog in the bog."

"Who is she exactly?" Gavin smiled but stared at the barred door, the light and shadows cast by his torch dancing across his inquisitive face.

"I don't know." He lowered his voice to just above a whisper. "I'm certain the name she gave me is false, but I am more interested in gaining her trust. She wants to see Princess Caityn and the baby. I have the impression she thinks the princess is the only one who can protect Bastien . . . or her . . .

or the princess herself? It's not clear to me, but Prince Theiandar wants to question her in the morning. He was anxious to check on his family."

"Yes, we met him there first before coming here. He said he knew you'd stay to guard the girl yourself, and here you are."

"I didn't realize how predictable I am."

"As the weather is to an old arthritic sailor," Gavin quipped, and Xavier stifled a guffaw.

Ahmad glared at them both, but a grudging smile graced his unusually somber-of-late face. "There are worse things."

"Such as not sweeping the woman you love off her feet and dashing away with her to live in wedded blissful peace."

Ahmad wanted to frown, but Gavin spoke true. Instead of anger at being called out for the coward he'd been, he laughed. The action grated, almost foreign and out of place in the stark bareness of the tower, but a fresh appreciation for his own stupidity slid into place, and in recognizing it, a weight lifted from his soul.

"What did I say?" Gavin asked in amused bewilderment.

"Nothing and everything, my friend," Ahmad said and slapped him on the back. "I'm putting you in charge of the prisoner tonight. I have a certain problem to rectify come morning, and I believe I'll need all my faculties rested and in working order."

"You are cryptic. Must be the effect of that girl on the other side of the door."

"No, Gavin. Tis only love that turns men to fools," Ahmad said with a confident smile, and he jogged down the steps to leave the tower.

"Almighty speed!" he heard Gavin call after him.

Ahmad jogged back the way he'd come. He had to return to the ball before a certain someone left, because he had one thing on his mind and one thing only: find Lady Hilde.

CHAPTER FOURTEEN
QUESTIONS WITHOUT ANSWERS

CAITYN PACED THE NURSERY WITH Bastien cradled to her breast, his tiny fingers wrapped in innocent bliss around her finger with sleep as his peaceful companion. "Did I say thank you for hastening here, Idra?"

"Four times already." Idra laughed. It came as a surprise that she lacked more distress over the situation. But she trusted Ahmad, and he said this Crescent Cave girl carried no personal threat.

"I'll say it once more, my dearest cousin. Thank you. I'm completely undone by the thought of someone hurting my son. Who is this girl to come threaten us so? What did she mean by Skotos lives?"

"Don't you remember the old fables Bimala used to tell us, Caityn?" Idra asked and Caityn shook her head. Idra hesitated as her arms broke out in goose bumps. "Skotos was the son of the great ruler of the Thryst who murdered his father and mother, then banished his sister to the deserts of Akha to die by the vulture. Only she did not die and instead raised a people of her own, here in the Twelve Realms . . . only then it had not been one nation. She gained her strength from the people of the twisting river and they named it for her. Solfen."

Lost in the story's remembrance, Idra pointed toward where the river Solfen wound its way from Taisce and around High Castle.

"Oh yes, I remember now," Caityn said. "Skotos hated his sister, and he regretted not having killed her when he had the chance. He vowed to live until her life and her descendants were snuffed out of existence."

"Do you remember any more of the story, Caity?"

"Yes. Solfen's strength and beauty enraptured the ruler of Taisce, and he wed her. They had many children, and . . .. Oh my." Caityn looked to Idra, her eyes wide. "It is said that my family line heralded from this union . . . I just never thought . . .."

Idra continued for her. "Skotos could not defeat them as they grew in strength and numbers, but he'd made his vow on the Mount of Oria with an ancient order who, once the pact was formed, would not let his vow go unfulfilled. Skotos battled against the people of the southern realms, but his fighting only brought the many clans closer, banding them together in one accord. It is said that he fled to the west in fear for his life and died in distant lands, but his legacy of hatred brought about the beginning of our peace in the Twelve Realms."

That was all they knew from the fables told to them as young girls of how the Twelve Realms became one, and Idra had the worst intuition that this girl, Sabine, hadn't brought up the ancient name for no reason. She shook her head free of the myriad possibilities the old stories conjured and returned to Caityn's original question.

"Honestly, I don't believe she meant it as a threat. I can't explain it, but she seemed to only want to warn you somehow.

Besides, she's just a young girl. What harm could she really do?"

She didn't miss Caityn's eyebrow shoot up in surprise.

"Is that so? I find it interesting that such a question would come from a certain lady-in-waiting who has been training to defend and fight."

Idra had the good sense to blush, since she hadn't told Caityn about her training with Gavin. "Did our dear cousin tell you?"

"He needed someone with which to talk, so yes. He told me, but only out of concern for you. I assured him of the merits. Please don't be angry at him."

"Oh, no. I only hope you are not angry with me for keeping it a secret from you," Idra said.

Caityn's quiet laughter came as a relief. "I suppose I can't blame you. I hid my hurt, at first, that you didn't confide in me, but I soon realized you would tell me when you were ready. Tis unconventional and something I never imagined you doing, but I see how the events of recent years have changed you . . . have changed us both. I am not that innocent and willing to see the best in people, and you are not so timid or willing to hide from injustices. I hope our changes are for the best, truly, and I think that you learning to fight will only strengthen you, for you are already one of the bravest people I know."

Caityn laid the baby in his cradle and faced Idra with crystalline tears shimmering in her eyes, and she became teary-eyed, too. Her cousin had just put into words something she'd not considered in any depth.

"Oh Caity, I'm sorry for the trials you've been through. I hate to think that you've lost your trust in people."

"Tis not that so much as I've learned to be cautious. I like to think 'tis maturity more than disillusionment. But if anyone should be sorry, Idra, it should be me. If not for me, you never would have suffered through the traumatic experiences of the past two years. You've traveled along dangerous waters, been taken hostage, had your life threatened at the end of a knife, escaped into a raging river, walked through the dead of night to find help for me, been kidnapped, held prisoner, almost sold into slavery, fought a mercenary, and countless things you doubtless have never even told me." She stopped to breathe and shrugged. "I think if I were you I would hide in my room, never facing the world again, but you . . . you stand like a warrior queen of old. In truth, I think I'm envious," Caityn said with a quirk of a smile playing at the corner of her lips.

"Caity, 'tis you who've taught me to have courage," Idra said with a half-laugh. "If not for your exemplary courage day in and day out, I would certainly be hidden in the safety of my parents' home at Tanfield. I would never venture beyond the pasture. What I know is you bring out strengths in people just by your presence."

Caityn shook her head but came to hug Idra. "Don't be silly."

Idra returned the embrace and said her good night. No sooner did she open the door than Prince Theiandar arrived. He pressed Idra's hand in passing, then went straight to his wife and son, where she noticed Theiandar's gentleness mixed with anxious purpose as he examined his sleeping baby. She hoped against hope Ahmad had some special understanding and this beautiful family would know no threat from the Crescent Cave girl. Idra didn't know what she'd do if anything were to happen to them. She and Caityn were close, even more than she and her sisters, and if her cousin's heart were to break, so would her own.

* * *

Ahmad heard the orchestra playing while still down the hall from the ballroom. If there were any luck in the world, he hoped he had it then, because he would need Lady Hilde's help to accomplish his plans to woo a certain lady-in-waiting.

No sooner did he walk through the door than Xavier charged in after, out of breath and calling his name. He gritted his teeth and stared at the younger knight with a look he intended would make a solid, lasting impression.

"This is no place to be shouting or flapping about like a crazed hen, especially after what happened earlier. You're going to scare the ladies. As it is, there will be countless whispers circulating about the entire event." He cringed inwardly, knowing his name would be among the stories told.

Catching his breath, Xavier nodded. "Yes, sir. I'm sorry. Tis . . . well . . . 'tis just that Gavin said he would take first watch at the door and suggested I come back to enjoy more of the ball, which I was happy to do, but when I came into the hall, I noticed Florian walking the opposite direction. He happened to look back and saw me, then accused me of following him and told me to mind my own business. Can you tell me, Sir Ahmad, is this normal for him? He seems different—brief though our acquaintance has been, as you have pointed out."

Ahmad, perturbed by Xavier's insolence and continued suspicion over Sir Florian, shook his head and walked away. He didn't bother looking back and didn't care what else Xavier said. The young knight, whenever he opened his mouth to speak, demonstrated his youth and immaturity were still too great to be considered one of Prince Theiandar's elite guardsmen, and until he proved otherwise, he would gain no special attention from Ahmad. Besides, right now he had his own matters of the heart with which to deal and had no time for Xavier's ill-advised intrusiveness . . . or Florian's supposed personal problems.

Midnight had come and gone, but the crowd of attendees lingered. Ahmad, even at his current fitness level, wondered at the stamina it took to dance the night away. Some of the dandies prancing about with ladies beautiful enough to tempt the eye had not missed a single promenade about the room. He didn't return to admire or deride their innocent pleasure, but to search amongst their faces for a sign of Lady Hilde.

He found her amongst a group of ladies reclining in the corner and hesitated. There were seven young women who seemed to clamor for her attention, certainly asking for advice over young men of interest. He wanted to shake his head, but Ahmad remembered when he had found the chase more appealing. He'd given it up quite a while before meeting Lady Idra, having decided true love came from more than a pretty face. But since coming to know Idra, he'd given over to the passion he'd suppressed. She embodied his ideals when it came to affection, attachment, love . . . a future.

In the midst of his thoughts, he found himself walking toward the ladies and decided his course, no matter the danger, could not be altered.

"Lady Hilde, I apologize for interrupting, but I hoped to have a private word with you." He bowed to the group at large.

Ahmad ignored the hushed giggles hidden behind fans and delicate hands, but catalogued the reaction for later reflection. In this moment, the only thing which concerned him had to do with gaining the help of Lady Hilde.

Her quick smile spread wide, and she stood, smoothing out the crinkles from her satin dress. "Of course, Sir Ahmad. I am at your disposal. Ladies, please excuse us."

Ahmad pivoted from the group and walked away, with Lady Hilde at his side. He looked over at the auburn curls stacked upon her head. He hadn't seen the new hairstyle before tonight, but it was becoming and soft. For the life of him, Ahmad couldn't understand why someone hadn't snatched up this spirited beauty.

"Thank you, my lady. I—"

"Before you tell me what mysterious mission I might embark upon, please answer me what has happened with that poor girl you dragged away? Is she really in the dungeon, Sir Ahmad?"

He leaned forward to better see her face and noticed the serious demeanor of her brow. Her question held none of her usual jesting.

"She is well and in the inner tower. The high prince authorized the change of location."

"That is a relief. I could not stand the thought of the poor urchin wallowing in that dank hole below the castle." She shuddered.

Ahmad's curiosity piqued. "Have you been in the dungeons?"

"Me? Oh heavens, no! But I've heard them spoken of in the vilest of ways. Tis a wonder anyone emerges from there with their skin intact."

Ahmad led Lady Hilde to the table, laid with an assortment of delicacies, and thought over how to best answer her perceptions. "Another rumor, I'm afraid. The dungeons are not as resplendent as a castle guest chamber, to be sure, but they are clean and mostly dry. The prisoners have beds of straw, regular meals, and fresh water. There are certainly worse places."

"It still sounds horrid."

She popped a strawberry in her mouth and chewed it with a thoughtful, far-off look on her face that Ahmad wondered about, but before he formulated a question, she spoke again.

"Now, sir, what did you need from me?"

"I feel horrible when you ask in such a way, my lady. It makes it sound as if I only seek your company when I am in need."

Hilde's amused smile made him frown more.

"Oh, don't be upset, Sir Ahmad." Lady Hilde pressed her hand to his biceps in a comforting gesture and pulled it away before anyone might notice. "We both know that is not true, and you know I would do anything to help you, however I am able. Please, I want to help."

Ahmad stared at her face and could not mistake her genuine offer in the kindly upward sweep of her lips and faint crinkling of skin at the corners of her eyes—the hint of future crow's feet—a sign of someone who smiled often; he thought it a becoming quality in any woman.

"You are too good, my lady. Thank you. I covet your offer of help because I have a plan for making my intentions known to Lady Idra."

"Ah, matters of the heart are my specialty. Say the word, my lord."

Ahmad smiled and relaxed, forgetting about the strange girl locked in the tower, about dead knights and their annoying younger brothers, and centered his mind on what it would take to win the woman he loved.

* * *

Florian spent most of the night of the ball searching for answers. After his run-in with Xavier in the hall, he attempted more caution but found it difficult, as many people seemed to wander the halls during the ball. He aimed to enter King Orn's rooms and those of his uncle to search for anything that could lead him to the whereabouts of his sister, but he was thwarted at every turn; first King Orn's rooms were locked, and then his uncle had already retired from the ball.

Their encounter had been less than pleasant, where Florian hurled insults at the man who had called his father "Brother" and who should have been a shield of protection to his sister. Jeron had let them down in countless ways. It hurt to admit they were related. He found it even more agonizing when he considered the fact that he'd run away and left Faye in the clutches of such a nasty, greedy, grasping man as their uncle had now proved himself to be.

After the failure of that exchange, Florian retired to his bed. He'd discovered nothing that could tell him where they held Faye, and his only meager comfort that allowed him the reprieve of a night's sleep were the words of Jeron when he summarily dismissed him: "If you know nothing else, Nephew, know this. Faye is safe, warm, and fed. Tis your mission to keep her thus." If not for his absolute exhaustion, he never would have fallen asleep, but that is exactly what happened when his head hit the bedding. Terrible sleep tormented him, riddled with strange and horrible dreams defying reality and yet still strong enough to make his heart hammer erratically, painful in its tempo and disrupting whatever rest he managed. When he woke, his eyes burned and scratched as though sand had been dumped in them while he slept.

But thankfully, the clatter of his fellow knights gathering their equipment in preparation for the opening tournament festivities interrupted his disturbed repose. He groaned and rolled to his side, swinging his legs over the edge and sitting up in one smooth motion. Florian leaned his elbows on his knees and rubbed at his eyes with the heels of his hands.

"Rise and shine, Sir Snores," Zaccur said and kicked Florian's bare foot with his booted one as he walked by.

Florian glared at Zaccur, in no mood for the jovial antics of the others. He heard the excited chatter of the other men as they laced on their gambesons and padding. Today would be a day of full armor and melee battles. The stands and the canopied box seats for the thirteen royal families of the Realms had been erected over the last few weeks, and the minute details of the festivities were prepared. But Florian faltered. He hadn't informed Raz that he'd be standing guard over him and his family instead of participating.

There would be no explaining that change. The guardsmen of the high prince were known to take turns at standing guard over the royal family, but not for the opening melee. He couldn't see himself avoiding it, but he was torn between fighting in the battles and protecting Raz and his family. Florian understood that if he didn't at least pretend to do what Orn wanted, the spurious king would find someone else to do it.

"Are you not going to prepare, Florian?" Gavin asked, his arms held out at an odd angle while Daray attached his chain mail sleeves.

How could he explain not joining the melee to them and not raise suspicion? On the one hand, he faced the impossible necessity of keeping a secret from men who were like brothers to him, and on the other he endangered his sister's life without first having done everything possible to save her, which included keeping this abysmal secret.

"I won't be taking part in the events."

"Not participating? You must be joking."

"No, Gav, I'm not. My uncle . . . he'll be seated with Raz and his family. He . . . he has requested that I stand guard over them during the tournament."

The activity in the room ceased, and everyone turned to listen to their conversation. Florian closed his eyes for a second and wished for a way out of this.

"Why would he ask that, Florian?" Gavin asked. "Does your uncle suspect danger for Raz or High King Dante?"

"No." He answered too quickly. Even Florian knew he sounded suspicious.

"If there's no danger, then the men who've been assigned to stand guard will be more than capable of protecting them."

He didn't know how to answer and nodded because he disliked the concern on Gavin's face. He did not relish the other knights worrying about whether something was awry It would only incite more conjecture if he abandoned them on the field, but there was no way to tell Jeron or King Orn that their plan would not work without also putting Faye in terrible danger. He needed to find her.

CHAPTER FIFTEEN
TOURNAMENT

IDRA WALKED BEHIND THE HIGH royals: King Dante, Queen Zoe, Princesses Caityn and Eliya. They were on their way to the tournament grounds, escorted by High King Dante's twelve guardsmen—men of valor who'd been by the high king's side from their youth. Prince Theiandar had gone to check on the prisoner in the tower and then to speak with his men, and Caityn had mentioned his disappointment that this tournament would be one in which he could not join. As the high prince and future king himself, Theiandar's position required he oversee the tourney in celebration of his son's naming ceremony.

His father's shoulder injury, gained during the war with the Dark Lands seventeen years earlier, kept High King Dante from participating in the tourney, but only because it had been a sore subject between himself and his wife, Queen Zoe, who'd been adamant that he not join the games. Caityn had relayed the story of their conversation at dinner the night previous, just before the ball, and Idra couldn't help smiling about it. Zoe displayed a fierce love for her husband, even after all these years, but Idra also knew High King Dante's reputation well enough to imagine he might win out in the end and have some part in the tourney.

The sun shone bright for the festivities and not a single cloud marred the blue sky, but the canopy would protect them from the unseasonably warm rays during the melees. The opening ceremonies would begin in half an hour, and Idra's mind kept wandering to the idea of seeing Sir Ahmad in his full armor. From her knowledge, they only ever put on the massive, heavy equipment when preparing for certain training or actual war, otherwise they most often only wore helmets, a thick gambeson, and various bits of chain mail such as shirts and sleeves. Even gauntlets were rare. Unless they knew they were going to be in a dangerous situation, the guardsmen wouldn't even have any of those items, preferring the classic, specially designed leather armor and chain mail for practice or the typical garb of leather vests or tunics for daily wear.

Full armor on these knights today would be hot and uncomfortable, and Idra had a stab of pity for Sir Ahmad. Her only goal today consisted of offering Ahmad a token before the melee. She hoped it would be possible, but at the same time, her heart beat a wild rhythm at the thought of such an open display.

"Lady Idra!" Hilde called from across the open court near the tournament grounds.

Idra raised her hand to shield her eyes from the sun and looked in the direction from which she'd heard her friend's voice. She stifled a twinge of jealousy as a picture of Hilde smiling up at Ahmad surfaced in her mind.

It was not uncommon for ladies to smile at him. His handsome face and being a knight of the Realms—not to mention an exceedingly eligible one as High Prince Theiandar's most trusted knight—put Ahmad in a special light. His position now and the one he stood to gain in the future, along with its inherent power, were enough to draw the attention of a good majority of maidens at court. Idra had always admired him for how he did not take advantage of the regard or show false interest to garner favors from ladies. He exemplified a knight of the Realms, the pride of their combined nation.

"Lady Hilde, come walk with me," Idra offered with a smile and a wave.

Her friend left her family and came to walk next to Idra. They clasped hands in a brief greeting and then Hilde twined her arm through Idra's, a mischievous look lighting her eyes. Idra gave her a dubious smile in return.

"What plan are you forming in that lovely head of yours, Hilde?"

"I wouldn't dare plan anything! Oh no, not I. But I do help my friends with the plans they make."

Hilde clamped her lips together and locked them with an invisible key. Idra had to laugh. "I am thinking you are up to no good."

"I'm up to the best kind of no good, dear Idra. I want to invite you to come stay with me the last two nights of the tourney. There will be a small gathering the eve before the jousts on the last day, and I hope you will consent to keep me company while my parents stay here at the castle. I would prefer my own bed and don't mind the distance between, but I've no interest in attending the archery contests the day before the jousts and would be pleased if you'd keep me company."

"I would love to do so, Hilde. Allow me to speak with Princess Caityn to be sure she will not miss me. My family won't arrive until the day of the ceremony. The castle and city are huge, but I feel the pressure of so many strangers about, and it would be a welcome relief. Thank you for the kind offer. But Hilde . . . whose idea was it, if not your own?"

Hilde opened her mouth a smidge as if to speak, the smile still in her eyes, but she said nothing. After a second, she grinned wider. "Oh, a little birdie told me you prefer more intimate settings and peace."

They walked a little further before Hilde excused herself to return to her family for the opening ceremonies. Idra took the short flight of stairs up into the raised viewing box erected for the high royal family and their special guests. Caityn had arranged it that the parents and any siblings of Theiandar's guardsmen who were present be seated with them. Idra sat in the front beside Caityn and appreciated the spectacular view of the open tourney field.

Gracefully, she lowered herself into her seat next to Caityn. "Princess," she said without lowering her voice, "on the night before the archery and the following, would you be upset if I stayed with Lady Hilde at Hamlin? She's invited and I would like to say yes, but I do not want to leave you if you need me."

"Of course, Idra, you must go. It is such a kind offer. Please do. You've already taken care of the preparations for the tournament, and Bastien is well. Though he will miss you, to be sure," she added with a teasing smile.

"Thank you, my lady," Idra said, and they shared a secret, sisterly smile.

* * *

Ahmad sat atop his horse in full armor, his helmet gripped under his arm and sweat dripping down his skin under the layers of padding and metal. Prince Theiandar would be the first to ride out to welcome everyone. Ahmad and the others would come out behind him, followed by the representing houses of each of the Realms that would participate in the tournament for the next five days.

Today would be the melee on horseback. The next day would be the melee on foot, and jousts would begin after that, lasting the rest of the tournament. The third day had also been assigned the single matches of sword and dagger. The fourth day brought archery and a running of the famed pertento objex, the latter of which extended pure entertainment to the onlookers as it was an obstacle course, or trial of skill, most often taken part in by squires looking to be knighted. Not a knight there had forgone the pertento objex. The final day would be the deciding jousts and the announcement of the tourney winners and the awarding of prizes: the realm that won the melee would receive the traditional golden goblet and the right to hang the banner of the Realms as a sign of their prowess; the knight who won archery, fifteen gold pieces; the single matches' winner, thirty golds; and the winner of the joust would receive a kiss from a maiden of his choosing from within the high royal's box at the tournament and fifty golds.

Ahmad didn't mind admitting that he hoped to win the jousting because there existed one maid in particular of whom he desired to claim the kiss, and he wanted to seize this chance with the witness of the masses. He had some misgivings about her willingness, but the confident part of him believed she'd not deny him if he won.

The cheer rose from the crowd as High Prince Theiandar rode his horse around the outer edge of the tourney field. He moved forward to get a look out from the entrance to the arena and saw Raz stop in front of his family's canopied seating box, where Princess Caityn leaned over the edge and bent to kiss her knight, her prince, her love. Ahmad thought to look away, but like the other spectators, he took pleasure in the sight of his future king and queen displaying their courtly love for the world to see. The symbol of their affection elicited peace and encouragement, especially when his eyes wandered to the sight of Idra in the seat next to Princess Caityn's. She smiled at her cousin and didn't notice Ahmad. The soft sweep of her jawline and graceful turn of neck would have been enough to bring him to his knees had he not been sitting on his mount.

He thought she detected his intent stare, but aside from looking his direction she didn't seem to notice him hidden in the shadows. Ahmad watched her remove the ribbon from her hair and work her braid loose, allowing her auburn tresses to float around her shoulders in a beautiful sort of chaos.

The trumpet sounded, announcing the time for them to race onto the open field, and Ahmad pulled his eyes and focus away from Idra.

He pressed his helmet on, held his lance aloft, and galloped onto the open field. The helmet muffled the sounds of the crowd, but he led the charge of Delphor around the arena. After a full pass, they each approached their home realm. Ahmad stopped his prancing mount in front of King Trygg and Prince Melvyn of Nevin. Both men stood and acknowledged him before he joined the rest of his unit in front of High King Dante and his guests.

Princess Caityn stood next to her father-in-law and placed a wreath of colorful flowers around each knight's lance as he passed before her. When Ahmad's turn to receive the flowers came, he removed his helmet and bowed his head, but his eyes were for Idra alone. She'd come to stand next to Princess Caityn, on her side opposite the high king. She clutched her hair ribbon in her fingers and let it billow in the soft breeze, a gift sent by Almighty to keep the morning in armor bearable.

Ahmad extended his lance toward the princess, who placed the wreath there and let it slide down the post, and quickly stepped back to press Idra forward. He held his breath as he watched her trembling fingers reach the end of the lance, wrap the soft red ribbon around the end, and tie it tight. Their eyes met for only the briefest second before she stepped back into the shadow of the canopy and away from the cheering hoots and shouts of the gathered spectators.

Ahmad couldn't hide the besotted look on his face. He had eyes for Idra alone, even when Princess Caityn had stepped back up in her place. He didn't care if he lingered there; he loved Idra and wished the world to know. Ahmad wanted her and only her. He needed her. Life without Idra looked more and more impossible.

He raised his lance above his head and galloped once more around the arena, to the great delight of the cheering crowd. Surely this signified the beginning of an excellent tournament and marked an unspoken promise for his future—one he'd wanted for far too long.

* * *

Florian rode onto the field last. He'd sent a squire to inform his uncle that he could not miss the melees, but that he would be in attendance at his side during the other events of the tourney. The message had been obscure, but without being able to tell anyone what secret he held, it left him little choice. If he did not participate in the melees, his fellow guardsmen would become suspicious. He hoped the boy had been clear and that his uncle would be smart enough to realize this would not interfere with their plans.

But now, watching Ahmad celebrate his token from Lady Idra, Thoughts of Faye's danger and how he may have signed her death warrant by not following King Orn's explicit orders flooded his tortured mind. Florian wasn't the praying sort, but he needed all the help he could get.

"Almighty, if you're out there, watch over my sister," he mumbled, the words trapped inside his helmet.

The horn blew again, announcing those knights who'd come to represent their own realms. Ahmad led the guardsmen of Delphor from the arena while the others entered to parade through. Florian kept at the rear but removed his helmet and gave King Orn a pointed stare he hoped the man would understand. Faye was off limits. Orn must have comprehended his look; though a dark cloud of ire lingered over his face, he nodded once to acknowledge the knight.

Once the knights had made their opening parade around the oval arena, the melee commenced. Florian joined in the chaos, forgetting his worries, taking out his aggression, rage, fear, and hatred on the men he battled.

CHAPTER SIXTEEN
KEEPING SECRETS IS HARDER THAN IT LOOKS

THE MELEE HAD BEEN A bloody affair. One knight in the first pairing had been seriously injured, but other than plentiful bruising and minor injuries, the ensuing battles had gone well after that. Florian realized he'd not been at his best during the fight as his eyes wandered between King Orn's box and High King Dante, both watching the tourney battle with different thoughts and motives of their own.

Orn had given him until the end of the tournament to murder the high king, but Florian knew he'd never be able to do it. His loyalty belonged to the high king, to his son, and now his grandson. Florian could not do what he'd sworn to do, even on his sister's life . . . he would not.

When he pounded his battle ax into the shield of another rider, the full import of the game he played set in; it truly was life or death. Unlike Orn or his uncle, he could not use the lives of others like pieces on a chessboard. But the problem remained the same: if he said anything to anyone or did not fulfill his part in the bargain, Faye would suffer the consequences. Thus Florian would expend the fullness of his effort to find his sister and be willing to give his life in the process. If he could not do so before the last day of the tourney, he resolved to tell Raz and High King Dante of Orn's plot before anything happened to either of them or their family. Risky move or not, he had nothing else.

Now Florian had received a summons to his uncle's apartments in the keep. He marched down the hall and came around the corner but made impact with another body, one that grunted in the most feminine way.

"My Lady Idra! I apologize. That is twice in almost as many days that I've run you down in the halls of High Castle. Please forgive my thoughtless meandering."

"Sir Florian, you are forgiven, and I must say you are just the man I wished to see. Will you take a turn in the garden with me? I find I need some fresh air not choked by dust, horses, or other wildly sweaty, um, beasts."

"Ah, well, uh . . ."

"Oh, please say yes, Sir Florian. I really must speak with you."

"I apologize, my lady, but I've been called to my uncle's chambers. I should be going."

Idra's warm smile held a gentle kindness that had the power to be his undoing. She'd always been a sweet sisterly sort, and something about her quiet demeanor reminded Florian of his mother, or at least what he remembered of her.

"Please give me just a few moments of your time then," she said and pointed down the hall to a table and chairs.

"Of course, Lady Idra. I'm at your disposal. What can I do for you?" he asked as they walked the short distance to the intimate seating arrangement.

"What has happened to your sister?"

The blunt way she asked sent Florian's mind spiraling. Exhaustion from stress, lack of sleep, and from the melee earlier that morning rendered his mind useless for anything but the treachery being acted out upon himself, his sister, and the high royal family. But what could Idra possibly know about it? He hadn't said anything to anyone.

"Sir Florian? Your silence and that look upon your face, be it shock . . . fear . . . dismay, whatever is wrong, please tell me. What you said while we danced, about your sister, has hung heavy on my heart. Is there anything I can do?"

He realized in that second that she knew nothing but continued to share concern over comments he'd made the night before. A strange mixture of relief and disappointment engulfed him. It would have solved a mountain of issues to have the ear of Princess Caityn's most trusted friend. He said nothing and shook his head.

"Please. If it is a delicate matter, I can see why you haven't gone to your fellow guardsmen. Your sister seems to be in some kind of trouble. What is it? Is . . . is she with child?"

"Wh-what?" Florian spluttered. "No. No! Faye would never—she would not disgrace our family or our parents, Almighty rest their souls."

Florian watched the color rising in Lady Idra's cheeks and realized his own were heated.

"I apologize, but you are hiding something and I would swear you need help. It has to do with your sister. I am sure of it. Has someone hurt her? Is it money?"

Florian stood and whispered, "Tis not your concern, my lady. Please forgive me, but I must go now. My uncle is waiting, and he is not a patient man."

He didn't wait for her to dismiss him or even to apologize again. He walked away with his throat constricting, unable to swallow. Florian ignored the tears welling in his eyes and rapidly blinked them away. Everything in him wanted to tell her what misery had befallen him. Even the taught sinews of his muscles screamed at him to beg for her help, but his fear for Faye far outweighed his trust in anyone other than himself. He was unsure of what King Orn might actually be capable, but if he could only choose between himself or Faye, he would die before he let anything happen to her.

He strode down the hall to Jeron's chamber, where he stopped and stared at the grain of the wood door where it snaked around a knot in graceful curves. It took him uncountable moments to work up his nerve. He knocked and his uncle's muffled voice bayed him enter, but Florian took one last deep breath before shifting the latch. He stepped in and closed the door with great care.

"You idiot! You confounded fool! You ingrate and stupid, boorish child!" Jeron's voice thundered. "What were you thinking today? King Orn nearly sent his runner to have your sister dealt with. If I'd not stepped in when I did, she would be doomed as we speak. What were you thinking, I say?"

Florian strove to remain composed while battling the urge to defend himself and rant back at this deceitful, arrogant blackguard who called himself an uncle. How could he be culprit and angry at Florian in the same instant? It took a mountain of control to keep from lashing out. Florian couldn't speak for fear of going too far.

"What do you have to say for yourself? Hmmm?" Jeron tapped his foot, his arms crossed like a disappointed father rebuking a child, which served to anger Florian further.

"Orn is insane, as are you, old man. If I didn't join in the melee today, the other guards would have suspected something. I tried to get out of it, but they were already questioning my motives, and I could do nothing else to protect the secret. I will not joust and can make my presence known within the high king's box tomorrow, except during the melee on foot, since we have placed in the top four units. Besides, Orn hasn't yet given me this weapon, this dagger, he said would kill the king."

"You will get it soon enough, but you must make your presence in the high king's box inconspicuous by constant attendance or you will seem out of place. Talk to Prince Theiandar. Make your presence there a priority, however you can. If not, Faye is doomed."

"Uncle, where is Faye?" Florian hoped he hadn't overstated his emphasis but would somehow resonate.

Jeron stared hard at Florian. The older man's gaze burned hot on his skin, searing him with the reproach of anger. Florian suspected it might be hatred, but Jeron soon sighed and stepped over to the chairs by the fire, where he lowered himself into a seat like an old man. He sprawled out there, arms limp on either side and legs spread wide, his chin resting on his chest.

"Faye is nearby, but I do not know where. I suspect she is somewhere within the city in order to access her at any time. I do not want to know and implicate myself in this."

"Are you having second thoughts?" Florian asked before he could stop himself.

"No," Jeron said without hesitation. "I have worked toward this goal, toward gaining lands and wealth and a name since . . . the time doesn't matter. It has been almost my whole life. Too many things have stood in my way, you being one of them. Orn can give me what I want. Dante refuses, and his hardness has cost him much loyalty from nobles and kings across the Realms. No, I will have my spoils in this, and if you play along, boy, I will make sure you gain what you deserve as well."

"All I want is Faye's safety, Uncle. Tell me where she is, and I'll keep my oath," Florian said, the false words passing his lips with ease.

"You lie. You never could lie to me, boy. No matter. I know a lie from you when I hear it. Faye is a silly, stupid girl who you should care less about. You're a fool, as I've always said. Fine. You may be absent from the box during melee on foot but for nothing else, or King Orn will not hesitate again to fulfill his promise against you by making Faye the object of pain. Do you understand?"

With great reluctance, Florian nodded and left without another word. He may not have gained much by the conversation, but Faye had to be somewhere close. That was a start. Next, he needed to find out what servant of Orn might be trusted with her location and follow them. He'd no idea how to accomplish this when he would be required at the tournament the entire time. There had to be a way.

CHAPTER SEVENTEEN
CURIOUSER....

IDRA WATCHED SIR FLORIAN STORM off again, but this time with a certainty of something far worse than she imagined looming over the horizon. Whatever that might be, he felt compelled to keep it a secret, which surely heralded some terrible downfall. That look of dire warning in Sir Florian's eyes, the oddity of his behavior, paired with the arrival of the soothsaying Crescent Cave girl and her threats upon the baby who would one day rule Twelve Realms, caused Idra to question her own sanity. What if following after the mystery manifested by Sir Xavier's request to help divulge Sir Florian's secret, out of genuine concern for his friend, had sent Idra into some silly fit of nerves? She'd never suffered such a thing before, but anything seemed possible after the things that had happened to her in recent years.

She rose from the chair in time to see someone duck around the corner. Idra second-guessed herself again. Had someone been standing there, or might she have imagined it? "Get ahold of yourself," Idra whispered, but an unpleasant warning of intuition snaked up her spine. "Maybe that girl is a real soothsayer. Maybe she knows something." With that thought, she wandered toward the tower where they'd imprisoned the Crescent girl.

Idra passed many strangers on her way. Some gave her an uncomfortable feeling, visceral yet unaccountable. She'd almost arrived at the inner tower when she realized why the hairs raising on her neck were familiar. The sensation of being watched hovered in her conscious thought, just as when Zaide had spied on her from the shadows of this same fortress city. She shivered and glanced around, an icy chill sweeping over her and raising goose bumps along her flesh.

She pressed the latch to the tower door and stepped in, slamming it closed behind, and leaned back on it to catch her breath. Once she gained control of her outlandish anxiety, she pushed off from the door and took the winding stairs with quiet purpose. Halfway up, she ran into Ahmad coming down the cramped stairwell.

"Ahmad! Oh, I'm glad to have met you in such a fortuitous manner." His presence immediately relaxed the tension from her shoulders. Ahmad would know what to do. At the same time, she grew shy at the sight of him, especially after the bold act of giving him a favor before the melee on horseback earlier.

Ahmad had not yet changed from his plate armor after the melee, and if she hadn't been so wrapped up in her own thoughts and worries, she might have heard his chain mail's soft *chinking* as he descended the stairs. She stared up at him on the steps above her. His chest and broad shoulders filled the cramped space. His dark hair appeared tousled, probably from sweat and being inside his helmet, but it only added to his appeal. The confused look he wore brought her back to her senses in a snap of embarrassment.

"Idra, my lady, what are you doing here?"

"I-I . . . uh . . .." She didn't have a ready answer, but settled on the truth. "I came to seek out the Crescent girl."

Ahmad took a step down, bringing him that much closer. Then another and another until he stood on the same step with her, crammed in the tight spiral stairwell, her eyes even with the gray chain mail resting upon the place where his collarbones met. With a sharp intake of breath, she peered up into his face and lost herself in the heated energy emanating from him.

"Why do you seek the Crescent girl?"

Ahmad's whispered words held curiosity, and Idra detected a hint of something akin to protectiveness. She tilted her head to consider who he meant to protect but remained undecided whether it was the girl or herself or both. But his continued proximity worked to wreck her sensibilities to the point her mind dismissed everything else as she wished for this moment to last.

"Idra?" he whispered in an amused tone.

She fluttered her eyelids and shifted as if she were waking from a dream. It had been a beautiful dream. She wanted to touch him to make sure he was real, but refrained. The jumbled thoughts of what she wanted to know about him, about what relationship endured between them even now, about Florian's strange behavior and her promise to Xavier to speak with Ahmad, all mashed about in her brain until her head hurt.

"Ahmad, I . . . I must ask you to speak with Sir Florian. There is something amiss with him."

He scowled, and Idra wasn't prepared for the hurt his obvious displeasure wrought.

"Did Sir Xavier put you up to this?"

"What?" she asked, caught off guard. "Yes, and no. Stop changing the subject."

"He brought his concerns to me already, and I'll tell you what I told him. If Florian has a problem, he will come to us."

"I-I'm sure you right," Idra said, hurt by the dismissal of his tone. She looked away and struggled to formulate how else to speak with him on the subject. If unable openly share her concerns with him over this, what could she share? The invading notion was disturbing.

"Idra," he said, lifting her chin with his index finger.

She softened and inwardly sighed as the gentle pressure of his fingers tempted her to melt into his arms. Her eyes closed for a brief second, but the moment had been lost. She looked into his face. "Tis well. I must speak with the maid in the tower. Please excuse me."

She executed an awkward half-curtsy on the stair, her skirts brushing up against his legs in the cramped space and her forehead less than an inch from his chest. She made her way up the stairs without looking at him again.

"Idra, wait. You can't—"

"I don't need your help, Sir Ahmad," she said.

Idra refused to look back, though she desperately wanted to see in his eyes the apology his presence exuded. She loved him. She would forgive his dismissal of her concern, but not this second. He needed to see that her intuition matched his. She wanted to show him her fortitude and how much she'd grown in courage, but not turning back wrestled against her deepest ache to soak up his warmth and rely on his strength.

She hated admitting disappointment when he didn't follow her or even reach out to stop her. She imagined his touch would be gentle, matching the regret in his eyes. The daydream of it carried her up the stairs and to the prisoner's door. Outside sat a guardsman she didn't know by name but recognized from the castle guard. He bowed to her.

"Good eve, sir. I seek the Crescent girl, Sabine. Please open the door."

"I'm under order to not open the door, m'lady."

"I'm no threat to her, and I am sure she's none to me. I see no reason to bar my entrance. You may lock the door behind me."

"I'm sorry, but orders, you see."

She recognized the apology in his voice, but wasn't pleased. There were many reasons she needed to see this girl. "I understand. Thank you," she said and realized that Ahmad had been trying to warn her when she cut him off.

The hour of the grand tournament's opening dinner neared, so she gave up and went to prepare. "I will be back with permission from Her Highness Princess Caityn," she said over her shoulder as she took the stairs.

"Yes, m'lady," the guard replied with a smile.

* * *

At dinner later that night, Idra's seat was next to Lord Jeron. Conversations around the table comprised discussions regarding the melee, and Idra found herself surprised at the techniques she recognized in the talk regarding fighting and defensive moves. She normally took no interest in mock battle any more than the real thing, but now she found herself intrigued.

Jeron never smiled, except when he laughed uproariously at his own jokes, belittling the knights of various realms. After the first three courses and several glasses of wine, he seemed to disappear into himself in quiet brooding. Idra chose that moment to ask him a question.

"Where is your niece?"

"What?" He flopped toward the table, slamming his fist down on the hardwood surface.

The intensity of his response stunned her. "I-I only wondered, since she is of age, why she did not accompany you to the tournament and ceremony."

He seemed to relax, but only a fraction. An uncomfortable wariness shifted about in his eyes, as if looking for an escape or an attacker to jump out at any second.

"Faye prefers her dog's company. She named the mutt after her brother, using that fool nickname. Fidget, she calls him. He's just about as stupid as my nephew too. Florian doesn't know what's good for him."

"Sir?"

"Hmmm?" he asked, seeming to have relaxed.

"Where is Faye? I'd like to send her a letter."

"Oh, she won't receive letters and she won't need them."

"What do you mean, she won't need them?" The hairs rose on the back of Idra's neck.

"You ask too many questions. Questions are dangerous in these times, my lady," he said, still relaxed but deadly serious.

Idra had mistaken his calm for drunkenness, and now she felt duped into revealing too much herself. "I apologize, sir."

His reply consisted of a pointed stare, but now a hardness not present a moment ago clouded his eyes' dark depths and caused Idra's scalp to tingle.

"If you'll excuse me, I will be retiring. Will I see you in High King Dante's box tomorrow, my lady?"

"Yes," she said and wished she didn't have to answer, even out of politeness.

* * *

Florian kept looking down the table to his uncle and Lady Idra. It had come to his attention that men had been set about to follow his every move. He hadn't noticed until leaving his uncle's chambers that evening, but it must have been happening since the arrival of Jeron and King Orn from Wyeth. If so, he believed the hushed conversation with Lady Idra in the hall had been witnessed, and from what he read on his uncle's face during the meal, his scheming mind did not take kindly to Lady Idra's questioning.

Because he'd watched with great care throughout the meal, he didn't miss it when his uncle stood and nodded to a man farther down the table. It looked like some kind of signal. He followed his uncle's gaze where he realized Jeron had been motioning to Havrik, and a sinking sensation settled in his gut.

* * *

Ahmad watched Idra throughout the night. Her graceful movements drew him in like a moth to a flame, but their earlier conversation on the tower stairs had caused a breach in his confidence. He knew he'd hurt her, but a way to fix it escaped him. Throughout the night, he searched for a way to tell her how he felt, to apologize for his short temper on the stairs, ask her forgiveness and so much more.

"Almighty, I barely recognize myself anymore," he said to himself.

"What did you say?" Gavin asked.

Ahmad didn't look at the other guardsman who'd sneaked up next to him. "I said I'm a fool." His gaze trained on Idra, who stood speaking with Prince Melvyn and his aunt. "I'm unworthy of her. I don't know what I thought. Who am I?" He turned to Gavin, unable to hide the self-doubt radiating from the depths of his soul and plainly written on his face.

Gavin laid a hand on Ahmad's arm. "You, my friend, are a brave man, a wise leader, and a compassionate soul. Idra loves you, and I, for one, am happy to imagine her with such a man as you. Stop second-guessing yourself. Have courage."

He lightly shoved Ahmad and nodded toward the lady. Ahmad stumbled a step, but his sight traveled back to her, to her elegant beauty, her radiant skin, her gentle smile. Could he live without her? He had thought he'd have to, but she'd given him hope, and deep down his gut told him she was the one for him. But before he could make a move, she took the arm of Princess Caityn and the two left the great hall. His renewed courage sank and the opportunity lost tonight, but he resolved to apologize first thing in the morning.

CHAPTER EIGHTEEN
WHEN THE PAST WON'T STAY IN THE PAST

"I WISH YOU WOULD HAVE SAID something sooner, Idra," Caityn said, dragging her along toward the inner tower. "To be honest, I've been wanting to go visit this Crescent girl since last night, but Theian strongly cautioned me against it because she insists upon seeing me and Bastien. I won't take my son, but if you are with me, I think we will be well. Sir Ahmad has assured us she will cause us no harm, and I am of a mind to see how I can help her."

"Thank you for coming, Caity. I feel for this girl, and there is something in me that wants to trust her."

"You mean aside from your feelings for Sir Ahmad?" Caityn asked with a skeptical look on her face that Idra frowned upon. "Yes, that could very well be, Idra, but we cannot be certain she is trustworthy. More than anything, I can't get the unsettling thought of Skotos out of my head. I must know what she meant by saying he lived." They arrived at the stairway in no time and were soon standing at the door. "Please, guard, open this door at once."

"Yes, Highness," he said as he bowed to her.

Idra followed Caityn into the room, which had settled into darkness. She stepped out and asked the guard for the torch in the wall, leaving him with the candle burning on the table. Once accomplished, she stood next to Caityn just inside the door and jumped a fraction when the wood tapped the frame, the lock sliding back into place.

"Sabine, is it?" Caityn asked.

Idra saw the girl sitting on the edge of the bed, a hand raised to shield against the brightness of the torchlight.

"Yes, and you are?"

"Princess Caityn and my lady-in-waiting, Lady Idra."

Sabine stood in one swift movement and stepped closer, so close that less than a foot separated her from Caityn. At first Idra wanted to step between to protect her cousin, but nothing in Sabine's presence spoke danger. In fact, the fiery look in her eyes as the reflected torch's flame danced there showed only pleasure and relief.

She took a step back and bowed at the waist letting her black-as-night, shoulder-length hair spill around her face. "Your Highness, I am glad you've come to me. Time is running out. Your son is in danger, as are you."

"How do you know this? From who is this danger to come?"

"You know him as a thief who steals the beauty of innocents."

"Nox?"

"His name is ancient, Princess. Nox is not his true name, but it is the truth hidden in plain sight. This is the man. Nox is Skotos from the legends of our ancients before the lands endured shame, before we were separated and joined anew."

"But I don't fully understand the connection to our present circumstances, Sabine. Nox died at Ophira's Peak," Caityn said.

"It did not end there, nor did he ever die, Princess," she said and tucked her hair behind her ears. "Skotos did not die in far-off lands. He found the key to his revenge, but it came with a terrible price even he could not withstand. The Order of Nokt bargained with him at great cost and sent him to find the sands of life. In gaining more life, he takes it from another. In taking it, he loses pieces of himself to the consuming darkness. Nox is not just a name, it is what he has become—eternal night, darkness—and greed led him to it.

"Princess, you have experienced what the sands of life have become in his hands. He returned with them, and the Nokt made for him the Amulet of Dai, but once they showed him the way of the power, he turned against them and unleashed his ten henchmen to murder the priest-like Order of Nokt."

When the young girl talked of an amulet, Caityn crushed her hand to the hidden scar on her chest. Idra stood there mesmerized by the story, the familiar elements frightful and enlightening at the same time. She watched as Sabine's breathing increased, labored by some unseen force, but she only paused for a moment.

"Before leaving on the quest to find the sands, he placed his kingdom in the hands of his elder cousin and did suspect in the fifteen years he'd searched, this cousin planned and schemed to keep the kingdom for himself."

"How do you know this? If 'tis true, why have we never heard the rest of this tale?" Idra asked, unable to leave it be. Something important in Sabine's attempt to resurrect this old tale remained unclear. It had merely been stories recounted to children at bedtime. "This is nothing but a fairy tale, a legend."

"No, my lady," she said to Idra, "Tis all true. The Nokt have kept faithful record of him, and Skotos has lived these thousand years. He did not heed the warnings given by the Order, and when he sapped his first victim of her beauty, the amulet of Dai took him under its spell, living for nothing but what he could gain by the amulet. He forgot his kingdom. He has forgotten his original oath in the midst of gaining life by the sands, but forever there remains within him the vow he made. He cannot undo it, and he will continue to seek, without knowing it, the end of his sister's line." She faced Caityn. "You. Your family. Your son."

"This cannot be," Idra protested but weakly. She could not trace the intricacies of her own family lines, let alone Caityn's, to test if this young girl spoke true. It mattered not that she'd heard the tales of Skotos from a young age. It mattered not that Caityn's family thought their lineage traceable back to the beautiful and strong Solfen of Thryst, the beloved wife of the first king of Taisce. It didn't matter that Nox had so desperately wanted Caityn's beauty that he'd risked the discovery of his cave to have her, a princess. It only mattered that Idra needed it to be false, a made-up tale. That way she would not have to worry for her cousin in the face of untold power and ancient revenge.

Caityn spoke, her voice far too calm for Idra's liking. "Sabine, if this is true, then what you are saying is Nox is Skotos, my uncle from generations past, and though he does not remember why, he wishes to end my life and that of my son."

"Yes." Sabine nodded and slipped to the floor as if the telling of the story had robbed her of strength.

Caityn sunk down next to her, but Idra stood awkwardly above them holding the torch in one hand and gripping the handle of her hidden dagger in the other. She took one step back and slid the torch into the holder on the wall.

"Is this why you've come? Is this why you sneak into the Realms?"

Sabine shook her head. "No, Princess. My reasons are far more selfish. But when King Ekreton sent his men to return me home, one night on the trail I dreamt. I couldn't return to my journey with a clear conscience if I did not warn you. Skotos . .

. Nox has awoken from his generations of slumber and is more powerful now than ever before.

"He has gained the magic and power of centuries. He has powers to wipe memories, induce eternal sleep, wrest a man to the grave with one swing. The stories of my people are unending. When you broke the sands of time and your beauty returned to you, it also cracked the power fogging Skotos' memory. Soon, he will remember his vow. Even now I fear I have come too late, but I have nothing more to offer and beg that you release me to return home."

"Nox is dead, Sabine. He fell from the mountain, down a cliff face. I must ask again. Why do you come within our borders?" Caityn seemed unperturbed by what the Crescent girl had just revealed, which bothered Idra. Something undeniable lived in the words Sabine spoke. And they'd never found Nox's body after his fall.

"He's not dead," Sabine said, ignoring the question.

"That's impossible," Idra said, her eyes focused on the top of Caityn's head. A simmering unease built in her chest.

"I feel him."

She looked to Sabine, and the two made eye contact. What Idra saw in the darkness were eyes of blue, sparkling in the flicker of light and full of dread.

"How?" Caityn asked, interrupting the tense silence.

Why did Caityn continue to humor the girl? In her heart of hearts, Idra knew. She wanted to deny every fantastical word. They'd never found his body, but still . . ..

"How, you ask, Princess? I think you are the only one who will believe me, which is why I asked to speak with you."

"Then tell me before I lose patience," Caityn said without an ounce of noticeable irritation in her voice.

Idra's legs wobbled, as if the invisible words of the story floated about the room, draining them of energy. She believed fear had that power, but why had she a need to fear? Unless Nox still lived, and he planned to come for her cousin and the baby. Idra sat on the bed behind Sabine, her body heavy, and listened as the Crescent girl explained.

"What was once Thryst is now Crescent Cave, and what Emlyn used to be before it became one of your realms in the battles against Skotos. We were not of your people, and because of that, I am cursed. My mother was cursed, her mother before her, and my great-grandmother before her, as the legend goes. I had been told the stories, warned of what would happen, but never suffered under it as sharply as I did beginning almost two years ago.

"But I should start from the first." Sabine rolled her shoulders back to sit as tall as possible. "My great-great-grandmother had untold beauty from a young age. She had a gentle soul and Nox wanted it. He stole her beauty and planned to use it, but he did not realize she carried a child in her womb. He also did not yet realize that the power's curse needed a maid of innocence and only one who came from the lands of his sister could be taken because of the vow he'd made. The Nokt had tried to limit his power in that way."

Idra's eyes strayed to Caityn as the princess turned away from Sabine, her hands press to her stomach and her head bowed. What must her precious cousin be enduring? Idra ached for her.

"But in his greed he chose my great-great-grandmother, one not under his sister's rule, whose body and heart were ravaged by the curse, but whose beauty he could not contain. On the night of the eclipse, horrible pain tormented her curse-damaged body, and she died, but in the midst of it she gave birth. Her baby, my great-grandmother, was born beautiful—seemingly untouched by the curse—but as she grew up, she had strange and frightful dreams even while awake. Her father feared for her, thus he approached the council of elders for help.

"The Nokt were not completely wiped out those centuries past, and some escaped to the far reaches of the north, beyond Crescent Cave. They kept the legends of Skotos, and her father went on a quest to find the Nokt. When he did, they informed him his daughter, though protected from the scourge of soullessness, would forever be inexplicably and irrevocably connected to the thief and this would continue as such throughout her generations. The Nokt who carried on the order's traditions regretted the actions of their ancestors and asked to be allowed to return to Crescent Cave."

Sabine paused again. Her shoulders sagged, and Idra wondered if the recounting of this tale somehow took a toll on her in hidden ways. She too felt heavy, but Idra had a strange ache to hold the younger woman in her arms and whisper that everything would be well. But with each word Sabine said, Idra rejected the lie that false comfort would be.

"I have always had the dreams, but never as when Nox came for you almost two years ago, Princess. Word arrived of the rumors dancing across the Realms like wildfire. I knew there was some truth to them because I saw your face. I witnessed your destitution. Sometimes I remained trapped in the dreams. I feared going to sleep until I could not hide from them even in wakefulness."

Caityn swiveled toward Sabine and kneeled next to her, placing a hand on her shoulder.

"My mother and her mother before her never suffered as heavily as I have under the weight of them, but they are both gone now. I cannot ask them, but in the years since my great-grandmother's father found the Nokt, they have returned to our people in Crescent Cave, hidden amongst the commoners.

"But they are not who they once were. They wish to undo the wrong their ancestors have done and regain their place among our peoples. They wish to take from Skotos his power and end his unnatural life and have helped me to learn to control the dreams, but I cannot escape them. I am cursed. I am so very tired, Princess. I know nothing else but that Skotos, this Nox, is going to seek revenge upon you and your son. Please let me go. I swear I will leave Twelve Realms and you unharmed."

She lay down on the cold stone floor and closed her eyes, her cheek pressed to the hard surface. Idra and Caityn stared at each other, both mirroring a look of incredulous disbelief. Sabine's story flew far outside the realm of reality and left Idra speechless.

No wonder she'd said no one outside Caityn would believe her. Magic, especially of this sort, was unheard of in Twelve Realms. Until Caityn's beauty had been stolen, no one would have believed it possible. In fact, many of the people of the realms did not believe it. Rumors still circulated about that there had been some sort of disagreement between the kings, or the princess had tried to elope with another man before the wedding, or that the real princess had been so ugly that Prince Theiandar had refused to marry her without a double dowry, or they'd replaced her with a distant cousin and proclaimed her to be the princess as a ruse to make the prince marry her. There were such numerous rumors floating about that Idra didn't know whether to laugh or cry for her dear cousin. Caityn had been through a great deal, yet she continued to show the doubting people love, patience, and compassion.

Idra imagined the rumors dwindling away with time, but if this magic was real and true, if Nox lived . . . nothing would stop the old doubts from resurfacing.

"Help me get her into bed, Idra," Caityn said while she attempted to maneuver the young woman up. Idra had been lost in her thoughts and not paying attention.

"Of course," she said and slid off the bed to kneel on the floor next to Sabine and Caityn. "I can't believe she's asleep. How can she not wake up?"

Caityn shrugged but looked worried. "I shall take her feet if you, her arms."

Idra nodded and the two of them struggled to lift Sabine's dead weight. Idra had barely settled her back on the pillow and reached for the blanket Caityn passed her, then Sabine's hand shot out and gripped Idra's wrist suspended above her chest.

"Beware the Fyll Blade. It rests amongst you even now, but soon it will make its indelible mark," Sabine whispered and closed her eyes in sleep once again.

"Fyll Blade? What is it? What does she mean?"

"I've no idea," Caityn replied, bewilderment and unvoiced worry twisting her pretty face into something unrecognizable in the shadows. "Come. Let her sleep now, and tomorrow I will ask High King Dante to release her. I cannot tell what to do with what she's told us, but I fear Nox is nearby and I will not recognize him if I see him."

She knocked on the door, and the guardsman let them out. Left speechless, Idra had been caught up in the strange recounting and forgot to ask Sabine her questions, but the more she thought about it, the more she realized it had been utterly ridiculous to think Sabine would know anything about Florian or his sister or King Orn. Sabine had been cursed with a gift of sight only connected to Nox. He plagued her sleeping and waking. And he wasn't dead.

CHAPTER NINETEEN
LOVE AND PROMISES

IDRA COULDN'T SLEEP. SHE AND Caityn had returned to the nursery where Caityn wept silently over her son. How might she comfort her cousin or protect them from one whose power went beyond that of mortal man? No matter how impossible it sounded, something in her knew the truth of his continued existence. When sleep continued to be elusive, she replayed the story Sabine told, and no amount of denial would undo the sneaking truth of his presence, no matter how impossible it seemed. Nox had already proved he lived outside the possible.

The jousts were soon to begin, followed by the melee on foot. Idra had to find Ahmad before then. Caityn had refused to tell Theiandar about what Sabine said under the pretense that he either would not believe it, or he would believe it and lose his mind with worry to protect them. She refused to be a catalyst of fear, taking solace in the idea that they were now surrounded by loyal subjects and knights from across the realms. She doubted even this betrayer Nox would attack during such a spectacle as the naming ceremony events.

Idra didn't agree, but Caityn refused to listen. Instead, Idra chose to approach Ahmad and tell all in hopes he'd believe her about this even if he didn't about Florian. She sneaked into the tent erected for the knights of High Castle, and the eyes of those present turned to her. Heat rose in her cheeks, but she held her ground, forcing her vision to search the dim space for Ahmad. When she saw him a surge of relief washed over her.

"Sir Ahmad, may I have a word with you?"

"I'm next in the jousts, my lady."

"I will not keep you long, but if I may, I'll stay here and speak with you while you prepare."

Her words had been timid but bold, but she kept her eyes focused only on Ahmad, knowing she'd surprised the five other guardsmen in the tent, not to mention herself. Ahmad's eyes were intense, but something in them seemed alive. He made one sharp nod and held out his hauberk to her. Idra's next breath caught in her throat at the invitation, but she didn't hesitate to move forward and take the heavy chain mail shirt. She bent forward under the weight of it; the hauberk probably weighed as much as a small-to-medium-size sleeping child.

"How do you wear this?"

Ahmad laughed and lifted part of the mail from her hands. "You get used to it. I'm assuming that you've never put it on during your training with Gavin?"

His question, posed innocently, held an unfamiliar tone. Perhaps jealousy? Or displeasure? She answered with care.

"No, and since I never plan to be in battle, I didn't think it necessary."

"I see."

She cocked her head. At one point in time, it seemed as though they read each other's thoughts, but now . . . she prayed they'd be able to regain that closeness. Idra raised the hauberk as far as her arms would go, and Ahmad ducked into it, his arms lifted to receive it. As he moved in slow motion to stand tall once again, barely any space separating him from Idra, his head raised and his face came so near hers she only need lean forward a fraction of an inch to brush his skin. She had the desire but held herself still with her fingers entwined in the chain mail, skimming along the padding protecting his ribs.

Ahmad's arms lowered and, in the passing, the back of his fingers swept along her cheek. Idra choked on the air she sucked into her lungs and took half a step back. She wondered if his heart hammered as hers.

"My lady, I must tell you I'm sorry for what I said on the stairs yesterday. There is no excuse, but I beg you forgive me. Whatever it is you are worried over, I will listen to and do my utmost to assist in."

His soft-spoken, sincere words were mirrored in his eyes, the answer to her longings of yesterday after their misunderstanding; she wanted to believe it but a doubt lingered. She glanced around to see they'd been left alone. She did not miss the kindness of the gesture, but she had business to deal with, and this man needed to hear her out one way or another.

"Ahmad," she said, a warble of intense nerves rattling her voice, "I want your help with Florian. There is most certainly a danger or problem that he is facing with his sister that he refuses to discuss. I sense fear in him, but I have more unpleasant news to share with you, and I need your help. How else shall I say it, except I will say it plain. Nox is alive."

There. She'd done it. She believed beyond a doubt that he lived, but there remained no explanation of how without having seen the evidence for herself.

He reached up and wrapped a loose tendril of her hair around his finger. "That's impossible. You did not see the cliff from which he plunged. No man could have survived that fall." His words were soft and distracted, as if he wasn't really listening to what she said.

"That is what I said, but the Crescent girl said it is true, that he is alive—" She took a sharp intake of breath when his fingers slid from the ringlet of hair to her jawline and neck. "Ah . . . and he is planning revenge . . . on Caityn and her son. Tis complicated," she said, her breathing shallow and her focus diminishing to only his gentle touch.

His hand stopped just below her ear, and his attention, which had been following the trail of his hand, drifted back to her eyes but kept their far-off look. "You spoke with Sabine?"

"Yes. Caityn and I went to her last night. She told us why she came to High Castle. It is a long tale and one I'm not sure anyone else will believe."

He placed his hands on her cheeks. The warmth of his palms on her face soothed and sent her heart rushing. She closed her eyes and let the worry of the unknown melt away, but she froze for half a heartbeat when she felt the soft pressure of Ahmad's lips upon her own.

When he pulled away, her eyes fluttered open, but as she glimpsed into his, his face inches from her own, she recognized her feelings mirrored there.

"Forgive me, Idra. I am completely irrational when you are near." His eyes traveled to her lips. "I could think of nothing else but . . . doing what I just did. Forgive me for taking liberties."

"There's nothing to forgive."

He must have taken that as a sign, because no sooner did her lips relax an inch than he kissed her again, but with an intensity she found herself returning.

The moment lingered, but the sounds of the tourney broke through the wall of silence that had temporarily filled their world. Without letting her go, he broke the kiss and a heavy sigh escaped his parted lips. He must know, like her, that there were important matters to be discussed.

His voice soft but tinged with the seriousness she admired, Ahmad leaned his forehead to hers and said, "I must make you understand I trust you and your word. You are more to me than my life."

Her wonderment at whatever had just happened drifted about them like a heady blanket of fog, even as Idra explained what she had learned of Nox, which was inadequate. She relished the feel of Ahmad's arms wrapped loosely around her waist and tried to focus on the most pressing difficulties to overcome, which were the protection of the princess and that whatever load Florian suffered under need be dealt with as soon as possible.

"If Nox is alive, our princess is in danger. I will speak with Raz after the jousts. And I *will* speak with Florian. I promise. I trust you, Idra, and I—"

"Ahmad, you're next," Xavier said, stepping in the tent door.

She stiffened at being caught in Ahmad's embrace, but it was his pained expression as his eyes closed for a brief second before taking a slow step back from her that kept her from flinching. Ahmad's eyes were trained on her, an intense, conflicted look crossing his face before he nodded. He and Xavier worked together to finish putting on Ahmad's armor, and there was little more to say or ask.

Idra picked up his helmet, and he took it from her, tucked it under his arm, and reached for her hand. She held her breath while he raised her fingers to his lips and placed a lingering kiss on her knuckles. His genuine smile brought one to her own face as she watched him stride from the tent.

Idra pressed a hand to her breast where the crazed beat of her heart seemed to pull her toward him by an invisible cord, binding them with more than words and promises. Slightly dazed by what had most certainly occurred, though it lingered like a dream, she made her way to the stands to watch the event with a mixture of anticipation and worry. The jousts could be fatal, but Ahmad's strength and jousting ability had been heralded across the Realms.

She slipped into the seat next to Caityn and offered a weak, if not guilty, smile. Caityn looked at her with an expression that said she knew Idra had spoken with Ahmad about Nox, but it quickly changed to one of acceptance and even gratefulness as she squeezed Idra's hand. The unspoken agreement between them eased the weight from Idra's shoulders. She hated to go against her cousin, but Princess Caityn would not want to keep the news of Nox from Theiandar for long, and who better to tell him than his most trusted knight.

The joust before Ahmad's took Idra's breath away. One man ended up being dragged away, unconscious. He didn't appear to be dead, but a hush of concern swept across the arena.

Ahmad galloped out into the open and took one pass around the joust field to the applause of most of the audience in the stands. His opponent, Sir Havrik of Wyeth, followed. Applause for the other knight mixed with boos as the man had gained a reputation for ruthlessness that followed him everywhere. Idra tensed, not realizing Ahmad would face this man in the jousts today. Havrik would be a worthy opponent, but that increased her concern by several degrees.

Idra held her breath and watched as the two were set up at opposite ends of the field. The blare of the horn telling the riders to race on made her jump out of her skin, but she leaned forward and gripped the rail of the box with such force that her knuckles turned white under the pressure. There would be three passes, and each pass would give the knights the potential to gain points.

Their lances lowered from the vertical starting angle and aimed with precision upon their opponent, but Sir Ahmad made the first blow, Sir Havrik's missing by what looked to be mere inches. The next pass seemed to take forever, but this time both men slammed the shield of the other, their lances shattering with the impact. Ahmad had the higher score, but if Havrik could unseat him he'd take the round.

"Almighty, protect Ahmad," she whispered and took Caityn's proffered hand.

They squeezed each other's fingers and waited for the last round of the session. Idra couldn't make eye contact with Ahmad through his armor, but she felt his attention on her as he raised his lance above his head. She waved to him, unable to contain herself or her pride in his ability. No other man in the world could she imagine loving like she loved him.

The last horn blew, and the men raced forward, their lances lowering for a last pass. It seemed that Sir Havrik took position first, but in the split second it required to hit the other, Havrik flew from the back of his horse and landed in a cloud of dust. The surprise of the crowd caused such a hush over the arena that Idra thought she heard his grunt when he landed.

She didn't care. She jumped to her feet and cheered with the crowd. Ahmad had unseated the one man the crowds thought would win. He'd won the round and would almost certainly face the intimidating knight again in the final jousts at the end of the tourney.

* * *

Florian slipped out of the box and made his way to the High Castle tent to prepare for the melee on foot. The jousts had taken up the entire morning and today's mock battle would determine the winner of the melees. His uncle had said that though displeased, King Orn had agreed to Florian's participation in the melee, but under no circumstances would he advance and attack. Instead, he should hold back near the rear to avoid injury.

Florian made no reply to the order and planned to ignore it. He met the others in the tent and congratulated Ahmad on his win against Havrik, but otherwise he ignored them, lost in his own problems and thoughts.

The melee consisted of a battle between four realms, the ones who'd come out on top at the melee on horse during the first day of the tourney. Wyeth, Berne, High Castle, and Tappen prepared to battle and stood at four points of the oblong arena. Florian glanced to where King Orn sat with his retinue, then toward his uncle in the box with the high king.

A sudden regret overtook him as he realized he'd left the high royals completely vulnerable to attack by not being there. He should have told his fellow guardsmen or, at the very least, bowed out of the melee, no matter how it might look to them. It was too late for regrets.

The battle began in the heat of the afternoon, the autumn sun beating down on them and adding the possibility of heat stroke to their discomfort while dressed in full armor. Florian fought his way to the front, slamming his battle ax into his opponents, knocking some aside while struggling to fend off blows from others. The chaotic and loud field of battle hid within a thick cloud of dust and made breathing difficult.

Florian ran into the thick of it just before a slamming weight struck his shoulder blades, knocking him to the dirt. He scrambled to his knees and attempted to stand, but another blow slammed into his shoulder from the side, sending him sprawling to the dusty ground. In mere seconds, Havrik stood over him with the long tip of his battle ax pressed into the space between Florian's helmet and cuirass, where his only protection came from the leather pixane at his neck.

"Stay down."

Havrik's growled command stood out over the deafening cries of the melee. Florian should have heeded the warning, but something in him snapped. He knocked the ax aside and kicked at Havrik's gut, successfully knocking him off balance and backward by a few steps. He rolled to his side and attempted to get to his feet. But full armor hindered the motion, making it slow and labored where he was already exhausted from the battle.

Ahmad appeared out of nowhere and gave him a hand, but before he had regained his balance Havrik attacked them.

Ahmad fought him off with a quick swing of his longsword. Florian watched him step in and grab Havrik's shoulder, at which point the Wyethian knight cried out in pain. He'd obviously sustained an injury, probably during the jousts.

Florian left them to battle it out and moved his way forward, looking for other knights to engage. Many had already fallen, but the realm of Tappen had the most men standing. That didn't surprise him as Tappen fashioned the best steel weapons and were renowned for their battle training. The Realms' best weaponry and armor were forged there too.

The melee on foot soon ended and Tappen indeed came out the winner. The crowds cheered, but Florian found no pleasure in any of it. At that precise moment, his sister languished under lock and key, guarded and in danger. He joined the other High Castle knights in congratulating the men of Tappen and made his way back to the tents to remove his gear.

After the battle, his sore muscles refused to obey, and it took a while to strip the layers. There were squires and pages on hand to assist them, but after a hard day of battle, dogged weariness still hindered the process. Once out of the heavy gear, he made his way toward the door and out into the narrow alleys between the numerous tents.

"Florian! Wait," Ahmad called after him. "Let me walk with you."

Florian let him catch up, and the two made slow progress toward the barracks.

"Florian, I've been told your sister is in trouble, and I want to help."

CHAPTER TWENTY
DIRTY CONSEQUENCES

FLORIAN STOPPED DEAD IN HIS tracks, his heart missing a beat, and grabbed Ahmad's arm to halt his progress. Florian faced him with a look of anger and fear he couldn't hide. He had no idea how Ahmad had found out, but he had to keep quiet. He valued his sister's life too much to let it be wasted because Ahmad couldn't keep his mouth shut.

"Be silent, Ahmad. Faye is well. She is safe," he said, hoping he'd misunderstood Ahmad's words.

"That is not what Lady Idra told me."

Now Florian was even more confused. Lady Idra knew nothing of what had happened to Faye. He'd made sure of it.

"What did she tell you?"

"Calm down, my friend. I might be wrong here, but I made a promise to Lady Idra that I would speak with you, and between you and me, I am afraid I've lost her trust. She warned me of trouble with your sister and that she'd deduced you might need a friend's help. Is your sister in trouble? Danger? You know we will help you."

"Faye is none of your concern, Ahmad. I beg of you to lower your voice," Florian said through clenched teeth, looking around. If someone—the wrong someone—heard, Faye's fate would be sealed. "Please, don't say another word."

Havrik stepped out of the shadows from behind a tent and grinned at Florian, whose heart stopped as he watched the other man tap a knife against his palm. But it wasn't just any knife; he held the one Orn had shown Florian the other day. Why did Havrik have it? He didn't know, but he wasn't about to let the vindictive oaf hurt his friend.

"There's a little birdie who begs your silence, Florian."

Florian knew exactly to whom the Wyethian knight referred, but he didn't know what to say.

"And there is a lady who doth protest too much," Havrik said with an amused grin while his eyes shifted to Ahmad.

Why the grin? He spoke of Lady Idra now, but why?

Havrik seemed to ignore Florian at that point and placed his attention on Ahmad, who stepped out in front of Florian.

"Why, sir, do you threaten another man of your realm, of our united kingdom?" Ahmad asked and rested his grip on the pommel of his arming sword.

Florian's mind went blank. He needed to avert a confrontation to protect Faye and his fellow knight by whom he stood. "Tis nothing," Florian stammered, "but an old rivalry between Havrik and me. You can ignore him." The edge in his voice stood out, and he doubted Ahmad had missed it, especially when Florian noticed his fellow guardsman's hand slide from the pommel to the hilt.

"Yes, Sir Ahmad, 'tis only an old rivalry," Havrik said, touching the blade in his right hand to his left shoulder where Ahmad's lance had struck him while jousting. "But you, I have a new grudge against, and there are certain things you need to keep your nose out of."

No sooner had he said the words than he slashed at Ahmad with the gently curved dagger in his grip. He moved quick, but in the span of seconds it took him to swing, Xavier jumped out of nowhere, the blade slicing across his chest, a rush of blood quick to rise to the surface. He cried out, taking the brunt of the attack. By instinct, Florian stepped close to Ahmad as well, but he'd not beaten Xavier to the blade.

Florian charged at Havrik who dropped the knife, and the two tumbled to the ground in a scuffle of grunts and punches. He pinned Havrik to the ground and leaned close, glaring into his face.

"Have you lost your mind?" Florian whispered in a voice closer to a growl.

"Tis you who've endangered your friends, *Fidget*," Havrik spat back, barely above a whisper, using Florian's childhood nickname as a jibe. "I'm not through with *Sir* Ahmad, and the king won't let him live knowing what he knows."

It took Florian several seconds to grasp the meaning of Havrik's words, but by then the knight had shoved him aside and stood. He pointed down at Ahmad who cradled an unconscious Xavier. "He attacked me!" Havrik shouted to the newly formed crowd.

Florian only pictured potential outcomes for Ahmad if he said or did anything. He completely froze, staring at Xavier's slack jaw and closed eyes. How could he protect Ahmad from a worse fate than the eternal sleep to which Xavier had just been sent?

Several others had emerged from the tents and come running because of the ruckus, but Havrik stood firm. "Sir Ahmad attacked me, and that boy jumped between," he said, his voice calm.

Florian wanted to deny it, but the idea suddenly struck that Ahmad would be safer under house arrest than wandering about where anyone might attack him. He looked from Ahmad to Xavier's deathlike slumber and back. He only had to corroborate Havrik's story and Ahmad would be well. His gut clenched at the thought of spreading the lie, of helping the enemy, but in the thick of it Florian had no better way to protect his fellow guardsman. The question became, how could he explain that to Ahmad?

"You lie, Havrik! You attacked me!" Ahmad's vehement tone hardened with anger. "What have you done to him? He won't respond. Is this blade poisoned?"

"How should I know?" came Havrik's smooth reply. "'Tis not mine. You attacked me."

"Liar!" Ahmad yelled and looked ready to jump from the ground if not for Xavier's head on his knees.

It was now or never. If Florian didn't step up and say something, even though validating a terrible lie, Ahmad's life would be taken when least expected, and Faye would certainly lose every vestige of herself and her life.

"He tells the truth. Sir Ahmad attacked him," Florian said, his voice quiet but heard by those standing near.

A hush fell over the group of men clamoring for an explanation, and all eyes turned to him.

"Sir Ahmad attacked? He threatened him?" someone from the crowd asked.

Florian swallowed the lump in his throat and nodded. With his mouth dry as sawdust and unable to utter a sound, he made eye contact with Ahmad and inwardly staggered under the full force of his betrayal thrust back in the look on his fellow guardsman's face.

Several knights pushed forward. Two took hold of Ahmad by the arms, dragging him away, while more came and carried Xavier toward the barracks. One ran off to find the physician, and Havrik was ordered to follow those escorting Ahmad.

Florian only wanted to run away, to leave, to die, to disappear. How could he have just done that? How could he have told such a public and defamatory lie? Ahmad would never understand; he'd never forgive Florian.

A dull ache throbbed in his head and bile rose in his throat, but after ten seconds standing in indecision, he jogged after where they'd forcibly escorted Ahmad. He just needed a few seconds to assure Ahmad and ask for his trust. That was all, just a few seconds. They'd taken him to the keep and into the dungeon where Ahmad would be detained while the high prince was summoned.

He'd been silent the entire time, but when Florian met Ahmad's gaze through the bars of the cell his eyes spoke volumes of his contempt for what Florian had just done. Florian already blamed himself, but having that look burned into his soul by one of his best friends seared like having a hot poker pressed to his chest, branding him worse than a liar. A horrifying thought crashed into his consciousness like a battering ram. What if he was just like Jeron?

Florian fought back the guilt and walked past Havrik, who leaned against a tabletop outside the cells with an unreadable expression on his face, his thick arms crossed over his equally muscled chest.

"I'll stand guard over Sir Ahmad until High Prince Theiandar arrives," Florian told the dungeon guard who'd locked the door after the others brought Ahmad in. The man looked terribly confused but backed away. Florian nodded his thanks and faced Ahmad who remained silent. He leaned on the bars and whispered for only Ahmad to hear. "I'm sorry for this. There is a reason for what I've done, and for now, I need you to trust me that this is the safest place for you right now."

Ahmad grabbed the bars and leaned forward, his own whispers urgent. "What have you done, Florian? You've got to tell the truth. Whatever trouble you've found yourself in, getting me thrown in here will not solve it. And what of Xavier? What happened to him?"

"I can't explain that right now. This is beyond you or I, but I am begging you to trust me. Please."

Seconds of silence passed, their eyes locked, Ahmad staring through Florian into some expanse beyond his reckoning. "By Almighty, I want to trust you, but this?" he said, motioning around to the cell. "If you're in trouble, how can I help you here?"

"I'll explain when I can. Just sit tight and play along. I'll get you out of here, but not yet. I swear to you, my friend. Tis the only way I can protect you and my sister. Can you trust me?"

"I don't know, Florian. I didn't consider you to be a liar or one to keep secrets from us, but I will try. You must swear to tell all."

"As soon as I can," Florian said, relief flooding his soul. Maybe this would work.

He reached through the bars and offered his arm to Ahmad, who hesitated before returning the gesture. "You are in danger, Ahmad, and this will keep you safe until I can find a way to—"

"What's going on here?" Raz's voice boomed through the low-ceilinged dungeon, echoing down the various halls.

His severe, angry gaze rested briefly on Havrik before traveling to Ahmad and Florian. He approached and stood next to Florian.

"Ahmad," Prince Theiandar said with urgency and concern. "What's going on here? Are you well?"

"I'm well, Raz, but Havrik attacked me with a strange blade that struck Xavier when he jumped between us. He's accused me of attacking him."

"What nonsense," Prince Theiandar said, conviction coloring his voice. "I'll have you out of here soon." He went to call to the nearby dungeon guard when his father, the high king, stormed down the stairs.

"What is this?" High King Dante bellowed, his voice booming. He strode past Havrik without a glance, even when the knight bowed at the waist. King Dante stopped in front of

Prince Theiandar. "What is going on? Your guardsman attacked one of your own?"

"No, Father, that's not what happened."

"Of course it is. Even another of your own knights has said." The king waved to Florian, who found he couldn't breathe. The high king already knew about the incident, and someone had reported his part in it as well. "Word of this is spreading, and if your own guardsmen can't be trusted—"

"There's been a misunderstanding, Father, but I'll handle it. These are my men, and I trust them with my life."

"Oh, and what of the lives of your people?"

"And the lives of my people. I tell you, Father, I will handle this. I will get to the bottom of it and make sure the right parties are dealt with properly."

"I cannot let our realms see any more discord among our family. This needs to be dealt with and swiftly."

"As I say, they are my men, and I will handle it." The firmness of Raz's response came close but didn't step outside the bounds of respect he held for his father, even if he challenged his word by way of assertion.

King Dante shifted and glared over his shoulder at Havrik. Florian watched the crooked knight stare back at the king with what appeared to be an innocent look had Florian not known the man to be a fraud.

"And what of him?" the high king asked. "How will you smooth this over with King Orn? He seems to think his knight would never have attacked another of the realms, let alone a man within your own guard. Tis common knowledge such an attack, provoked or not, would be severely punished."

"I realize that, Father, and you may assure King Orn that if his man is innocent in this he will not be held, though I think it wise he no longer participate in the tourney and that he should leave the city immediately. I will assign a guard unit to escort him away as soon as I've questioned him."

Florian watched the high king evaluate his son. Raz stood under the scrutiny of his father with dignity and a piercing stare to match that of the older man. Though heartening, it also drove guilt further into Florian's gut, knowing he'd have to lie to protect those involved, including Raz and his family.

The king nodded and left the dungeon. He only said, in the same booming voice, "I hope you do not fail, Son. If you do, your people will lose faith in their future king, and that would be detrimental to our kingdom's strength and peace."

Hearing him speak to Raz that way in front of the men who were present kindled a fire of indignation inside Florian. For all Raz had done to please his father and become the strong man he was, he deserved better than that. From where the high king's dissatisfaction had come, Florian had no idea, but it baffled him.

Raz sighed and glared at his father's retreating form but quickly turned to look at Ahmad. "I'm sorry, Ahmad. Father hasn't been himself of late, but I'll have you free of this momentarily."

"Wait!" Florian said in a strangled yell, choking on the word at the same time he glanced back at Havrik to see if he listened. He might not hear them, but the dastardly knight watched with eyes like a hawk. "Sire, I would like to say that what Ahmad tells you is true, but Havrik was the one attacked, and Xavier getting hurt was by accident." He spoke loud enough for Havrik to hear, then lowered his voice to a whisper. "Ahmad, please tell Raz."

Ahmad glared hard at him, and Florian watched the muscles tense in his jaw. He gave a slight nod and said, "For now I am letting the accusation sit as is, but know that it is only for a time, Raz. Florian has said there is a reason for this but has yet to explain himself."

"I only need more time. Please, Raz, just keep Ahmad here for his own safety and get Havrik out of the city."

Prince Theiandar glanced between the two. "If you do not explain the entirety of your mysterious behavior to me before the next day dawns, Florian, you will find yourself in this cell instead of Ahmad. Understood?"

"Yes, Highness." Florian nodded and swallowed the desire to tell more lies. How could he continue to protect his sister, the high king, Ahmad, and Raz, if he were to tell all? Who could help him without drawing suspicion from Orn or his uncle? He backed away and left the dungeon as if he were drowning.

Once outside, he ran to the barracks. His heavy-laden steps crushed him with guilt and fear, like the short distance had become a thousand miles, and when he arrived, he found the physician stooped over Xavier's prone form on the table in the main room.

This cannot be happening. This isn't happening, he thought over and over as he stood in the doorway.

The physician had patched up the cut to Xavier's chest, but Florian noticed where blood seeped through the cloth. A strange pallor washed out Xavier's skin under the torchlight, but a steady, shallow rise and fall to his chest proved he lived on. The wicked enchanted blade must have been retrieved by another knight, for it sat on the table next to Xavier where he slept on in what Florian understood to be a deathlike sleep.

There were several knights milling about, whispering their speculations to each other, but none had seen it firsthand. Florian tried to ignore their stares as he approached the table with Xavier laid like death upon it. He couldn't resist reaching toward his friend in a comforting gesture with one hand, while with the other he aimed for the blade laying near Xavier's hip. The physician looked up at him but the distraction of Florian's hand on Xavier's shoulder kept his eyes averted from Florian's true purpose. His face tilted toward the sleeping guardsman's, and he did not see Florian swipe up the knife and slide it into his sleeve.

"I cannot comprehend what has happened to him, sir," the physician said, shaking his head. "He sleeps but cannot be woken. Do you know? Did he hit his head when he fell? There is nothing on his scalp to indicate such a terrible blow. I think poison has caused this sleep, but I know not what poison could do such a thing in this way. Nothing wakes him. Not even a flinch when he is poked or pinched. It is beyond me."

The physician asked Florian, but he didn't really seem to expect an answer as he rambled on about the oddity of the case.

"I am moving him to the keep where I can better look after him until he wakens."

"That is wise," Florian mumbled.

"Hmmm? Oh, yes, yes. Quite," the physician said absently as he lifted Xavier's eyelids and leaned over to examine his blank, staring eyes. "Such strange behavior. They should not stare so in sleep. It is as though he is alive but dead. I cannot make anything of it. Never seen this in all my years. Never. Well, come, gentlemen. Let's get him to my rooms within the keep." He motioned to two knights who brought a large cloth over and slid Xavier onto it to carry him away. "Oh me! Where did that strange blade get to?"

"There was no blade," Florian said, his heart racing as the other man searched around and under the table.

"I thought I left it right there. Are you certain you did not see it when you came in?"

"No. There was only Xavier. Mayhap Sirs Jarl or Gavin took it to the armory for safekeeping?"

The explanation seemed to satisfy the good physician. Florian mentally worked to relax his muscles and walked with them, but it felt more like he walked Xavier to his grave to be buried. On the way, a boy ran up to him. "Sir Florian, sir. Your uncle has asked for you to join him this instant."

He stared at the boy until the words sank into his muddled, slow-as-molasses brain and nodded. "I'll check in on Sir Xavier after a time," he said to the physician, who nodded and kept walking on the other side of his patient.

The boy ran off before Florian had a chance to ask any questions, but it didn't matter. He was overwhelmed, and with each second Ahmad stayed locked up in the dungeon, his anger rising, Florian's will to overcome diminished. He hated the iniquity. He hated the very wrongness it created as it highlighted everything evil in the world. Florian saw no way clear of his predicament no matter how many ways he looked at it, and without exception he found himself deeper and deeper in the darkness whenever he tried to protect the ones he loved. What could he do to save them all?

He arrived at his uncle's chamber door before long and shoved the blade he'd swiped from the table further under his vest, wedging it between his side and the belt securing his tunic in place and holding his sword on his hip. He inhaled deeply and walked in without knocking, but more than Jeron greeted him. There, pacing back and forth at the foot of the bed, stomped King Orn. As soon as Florian latched the door, the king turned on him with pure malice seeping from every pore.

"You are more of an idiot than your uncle says. I knew I shouldn't have trusted you with this. You see that man standing behind you?"

Orn waited for Florian to look to the man standing in the shadows by the door. His face stayed hidden in the darkness, but Florian nodded anyway as he squinted hard at the man, attempting to make out his features.

"That man will relay a message for me to another, who will make sure Nox gets his next victim. Remember how last you saw Faye's face, because it will be hideous in its transformation the next you see her."

Florian jerked forward, ready to take a hefty swing at the king, but two men closed in and grabbed his arms.

Jeron approached Florian, who struggled against the grip of the two knights. "Nephew, do not make more trouble for yourself or me. Calm down."

"Calm down? Calm down! Are you out of your mind?" Florian stopped pulling against the men and leaned toward his uncle's face. "You're playing with other people's lives here. Xavier is just a boy. Your accursed knife has wounded him and now he lies as if dead. My friend is imprisoned. Faye is innocent, and yet you would give over your own niece to the depravity of this man? No, sir, I will not be calm."

Without warning, Jeron slammed his fist into Florian's stomach, well-placed just below his sternum. The unexpected blow landed hard, and he buckled at the waist. Gasping for air, he tilted his head up even as his uncle's palm came in contact with one cheek and then the other in rapid succession.

"That young knight should have minded his own business. Sir Ahmad asked too many questions, and as far as my niece is concerned . . . I will protect Faye, but you, my boy, must shut your mouth if I am to do so," he said in a low tone, his breath tickling Florian's ear.

He slapped the restrained Florian once more and then backed away, turning to face King Orn. Florian labored for breath, but gave up the fight against the strong grip of the other knights while he waited to see how Jeron might protect Faye. Part of him hoped his uncle might be just as much a prisoner of King Orn as he found himself, but Jeron's next words betrayed the wish.

"You may use my niece however you see fit, Highness, but before you give her over to Nox, I would beg you, reconsider." Jeron looked over his shoulder at Florian, a gleam of triumph in his eye. "Florian may be stupid, but he is not yet useless." He looked back at King Orn, then stepped toward a decanter on a high table in the corner where he poured himself and the king glasses of amber liquid. "I have been informed that Florian accused Sir Ahmad of attacking, and now that knight is locked in the dungeon. If Florian wants to keep this friend alive, he only need continue to speak thus against Ahmad, and Havrik will be free of danger." He finished speaking and handed the glass to the king, who stood in full view of Florian.

Orn released the stone dangling around his neck, took the proffered glass, tipped it back and drained its contents. He visibly relaxed and stared at Florian. "Make it happen, Jeron, and you will have the headship of Wyeth plus much riches and lands held by the high crown. You are going to be a very wealthy and powerful man, my friend."

"That is all I ask, Sire," Jeron said and bowed.

"You bastard! You would sell your own family into slavish treachery for a bit of land and money?"

Jeron made eye contact with Florian, but the depths of his uncle's eyes held nothing but a glint of pure selfishness and greed.

"You still have a chance to rescue Faye, you imbecile," Jeron said with a hint of anger. "Isn't that what you wanted?"

Florian gaped at Jeron; the man was a depraved lunatic, in good company amongst that of the capricious king of Wyeth. Instead of answering, he yanked his arms free of the now relaxed hold of the two knights, stood tall, and stormed from the room. His temples throbbed with pain, but only his jumbled thoughts drove him slightly mad.

Without the ability to give an answer to any of them, his heart pounded in his ears. He would not help them commit treason, and he could not let them hurt Faye. He would not let them get away with Xavier's death or Ahmad's imprisonment, either.

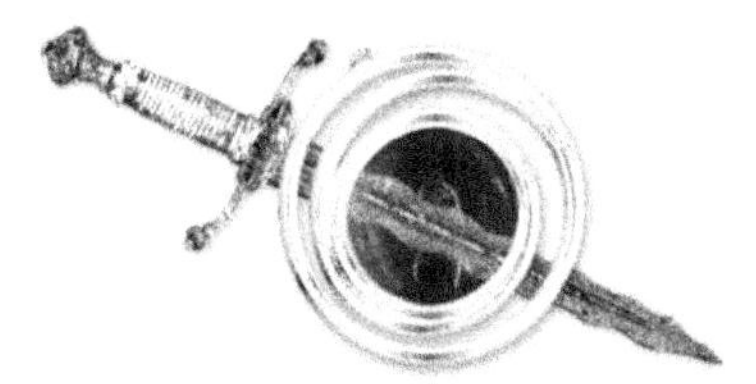

CHAPTER TWENTY-ONE
DESPERATE TIMES, DUPLICITOUS MEASURES

IDRA STOOD OUTSIDE THE BARRACKS, full of indecision. One of the other knights of Delphor informed her that Ahmad had been taken to the dungeon on false charges but that Prince Theiandar had agreed to detain him there. It was forbidden for her to visit the dungeons, even for him, but part of her fought desperately to ignore the rules and do it anyway. She took a step to follow in the path of Sir Jarl when Florian burst around the corner, something grasped tight in his hands that he quickly tucked into his vest.

"Lady Idra, what are you doing here?" Florian asked as he approached from behind.

She noticed the same tension and brooding anger on his face she'd witnessed several times over the course of the last week. "I'd come to find word about Sirs Ahmad and Xavier . . . for my princess. You were there when it happened were you not? How should Sir Ahmad be accused of such a thing? I'm at a loss. And what of Sir Xavier's condition?"

Before she took another breath, Florian grabbed her arm and dragged her around the barracks. She considered protesting, but no harm would come to her in Sir Florian's presence. He looked around—for what, she did not know—but when he seemed satisfied, he spoke in hushed tones.

"My lady, you have been right from the start, and I cannot believe I am revealing this to you, but I am desperate. Xavier was right to question me. He's in terrible danger now, but so is my sister, as you've discerned. And now Sir Ahmad. What I am about to say must not be repeated to anyone, anywhere. Do you understand?"

He waited and she nodded. Florian glanced around and pulled her further into the dark. "Faye is being held prisoner somewhere, and I need your help. There's none I can turn to that I trust outside Delphor, but as you see, just the mention of anything to them and harm comes their way."

He stopped for a breath and lowered his voice even further. "Xavier has been injured by an enchanted knife. If stabbed, it causes instant death; if sliced by the blade, a deep, eternal sleep is induced. I'm aware of no cure for this. I fear Xavier is gone from us forever. And now, when I thought enough had transpired to make my head spin, Ahmad has asked too many questions and got himself in the thick of it. The only way to protect him from such a terrible fate was to have him locked safely in the dungeon."

"No!" Idra said, not wanting to trust any of it. If what he said proved to be true, that meant she shared the blame for Ahmad's current location in the dungeons. He'd not wanted to ask questions but for her prodding. "No," she repeated with less conviction. "None of this makes sense. Do you speak true?"

She held her breath, wishing she'd not heard him right, but he convinced her with the slow nod of his head.

"There must be something we can do." She waited, imploring him further with silent entreaty. Idra had listened to his brief recounting, but there were still details missing, things he must be hiding. Idra just didn't know which questions to ask, and her stomach tied in knots. The worry she already felt for Ahmad tripled at the idea that he could be injured as Xavier had been.

"I'm sorry, my lady but I have no knowledge of it but what I was told."

"By whom?"

"I cannot reveal that to you. Anything else I speak on the subject puts my sister in further danger, and now I am putting you in more danger than you had already done yourself by asking questions. But I will tell you one more thing. Nox is not dead. The Beauty Thief is alive and hidden within the realms, gaining strength and more power even as we speak."

"I know," she said, meekness and fright entering her heart at hearing Florian say the same thing Sabine had said the night before.

"You know?" he asked, all astonishment. "But how?"

"The Crescent Cave girl told us. She said he is coming for Princess Caityn and her son, to finish them off for ancient revenge. She said—wait! She mentioned the Fyll Blade. Do you know anything else of the knife which injured Xavier?"

"Nothing."

"What if that is the blade she warned me of? I must go speak with her. Will you come to the tower with me?"

"I cannot, my lady. There is something I must do first, but I will come find you when I'm done."

Idra offered her gentlest smile to Florian, wishing to dispel the look of agony he wore. With a nod, she left him and hurried toward the inner tower to ask Sabine about this blade. It frightened Idra to think that Sabine's presence might now give light to other, seemingly unrelated, circumstances. But wondering at the possibility that Nox had in some way been the catalyst of each dilemma gave her a worse foreboding chill.

The same guard who'd been present when she and Caityn last visited Sabine stood in attendance and allowed Idra access with no preamble. Once she'd explained the details of her mission, Sabine disappointed her with her reticence to answer the questions. And most of what the young woman did share wasn't helpful, except what little she knew about the blade. After gaining what she could from Sabine, Idra left the tower feeling a weight heavier than before pressed down on her shoulders. Once outside, Idra dashed toward the barracks, but again she nearly ran into Florian.

She stumbled and said, "Oh! Sir, we really must stop meeting this way."

Florian's weak smile spoke volumes about his state of mind, but Idra appreciated that even amid the gravity of the situation, he saw a glimpse of light. That meant he still had a flicker of hope in him.

"What did you find? Did the Crescent girl know anything?"

"Yes, but I'm not sure how helpful it is. I'm afraid Sir Xavier is lost to us, as you said, for it was surely this Fyll Blade of which she spoke before. The only answer she gave regarding him requires asking for the help of an ancient order called the Nokt."

Saying it out loud, hearing the words from her own lips, gave her yet another surreal moment in the turn of events her life had taken over the last two years. But she'd experienced enough of the unimaginable, that this—while outlandish—aligned with all the rest.

"What does that mean? Who are they? Where?"

"I wish I knew, Sir Florian. If only we could capture the enchanter of the blade."

"Nox."

Idra blinked and frowned. "How did you know?"

"It doesn't matter, but he is at the root of all this treachery. And my uncle is helping him. This much I know for certain." Florian grabbed his hair and thrust his fingers into the unruly auburn-and-gold locks. "I've got to find Faye. You cannot say anything to anyone."

"But your fellow guardsmen would help you. They are strong and capable. They would protect her like their own. You know that. Why won't you ask them for help?"

"Because I cannot risk any more of them being injured or, worse yet, killed. Ahmad's life is already in great peril. You and I have not been overly close, my lady, and you are a woman. No one will suspect I've spoken with you on this matter. I hope. And if anyone finds out that I've breathed a word in regard to what is happening, even a hint, Faye will pay the ultimate price. Do you understand how serious this is?"

"I . . . I think I do. Sir Florian, I want to help. I must help, for not only you sister's sake, but that of Ahmad and Sir Xavier. I'm only afraid I don't know how."

"You would help me rescue my sister?"

"Of course," she said without a second thought and meant it. "Will you tell me what exactly is going on here?"

"I . . .. No. It's too dangerous," he said, vigorously shaking his head.

"Sir Florian, I would feel much better if we apprised the situation to High Prince Theiandar. He can keep your secret and keep you safe."

"I cannot share this with him; the less who are aware, the better. As it is, I fear for your safety, and every second am reconsidering—no, regretting what I've told you. Do not do anything. Stay far away. Take the princess and the baby far from here. Do not hesitate. Do not ask questions. Only do this and be safe. Almighty protect you and give you speed."

"I would say 'and you as well, sir,' but you know I cannot do that. I will help you because running away will save no one in the end. Princess Caityn would never agree to leave without an explanation, and she knows already that Nox is alive. It would do no good. Instead, I will try to help you find Faye, and you will help free Ahmad so that we might find a cure for Xavier's illness."

Florian frowned but bowed. Idra had no idea how he truly felt about it, but she thought she saw a flicker of relief cross his face in the midst of the turmoil. "As you wish, my lady. I must go before we are seen together."

She nodded, and he ducked around the corner a second later. Idra stood there for a minute, trying to work up the courage to walk back toward the keep. Jeron would be at dinner, and his involvement led her to believe he represented the best source from whom to gain information. She just needed to figure out how to go about it.

Idra dashed for the keep and toward her chamber, but instead of going there, she tiptoed around the corner of the hall that led to Lord Jeron's. She froze when she heard something like heavy cloth brush the wall behind her, and after a second more hesitation, she took a step forward. Suddenly, rough hands grabbed her and covered her mouth before she uttered a scream. A sickly-sweet scent filled her nose.

The world melted into blackness.

* * *

Florian jogged for a short time, worried that the place he'd stashed the Fyll Blade while Idra was speaking with Sabine would be found. He wondered when they would track its absence back to him, if they would even consider it. The physician hadn't a clue what poison Xavier had succumbed to, and he didn't seem concerned over the blade's actual whereabouts. Of course, the man had been distracted, more than usual.

Florian slowed his pace to a walk as he approached the keep's main entrance. If there weren't eyes on him before, there definitely were now. He sensed someone lurking and lingering, eyes boring into his flesh, but he had to ignore it and pretend he hadn't noticed. Raz expected a report from him explaining why Ahmad needed to be kept in the dungeon for his own safety. Nothing he thought of would protect his sister, the high king, the prince, and Ahmad. The list continued to grow. Somewhere in the back of his tortured mind he comprehended the bitter truth of his predicament, but he refused to admit that Orn's words and wasted breath carried an infinity of lies; if he would acknowledge it, he'd be forced to concede that his sister's life was already lost to him. Again, he begged the Almighty to give him the right words and strength to continue, to rescue Faye.

Florian made his way to the dungeon in search of High Prince Theiandar. At the top landing, just within the doorway, a guard inspected Florian with a look up and down before moving aside. Each step down crushed him as though the burden of what he had done and what he still must do were too much of a load to bear.

There were a few other men lingering about. Unit Delphor congregated there, but as soon as Raz noticed Florian's presence, those not a part of the elite unit were dismissed. The dungeon had no other inhabitants, which only made Ahmad's location all the more stark. Florian watched Raz throw a ring of keys to Gavin, who unlocked the door and allowed Ahmad to exit the cell.

Florian stood ten feet away from the group and most of them, along with Ahmad, turned to give him glares of disbelief and anger, as though he'd betrayed them all; in a way he had. But he'd wanted to protect them the only way he knew how, to be brave and press onward with whatever meager plan he mustered. With Lady Idra's help, he might pull this off without putting anyone else in harm's way.

"You're angry," he said to the knights at large. "I don't blame you, and I'll do my best to explain. Are you sure that we're alone?"

"Yes, Florian," Raz replied, his temper short and the effect of it clipping his words. "The others swept the halls to verify. We're alone."

He acknowledged the high prince with a slight nod and steeled his nerve to continue. What he was about to say was the truth, but only the half of it, and he needed it to be convincing enough to protect Ahmad and keep Havrik from wreaking havoc.

"Where's Havrik?"

"I listened to his story—something about Ahmad picking a fight with him, and you and Xavier happening upon them. He gave the impression that you were the only other witness."

"Yes, I believe that is true."

"Then you had best explain what really happened and why you lied in order to get your fellow guardsman thrown in the dungeon," Raz said.

Florian flinched at the description of what he'd done but ignored the change of topic and went back to his original question. "Is Havrik gone from the city? Did you have him escorted by high castle men?"

"Why are you concerned? Yes, I informed him that because he was involved and his story did not align with Ahmad's, he must leave the city for the duration of the celebrations and that he would be required to attend a trial after the ceremony concluded. I believe the men escorted him to the village to stay at the inn there."

While good that Havrik had left the city walls, he gained no comfort by having him stay that close. It would be better for Havrik to disappear altogether.

"Thank you, Highness. Now I'll do my best to answer your question." His throat constricted, and sweat greased his palms, upper lip and the bridge of his nose. "Nox is alive and seeking revenge by first attacking your guardsmen, eliminating them one by one. Ahmad, you were first because you are closest to the prince."

"What is this? How would you come by such knowledge?"

"It was your Crescent girl," Florian said, looking at Ahmad for half a second. "She spoke it to Lady Idra, who I happened to meet by chance just after their conversation."

He hoped they wouldn't realize the impossibility of that timeline, since Lady Idra had spoken with her after this had happened. He'd need to approach the lady and ask her to second his story, but the thought of more lies and asking her to bear false witness to the high prince seemed to take it too far; he just had no notion how to stop it and save his sister with no one else getting hurt.

"Raz, she spoke of the Fyll Blade, which can cause a deathlike eternal slumber if sliced with it. That is exactly how Xavier is now, and I believe her. Nox wants revenge, and he's starting with us — with Ahmad. The only way to stop him until we can find him is to keep Ahmad safe, and this seemed the best way to do it without Nox finding out we know he's behind the attack."

Florian held his breath. He'd said it and held loosely the hope they'd believe every word. *Almighty, please let them believe it until I can fix all this. Please, Great One.*

"You mean to tell me Havrik is working for Nox?"

Florian hadn't considered that point and opened his mouth without the right words to say. "I . . . uh . . . I would have to assume so, Sire. I don't know that for certain, but it would seem so." He had nothing else to say; Florian knew Havrik served Orn who worked with Nox. He dared not come any closer to the whole truth.

"Are there others working for him as well?"

Florian looked to Ahmad and willed him to be forgiving, but the stoic look on the other knight's face remained undecipherable. "I believe there are many, Sire." He almost added "but I have no idea who," but stopped himself before another lie escaped his lips.

"I think we should cancel what remains of tourney. The danger is too great."

"But, Raz," Ahmad said, still staring at Florian, whose heart had stopped beating upon hearing the prince's pronouncement, "if you did that, Nox would realize we are aware of his existence and his plans. We will lose any opportunity to find him if you halt the tourney."

"Not to mention," Gavin added, "it will also send a terrible message across the realms, a bad omen of sorts for the beginning of your son's life and his future as king. That may well be part of his plan, or benefit him at least, from what you relayed about what that Crescent girl told Princess Caityn."

Theiandar looked to be contemplating their arguments, but he sat in obvious opposition to anything that would jeopardize any of his men's lives.

"I agree with Gav," Ahmad said.

Florian noticed some of them nod and that just slathered on another layer of wretched guilt. He'd told them the truth, but only part of it. The rest would make what he'd said inconsequential, and they'd string him up by his toes if they knew.

"I see what you are saying, but I cannot endanger any of you hoping to catch a madman."

"We would do it of our own free will, Raz," Gavin said, and the rest voiced their agreement.

"You are each of you brave, and your willingness to protect my son and the future of the Realms is worthy of much praise. It will be done just as we've discussed. The tourney will continue and we will begin a quiet search for Nox and his cohorts." Raz turned to Ahmad and laid a hand on his shoulder. "Ahmad, I am having you moved from here to the inner tower to occupy the cell opposite the Crescent girl. Tis smaller, but you'll be better there than here, and the door will remain unlocked. Consider it house arrest. That should still maintain the appearance that we suspect nothing."

"Thank you, Raz," he said and looked over at Florian with a stern countenance.

"I'll continue to stand guard over you and your family at the tourney, Raz," Florian said, wanting to cram the words back down his throat knowing that they carried a double meaning. He would need to spin another story for his uncle to keep him from discovering how much he'd revealed to High Prince Theiandar and Delphor. The prince acquiesced and Florian watched as two of the others escorted Ahmad out of the dungeon.

Their fellow knights followed, and their shoulders drooped as if they also carried the weight of Florian's guilt. He hated himself for lying to them. They were like brothers to him, much more like family than the uncle he'd been given by Almighty. Deceiving them tore him apart, even if only withholding part of the story. The only modicum of sanity in his head came from the thought of his innocent sister and the potential of her wasted soul at the hands of Orn and Nox. The nightmarish picture it presented induced him to evade that outcome at all costs.

CHAPTER TWENTY-TWO
WAKING NIGHTMARE

IDRA GROANED AND REACHED FOR her aching head, only to find her wrists restrained. Groggy and in pain, she cracked open her eyes into slits and attempted to make out her surroundings She could tell she lay on hard-packed earth, but there was no way to discern the time of day beyond the fact that light slipped in from outside. Her mouth was dry as cotton, and her eyes burned like someone had dumped ashy soot into them.

Idra fought the pain in her head and worked to open her eyes wide. She'd been trussed up like a stuck pig ready for the spit, and once fully aware, she recognized her location as a dilapidated cottage of some sort. A thick layer of dust covered the floor except where footprints disrupted its smoothness. There were two men present—one standing at the meager, boarded-up window, peeking out between slats, and the other sitting on a stool, whittling wood and ignoring both her.

Her memory slowly returned, but the pounding of her headache impeded the process. The last thing she remembered was speaking with Sir Florian near the courtyard by the keep entrance. She had a vague memory of going to Lord Jeron's chamber, but that's where her memory faded. Everything went dark. The next thing she knew, she woke up here . . . wherever *here* was. She had no answers and no help. Someone would miss her, which gave her comfort, but not much.

If only her feet weren't bound and her hands, she'd attempt to escape. If this were a cottage, they must be within scant miles of civilization. A bright swath of light spread across the dirt floor in front of Idra when a third stranger opened the door, his silhouette and shadow stretching tall. He closed the door behind, and the light of the world instantly disappeared along with most of Idra's remaining hope. How could this be happening . . . *again*? Had something about her twenty-second birthday opened up a world of misfortune upon her? She realized she might have asserted herself more around that time. *Oh dear*, she thought, *I've brought this upon myself.*

"No screaming," the newest arrival warned, while removing the gag from her mouth and the rope from her feet. He then wrapped bony fingers around her upper arms and hefted her to stand.

"I will not scream, but I suppose it would do no good to ask to be returned to High Castle."

"None whatsoever."

He went to the door, opened it, and gestured for her to precede him out. Feeling pert and perturbed, Idra looked to the other two men and curtsied. "Good day, sirs," she said, then walked out the door with her head held high. The sky shone bright with the midday sun. She must have been out for at least a night and half the next day. *No, no, not good.* She didn't recognize the place.

"Where are we going? Who has commissioned this kidnapping?"

"We are going a few hours north, and I believe you already know the answer to your other question," he said and offered his hands as a step to mount the second horse.

They were alone, far from civilization, and Idra didn't even see any horses belonging to the two men still hidden within the abandoned cottage. She considered who would have her kidnapped and remembered Florian's warning about what might happen to anyone who knew about his sister. She remained unsure of the answer, except that she believed it had something to do with Nox. A shiver ran up her spine, causing her to jerk a bit. Words failed her as she realized she might be headed into the Beauty Thief's grasp. The only word she could utter slipped past her lips.

"Almighty."

"You should say a prayer, my lady. If Jeron's nephew fails, you can be sure yours is the first beauty the king will have the pleasure of taking."

"Hold a moment." Idra didn't fully comprehend what he'd just said, but he mounted his horse, no longer paying her any heed other than to make sure her horse's reins were attached to his saddle horn. "Sir, what king do you speak of?"

"You don't know?" he said, a glimmer of amusement in his eyes. "I'll let him tell you then."

She'd never questioned Florian about why his sister, of all people, had been captured by the Beauty Thief, or why his uncle might help Nox, or any of it. She'd blindly accepted it as part of Nox's plan to hurt Princess Caityn and her son, never once thinking a king would ever be involved, making threats against Faye to induce Florian to obey whatever command he'd been given. The jumble of thoughts sent blood rushing through her head, making it throb even harder.

The man with her brought his horse parallel to hers, slipped a sack over her head, and then chirruped. Her horse lurched forward, throwing Idra off balance. She kept her promise and did not scream or cry out, but from what she ascertained, no one would hear her anyway. It would be wasted breath since it appeared they were miles from any other people. They must still be within a day to a day-and-a half's ride of High Castle, which gave her some encouragement, especially after their trip took them over a bridge, one that most likely spanned the river Solfen.

After what time dragged on forever, but must have been five hours, Idra found out why the man thought she should be awake for the ride. He halted her horse and pulled the bag from her head. The afternoon sun assaulted Idra's vision and caused her to squint. They were at a thin trailhead that stood sixty feet up on the edge of a cliff face overlooking the river. One side rose a hard rock wall; the other offered a sheer drop-off. The horse seemed familiar with the trail and reluctant to travel down it. Idra's heart raced and unbidden tears fell from her eyes as she tried to keep the nervous horse on the narrow ledge and not look down.

The clunking and clattering of gravel and rocks sloughing off the cliff brought her one step closer to believing she would die each time the hoof of her equally tense mount clopped down on the loose terrain. The trail widened and curved around to the left, where she could not see beyond her captor's head. They turned the corner and the opening to a cave large enough for the horses to enter came into view.

Once through the wide gap, Idra counted three other horses huddled in the expansive cavern. Behind them, the ceiling lowered and extended into darkness.

The black-clad man dismounted and reached up to assist Idra off her horse. She accepted his help, exhausted from the effort of keeping her wits about her. "Thank you," she said, mostly out of habit but also because she was truly grateful for any kindness. But as his hands lingered on her waist and she noticed the lustful look in his eye, she regretted having said it. A knot formed in her stomach similar to what she'd suffered on the ledge, and she stepped back to free herself from his grasp.

Though not bothering to mask his disappointment, to her profound relief, he respected the distance.

The stranger dressed in black pulled his sword from the saddle and slipped it into a second sheath on his waist. He carried both arming and longswords with him and led her further into the cave, into the darkness.

Once again, Idra's heart rate picked up and her breathing shallowed. She thought she might pass out, but soon light from up ahead illuminated their path until they came into a huge grotto. When her eyes adjusted, Idra spied two men near a small fire. Another human being huddled against the wall. Upon further inspection, Idra made the form out to be a woman.

Things started making sense to her now. Nox had somehow gained the aid of people within the Realms and had kidnapped Florian's sister to hold her soul over her brother's head, to coerce his obedience by the easiest means possible while also ensuring access to unspoiled beauty. But what king had the man been referring to? She couldn't be sure, but it must be one among the twelve of the Realms . . . thirteen if she included the high king.

The men at the fire barely looked up except to reveal the ugly leers contorting both their faces. She did her best to ignore their expressions and stared around the expansive, high-ceilinged cavern. She didn't see any exits other than the dark abyss of an entrance they'd walked in through, but she saw stashes of weaponry along one wall and stores of food along another. They cordoned one spot off with a blanket attached to a rope, but she got the impression it acted a screen for privacy while using the privy. Or at least that is what she hoped. There were no other rooms to be had.

The man who'd brought her prodded her toward the back and pressed her down next to the young woman, who didn't raise her head from her knees. He pulled out a shackle and clamped it upon Idra's wrist. She wouldn't be able to wriggle from the tight metal bracelet, but as she examined the chain, she realized the other end was attached to the girl and not to the wall. It raised her hopes half a second until she noticed the ugly addition to the chain on the girl's ankle—an extremely heavy-looking ball the size of a man's head. And the sight of the two men by the fire, not to mention the double swords kept by the one who'd brought her, was enough to remind Idra they were out-manned in this situation and escape would be next to impossible.

She had to return to High Castle. Ahmad was locked up; Florian thinking him safer there. Princess Caityn was in danger, and so was Bastien. Idra couldn't . . . no, she wouldn't let anything happen to them. She'd never forgive herself. She refused to think they were trapped here or that no one would come to their rescue, hers and this girl she assumed to be Florian's sister Faye.

The first captor stood over them and stared down at Idra, who returned his stare with an apathetic one of her own. Once upon a time, she would have been frightened out of her wits. She'd have cowered and cried, but not anymore. Idra had learned to be strong through trial and hardship, and she discovered an ability to withstand much more than she ever thought possible. This would not overcome her. Not today. Not when the ones she loved were counting on her.

"Hello," she said to the girl next to her when the man walked toward the fire. "My name is Lady Idra of Tanfield. Who are you?"

The girl peeked up over her folded arms and stared at her. Idra saw that the girl was the right age, about sixteen. The shadowy cave made it difficult to tell, but the color of the girl's hair seemed to match that of Sir Florian.

"Tis well, for I think I know who you are. You are Faye, sister of Sir Florian, daughter of Lord Westland."

"My father is dead, and if not yet, my brother soon will be," the girl whispered, her head still tucked down into her arms.

"I spoke with your brother only yesterday. At least I think it was yesterday. But . . . he is well and desperate to find you, commissioning my help in the effort."

"If you are supposed to help, how is it you are also captured?"

Idra couldn't resist a quiet laugh. "You are as quick-witted as your brother says. Let's consider this part of the plan, shall we?"

The girl's head raised another inch, and Idra continued to find her reluctant curiosity humorous.

"You didn't mean to be taken, did you?"

"No, I did not," Idra said, "but I've heard it said, Almighty works everything out, even the difficult and terrible moments, according to his purposes and for the good of those who love him, though in the midst we might not always understand it. And I, for one, trust him at his word. The question becomes, do you think you might be able to trust me, Faye?"

"How do I know you aren't brought here by them," she motioned with her head toward the fire, "and are a trick to amuse and give them reason to hurt me?"

"I wish I could reassure you, but I have nothing to give you except my word. I am lady-in-waiting to Princess Caityn, and if I do not return there will be a manhunt for me."

Her mind wandered back to Ahmad, locked away and unable to come for her. She wanted to add, "Not to mention a certain guardsman who will not rest until he has found me. This I know with all my heart, because he chased me across the Opal Sea and kissed me with a passion I shall not soon forget," but unless he'd been set free, he could not do what she knew he would.

Thinking of Ahmad and how much she felt sure he loved her bolstered her own waning confidence. She had no idea how they'd escape and wished Caityn were there to come up with some plan like she had done for them when Idra took a dive into the Bear River. Without thought, she let the dream-like hope tucked away inside flutter on a whispered breath from her mouth. "He'll come for me . . .."

"What?" Faye asked, lifting her head and tilting it. The look on her young, beautiful face held a mixture of hope and confusion. Her wild, unkempt hair drifted about her cheekbones and ended abruptly an inch above her shoulders.

"I said we will get out of here. Just you wait and see."

CHAPTER TWENTY-THREE
WHERE THERE'S A WILL IT CAN BE SQUASHED

AHMAD WOKE FROM HIS RESTLESS sleep with a crick in his neck and a headache to rival any. He rolled to the side, sat up on the cot, and rubbed his neck with one hand, his eyes with the other. A soft moan passed his lips as he worked out the tightness.

As much as he wanted this plan to work, he felt helpless sitting in this tiny cell of a chamber if Nox roamed about alive and free. He should be aiding in the search. He should be confronting Havrik about Nox and the knife that sliced Xavier. And what of Xavier? Would they ever be wake him from whatever spell he rested under?

Ahmad stretched his arms high overhead, then retrieved his clothing, pulling it on. He had a table and chair along with candles to light the room, but the sparsity brought with it far too much quiet to contemplate the magnitude of circumstances he'd encountered since returning from the north.

Though danger lurked, he allowed the image of Idra after he'd kissed her in the tent to linger strongest in his mind's eye. He wondered if she'd heard about what happened and if she'd try to visit him here in the tower. Part of him wished she would; the other begged her to stay far away and be safe.

Ahmad sat, stretched out his long legs, and rolled the unlit candle back and forth on the rough surface of the tabletop. It took all his self-restraint to keep from getting up and walking out of that room—to hell with Florian's mysterious plan. His inner battle was put to rest by a knock at the door. It opened to reveal Raz carrying a tray of food. He arranged it on the table in front of Ahmad then took a seat on the bed.

"Good morning, my friend. I hope you slept."

"I thought you'd add 'well' to that statement," Ahmad said with a crooked smile.

"I know better." Prince Theiandar leaned back against the wall, his hands laced behind his head. "I'd be surprised if you slept at all, knowing you."

"I slept some. Thank you for bringing me a meal." He took a bite of a sausage and savored the spiced, salty flavor. "My stomach began to protest its lack of food since the midday meal yesterday a half hour ago."

"I came to bring you food, but I also came to tell you we've already begun a search of the castle for any sign of Nox. I've enlisted the help of Saar's unit as well. This feels egregious, keeping you locked up in here. I realize too late that Florian chose the wrong path for the right reasons; there had to have been a better way than this."

"What's done is done, Raz. All we can do is move forward and stop Nox before he can do any more damage." Ahmad ate more and contemplated Florian's actions over the past week. Something didn't quite add up, but he couldn't figure out why. "Raz?"

"Yes?"

"I hesitate to ask, but could you tell me how Lady Idra is taking this? Florian mentioned Sabine told her about the blade."

"I don't know. I've not seen her since yesterday." Prince Theiandar stood and placed a hand on Ahmad's shoulder. "I'll speak with Caityn and find out for you."

"Thank you. If possible, pass on a message for me?"

"Of course. Anything."

"Tell her . . . tell her it is her unwavering strength of will and honor that guides me."

Raz looked confused for a second but nodded. "I'll pass it along. I'm not sure what excuse to give about your absence at the tourney, but at least you were not scheduled to joust today. I'm sure there are stories circulating as we speak, and I don't feel right about any of this. In fact, I'm going to make different arrangements. Just give me today and I'll have you out of here. I cannot have your name whispered about falsely, Ahmad, and not just because you are my guardsman."

Ahmad stood and took Raz's outstretched arm. "You are a good man and a worthy prince."

"I'll return as soon as I can."

His mouth broke into a relieved smile. "I'll be here."

* * *

Florian gritted his teeth with such force a headache pounded to the beat of the imaginary battle drums within his skull. The morning jousts were over, and a short midday break came before the single combat would begin. He stood in his uncle's chambers, once again staring down the betrayer and the treacherous King Orn.

"Find someone else to do your dirty work. I will not retrieve the blade. Haven't I already done enough?"

"Florian," the king said in a condescending tone. "You, dear boy, will do exactly as you are told. Do you think we do not know what you've already done, to whom you've spoken out of turn?"

Florian tensed. He suddenly pictured his conversation with Lady Idra and the things he'd told Raz and the others of his unit the evening before; he'd done something he would regret.

"Lady Idra is a beauty in the classic sense, but her heart . . . that is what most inspires life. Nox and I have made a deal, son."

"Don't you dare call me that!" Florian said, spittle flying from his lips in the heat of his burgeoning anger and frustration.

"Tut, tut. No need to lose your temper. You . . . are not worthy to be a knight, and your scheming against me has caused not only the sad state of that young guardsman, but it has also brought about Lady Idra's current, shall we say, predicament."

"What do you mean?"

"Did you not notice her absence from the jousts this morning?"

"What of it?" he asked, but the sinking sensation in his gut told him all he needed to know.

"The lady finds herself rather indisposed at this time, rather far from home, in fact."

"What have you done?" Florian said, taking a threatening step toward Orn.

The king raised a commanding hand to keep his knights from taking hold of Florian. "It's not what I've done, but what you've done. You are to blame. You were warned, and here, by taking custody of Lady Idra, I have spared your sister yet again. The lady has meddled too much in our business, but you inviting her to locate your sister sealed her fate. Her beauty," Orn paused and admired the gaudy rings on his fingers, "will not be wasted, I assure you."

Florian listened with agonized restraint. He wished to melt into the floor, to be buried deep within the rock below the castle, and never see the light of day again. If he could die at that moment and know it would save Faye and Lady Idra, the high king and his family, Ahmad and Xavier, he would do it. Everything he'd done up to this point only made it worse. He couldn't be responsible for them all, but if not him then who? Did he really have to choose between protecting innocent women and the sanctity of the crown and realms?

"I see you are deep in contemplation, sir. You will not go against me again."

Florian glared at Orn with an endless supply of hatred and watched the grinning king massage the jade-colored stone on the necklace he always wore. His thumb rubbed over it, up and down, down and up, over and over again.

"I cannot do it," Florian said through gritted teeth, angry fear seething just below the surface. He found it easier to lie to Orn than anyone. "I will not retrieve the knife, and without it there is no guarantee the high king will die." Florian couldn't understand why he even shared in this conversation.

"You will obey, Sir Florian. You will gain the blade, and you will kill the high king. I will not be gainsaid, and you will speak to no one else."

Florian stared at the king's finger on the stone and swore he saw something move within. A dull ache worked its way up his back, and he lost the will to fight. Faye's safety consumed him. His anger had faded into despondence, but some fight persisted in him. He used his last bit of will to glare at the king and his uncle before leaving their presence.

* * *

Orn turned on Jeron and whipped the point of his knife up against the soft spot beneath his chin. "You swore he would do as required. What say you, old man?"

Jeron's eyes flashed and he grabbed Orn's wrist, forcing it down with more strength than his round, aging body belied. "And you said you could control him."

Orn growled and stood to his full six-foot height. "He resists at every turn. Nox assured me the stone would work, that I had power to persuade anyone with a weak will to my bidding. But your nephew continues to fight against it. I thought I saw a weakening in him, but unless his will is broken, I cannot be sure of his puppetture." He swung around to face Jeron again and glared. "The boy is not what you think he is. I suggest you find a different way to ensure Dante falls or take care of it yourself."

Jeron jumped to his feet, almost tipping over with the force of his movement. "Sire! I would die if I did such a thing."

"So be it," Orn said and stormed from the room in much the same way Florian had minutes before.

* * *

Orn grimaced at the blood throbbing through his temples. The rush of it pounded against his brain, and the hard press of his hands to his scalp did not lessen the dreadful ache. Princess Caityn had come near to ruining the whole conspiracy with the note she dispatched to Hamlin House the previous night, inquiring after Lady Idra's whereabouts, and if not for quick thinking on his part, she would have succeeded.

"You're certain?" he asked through the fog in his brain.

"Yes, Highness. One of Queen Moira's men intercepted the messenger, paid him a hefty sum to leave the Realms, and made sure the fellow went on his merry way. Hamlin will never receive the note."

"And what of tomorrow, Havrik? Hmm? What about when the princess doesn't hear back? What then?" Orn collapsed into a chair at the table in his chamber and laid his head back, the heels of his hands pressing into his eyes, attempting without success to ease the splitting pain of his skull.

"I'm sorry, Sire, but I don't know what to make of tomorrow."

Orn stood up in a flash. "If I was not fond of you, you'd be dead right now. We know from our spies that Lady Idra planned to travel to Hamlin House to stay for a few days, hence we must use this to our advantage. You must have a note forged and sent to the princess indicating that Lady Idra is well and staying at Hamlin. Then you must also forge one to Lady Hilde at Hamlin saying Idra changed her mind, is under the weather, and to forgive her absence."

"Fine plan, my lord. I'll take care of it." Havrik bowed, pulled his hood over his head, and hurried from the room.

Orn thought he'd overreacted, but his head hurt too much to care. The headaches were getting worse, and he had no idea why. He moved to the nightstand and searched through the assorted items stowed there until he found the miniature vial of gray powder and dumped half the contents of it into a glass of water. He swirled it around then tipped it back, draining it to the last drop.

* * *

"Florian," Ahmad said when his supposed friend showed up at his cell. He repressed the lingering anger toward the other guardsman. "Did you happen to see Lady Idra in the box? I've not heard anything of her since yesterday."

"Lady Idra?" Florian asked, his tone unusually high pitched.

"Yes." Ahmad looked sideways at Florian, concern refreshed in his consciousness.

"N-no. Not since yesterday."

"I know she is going to Hamlin House this evening, but I assumed you'd see her at the jousts this morning."

"I couldn't say."

"What *could* you say?" Ahmad asked, his frustration with Florian winning out over patience. Florian wouldn't miss his underlying intent, surely.

Florian's face grew red. "There's much I could say, but will refrain."

"You are walking a dangerous road here, my friend," Ahmad said, not bothering to mask his threatening tone.

Florian looked away and mumbled, "You have no clue."

"Just tell me. Was Lady Idra there? Did she look well?"

"I . . . she . . . I didn't see her there, Ahmad," Florian said as though the words were trapped in his throat.

"That can't be right."

"'Tis true. Mayhap she was ill."

Ahmad's brow furrowed as he thought on that possibility. "Mayhap."

"Listen, I-I only came to say one thing. I need you to know there is more to what is happening than I spoke of last night, things I want to tell you, but . . . and there is a great deal I cannot tell you without risking more lives. I need to tell you I'm sorry for this, but I cannot say anything else. Please believe me when I say I am doing all I can think to make it right."

"I don't understand why you continue to be cryptic about whatever is happening. I only know you are adding further danger with your secrecy. You must trust someone. Why not me? Why not Raz and the rest of Delphor?"

Ahmad expected Florian would reconsider and relate the sordid details of his machinations; the contorted mixture of pain and hope on his face seemed to imply it. Ahmad's urgency drove him to extremes, but he held off on shaking the truth out of Florian in hopes of answers being forthcoming. He had to push away a sense of betrayal when the other man shook his head.

"I'm sorry, Ahmad. Truly. This is not over, but when it is you will hear all. I swear."

Florian's desperation and resolve were written on his face, plain as day, but the firm nod he made before exiting the room sent Ahmad over the edge of frustration; he slammed his fist onto the table with a loud crash and hefty rattling of wobbly wooden legs.

* * *

Florian's chest tightened and he couldn't breathe. Sir Ahmad would get himself killed if he continued to pursue Lady Idra's whereabouts or the need to unearth the sordid deeds to which Florian found himself a party. He desperately needed help and to tell the high prince and his family the truth of the events right under their noses, but his sister's and now Lady Idra's safety had to come first.

His uncle told him about the story they'd concocted for Lady Idra's absence based on reports from Orn's spying henchmen, but it would only work for so long before the flimsy excuse would crumble under further scrutiny. Even Florian saw that, and because of his desperation to preserve the trust of his friend, he'd run off to Ahmad's cell in the tower. Now he regretted it. He couldn't believe all was lost.

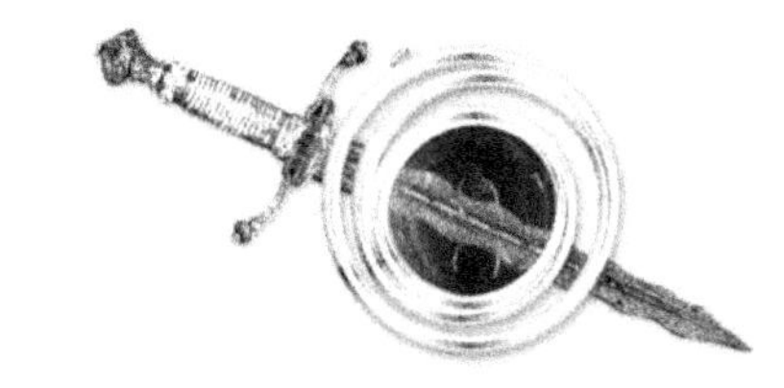

CHAPTER TWENTY-FOUR
FREEDOM WILL BE HAD
BUT AT WHAT COST?

IDRA COUGHED AND ROLLED OVER on the thin bedding provided for her. She'd just finally lain down as exhaustion overwhelmed her. Sleeping draughts were not conducive to actual rest, and the day had proved much more stressful than she let on. She had no knowledge of where they were except by the river Solfen. At least she hoped it was Solfen.

There would be something ironic and appropriate about Nox's henchmen secluding them near the river named for the ancient villain's sister. Instead of making her more afraid, it gave her a sense of strength, a reminder from the tales of old . . . of how a mere woman overcame her brother's hatred, found the love of a good man, and built a nation. These were reasons for hope, not for despair.

"Are you well, my lady?" the young girl asked.

Idra rolled to face Faye's shadowed form, the only light from the flickering of the fire near where the soldier's reclined.

"I'm well enough, Faye. But please call me Idra. Circumstances being what they are, I consider we are already friends," she said with a reassuring smile, even while knowing Faye probably couldn't see it.

"I've been here . . . I do not know how long. Can you tell me what day it is?"

"It is almost three days to the naming ceremony, if I am correct. The fifty-second day of autumn."

"Oh my."

"What is it?" Idra asked, concern for Faye's state of mind and health causing her to use great caution in her questioning.

"Tis nothing. I . . . I've been here for almost two weeks in this dark hole. I can barely imagine the world outside these damp walls."

The import of Faye's words wrenched Idra's heart. Nearly two weeks as a prisoner within this place would drive most mad, but Faye only displayed melancholy and calm. Her quiet voice reminded Idra of herself in a way, which gave her hope that, like Idra, Faye would also rise above and find her strength.

"I'm sorry, Faye. As soon as your brother found out about your predicament he vowed to find you. I am sure he is, even now, desperately searching."

"But he mustn't, Lady Idra," Faye said with surprising vehemence. "He must not do the things they are demanding. I heard their awful plan, and I cannot allow my life to be exchanged for those of the high royal family."

Idra sat up with a start. "What?"

Faye moved to a sitting position as well and wore a surprised look, illuminated now by eerie flickers of light from the waver of distant flame. "You didn't know?"

"Know what?"

"They want my brother to kill High King Dante and frame his son in exchange for my life."

Idra's mouth dropped open, but on a gasp, she choked on stale air. Insanity. Treason. Would Florian do such thing?

"This cannot be."

"Tis true, my lady. I have already cried all the tears I can. I have begged the Almighty to stop Florian, to keep him from doing the undoable. I've tried to escape to no avail, and I've given up hope. They always watch me." She glowered at their captors with an expression near hatred.

"You believe Florian would do this?"

Faye's grim countenance told Idra all she needed.

"He would do whatever it took to protect me. After the way our parents died . . . before his very eyes . . . I'm sure he will do what he thinks he must to ensure my safety. I'm afraid that if he cannot find me he might do it, but I can hope that his head will overrule his heart, or that his heart can withstand the blow. I would rather die than see him fulfill their demands. Surely he must recognize this about me. I could never forgive myself if my life took precedence."

"You and I are getting out of here in order that he will not face this alone," Idra said, the thought formulating in her mind, solidifying into a truth she would cling to until her dying breath. "Rest now, for soon you will need all the strength you can muster."

She lay back upon the thin pallet and stared at the two men by the fire. One slept; one kept vigil. The pieces were sliding together in her mind. Nox had been lost in Wyeth; Florian, his uncle, and Faye were from Wyeth. Jeron's connection to King Orn made Idra almost certain that the king to which the man in black had referred must be Orn. There had to be a way out of this mess. Idra felt to the core of her that Almighty had brought her here for some purpose. Rescuing Faye seemed the best reason and the one she would cling to for sanity's sake . . . and because hope had become her way, her strength.

* * *

Raz had showed up at Ahmad's cell later that afternoon and escorted him from the tower. It had been decided that not enough evidence was garnered, and Florian's statement wasn't sufficient to hold Ahmad, especially in light of the fact that the high king decided not to release information about Xavier being under some kind of curse. The physician and the royal family were the only ones allowed to visit Xavier, and when asked if the rumors about his injury were true, people were told that he would recover; his injury healed even though he continued to sleep.

High King Dante's displeasure about the situation had been made abundantly clear, but he recognized Sir Ahmad's presence, his public visibility, played an essential role to maintaining order and peace. He would not risk disunity over Xavier's life, though he expressed sorrow for the young knight's current state. Dante's only demand on his son came as a requirement that once the ceremony concluded, Prince Theiandar would hold a private hearing regarding the incident and officially clear his guardsman's name of wrongdoing.

After seeing the high king, Ahmad had gone back to the inner tower to speak with Sabine, but she'd been unwilling to tell him more about her conversation with Idra. Now Ahmad sat in the great hall awaiting the prince and princess at supper, thoughts of Idra filling his head, mingling with his steady concern over Xavier. He'd come early expecting to see Idra, but she wasn't there. He had thought she'd been planning to go to Hamlin House to stay just as he and Lady Hilde had planned, but he didn't think she'd have left under the current circumstances.

He saw the prince and princess enter together, the nursemaid carrying the baby prince just behind them. They picked at their meals, both looking preoccupied until Ahmad caught Princess Caityn's eye. He made a gesture to meet and watched the princess pull Raz from the table. They met him by the wall.

"Highnesses," Ahmad said with a bow. "I'm sorry to bother you after such a trying day, but I haven't seen Lady Idra. Is she well?"

"You were unaware?" Princess Caityn asked.

Ahmad stared in confusion.

"I understand your concern, sir. After a bit of a fright on my part, I learned she went to Hamlin House early. I hadn't seen her since yesterday eve—after what happened to you—and every wild, terrible thought imaginable entered my head. I didn't want to start any more hysterics about the castle, so I sent a note to Hamlin's inquiring as to whether she went there when I did not find her in her chamber. Her lady's maid said she'd not seen her but that several gowns and other items had been taken from the room. I finally received a note back this afternoon. She was distraught and decided to go to Lady Hilde's early and will not be returning until the end of the tourney."

"But that's three days when all is told."

"Hmmm. Yes. between you and me, just before I received the note, I was ready to send out a search party. She's not been gone a day since Bastien's birth without seeing him. I thought of no reason except the possibility that what happened, paired with the news of Nox, caused her such anxiety she felt the need to escape. The Hamlins have already come to stay at the castle, all except Lady Hilde, so they didn't know anything was amiss. I hope Idra is well. If I were able leave the celebration myself to check on her, I would."

Princess Caityn sounded unsettled about the whole thing, but it seemed plausible. There was no indication that either of them should feel unnerved, but Ahmad certainly was. Still, Princess Caityn knew Idra better than anyone. Who was he to question?

"If she is well enough, I must leave well enough alone."

"I expect her back for the last day of the tourney. To be honest, with the news that the young woman Sabine brought to us, I'm wishing she'd stayed at the castle, but Hamlin assured me he left a contingent of knights at his home. And surely she won't miss your final joust." She looked at her husband. "He will joust, will he not, my love?" she asked Prince Theiandar.

"Of course, Cait. Father was displeased by the idea, but he also saw no way around keeping things quiet and as normal as possible. I'm only sorry that this has put you in a poor light in my father's eyes, Ahmad," Raz said, his apology sincere.

Ahmad wanted to sigh, to shake his fists at the sky, but nothing within his ability would help aside from praying that all would turn out, that Florian's secrets would come to light, and that everyone would be safe. "Tis well, Highness. To everything there is a purpose."

Hard as it was to admit, and strange as the circumstances, having Idra at Hamlin House was actually a good thing. He'd have to let go of the uneasy feeling. There, she would be distanced from whatever evils were lurking within the city. It also meant he could move forward with the plan he and Lady Hilde had made days before. If events went according to plan, he'd be proposing to a certain elusive lady-in-waiting in the lush gardens of Hamlin House at this exact time on the next day.

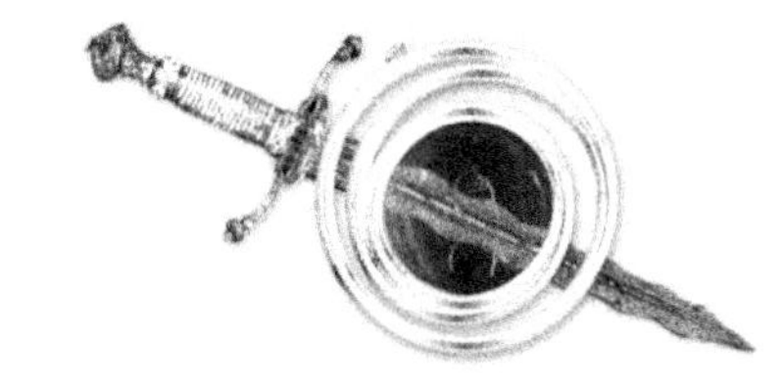

CHAPTER TWENTY-FIVE
BATTLING DEMONS

THE MAN WHO'D BROUGHT IDRA here had left almost immediately upon securing her. One guard sat in wakeful duty while the other slept, his loud snores competing against the crackle of the dancing fire. Idra analyzed the drowsiness of the one as his head drooped and he shook it. Soon he would rouse his friend so that he could take a turn at slumber, and they'd have a rested man interrupting the insane plan she'd concocted. If they were to escape, she would have to act soon. She rolled away, reluctant to turn her back on the men at the fire, but with little choice if her shackle-mate was to help her.

"Psst. Faye," she whispered as she gave the girl a teensy nudge.

It didn't take any more than that to wake her, as she seemed to sleep on pins and needles and jumped at the slight touch.

"Be still, child. We don't want to gain their attention just yet."

Faye took a shuddering breath and nodded, obviously doing her best to calm down.

"What's going on?"

"We're going to get the one guard who is awake out of the way as quietly as possible. Then you're going to pick up that ball at your ankle and carry it over to the wall where I can get one of those swords. Do you understand?"

"I-I think I do, but do you know what you're doing?"

She wanted to say no right then and give up, but Idra couldn't allow herself to think that way. "I've had a little training. Don't worry, Faye, I'm better with a sword than with the bow and arrow. You're in good hands," she answered with a rueful smile, relieved to be thinking about her training with Gavin.

"As you say, my lady. What would you have me do first?"

"Very good. And please call me Idra. Remember? But what we must do first you will not want to do, and I'm sorry for it, but we've little choice if we're to escape, find your brother, and save the king."

"You make it sound like an afternoon picnic."

Idra stifled a laugh, the nerves and adrenaline already building in her system causing the slightest joke to seem ten times more amusing than in actuality. "Yes, an afternoon picnic, Faye. Keep that in your mind." Faye nodded and Idra continued. "We must wrap this chain between us around the man's neck and squeeze."

Now that she'd said the words, her stomach roiled and bile rose to burn her throat. Images of men screaming and blood oozing from around a jagged sword filled her mind, but she pushed them away. The opportunity to be squeamish had passed; now she needed to act decisively, to be the brave girl everyone needed her to be. For her sake, for Faye's sake, for the sake of the ones she loved the most in the world.

"All I need you to do is pretend to be ill, and I'll do the rest while he's distracted. Can you do it?"

"I think so." Faye's accompanying nod trembled. "Yes. Yes, I can."

"Good girl." Idra nodded back and sat up on her pallet. She whispered to the guard, hoping not to wake the other just yet. He didn't even flinch, so she raised her voice the slightest notch. "Soldier."

He looked over at her then, his posture slightly more alert but still relaxed enough to make Idra assume he didn't suspect anything untoward. She gestured for him to come closer, and without a second thought the man came. His only hesitation arose when passing his sleeping mate who he did not bother to wake.

He towered over them, but even in the darkness enough firelight reflected off the wall that Idra saw the sinister manifestation upon his ugly mug, the expanse of his wide grin dark from broken and missing teeth. "In need of a midnight kiss, my lady?"

"Uh, no, soldier," she whispered, her eyes darting to the other man who continued on in blissful slumber. "This girl is ill, sir. Please look for yourself. She's burning up."

Faye moaned on cue and gripped her belly with her free hand. Her other laid out toward Idra to give the chain plenty of length.

This happened as surely as Idra breathed, but it didn't feel real. It couldn't be real. She'd never thought through a plan to hurt anyone in her life. The other times it had been spur-of-the-moment, heat-of-battle, gut reactions. Never this. Never the willful desire to injure, maim, or kill a living soul. All the sudden, she doubted her ability to follow through on the plan, but things were already set in motion, and Faye needed her to be strong. *Please be strong*, she begged herself.

The guard kneeled down. He landed on one knee and bent toward Faye, his hand outstretched.

Idra's breath caught on the lump in her throat, but it was now or never. She moved like a flash of lightning, even faster than she imagined possible, and stood at the same moment she whipped the chain up around his neck, using her full weight to pull against it. Until then, the only sound was the *clank* of the chain's links against each other.

Their captor gasped, releasing what air he might have had. He grabbed for the chain and simultaneously clawed at Idra's arms. Faye did her best to pull the chain from her side, too, and the man showed signs of flagging in a matter of seconds. They'd completely cut off his air supply, and within less than a minute he stopped struggling, went limp as a wet rag, and slipped to the floor.

Overall, Idra thought they'd been quiet, but the next thing she knew, the other soldier angled at her from behind. He made little sound, but Faye saw him coming and screamed. That gave enough warning for Idra to lean out of the path of his mace, which, had it made contact with her head, would surely have been a fatal blow.

He stumbled with the near miss and lost his footing.

"Quick, Faye! Get the chain off from around his neck. Hurry!" Idra cried, struggling to reach the dagger she saw protruding from the strangled man's boot. Her fingers were almost too far from it, but her urgent grasping was rewarded as she latched on and yanked it free.

In the time it took her to do that, the other man regained his feet and came at her again, but this time she was ready.

Idra leaned back and used her legs to land a hard blow to his stomach. He stumbled but in the next second he jumped toward her, and on instinct she went for his closest leg, striking his thigh with all her might while his mace slammed into hers in the same second.

A cry ripped from her parted lips, but pain from the blow delayed by mere seconds until the agonizing sensations from her nerves traveled to her brain. Miraculously, she still held the knight, but dropped it and grabbed her leg, her other arm's movement arrested as it stretched over her head where Faye struggled to remove the chain from around the man's throat.

Tears brimmed in her eyes, and she could barely breathe due to the torturous blow to her leg. *Not broken*, she thought, but the sharp points of the mace had torn wide her skirt and ripped through her flesh. Her only consolation came knowing her blow to the man's knee must have caused some damage as well because he sprawled on the ground, grabbing at his leg too.

"I've got it!" Faye said as she freed the chain, and Idra felt the release of tension there.

She took a deep, ragged breath and suppressed her need to focus on the pain, instead forcing her will into survival. Idra rolled to her side and gasped.

She reached for the knife she'd dropped and fought back tears, but the soldier she'd just injured wouldn't leave well enough alone. Midway to her feet, she crumpled to the floor. Idra's chest throbbed with the need to cry as she attempted to balance on her good knee. Faye cried out again.

"M'lady!"

Idra twisted to her left, her right hand thrust in the direction she turned, and grazed the man's ribs as he stumbled by. He tripped over the chain and pulled Idra down on her stomach. She grunted and sobbed when her chest slammed into the hard rock floor.

Faye appeared at her side and reached out to grab her arm while she gritted her teeth and struggled upright.

"The ball," Idra said between gasps.

The traitor-soldier, now pressing an arm to his ribs, worked himself up the wall and pushed off, limping toward them, his pantleg dark with blood, his eyes a storm of rage.

Faye scrambled to pick up the ball, and then she and Idra limped toward the weapons store.

The man stalked after them slowly.

Idra glanced over her shoulder to make sure they traversed the cave in the right direction.

The whole time, the man hadn't said a single word. He carried a look of murder and nothing more. He wanted to kill them, and the pleasure of the idea reverberated from his dark soul.

"Don't do this," Idra found herself saying as they backed up and he pursued them like prey. "You don't need to do this."

His evil smile only widened, blood covering his teeth.

They were almost to the weapons, but Faye struggled under the weight of the ball; the distance might have been too much for one not used to lugging such things.

"Tis slipping!" she cried out, grasping at the round, black hulking weight attached by a chain to her ankle.

"We're almost there, Faye. Just hold on."

Urgency brought renewed strength for the last push to the weapons only six feet away. But the man persisted, not about to let them get there without a fight. He pulled himself to his full height, and after puffing out his chest with a loud breath of stagnant cave air, he ran-limped at them with a hobbled gait but with frightening speed.

Faye screamed, and the ball slipped from her fingers. She stepped away from her anchor, while Idra almost threw herself as far as the chain between their arms allowed.

But not toward Idra did the man race. He charged after Faye.

Something inside Idra snapped. She roared like a mother lion, and instead of grasping at the swords behind her, she took the knife in her hand and lobbed it at the soldier, his face a mask of malice and unadulterated malevolent pleasure.

She'd been practicing but had never been good at hitting the mark more than half the time. Without blinking this time, she watched the knife, and with the speed of a raging bull, she ran toward where she'd thrown it.

The knife hit his shoulder seconds before she did. She raced with a stumbling gait past Faye, and when Idra knocked the man to the ground, her arm flailed back as it reached the end of its tether to her fellow prisoner.

She cried out at the sensation of having the limb ripped from its socket but couldn't arrest her forward momentum. The man's mace clattered to the floor, and as tears streamed down her face and loud sobs rent the air, she reached for it, knocking his hand away. Idra had landed on top of him, and Faye scooted closer to give her shackled arm slack.

With her free arm, Idra raised the mace over his head and panted and worked to suppress her tears, but looking down at him, she saw his humanity. She hesitated. "Give me the key to these shackles, or I'll be forced to kill you," she said, losing the will to fight.

With his arms resting on the floor but raised above his head, he studied her with vengeful eyes, but she saw terrible pain etched upon his face also . . . pain that likely mirrored her own. He slid one arm down along the dirty floor.

"Easy," Idra commanded, her eyes darting to his shoulder where she'd hit him with the knife.

He moved with extreme caution and pulled the flap of his tunic aside to show her where the key rested against his breastbone. He grinned at her, more blood filling in around the cracks between his teeth.

"Faye," she said without taking her eyes off him or lowering her weapon, though her arm muscles burned with holding it aloft, "take the key."

Faye, crying, sidled up next to Idra and reached with a trembling hand. Her long slender fingers wrapped around the warm metal key and pulled it, breaking the chain fastening at the back of his neck. In the next second, he reached up to grab Faye, but she stumbled away, outside his grasp.

Idra hadn't missed the imperceptible look of intent upon his face just half a second before he did it, and at the same time he reached she lowered her arm, dropped the mace, and twisted the knife protruding from his shoulder further in. The force of it made his back arch as he cried out at the renewed assault.

Idra, with her useless arm dangling, did the only thing she could think of; she punched him over and over with her fist until Faye grabbed her shoulder and caused her to cry out too.

"My lady." Faye whimpered and Idra barely registered it. "You've done enough, my lady," she said around tiny sobs.

Idra, reeling and unsure what she'd just come through, stopped and stared down at the unconscious man. She swallowed hard and fought down her own need to cry, to roar, to hide from the horror of what had just happened.

After she had a second to calm herself and gain a sense of control, she looked to Faye, who fumbled with the key again, trying to work it into the lock on her wrist. Idra wanted to stand, but the excruciating pain in her leg caused her body to dissent when she tried to put weight on it.

"Give me the key, Faye," she said after taking another deep, shuddering breath.

The younger girl handed the key over and held out her wrist for Idra to unlock the restraints. Once accomplished, Faye did the same for Idra before they slapped the manacles and ball to the unconscious man.

"Help me up, Faye," Idra said, her tone weary but her words and use of the girl's name commanding her attention and meant to keep the overwhelming distress at bay.

Once Idra struggled to her feet and suppressed the need to cry more as the pain lanced up and down her leg and into her brain, she examined the place with her eyes, searching for something to wrap around her leg wound.

"Tis well, Faye. Rip my skirt hem for a bandage and then you can see the wound better," Idra said, watching as Faye did what she was told. The temporary bandage coiled tight around Idra's leg, but blood seeped through it as soon as it was applied.

Nothing else could be done there. They had to escape before any unknown legions of other traitors might appear.

"What about your arm, my lady?"

As long as she didn't move it, her shoulder and upper arm didn't hurt, but if she tapped it even a little, it sent awful, stabbing pain to her fingers, along her shoulder, and up into her skull. "I'm not sure what's wrong with it," she mumbled. "I think we should secure it for now. Find another piece of cloth or something."

Faye scampered about to do her bidding, and Idra stood in a haze of agony, waiting for the girl to find something, anything. If only there was a way to whisk away the pain. She watched Faye move hesitantly toward the bedding and then jump back.

"H-he just moved!"

"What?" Idra asked, incredulous and relishing the immense weight of relief flooding her soul. "Grab that rope and tie him up before he wakes."

Faye looked where Idra pointed near the pile of weapons and dashed over, grabbing the rope and running back. She rushed to tie knots in the rope around the man's hands and feet. It lacked mastery, but it looked as though the ties would hold, so Idra found Faye's work satisfactory. She experienced a sensation of hovering between consciousness and some lofty plane of existence but fought against the urge to escape reality.

Faye whimpered. "Please, Lady Idra, I can't do this by myself."

Idra nodded and fought off fresh tears. "Something to wrap my arm," she gasped when a surge of pain ripped through her shoulder.

Faye gasped too and ran to grab a thin blanket. She brought it to Idra, throwing it over her shoulder and tying it in such a way to secure Idra's arm to her side and stomach. At first, Idra wanted to weep from the searing torture of it. Faye hesitated, but Idra grabbed her arm. "No, you must do this," she said, her voice just above a whisper, every word labored.

Faye nodded and swiped at her tear-stained cheeks. Once she finished, Idra's arm didn't hurt as much, and she felt more able to move, but unbidden tears escaped and slid down her cheek. After catching her breath, Idra glanced around the dark cavern. She knew what needed to be done, but fear settled in, ready to arrest her ability to move forward.

"Faye, we must get out of here now. Take whatever food you can carry. I'll acquire weapons."

"Yes, my lady," Faye said in a trembling voice, and made her way toward the food stores.

Idra observed her for a second, then hobbled to the weapons where she procured three knives. She then reached for a sword but couldn't take any more with only one good arm. It would have to do.

Faye approached with a smart sling of her own holding the foodstuffs she'd taken, and then she ducked under Idra's good arm to help her get out of the cave. They worked their way toward the opening, but as night still ruled outside, they had to rely on the horses' soft whinnies to alert them as they neared the entrance.

Finally, Idra made out the mouth of the cave and quelled a fresh wave of anxiety to see the lightening of the sky as morning approached. They were running out of time, and she had no idea how far they truly were from High Castle. *South, as the river flows,* she thought.

Surely the cave was somewhere between High Castle to the south and the place they'd landed at Conleth coming west on the river two years ago. It had to be. She didn't remember there being terrain such as this anywhere near Glass Lake to the west of High Castle.

"Almighty, I pray I am right," she said out loud.

Faye certainly heard her but said nothing in response. The three horses still wore their saddles, and though the number confused Idra, she didn't want to think about it. She patted one mare's rump to send her on her way along the thin, winding path.

"We'll ride the other two. Come, Faye. Can you help me mount? I'm afraid I can't do it on my own."

"Yes, my lady," Faye said and ducked back under her arm to shuffle toward the other two horses.

Faye put her hands out like the man had done the day before, and Idra stepped into the stirrup she created between her clasped fingers. More pain sizzled along her arm, and her damaged leg burned as she threw it over the mount. This time, Idra couldn't stem the rush of tears.

Great sobs wracked her body and sent fresh stabs of torment through her injured shoulder. The torrent blinded her, and her existence became a dark blur—pain her only company.

Without her realizing it, they were moving forward. Faye led Idra's horse by the reins until they reached the narrow ledge of the cliff trail. Several minutes passed before Idra regained control of herself. She thought herself strong and capable now, after everything she'd been through before, but the throbbing and stinging and burning of her injuries overwhelmed her with uncertainty and the truth of her utter weakness.

The thought of making it back in time without being overtaken by the enemy, the fear of infection setting in, the self-doubt in the face of her misery, caused her no end of fright.

All she could do was pray. Pray. Pray . . ..

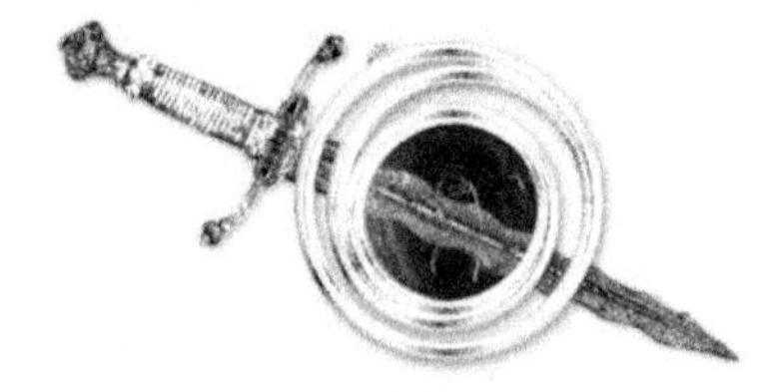

CHAPTER TWENTY-SIX
THE TRUTH HURTS. LIES KILL

TWO THINGS CONTINUED TO WEIGH heavy on Ahmad's mind. The first being Xavier. He had been nothing but unkind to the young guardsman since discovering he'd been chosen to replace Hanif. He hadn't even given him a chance, and yet Xavier had stepped out to protect him, risking his life for Ahmad even after practically being told he didn't belong and never would. Deep down, Ahmad knew he'd reacted the way he did to Xavier's presence out of guilt and fear; he didn't want to be responsible for the safety and health of Hanif's little brother. It was an excuse, to be sure, and he wished with a heavy heart for the chance to take back all he'd said and how he'd treated Xavier.

The other weighty distraction to his mind was Idra. Her note had said she went to stay at Hamlin House for the duration of the tourney, but he couldn't quite accept it. Something about the way she'd just up and left, telling no one, still festered at the back of his mind. He wanted to check on her and speak with her about how he regretted his treatment of Xavier. He wanted her forgiveness, since he'd been a fool in that regard as well.

He'd come to the archery contests but did not participate for two reasons—the first reason was he hunted for any sign of Nox, and the second, that he needed to keep a low profile during the tourney while still making his presence known for morale's sake. He walked around the grounds, searching the faces of those watching, looking for any sign of Nox amongst the crowd. He'd come up empty, and his mind continually wandered back to Idra.

The people vacated the arena and moved toward the city exits to where the pertento objex course of obstacles had been erected. There, the young squires trying for knighthood would run the course. His current state of affairs perplexed him. Did he stay, watch the young men compete, and continue to spy for the Beauty Thief along with the others who searched in secret, or did he leave early for Hamlin House, where he hoped to finally have a private moment with Lady Idra?

There was no question about which option appealed to him the most. Seeing Idra and ensuring himself of her welfare were the things that filled his every waking thought. With his mind made up, Ahmad followed the crowds to seek Raz, his mind focused on Idra to the point he temporarily forgot about the nagging mysteries of Xavier, Havrik, Sabine, and Florian. If Idra would only say yes, the rest would fall into place.

He wanted to change his clothing, but first he'd make his request to Prince Theiandar. Ahmad kept his pace in check as he jogged toward the gates of High Castle and out to the open field where the pertento objex had been built.

* * *

Florian stood behind the seats of High King Dante and his wife, Queen Zoe. They sat upon the royal platform shaded by a canopy. He watched Ahmad step up onto the raised structure and bow to Prince Theiandar and Princess Caityn.

He wasn't exactly angry that Raz had released Ahmad from the tower, but he worried after his friend's safety wandering free and alone. Florian would not make any more false claims against Ahmad since the original idea of protecting him by implicating him had been a rash move, one that carried the risk of lasting consequences. He only wished Raz would assign two or three other guardsmen to protect Ahmad, but he did not know how to ask without drawing more unwanted attention.

"Highness," Ahmad said, "if 'tis acceptable I would like to leave for Hamlin House. I've seen nothing of the one for whom we search. I'm to dine with Lady Hilde and Lady Idra, who I'd like to check on . . ." he glanced at Caityn, "for you, Princess, that I may report back to you on her well-being."

The royal couple looked at each other, but Florian missed whatever passed between them, since he stood to the left and behind, but he heard the princess's response.

"It would please me greatly if you would do me the favor of checking on my cousin, Sir Ahmad. I've not been able to shake this uneasy feeling in her absence. Please tell her we hope she is well and having a restful visit with Lady Hilde."

Ahmad bowed again. "Thank you, Highness. I look forward to reporting back to you. Until then." He stepped back once before practically running off the platform and out of sight.

Florian's heart rate had sped up as he eavesdropped on their conversation. If Ahmad went to Hamlin House, he would soon discover the absence of Lady Idra. If that happened, there would be hell to pay. Lady Idra's life—and Faye's—would be forfeited if Ahmad were to shout foul play regarding her whereabouts. He had to do something before Ahmad blundered into trouble, but no excuse to leave came to mind. Florian's stomach lurched with anxiety. There had to be something.

"Prince Theiandar?" he heard himself asking. "Sire, you are well guarded here, as most of your men are not taking part.

May I beg off attending you at the pertento objex? I'll ask Sir Gavin to stand in my place."

Raz turned to regard Florian over his shoulder. "Are you unwell?"

"Um . . . my uncle has asked me to handle a business transaction with a local farmer near the village." The lie tripped off his tongue, but it was the best he could do. "I would be gone until the evening, if that is acceptable. I thought to wait, but I'd like to get it over with."

"You are free to go. Send Sir Gavin," Raz said without hesitating, then turned to his infant son wrapped in his wife's arms.

Florian watched him lean over and kiss little Prince Bastien's head. It was a relief that he'd not given the high prince further cause to be anxious.

Florian bowed and searched his memory for where to find Princess Caityn's cousin, Sir Gavin. He realized Gavin had participated in the archery contest and either now finished up with removing his gear or already arrived at the pertento objex. He stepped to the corner of the platform and searched the crowds, mainly within the nobility. If Gavin wasn't near the prince, he'd be with his family, who had come from Taisce to celebrate the birth of their cousin Caityn's baby.

He found Gavin with the other guardsmen near the platform. They and High King Dante's men were the only knights allowed to carry weapons during the remaining days of the tournament. Havrik's attack had at least given the high king enough reason to remove unknown weapons from the occasion. It also meant Florian garnered special treatment as one of the few men allowed to carry a sword and dagger, which kept him out of suspicion when near the high king. That worked in King Orn's favor, but only because he remained unaware Florian refused to fulfill the commanded treachery. At least he convinced himself he wouldn't when far from either king's presence.

He brought his scattered thoughts into submission and asked Gavin to take his place before running back through the gates of High Castle. He would make a mad dash toward Hamlin House in hopes of waylaying Ahmad before he discovered Lady Idra's absence from that place. The other guardsman wouldn't have left for a dinner invitation without having first changed his clothes, and this gave Florian a bit of an advantage.

He swung open the door of the stables and dashed for Ahmad's horse's stall. Empty. He slammed his palms down on the gate and ran to saddle his own horse, ignoring the stable boys who watched him with looks of curiosity and amusement. The time it took to saddle his mount took too long, but once finished, he swung onto his steed's back and trotted out of the stable.

The streets of High Castle were like a ghost village with most of the inhabitants and guests outside the walls watching the pertento objex. Florian feared Orn's reaction, but he'd spoken loud enough for his Uncle Jeron to hear him, which ensured he wouldn't be likely to protest the story in front of the high king. He had one chance to prevent Ahmad from breaking the whole thing wide open or risk him thwarting Florian's ability to save both his sister and Lady Idra.

He galloped down the blessedly unoccupied path toward Hamlin House as the sun beat down on his back.

"Faster!" he cried over the pounding of hooves, dust flying out behind them. The horse, seemingly in response to his shout, pushed harder, flying down the empty lane like a hawk diving after prey.

Within minutes, he thought he made out the form of someone else on the path before him, but the other rider cantered along and soon he overtook him, since he'd stopped by the way to let Florian pass. He recognized Ahmad but was too late to stop next to him. He'd worked his horse into such a frenzy that it took a moment to slow and calm the heated beast.

He pulled back on the reins and his mount stomped, dancing in place while Ahmad came to a halt nearby.

"Florian! Have you gone mad? Is there something the matter? Is the prince in danger?"

Florian shook his head, working to get his breathing under control. "No, they are well, but I must stop you. It's not them who are in harm's way. I need you to listen carefully to—"

He broke off when he realized they were out in the open and he'd been followed at every turn. It was becoming difficult to shake off the paranoia. Within the realm of possibility, there existed the chance that even now someone might overhear what he came close to saying.

"Florian, what is going on? I didn't believe Xavier when he expressed concern about you. Now he's beyond my help, and I cannot tell him I was wrong. Do you not see how your actions have led him to ruin? There is something wrong, and you must tell me now or I will be forced to go to Raz. The prince has no time for your foolishness."

"I understand," Florian said, unable to think of an appropriate, worthy response. Ahmad, Prince Theiandar, everyone deserved the truth, but too many lives were at stake. He didn't know where to start. His horse brayed and stomped, shaking his mane. Florian did his best to keep the animal calm, patting his neck and speaking in low tones.

"Please, Florian. You can trust me. Whatever is going on, I want to help you."

His imploring tone and the heartfelt concern written across Ahmad's face nearly broke Florian's will. The overwhelming sense that many precious lives were in his hands brought him near to tears as he shook his head.

"Not here," he said and drove away the sorrow with a shuddering breath.

Ahmad gave a clipped nod. Florian searched the distance for any sign of man or beast while he contemplated the best direction to head. The walls of Hamlin House would be safer than within High Castle where his uncle and King Orn seemed to have spies hidden in the woodwork. The two of them rode at a fast pace toward the manor.

Neither of them spoke, but Florian felt Ahmad's tension. He somehow needed to prepare the other man for the fact that Lady Idra would not be in attendance at the manor, but he needed to do it without causing a scene. He cleared his throat and peeked over at Ahmad, who kept looking his way with a wary eye.

"Ahmad, listen. I need you to keep calm."

"You make that difficult, Florian. Out with it."

"Remember. I warned you."

"Fine. Just speak."

He hesitated for a second more, but the chagrined look on Ahmad's face said he could strangle him.

"Lady Idra is not at Hamlin House."

Ahmad pulled up on his reins and Florian followed suit. The two of them stared at each other for a few seconds.

In a deadly calm voice, Ahmad asked, "Where is she?"

Florian swallowed hard, choking on the lump that had formed in his throat. "She . . . I don't know . . . exactly."

"A note arrived from Hamlin House that said she had come here. She is in attendance with Lady Hilde. Are you saying this is false?"

"Yes." Florian glanced around. "I'm afraid we'll be overheard. I cannot tell you more now, but I need your help and promise to tell you the whole."

"No." Ahmad dismounted and reached for Florian's reins. "You tell me everything. Now! I will not wait." His words ground out in a deep, guttural, suppressed rage. "You tell me Idra is not where she is supposed to be, that a false note has been given to the high princess, and that someone who shouldn't might overhear. I cannot give you any more time. Tell me now." He reached up with his free hand, yanking Florian from his horse. "Where is Lady Idra, and what is going on?"

Ahmad readjusted his hold on Florian, who stumbled about and was kept from falling in the dirt by Ahmad's grip on his clothing. They stood eye to eye, Ahmad's telling Florian he neared losing what little of his composure still lingered.

Hamlin House sat within sight. Florian glanced from Ahmad to its gates to the road behind and into the wooded area nearby. He sighed because he had no choice. He had to tell Ahmad now or risk losing more than he'd bargained for. He had no doubt the other man would help him, no matter what, even if Lady Idra weren't involved. But Florian suddenly realized that because of how deep he'd dug himself in this mess, he could easily lose something else he valued more than his own life: the trust and friendship of his fellow guardsmen.

Florian disengaged Ahmad's grip from his tunic and walked into the forest cover. Without looking, he knew Ahmad stayed right behind him, bringing both horses along. The air cooled under the canopy of trees, but Florian barely noticed the difference. He'd gone frigid inside. He felt lightheaded.

"Well?"

Florian turned to face the anxious, seething knight and nodded.

"King Orn and my uncle have taken Idra. She was getting too close . . . and they wanted to teach me a lesson, I think."

He watched the color drain from Ahmad's face.

"Taken? Taken where? What are you talking about?"

The veins on Ahmad's temple protruded from the skin there as he gritted his teeth together. Florian opened his mouth, closed it and shook his head. Where to begin?

"So help me, Florian. If you don't start talking, I'll beat the truth out of you."

"I'd deserve every bit, Ahmad. Every bit."

Ahmad's expression transformed from anger to concern as he stepped forward and laid a hand on Florian's upper arm. The reassuring gesture lathered on another thick layer of guilt.

"Florian. Tis obvious how difficult this is for you to articulate, but you are speaking of Lady Idra ... my Idra. Please, tell all. I cannot help you, or her, if I don't know what is happening. And if she is in danger, I will move the heavens to reach her."

Only three years separated the two of them, but Florian felt like a child under Ahmad's steady, imploring gaze.

He stepped back out of his reach. "You are right. I'm sorry, Ahmad. I never meant for her to be put in danger. I kept as much of this from her as possible, thinking it would protect her from . . .. But it did no good. Listen. You are aware that Nox is not dead." He waited for Ahmad to acknowledge this before moving forward. "Raz tasked King Orn and his men with searching the caves at Ophira's Peak for any sign of Nox. You'll remember they were tasked with breaking into the locked room."

Ahmad nodded.

"They found Nox alive, but King Orn kept it a secret. He's had Nox with him this entire time, supposedly locked away. But the two of them have been scheming, along with my uncle." That last bit had been difficult to swallow and burned in Florian's gut. "They've taken my sister, Ahmad. This is why I could not speak. Don't you see? My sister is at the mercy of Nox and his powers."

"Do you know this for certain?"

"My uncle has no reason to lie to me about it. He's never truly loved me or Faye. Somehow I feel it, a power I can scarcely fight against, telling me there is no doubt of the truth in it. And Orn showed me a braid of hair the same color as my own, the identical color of my sister's. Then there are the things your captive, Sabine, told Princess Caityn and your lady about Nox. And you saw what that knife blade did to Xavier."

"What? The knife? You mean King Orn and your uncle were behind that attack as well? That blade was meant for me, Florian," Ahmad said, stepping closer in a menacing way.

Florian stood his ground, accepting Ahmad's response, for in truth, it signified exactly what he deserved. "You're right. You were asking too many questions. Havrik had been spying on me. You got in the way. If Xavier hadn't stepped in when he did, it would be you lying in a sleep of death."

Ahmad grabbed the front of Florian's tunic and yanked him close, breathing heavily upon his face. "Xavier shouldn't be in such a place, either. And you vouched for that worm, Havrik. Maybe the dirt is where you should be."

"You're right, Ahmad, but if I die before doing what King Orn has ordered of me, Faye—and now Lady Idra—will suffer a fate worse than death at the hands of Nox. They warned that if I said anything to *anyone,* that is exactly what would happen. I tried to keep you out of it! I have tried to do this on my own."

Ahmad let go and shoved Florian, causing him to stumble a few steps before he caught himself. He watched Ahmad bend at the waist as he pressed his palms to his eyes, his fingers coiled in the dark hair tumbling over his forehead. Florian empathized with the turmoil he saw in his fellow guardsman, but he'd had more time to come to terms. He waited for Ahmad to right himself and mightily wished for the ability to take the suffering from his friend.

"Xavier saved your life, and I'm sorry he's been put under this enchantment, but that blade is meant for High King Dante. And what Orn wants me to do to him with it is far worse than an eternal sleep that might be broken. It would be death with no chance of saving."

"Florian, you're playing with people's lives!" Ahmad threw his hands up in the air, his frustration more than evident.

"I'm sorry for this, Ahmad. Truly." Florian's stomach felt as though it rose into his throat. "I'm trapped in a hell. I tried to protect my sister, and that's why I haven't said anything. I couldn't let her down again. I can't let her end up like my parents. But I need your help to find her and Lady Idra before the end of the tourney tomorrow. I've searched the city while everyone slept. I've scanned the crowds, I've followed Orn's men. I think she's close, but I can't find her. Tomorrow—that is when I have been ordered to kill High King Dante and frame Raz for it, in front of the entire assembly of countrymen."

Ahmad had turned his back to Florian during the midst of his explanation, but now he swung around. "You're telling me Orn plans to overthrow the high king and his son by double treachery?"

"Yes," Florian answered, relieved that he'd made some sense. He stepped closer to Ahmad. "If he can frame Raz for his father's death, the high prince will be convicted by the Duodenocourt and hanged, then drawn and quartered for treason. Orn plans to place himself on the high throne and claims to have the support of other kings and nobles in the realms. I don't know how much of that is true, but he's had help from someone."

"You should have told us sooner."

"I know." Of course he knew, but every word had felt like another curse upon his sister, betraying her trust and her life.

Ahmad blew an exasperated breath and punched Florian square in the jaw, his fist like a battering ram. Florian saw it coming, but it still sent him reeling. He deserved much more than that, so he took it with little more than a grunt. Ahmad shook out his fist and muttered under his breath, then took another deep breath.

They stared at each other for nearly half a minute before Ahmad finally spoke. "Do you have any intelligence of where they've taken Lady Idra or your sister?"

Florian shook his head. He'd been able to find nothing regarding the whereabouts of either of them. "I don't know what to do. I . . . I cannot do what they've ordered me to do, but I cannot risk letting them hurt my sister. Or now, Lady Idra. If I don't murder the king, they'll find another way, torture my sister before my eyes, and either kill or imprison me. My life has no worth to me if all I have loved and devoted myself to is ruined. I have no doubt Orn is capable of more than he has threatened. Until now, I did not think my uncle capable of such evil, but now I have no uncertainty."

It hurt in his chest to speak of such things, to recognize cowardice in the face of these men kept him silent. He couldn't admit to Ahmad that the thought of seriously doing what Orn had commanded had crossed his mind and doubted he'd ever be able to admit it to anyone. The thought made him sick, but an infinitesimal part of him—especially when in the presence of King Orn—seemed to want to follow through with it, to take the life of the high king and frame his commander and future high king. It made no sense, but with each new occasion he drew near to either king, Dante or Orn, the desire to fight against the very thought of treason lessened. But now, away from their presence, he hoped he would never do what Orn ordered.

Ahmad wore a look of agitated contemplation on his face while Florian waited for a response. A minute of silence passed. "I must see for myself that Lady Idra is not at Hamlin."

Florian nodded and went to mount his horse but stopped short when Ahmad said, "You will not go unpunished, Florian. I think you know this, but you should have gone straight to the high king and prince with this information, no matter the consequence. You have not only put the lives of Lady Idra, your sister, and the royals in grave danger, but you've placed the entirety of the Twelve Realms at great peril."

Florian acknowledged the truth of it and stepped toward Ahmad. "I accept my fate, but I will let nothing happen to anyone else if I can help it. The king and prince can protect themselves, but my sister and Lady Idra are at the mercy of killers and thieves. Please understand, I would do anything to protect them. I have come up short in every respect. And though I have not been able to locate them, there is one man, a knight from my uncle's household, who may be able to help us."

"You trust one of your uncle's knights?"

"Only the one. He was a friend to me and to my sister."

Ahmad nodded, but the angry, determined look had come back, replacing any remaining bits of concern outside that of rescuing the women and protecting the high king. Florian knew him well enough to believe Ahmad would go to great lengths to protect the ones he loved. At least they had that in common, and Florian hoped it might soften the other man's heart toward himself.

They mounted and together galloped on way to Hamlin House. Afternoon shifted toward evening and Florian bore the weight of the sands of time which stop for no man.

CHAPTER TWENTY-SEVEN
WHERE THERE'S A WAY

IDRA SHIVERED UNCONTROLLABLY ON THE back of her horse. She was weak. So weak. They'd escaped the cave, made it along the treacherous cliff path, and galloped through the wood until the horses slowed with fatigue. Idra wanted to stay near the river, but there they risked far too much danger if their captors used that path. As it happened, they'd journeyed farther north after leaving the Solfen's winding path to avoid danger.

Her fingers were numb from gripping the pommel of the saddle.

"My lady, we must stop."

"No, Faye." Breathlessness kept her words soft as she battled unconsciousness and pain. "We cannot stop. If I am wrong about the day, we might already be too late."

"And if we are, then we will have come near death for nothing."

Idra frowned, too tired to argue the point.

"Lady Idra, if we do not stop and let the horses rest, they will not make it, no matter how much you wish it. Please. You look near death, and there is a creek just over there. Please," she begged, her voice full of unshed tears.

Idra relented and nodded. Too weary to argue, she accepted the soundness of Faye's reasoning. They cantered toward the creek, down a short, gentle slope, and dismounted. Faye had to catch Idra as she slid off the horse. Faye more likely broke her fall. They both lay on the ground for a minute to catch their breath. Idra couldn't stand right away, so Faye brought her sips of water in the cupping of her hands.

After she'd had enough, they sat there while the horses drank from the stream. Faye pulled out the dried meat she'd grabbed from the cave and handed a piece to Idra, who accepted it and ate greedily. She'd not eaten for a day or more, but once she'd scarfed down three pieces of the tough jerky, her stomach protested. It took at least five minutes for her to convince her body not to reject what she'd eaten. At the same time, she looked around to gauge where they were and how far they might be from High Castle. The effort overtaxed her and brought fresh tears to the surface, but she refused them passage, blinking them back.

She hurt in ways she'd never experienced and couldn't think beyond the next minute, let alone to a time of seeing her home and the people she loved most in the world. Her only consolation came by thinking she'd surely been missing long enough that people were searching for her . . . that Ahmad searched.

"Come, Faye, we must go. Time is never with us. I feel I am always against it, an unseen foe who will not let me rest," she said with the threat of tears disrupting her voice. Melodramatic though it might have sounded, she felt it at the core; she seemed to constantly fight against the pull of time, and the invisible battle drained her.

****

Lady Hilde emerged from the entrance to the manor, pulling a shawl around her shoulders even though the autumn day warmed her skin. "Sirs Ahmad and Florian. To what do I owe the early pleasure of your company?"

Her parents were both staying at High Castle, and he'd expected that their twenty-two-year-old daughter would take on the responsibility of receiving guests. Ahmad dismounted, handed the reins of his horse to the stable boy, and strode toward the lady. He took her proffered hand and bowed over it.

"My lady, I must ask, is Lady Idra here?"

The look of confusion that passed over her face answered his question, but broke his heart. He had wanted to deny what Florian said. Her absence meant he'd let her down once again.

"I'm sorry, Lady Hilde, but we cannot stay."

Ahmad turned to go, but her question stopped him short of mounting.

"I received word that she changed her mind. If you are here looking for her, then that must mean something has happened. Where is Lady Idra, Sir Ahmad?"

He turned around and came near, speaking in hushed tones. "There is nothing to fret over. I haven't seen her and assumed she'd come, but I must speak with her. All is well, lady. Will you attend the Winner's Ball tomorrow eve?"

She frowned at him, but he couldn't drag Lady Hilde into this disaster, too. Ahmad hoped the lie-that-wasn't-a-lie would be enough to satisfy her and keep her safely out of the mess.

"Yes, I'll be at the ball. I'll be at the final joust as well. Will you be competing tomorrow, sir?"

"I will, unless circumstances dictate otherwise." He'd said it and knew it was a mistake, but he couldn't take it back.

"What circumstances? Sir Ahmad, I can read you like an open book. There is something you are not telling me, and if it has to do with Lady Idra, I charge you to speak true."

She used that commanding tone of voice she often wielded when she would brook no argument. She wouldn't let it rest, and he knew it. "Please gather a few of your father's household knights, Lady Hilde, and do not leave without an ample escort. Lady Idra has been abducted in connection to a plot against the high king. But I beg you to keep quiet or risk the lives of Lady Idra and any other maiden currently held hostage. Please, do this for me."

"But is there anything I can do?"

"That's all? No incredulous retort of disbelief? No demand for more information or . . . or anything?"

"Sir Ahmad, do you know me so little? If you say I should keep quiet, you have no reason to think I will do otherwise. I've told you, I will do anything I can to help you. Lady Idra is my friend, which is a trusted commodity, difficult to find in this place, and if she is in danger, then I must make myself useful. What can I do?"

"Nothing except stay safe, my lady," he replied, a little surprised by her no-nonsense statement of support. "I could never forgive myself if something also happened to you because I dragged you into the middle. I need your silence and for you to surround yourself with a shield of protection in the form of your father's knights. I know not who can be trusted within the city walls."

She looked ready to argue, but must have thought better of it. "If there is anything else I can do, you will not hesitate to call on me?"

"Thank you, Lady Hilde. You are a star in the night sky. If we need you, we will call for your assistance."

"That is all I can ask," she said and stepped back. "Go now and save my friend. I will pray for you."

He studied her determined face and shook his head. Hilde was too spirited for the people of High Castle. None of them grasped her true worth, and he regretted her loneliness, which he saw where no one else did. It lurked hidden in her eyes, deep and dark as the midnight sky.

"Be well and safe, my lady," he said and mounted his horse. "Come, Florian. I think there is a man at the castle with whom we must have a conversation."

They rode out the front gates of the manor and toward the city of High Castle. Ahmad soon forgot Lady Hilde's fortitude in the face of Idra's uncertain fate. Once again Idra had come in harm's way in the endeavor of helping someone else. The woman didn't seem to know how to stay out of trouble, and though he hadn't known her so well for long, he found her willingness to risk her life for others both appealing and aggravating. He just hoped she didn't use the meager training she'd gained with Gavin to actually attempt fighting anyone off. He did not foresee that turning out well. Wherever she dwelt in captivity, he determined to find her. By Almighty, he'd done it before and he'd do it again.

"Ahmad, why did you lie to her?"

"I didn't."

"But you were going to." Florian chided him with the reminder.

"What? And you haven't lied to us all? I tried to protect her from—"

"I did no different. He has my sister, Ahmad."

Florian looked self-righteously at him, obviously fighting the desire to defend his actions. But a hint of a sparkle in his eyes could be mistaken for restrained tears. Ahmad watched him shake off everything but humble entreaty and continue speaking his case.

"Orn is using her to get to me, and I broke down and told Lady Idra about her, but only that much of it—just about Faye—and now look what's happened. What can you expect from me but to protect the ones I care most about in the world? I didn't mean for Havrik to attack you or for Xavier to be sliced by that blasted blade. I didn't mean for Lady Idra to be taken. I wanted to prevent the possibility, and that's why I didn't speak. Can you understand what I have been up against? I cannot fathom the depths of betrayal running throughout the Twelve Realms."

"Stop," Ahmad ordered, though not unkindly. "I begin to understand, Florian. I'm sorry I was harsh with you, but Idra . . . I cannot think straight when it comes to her. I thought I'd lost her. I won't be able to live with myself after what we've been through if something were to happen to her now." His mind tumbled about with images of Idra covered in blood and dirt, shock and sorrow written in the smudged curves of her beautiful face.

"I'm sorry, Ahmad. I'll do everything I can to get her back. I promise."

Ahmad looked over at him and grimaced. "Don't make promises you are unsure you can keep."

"What's the point of promises unless you strive, full of determination, to keep them? A promise is my word, and I stand by it."

"I'll hold you to it, then."

They grew silent after that. Ahmad found himself deep in tormented thought, sifting through the conversations he'd had with Idra since returning from the north. Nothing stood out in his mind other than her strange obsession with helping Xavier discover what bothered Florian. Then he recalled her anger after being discovered learning to fight with Gavin. She'd said she never again wanted to feel helpless. *Almighty, Great One above.* He prayed she not be rendered so.

"You mentioned a knight from your uncle's household. How is it you think you can trust him?"

Florian's mouth twitched down further, but he said, "He brought me a letter from my sister. One she'd written several days before they departed the castle of Wyeth. Though I cannot be fully sure of his loyalties now, he and I were friends growing up. We were knighted at the same time, and though I have not been close with him for many years, I think he can be trusted. My sister trusted him enough to place a letter in his care."

Ahmad would have to take his word for it, but the explanation had been thin.

* * *

Florian and Ahmad arrived at High Castle, left their horses at the stables, and strode toward the keep. At the dinner hour, Florian thought Sir Dennan would be in the great hall with the other knights. He'd no idea how they'd get the man alone, but they needed to start somewhere.

"Sir Ahmad," Florian whispered as they ducked between buildings in an attempt to go untraced, "there's something else I didn't tell you."

"Out with it."

"Orn threatened to have King Dante killed another way if I do not fulfill whatever obligation he seems to think I have to him. I thought if I kept up the ruse, I would be able to buy the time necessary to save my sister and protect the king from any assassination attempts."

Ahmad looked like he wanted to reprimand Florian, but he took a deep breath in, flaring his nostrils in the process, and nodded. "It makes sense, though it is stupidity on your part. You should have trusted us with this. You could have come to me, Florian. We could have helped you."

"The risk felt too significant. I swear I've been followed and tracked ever since they dragged me into their treachery. To share risked putting Faye, and even my fellow guardsmen, in danger."

"But you would risk the woman I love?"

He cringed at the honesty of Ahmad's blunt question. "I wasn't thinking. She seemed to know more than I realized, and

I blurted out too much. Then it was too late. When I told her to leave the castle, to take Princess Caityn and the baby to keep them safe, she said it would never work and vowed to find Faye. I couldn't stop her."

"That sounds like the Idra I've come to know." Ahmad shook his head.

Florian couldn't tell if he was proud or upset.

"I'm truly sorry."

"I don't completely blame you. Lady Idra is her own woman, with a strong will hidden under a quiet exterior. Do not be fooled. She's made of diamonds, a gem of Taisce; she is strong. I cannot forget this, or I will die in my fear for her life. By the Great One, she is a fearless champion."

Florian watched Ahmad lose himself in his thoughts; they were probably more of Idra. The guardsmen of Delphor unit were well aware of Ahmad's love for the lady, and at this moment, Florian found himself with a deep respect for the other man's devotion. Instead of a desire to tease him, he wished to emulate him.

Ahmad was right. He should have gone to his fellow guardsmen right away. There had to have been a way to do it without Orn or his uncle finding out, but he'd been too much of a coward to attempt it. Now his friend suffered under the uncertain fate of his beloved, and that added another weight on Florian's shoulders.

But he could not dwell on his guilt. He had other problems to solve, one of which involved how to appease Orn in regard to the blade for the time being. He certainly didn't want to hand the accursed weapon back over to the devil himself.

"Sir Ahmad, you should know I have the dagger hidden in order to keep Orn from doing anything else drastic."

Ahmad stopped outside the door to the great hall, his glaring stare boring into Florian's eyes. "How can I trust the blade will not fall into the wrong hands?"

"There is a risk, to be certain, but if I cannot show proof that I control it, Orn will look for other ways to overthrow the high king, and Faye's life will be lost to the Beauty Thief."

"Florian, has it occurred to you it might be too late for your sister? That Nox will probably take her beauty, if he hasn't already, no matter what? I think we must halt this sneaking about and go straight to the high king and Raz."

Florian panicked and gripped Ahmad's arm. "No," he said in a gasp. "No, Ahmad. I have no proof of any of this. It is my word against a king of the realms who will also have the backing of my uncle if it comes down to it. I will be sentenced to a whipping and then the dungeon for accusing a king, and then I'll never be able to rescue my sister. Please tell me you won't do that—not unless it's our only choice."

Ahmad seemed to consider his words, and Florian held his breath while he agonized over the other man's response. Ahmad grasped Florian's hand where it rested on his arm, but instead of ripping it off, he gave it a firm squeeze.

"I give you my word. I will not speak of this to the high king unless the sum of possibilities has been exhausted. I will leave you to find this knight. And, Florian?" He paused, obviously wanting to make sure Florian didn't miss his next, stern words. "When it comes to that knife you possess, you must not turn it over to Orn or any of his men. I realize you must prove to them you have it, but keep it safe or I will kill you myself. Understood?"

Florian nodded. Ahmad certainly meant his unmistakable, serious threat, and Florian didn't blame him for it. He thought he himself cared just as much for his sister and Lady Idra's safety. Florian would die for them if it meant they'd be safe, but maybe Ahmad's devotion ran deeper still.

"I need to search Idra's room for any clues. Meet me on the south wall after dark." Ahmad left Florian standing there as he ran down the hall, away from the sounds of clanking dishes and raucous amusements within the great hall.

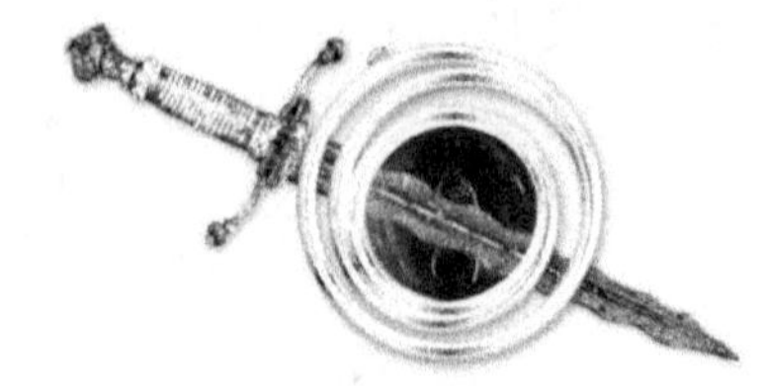

CHAPTER TWENTY-EIGHT
THE WORK OF SPIES

THE SUN HAD SET TEN minutes before, but Ahmad's outlook had gone dark long before the shadows of night overtook the cityscape. He stood on the south wall, as far as possible from the north tower where the treasonous King Orn and his men were housed.

Florian would escort this knight from Jeron's own people. Ahmad and Florian planned to meet at this spot, between guard patrols, and they hoped to find who had knowledge of Idra's whereabouts.

The landscape melted into the darkness, minute by minute, as the sun's last rays disappeared over the horizon. Ahmad shouldn't be here waiting for this clandestine meeting. He should be in the lamp-lit gardens of Hamlin wooing the woman who'd forever stolen his heart. The thought of yet another moment pulled from her hopeful embrace and tender kisses wrenched at his heart, but imagining her peril twisted his gut into knots.

"Sir Ahmad," a hushed whisper called to him from the shadows of the tower stair door.

He looked in that direction to see Florian emerge, another man following. The knight appeared to be around the same age and walked with confidence. His hand rested on the empty sheath where his arming sword would normally be. Ahmad looked from one man to the other, a wariness once buried now rising to the surface.

"You're late."

"I'm sorry," the other man said, leaning from behind Florian. "Tis my fault. I was at the tavern instead of dinner."

"It took some time to locate him, Ahmad, but Sir Dennan might have the information we need."

"We don't have all night."

Dennan frowned. "What? Florian didn't tell me anything."

"You are familiar with Orn and his closest knights, are you not?" Ahmad asked, his patience running thin.

Dennan looked relaxed and unfazed by Ahmad's brusque manner. "I wouldn't say 'well.' They're a secretive lot, but I suppose I know them well enough. As much as I'd like to, that's for certain."

Ahmad sensed from the knight's posture and the easy way he answered, Dennan spoke the truth. Florian seemed to trust him, so he went on. "We need to know who his most trusted men are. The ones he'd tell his darkest secrets to or would entrust with the most important missions."

Sir Dennan rubbed his chin and leaned back against the stone. "Can I ask what's going on?"

"We've told you enough, Dennan. You'll have to forgive us for the secrecy, but 'tis truly for your own good," Florian said.

Ahmad waited, impatience and distrust sprouting deep roots with each passing second, until the Wyethian knight stood rigid.

"Alright, Florian, but only because we've been friends a long time." He looked back and forth between the two of them.

"Tis quite clear Havrik is a favorite, but you've got him banned from the place. There's only one other man who would have the king's ear and trust." He paused and Ahmad wanted to shake the answer from him. "His personal valet. Merin is his name. Supposedly, he's a distant cousin to the king who'd fallen on hard times, and he's a twisted fellow if ever there was such a one. If anyone knows anything about King Orn's secrets, 'tis him."

"You're certain?" He had to be sure before he started knocking down doors.

"Do you take me for a fool, sir? I've spent enough time at that blasted castle to know what color the king urinates, and 'tis far more than I'd wish to know. The king has always been an idle rogue, but in recent months, he's verged on a sort of excitable lunacy. That Merin is always whispering in his ear, and the two of them have had someone stashed in the castle tower for months. If you need more, get to Merin."

"I hope you're right." Ahmad's tone held the distinctive edge of a man on the brink.

"I am. You wait and see," Dennan said, his voice bolstered by confidence and a hint of defensiveness as he stepped up to Ahmad, their chests a mere foot apart.

Florian came near the two and pressed them away from each other. "Thank you for your help, Dennan. Tis best we part ways here, but watch your back. There are things afoot to put a man in the path of violence."

"Thank you for the warning, Florian. You watch your back as well. Keep each other safe. Whatever foolishness you've got yourselves in the middle of cannot turn out well if you don't." He nodded and walked away, into the turret stairwell.

"You really believe we can trust what he said?"

Florian faced Ahmad and gave a solemn nod. "He's never given reason not to. I think he's right about Merin. I've met him once or twice. Besides Wayne, his steward, I think Merin has been the one to run more errands for and speak on behalf of the king more often than anyone else. What should we do?"

"Is he the one that always wears black and shadows the king wherever he goes?"

Florian answered in the affirmative and Ahmad acknowledged he knew of the man.

"I'll follow him. See where he goes. You said they claimed to have your sister close, did you not? If need be, I'll ask him where Lady Idra and your sister are being held."

Florian smiled. "You'll *ask*?" he was clearly amused by the jesting but hard tone of Ahmad's voice. Ahmad would not ask nicely. "Yes. My uncle says he doesn't know the exact location, but he seemed to think her within the city. But I've been able to find no trace of her, and I've not come across any place other than public houses where Orn's and my uncle's men have frequented within the castle walls. My gut tells me she's not here, but that's the best I can do."

Ahmad exhaled and closed his eyes for a second. "I will track this Merin, and you do whatever it takes to keep your uncle and Orn from becoming suspicious."

"I understand," Florian said.

"This plan had better work, or not only you and I will pay; the citizens, down to the last man, woman, and child in the Realms will suffer. And, Florian, do not lose that dagger."

He couldn't impart the serious nature of this secretive mission more than he already had. He also couldn't go the night without warning the prince, no matter what he'd told Florian. Raz had to know what intrigues befell them all.

Florian had pulled the dagger out to display his possession of it, but now put it back into his belt and hid it beneath his cloak. Ahmad watched him leave the way Dennan had gone minutes before, while he went the opposite direction.

* * *

Orn glared at Jeron, displeased with the other man's lack of foresight. If he truly knew his nephew the way he said he did, they wouldn't be having the problems they were then. If Florian had been as malleable in the face of his sister's need as Jeron had purported, Havrik never would have had to do what he'd done, nor would the Fyll blade have ever ended up in the wrong hands.

When Orn had received word of Florian's dash from the pertento objex earlier in the day, he'd sent Havrik to follow him. The now-disguised knight hadn't been able to locate Florian until he witnessed him dragging one of Jeron's own household men through the darkened streets toward the south wall.

Merin had sent of Queen Moira of Emlyn's men, who now trailed after the knight Dennan. She proved to be Orn's best ally in his plans, her loyalty influenced by the promise of eternal youth. Her husband, King Ekreton, was far too loyal to High King Dante, but his wife had been a lustful woman in her youth, and one Orn had once had a fancy for before Dante arranged her marriage to the loyalist king of Emlyn.

Back at her home in the north, she'd been forced to kill Orn's messenger when a servant walked in on them unannounced, as he'd been in the process of delivering word of their schemes to her. Moira had used the excuse that he'd broken in as a secret spy of Crescent Cave set on murdering her. Their current tension with the Crescents had certainly worked in her favor, and it appeared Ekreton didn't suspect a thing in regard to his wife's duplicity.

"When will he arrive, Jeron? I don't have all night," Orn said, slapping the tabletop.

"Florian will be here soon. He sent word that he has the blade."

"I certainly hope he is not stupid enough to use that particular phrasing."

"No. The boy who delivered word said Florian has what I need and will be bringing it. That is all. My assumption is that he spoke of the blade. I can think of no other reason he would need to bring something to me or you."

"Very well," Orn said with a dismissive wave of his hand. Speaking with Jeron became tedious. The man might soon outlast his usefulness.

A soft knock rattled the door before Florian entered.

"Where is it?"

Florian looked at him but did not feign respect with a bow or nod. He reached under his cloak and pulled out the Fyll Blade. Orn sighed with relief. The plan could move forward. Dante would die and Theiandar would pay the price. It would work exactly as he and Nox had designed.

"Give it to me." The vigorous flapping of his outstretched palm emphasized Orn's demand.

"No," Florian said, his response clipped as he slid the knife back into his belt.

"What do you mean, no?"

Florian looked at the other men in the room, some hidden in the shadows along the wall. Orn knew Florian counted them, six including himself. If they wanted, they could take the blade from him.

"I mean I will hold on to the blade. I will need it tomorrow, will I not?"

Orn reached up to rub the stone amulet and smiled as he let his mind do the talking for a moment. He witnessed the new hesitation cross Florian's face, but it didn't signify enough. He wasn't yet convinced the boy would obey to the last breath.

"Yes, you will use the knife to stab the king at the end of the jousts. You will do this and save your sister's life. She is on the brink of a living death, but you can save her. Only you," Orn murmured in a soft, calming voice as he stepped nearer and nearer to the knight, still rubbing the stone.

Florian's eyes flicked from the necklace to Orn's face and back. "What of Lady Idra?"

"Mmm. You've no legs to stand upon, let alone the ability to negotiate. But rest assured, I am feeling magnanimous since you've brought my blade."

Florian appeared to be struggling, but a softening of will emerged there; Orn was certain he'd seen it. He had to believe it worked. "Kill Dante and Faye lives a full and beautiful life. You love your sister, and you will do this for her."

"Yes. I will."

"Now rest, for tomorrow will be an eventful day."

"Yes, Sire." Florian bowed.

He left the room without a backward glance, and Orn fondled the trinket around his neck. It had finally worked its magic on the willful young man.

Orn turned to the shadows near the doorway and motioned for the man there to approach. "It is time, Merin. Bring me Faye and the Lady Idra. By the time I've bent their wills, they will want to give their beauty. Bring them so that there can be no excuses. If he even hesitates, we will show him the real power he is up against."

"As you wish, Highness," Merin said and walked out of the room.

* * *

Prince Theiandar's words still rang in Ahmad's ears. He'd relayed Florian's story to Raz, revealing everything Sabine had exposed regarding Nox. Raz was angry—angrier than Ahmad had ever seen him. Princess Caityn stayed in the nursery with the baby, which saved her from witnessing her husband's tirade as he ranted over the unacceptable secrecy of his men. Ahmad attempted to reassure Raz of the reasons why Florian had kept the secret, of the fact that none of them knew exactly where Nox was, or where Faye and Lady Idra were being held.

They hoped the two were together so that there would only be one trail to follow.

After Theiandar calmed down enough, he agreed to keep the secret, but to include the other knights of Delphor in the plan, as well as Raz's father. King Dante deserved the truth of their dire situation, but it would have to be done without alerting anyone else to the danger. The high king would want to see if Florian told the truth, and Theiandar didn't believe he'd act rashly or imprison Florian. If Dante knew, they could have Orn and his people surrounded without drawing attention, and if it were true, the sub-king would be apprehended and arrested for treason.

Now Ahmad hid in the shadows waiting for Merin to appear at his chamber in the tower where Orn's people were housed, since the place had been empty when first Ahmad arrived. Half an hour passed after his meeting with Raz before Merin finally showed up. Ahmad considered forcing Merin to take him to Idra, but he thought better of it, not wanting to cause the plan he'd made with the high prince to fail.

Merin soon reemerged from the tower wearing a black hooded cape and walking like a man with a purpose. Ahmad glanced about to make sure no one noticed him and followed after Merin, who went to the gates of the castle and out toward the forest.

Stealthy and sure-footed, with years of knowledge of the woods surrounding High Castle, Ahmad followed the man illuminated only by the trickling shafts of moonlight filtering through the half-naked canopy of late-autumn-ravaged tree limbs overhead. They went on this way, one unaware he was followed and the other mindful of every breath he took, for an hour before Merin stopped and whistled like a bird. He waited there for the span of several seconds before a similar call returned from beyond. At the edge of the wooded area, a dim light outlined a door and a small boarded-up window.

Merin moved forward again and entered the dilapidated little cottage lost to the forest. Ahmad moved as close as he dared and surveyed the area. There were four horses tied off near the cottage, and none were saddled. It could mean there were five men inside, but the place didn't seem big enough for that many. Still. This could be where Idra and Faye were being held captive. And as the thought worked its way through his consciousness, hope lifted his spirits and made him bold. He slinked closer until he leaned against the wall of the cottage, away from the door.

The walls were thin and the men within, though speaking in soft tones, could be heard through the almost useless boards.

"Don't be daft. Merin's a far better rider than you, and you saw how she looked at him. That woman, Lady What-was-her-name, was more afraid of him than she ever would be of you, Kelor," one man spoke, derision filling his voice.

"Kelor, the king has other plans for you. Go to the castle and wait for my return. I'll have the women with me, and I'll need your help getting them secured. Jass, you'll stay here and await my return."

"Yes, sir," the other men said in unison.

Ahmad held as still as possible as he crouched outside the thin wall of the mossy cottage and eavesdropped on their plan. It seemed there were only three men. Idra and Faye were not within. That much was clear, but nothing had been said about where they were. They must not be too far away, but Ahmad had no way of following Merin. He thought his best bet would be to corner this Kelor at the castle, question him, and return to this cottage with a unit of men. If Merin returned here before going back to the castle, they'd be able to apprehend them at this spot.

There were rustling sounds coming from within the cottage, and then the door slammed open. Ahmad stepped away from the swath of yellow light that issued from the doorway and flattened himself against the wall. He held his breath and waited.

Three men emerged. One of them stopped in the doorway, making an imposing shadow drift across the ground. The other two grabbed saddles and prepared their horses. With the man dressed all in black, Ahmad identified Merin's face, but the other man needed memorizing. He wore breeches and a gray tunic, a sword belt strapped to his waist, and short leather boots. The man's dark, greasy hair framed his pale, angular face in the low light from the doorway and filtered moonlight.

Instinct screamed within Ahmad to follow Merin, but it would be hopeless, that he'd either be seen or never keep up. He leaned his head back on the wall and squeezed his eyes shut as he prayed to Almighty that Idra be safe, and Faye too. He begged the Great One to bring his beloved here to him, where he swore he'd never leave her side ever again.

"Don't forget to bring back a bottle of that ale from the Emlyn queen. She has good taste, that one," the man in the doorway said, laughing.

"Queen Moira has more than good taste," Merin said from the darkness, but Ahmad judged the intimate implication of his light tone and a new anger pierced his gut.

"She's got a wicked and mighty blow! I'm only glad I wasn't picked to carry messages between her and King Orn."

"Count yourself lucky and keep your head down," Merin replied.

The door to the cottage shut once again, darkness enveloping the landscape where it had once been illuminated by the firelight. Both riders trotted out, and Ahmad leaned against the house, wondering what he should do next while he waited for them to disappear beyond sight and sound.

Merin had ridden off to the north. Ahmad would hold on to that knowledge as the best thing to give him hope of knowing Idra's location. The question became, what to do with the man in the cottage? He could leave him be, sneak back to the castle, and report to Raz as planned. Or Ahmad could capture this man at the cottage and get him to speak, out here, away from prying eyes. He leaned forward with that last thought pressing hard on his will but stopped short as he realized if anyone else came out to the cabin and found them or if the knight were missing that it would be an alert to Orn that they were onto him. This outcome he wanted to avoid, come what may, if they were to gain any evidence to the fact that King Orn and his cohorts were behind the treason against High King Dante and his family.

Ahmad reached inside his vest and gripped the tattered cloth of Idra's handkerchief. "I'll come for you, Idra," he whispered with such quiet even the wind did not carry his words. "Stay strong."

His entire body tensed with reluctance to leave when he considered the off-chance existed that this man inside could lead him to Idra, but if he understood the plan, they were bringing Idra and Faye here. He needed to make haste. Ahmad tiptoed back into the forest, and when he'd gone far enough from the deserted house, he dashed for the castle.

CHAPTER TWENTY-NINE
WHERE EVIL MEN LURK

FLORIAN GRABBED HIS HEAD AND squeezed. Terrible pain wrenched at his brain, and his thoughts were a jumble. King Orn's words were ringing in his mind, and he believed in what the man had offered, as if his promise of Faye's safety in exchange for killing the king was real. A warring thought banged at the heavy door of his consciousness, yelling that Orn lied and broke promises, but the distant thought grew dimmer by the second.

He stumbled down the hall toward the main door out of the keep. He had to get as far from there as possible before he completely lost his mind. The overwhelming desire to kill the high king and save his sister, the irrational idea that it was the only way, increased. He almost made it to the door when a hand grabbed his arm. He jerked away and reached for his sword, but another hand gripped his on the hilt.

"Raz," he gasped. "I thought you were someone else."

Prince Theiandar looked at him with a curious expression, then in a hushed voice said, "I didn't mean to sneak up on you. Come with me."

The prince motioned with his head, then walked toward the wing where the high king's private chambers were located. Florian hesitated when a foreign and disturbing thought entered his mind. He could kill the king tonight if that's where they were going. But then he'd have to kill the prince as well, and his insane thoughts stopped dead. The pounding grew, but still he shook his head about in an attempt to clear the murderous images from his mind. He would not kill the king, no matter what. They were close to freeing Faye and Lady Idra. His bones ached for that to be true. If he just kept his wits for a little while longer, this would be over.

"Florian," the prince whispered urgently. "Come."

Florian nodded and followed after. He glanced about, wondering who had seen them and might be following. He had the impression Raz knew something and wondered if Ahmad had gone to him anyway. It wouldn't surprise Florian, but if so, the other knight might have already signed the death warrants of both Faye and Lady Idra.

They hastened down the halls where they passed the castle's steward, Breg, and then two of High King Dante's most trusted royal guardsmen. Florian got the impression lines of defense had been set up in the form of those men to keep prying eyes away. He doubted the wisdom of such a move, but at least none of King Orn's people would be poking about down this wing. That was a tenuous sort of saving grace.

They arrived outside the door to the high queen's private sitting chamber, and Raz stopped with his hand resting on the handle. "Ahmad told me the whole of it, Florian. I wish you would have come to me sooner."

The simple reprimand hurt far worse than if the high prince had rebuked him with every true word of his deceit and culpability. He swallowed the lump in his throat and nodded, unable to form a word, let alone string a sentence together. This man before him, High Prince Theiandar, epitomized the exact opposite of men like King Orn or his uncle Jeron; Raz's honor included his word. He could be trusted with Florian's life—with Faye's life—and Florian had let fear overshadow the truth and break his trust in the goodness of his fellow man. Now he may never again have the trust of a man who was like a brother to him, and it stung like the deadly bite of the black widow. Florian sensed the slow spread of the poison in his veins, but no cure existed for such a bite, such a visible lack of trust as he'd made clear to Raz and his fellow guardsmen.

Raz let go of the door's handle and grabbed Florian's shoulders, forcing the knight to look him in the eyes. "I understand, Florian. I know you'd never do anything to hurt my family, and I trust you with our lives, but we would have helped you from the first," he said, his voice passionate but quiet.

"I'm sorry," Florian squeaked out. Now that the floodgates were open he couldn't stop. "I wanted to tell you as soon as the threat became clear, but I have been followed and spied upon no matter which way I turn. They said Faye would pay the consequences if I said anything. If Nox were to get to her, to do what he did to Princess Caityn . . ." He swallowed. "How could I live with myself if I didn't do everything possible to save her first? Tell me you wouldn't have done the same thing."

He thought for certain that Raz would—no, that he *should*—deny the wisdom of keeping the truth from those most in danger of its consequences, and that he would reprimand him further—accuse him of being a traitor too—but he didn't.

Raz nodded in slow motion. "I think I would have done the same thing. If it were Eliya, I would have attempted anything to rescue my sister before I risked her becoming the next victim of the Beauty Thief."

"You would?" Florian asked, at first not recognizing the sound of his own voice.

Again, the prince squeezed Florian's arms where his hands rested. "Yes. I know why you did it. Do not forget, I saw what that monster did to my beloved Caityn.

"I lost my temper when Ahmad told me, but I am nearly certain I would have done the same. If it lessens your pain, I have not told my wife of her cousin Lady Idra's current circumstance. I can only imagine how she would react and worry if she knew the truth, and there is nothing she can do. I will not add to her anxiety over our son by revealing that her cousin has been captured."

Raz took a huge breath, his chest expanding to the limit, and let it out in a huff. "Come, the others are inside my mother's salon. We're awaiting Ahmad's return and then we'll make our plans for the morrow. And in case you're wondering, I made sure to spread the rumor that I gathered my guardsmen with the purpose of strategizing for the final jousts tomorrow, since two of my men will be participating."

Raz donned a halfhearted but kind smile and slapped Florian's shoulder.

He flinched and nodded. "Yes, Sire. I don't know how to thank you."

"Your thanks can be in protecting my family from the traitor and his conspirators and helping to capture them before anyone else is hurt."

"Yes, Sire." The problem remained, Florian felt a part of himself shifting in a dark direction, even as he heard Raz speaking, and he feared he did not have complete control. It left an empty pit in his stomach and placed an invisible seal over his mouth.

* * *

Ahmad panted, tipsy with exhaustion by the time he raced back to the stables. He'd hoped to catch the man called Kelor there, but he'd missed his opportunity. Instead, he found a stable boy who took some convincing, but after a coin or two and the freedom to return home for the night he opened up about where the stranger had gone: toward the keep's kitchens.

Standing in the stables, still slightly out of breath, Ahmad dismissed any thought but that of rescuing Idra and Faye. He pressed his hands to his knees, looked toward each door of the stable, and contemplated the choices before him. Follow the stranger or go to the prince with the information he'd obtained from his spying. Both were viable choices, but he was aware that Raz awaited his return. He remained unaware of Kelor's final destination other than possibly sneaking his way to King Orn, and if that were the case, he'd not be able to waylay or question the man.

He pushed off from his knees to stand tall and rushed toward the keep, where he planned to give his report and gain the insight of the prince and the rest of unit Delphor.

* * *

Florian didn't know whether to cry from joy or from humiliation, but he hesitated at the sympathetic response of the other guardsmen when he walked into the room. If not for the twinge of anger they shared over how Florian had handled Xavier's plight and had Ahmad thrown in the dungeon, they might have never given his deceit a second thought, but he'd gone too far when he'd done that. Florian's heart sank at how this would forever be a stain on his reputation, but he justified it by mentally arguing that it had been for the sake of protecting the innocent, and wasn't that what they'd all vowed to do when they became knights?

Not long after Raz and Florian arrived at the high queen's salon, Ahmad showed up. He burst in but must have thought better of slamming the door, as he paused and deliberately leaned back on it in slow motion until it clicked in place. Florian stared at him with a sense of unease and anticipation, thinking Ahmad believed he'd discovered something.

"There is a cottage in the woods that they are using," Ahmad said without another moment's delay.

"Lady Idra and Florian's sister are there?" Raz asked.

Here Ahmad hesitated and glanced at Florian, who felt a crushing weight at seeing the brief disappointed expression in the other man's eyes.

"No, Raz, they are not."

Florian stepped back and shook his head, his life feeling like a child's ball, spinning wildly out of control. Ahmad seemed to expect his reaction and already walked toward him with his hand outstretched in a placating manner.

"But they are being brought there, to this cottage, by King Orn's man. He has traveled north to retrieve both of them, but I do not know for what purpose. And at this time, there is only one man left there." He stopped a couple of feet from Florian and nodded. "They are going to be well. We will be there. Faye will be well, Florian."

He swallowed hard and his eyebrows rose in hopeful question. If therein lied truth to what Ahmad shared, he had done the belatedly right thing in finally revealing all, gaining the help of his fellow guardsmen. Could he have done this on his own? Maybe. But who could say he wouldn't have been followed and then ruined any chances of saving Faye from the Beauty Thief.

"I do not know what to say, but thank you, Ahmad. I'm sorry for what I've done. I never should have kept this secret."

"No, 'tis not the secret that is the problem, but that you didn't trust us enough to help you carry it," Ahmad answered.

A hushed round of consensus passed from the men in the room, but when Florian chanced to look around at them, none had a look of malice or anger, only pity. That might have been worse. Florian didn't want to be pitied. He was a knight and brave enough to risk his life for his king, his friends, his family, and the realms.

"Enough of this. We need to discuss what we will do to keep our knowledge hidden and entrap these scoundrels," Raz said, interrupting the silence. "Please sit."

They obeyed, taking seats around High Queen Zoe's private sitting chamber. Where to sit without awkwardness amongst the group? Florian had a sense of being an outsider, though no one had said anything to make him feel thus. His actions had driven a wedge between them, but in the recesses of his mind, he hoped for reconciliation. If only that were possible when trust had been broken. He chose a place by himself next to the fireplace, his body heavy upon the hard seat.

Raz took charge, planning and shaping the course of events starting with the continuing of the jousts to cover up their knowledge. Only two of his knights would participate on this last day, which left the rest of them to head up the units of guardsmen that would surround King Orn, stand guard outside the high king's box, travel out to surround the cottage in the forest, and lastly, the tower where Orn's household stayed for the duration of the tourney and ceremony.

"I should be there, Raz," Ahmad insisted.

"No, Ahmad, you must joust. If this man of Orn's has not returned with the women by then, we will still need to keep them believing we do not know their plans. If you don't participate, they will detect something is not right. It has taken much to douse the rumors of what has happened to Xavier, and if you do not joust, it will cause a stir. I'm sorry. Trust that these men here and those of the castle can and will exert profound effort to protect Ladies Idra and Faye. Do not fear, but trust in the Almighty. There is nothing else for us to do but our utmost."

"Yes, Sire." Each syllable was pronounced with reluctance as he crossed his arms over his chest.

"Then 'tis settled. You each have your assignment, and you must perform it without fail, or our plan will dissolve. There will be many unarmed, innocent people at the tourney, and it is our mission to protect them as well. Do your best to keep them from harm."

"But we don't know how far this treason reaches. What if there are many spread throughout the crowds?" Gavin asked. He'd been silent throughout the evening.

"That is a good point," Theiandar said, his acknowledgment accompanied by a hand to Gavin's shoulder. "Be wary, but do not assume the worst. You remember that beyond Conleth's monarch, and some lords, the queen of Emlyn is also involved. Keep watch over their seating area as well. I'll have a dispatch sent to King Ekreton immediately. Ahmad, are you certain he is not involved?"

"I'm certain, Raz. He genuinely believed his wife was attacked by someone from Crescent Cave, when, in fact, it was one of Orn's people carrying secret messages between the two. She has deceived her own husband. I do not know the extent of her influence with the knights who accompanied her and her daughters to the tourney, nor do I know her daughters' involvement."

"Fine. We must watch them with care." Raz leaned back with a terrible invisible weight on his shoulders. "I'll speak with my father, who is even now preparing his own men for tomorrow's events. I'll then gather the captains of four other units to command their men."

Prince Theiandar stood and paced by the window. His tension emanating near and far. "For now, I would like you to contact Captain Saar, Ahmad. Take him outside the walls with his men and tell them the plans. Head south of the castle and around to the north, but stay away from this cottage to avoid suspicion. One of Saar's men can return to the castle for a second unit once you've taken them to the place."

The prince's head bobbed and his pace quickened as the plan formed in more detail. He stopped and stared at Florian, but his look stayed unreadable, setting Florian further on edge.

"We'll put a few men on guard at the cottage while the rest keep a distance to the northwest. One of them can act as a runner to gather the two units after Orn's man returns there with the ladies." He shifted his attention back to Ahmad. "If you scatter a unit throughout the forest north of this cottage, you might stop the man escorting the ladies before he arrives.

"The rest of you get some sleep. If anything happens in the night, you'll be informed with great haste." Raz jerked his head toward the door and watched the men file out, but Florian hung back when the prince tapped his shoulder.

"Florian, I am counting on you to bring me any news or updates as soon as you have them. My father is expecting regular reports as well. Do not let me down."

"Yes, Sire." Florian had said the same words to Orn not long before, but this time he wished to mean them.

CHAPTER THIRTY
TELL ME EVERYTHING

AHMAD DIDN'T SLEEP THAT NIGHT. He stayed in the woods with the other men until the sun peeked over the horizon. He had to return to the castle or risk ruining the plans they'd made, but he longed to stay there and see Idra emerge from the north, to wipe the dastardly traitors from the face of the earth they stood upon, and kiss her until it felt their lips were not two pairs but one.

"I must return," he said with reluctance spilling from every fiber of his tense body. "Please do all you can to keep the ladies safe."

"You have my word," Captain Saar responded while squeezing Ahmad's shoulder.

He crept from the bushes outside the cabin. The man who'd stayed behind had never emerged, and the light had gone out some time ago. Ahmad feared wherever Idra and Faye were being held might be farther than he imagined. Florian had been so sure they were not far; Ahmad had to hope and pray for a distance of less than a day. The meticulous plan hinged on them being nearby. If not, a blunder would prevent them from ever finding the two women, but Ahmad refused to entertain such a provoking thought.

Once back at the castle, he went to the armory to gather his weapons and then headed to the arena to prepare for the jousts, scheduled to begin in two hours. He needed to eat something, but his stomach rebelled at the idea of food when he so dreaded the thought that Idra might not be able to eat.

Ahmad half-yanked his tunic off to put on his gambeson when a thought occurred to him. He pulled the tunic back on, replaced his sword and belt around his waist, and dashed from the tent. Several men, too many to count, watched him jog by, but no one stood in his way. He slowed his pace once he neared the inner tower and looked around to see if anyone watched with more interest than necessary, but it seemed no one cared one wit about his presence there.

He opened the tower entrance and took the steps as quickly as possible given the cramped space available to move within. Ahmad motioned for the guardsman to stay put. The man obeyed while Ahmad opened the door and stepped inside, closing it behind.

"Sabine, are you well?" Any competing thought dashed from his mind when he saw her on the bed, pale and seemingly lifeless. "Sabine?" he asked again, crossing the room in two quick steps to kneel beside the bed.

She blinked at him, but her lips were drained of color, cracked and dry. He reached for the bucket of water nearby and ladled out some of the cool liquid, holding it to her mouth. Her lips were already parted, but she didn't move them to accept the water. He poured a few drops in any way and waited for her to swallow. When she did, he let out a breath he didn't realize he held. Once she'd had that tiny sip, she reacted like a parched desert and opened her lips wider for more.

It took more than a minute for her to finish the entire ladleful, but she finally did. Ahmad set it aside and sat down on the floor next to the bed. "What's happened to you? When was the last time you ate or drank?"

He waited for an answer but she just stared.

"Haven't you been eating?"

"No."

"Why?" He wanted to shake her, but she looked fragile enough to break.

"Nox will win. I'm certain of it. I cannot make him stop." She stopped and Ahmad sensed her desperation. "I do not want to see his horrors anymore." She coughed, her hand slowly reaching toward her throat. "Please, let me go home to my people to die."

"You will not die, Sabine, and Nox will not win. We won't let him. You must believe this."

"How can I?" Her voice rose barely above a whisper. "What I see happens."

"That can't be true. Look at Princess Caityn as proof. Have faith. Nox's plans are not for anyone's good but his own. With your help we can stop him. You must eat. Drink." Ahmad didn't wait for her to reply. He tilted his head toward the door and yelled for the guard outside. When he entered, Ahmad said, "Bring this prisoner some broth, and send a girl to care for her. Send for Noreeta, Lady Idra's lady's maid."

The guard nodded and dashed off to do as ordered.

"Rest and we'll have you well soon enough." He stayed there next to her for ten minutes, watching her, before speaking again. Sabine's eyes were closed as if in sleep, but unrest marred her young features. When he couldn't wait another minute, he said, "I must ask what you know of King Orn. Are you strong enough to tell me?"

"I do not know him." Her eyes fluttered open and closed, but she appeared more peaceful than she had a few minutes before.

"Have you seen where Nox is? Have you seen anything else of what he's done?"

"No. I only see the babe, sprawled upon a wooden floor, alone, his face red with crying, and the banner of Twelve Realms burns nearby."

"Nothing else?"

Her head drooped to the side, irritation glaring forth from her eyes. "Nothing? Tis everything."

A brief knock interrupted further discourse, and Noreeta entered. He chose her to care for young Sabine before anyone else because Idra trusted her.

He ordered her inside, and she curtsied low.

"You will care for this girl. Her name is Sabine. She must have sustenance, but be gentle with her, Noreeta. She looks a prisoner, but by our high prince she is a guest with us."

"Yes, sir." She curtsied again and her eyes flickered to Sabine. "I heard the princess and Lady Idra speak of her, sir, and my lady seemed to speak with gentle regard."

"I'm not surprised. Your lady has a generous heart." He stood and stared hard at Noreeta. "Thank you. I must go, but I trust you to do well." He looked down at Sabine, whose eyes were finally alight with a shimmer of life. "Are you certain you have nothing else to tell me regarding Nox?"

"He's betrayed the trust of those who sheltered him. He wanders in secret among your people, but he will be gone before you realize. Though he will not stay gone. He is driven by a force even beyond his own reckoning."

"Eat and rest, Sabine. Gain your strength. I know you want to return home, but if what you say is true, we will need your help. Can I ask it of you?"

"If it means my suffering has purpose, yes." A tear slipped across her temple and pooled in her ear, the shimmer of it caught in the rays of light slicing through the window above.

Ahmad worked to ignore the misplaced guilt he shouldered over having captured Sabine to begin with and left the two of them alone just as a kitchen maid arrived with a tray of broth and bread and a few other light morsels. The only thought to bring him a scrap of peace over her captivity came from the knowledge she held regarding Nox and her willingness to help them.

He'd hoped Sabine could tell him more about the intrigues and treason, that if Orn and Nox were working together, she'd be able to explain the connection, but it had proved a false hope.

* * *

With a half hour left until the jousts, Ahmad stood alone in the tent where the High Castle knights prepared for tourney events. Fully armored, he didn't notice the weight of steel, but it didn't drag him down so much as the austerity of the situation in which they found themselves.

No word had returned from the cottage yet, which meant the man Merin had not returned with Idra and Faye. His heart sank further and further. The longer this went on, the less chance of getting Idra back.

"Almighty," he prayed, "what would you have me do? I am learning but also floundering in doubts. Your will be done, but let me be a lightning rod in your arsenal of purpose."

"Amen."

That half-whisper did not fool Ahmad. He jerked his head up to see Prince Theiandar standing nearby, a solemn look on his face.

"Raz, shouldn't you be in the stands? Has there been word from the cottage?"

"No word, but I've sent a rider. I only came because I needed to warn you. After discussing all with my father, he reckoned it important to bring Havrik back for your last joust to dispel any more gossip or dissension."

"What?" Ahmad asked, a sinking weight in his gut. The last time he'd seen Havrik, there had been a definite bloodlust radiating from the man's eyes. He didn't fear meeting him in the jousts, but an added danger waited now that Ahmad recognized the fact that Havrik's loyalty belonged to a man who would rather see Ahmad dead than have his plans ruined.

"Father seemed to think that by not allowing Havrik to take part it sent the wrong message to the Realms. He made it clear that by keeping Havrik from participating, while having you here, it would raise suspicions of which he did not want to be a part. I was not aware there rumbled so great a discord across the Realms, but Havrik's participation will ease much of the doubt that's been perpetuated."

"He's a traitor, Raz."

"You don't need to tell me twice, but I have been overruled. And I must admit that part of me agrees with my father. Please hear me out," Raz said, a pacifying hand raised.

Ahmad stayed silent, though with great reluctance.

"I must look to the future of the Realms, not just the few I care most for in the world. No matter how much I care for my guardsmen and for my wife's cousin, I cannot risk the sanctity of the kingdom for the few. I must protect my son, the future of this kingdom, first and foremost. I must squash rebellion and the ill effects of rumors spread abroad."

Ahmad gritted his teeth. He understood, but hated to admit it. Twelve Realms and this prince before him were those to which he'd committed himself, and before anything else, they were what he must honor. He nodded with heavy reluctance, and Raz returned the gesture with the same weightiness.

"We are prepared for Florian's signal. He will alert us to when the attack is to begin. The others are in place."

"Sire." Ahmad bowed his head a fraction.

Raz reached out his hand and, after a slight hesitation, Ahmad grasped his arm in return. Above all, the high prince was his friend who deserved his trust and his fealty. He could not control Idra's fate and had to leave her in the hands of the Almighty. Ahmad had been positive he had trust in the Great One, but everything about his love for Idra tested the truth of it. Was Almighty asking him to give up caring for his closest friends in exchange for something greater? He couldn't imagine the creator of all asking him to stop caring for any of his creation, thus he reasoned it wasn't giving them up so much as trusting them to Almighty's care. Ahmad needed to stop trying to be their savior.

Prince Theiandar interrupted his musings. "Be safe. I'm sure you'll agree Havrik is out for blood."

Ahmad grimaced at the thought. Havrik didn't concern him, but jousting against a cruel man with a wish to kill him did not rank high on Ahmad's list of enjoyable pursuits.

"Yes. There's little doubt of it."

"You beat him once before. You can do it again. Do this for the kingdom, Ahmad."

"But what of Idra? What of Nox and his amulet? Did not your wife explain he has the sands of life and will make a new amulet?" Ahmad shook his head. "I shouldn't be here. I should be out there, searching for her."

Prince Theiandar stared at him, and he returned the piercing look without speaking. The prince had to know by now how important Idra was to him. How could he not?

"You're right, Ahmad. I've been foolishly blind. I should have spoken up to my father and stood my ground. What kind of king will I make if I cannot stand for what I know is right?"

"You will be a great and worthy king, Raz. Of this I am sure," Ahmad said, the reassurance of the truth of it resounding through his chest.

"Thank you, my friend. As such, I release you from this duty and order you to the forest. Take the men already stationed there and apprehend the traitor in the cottage. Make him lead you to wherever they are keeping my wife's cousin and Florian's sister. Glean from him any knowledge of Nox. You are my right hand. We will show the Realms that we are strong and united, that treason is only for the weak."

Ahmad couldn't believe what he heard. He trusted the prince, but this act would go against his father, the high king of the Twelve Realms. It was a bold move.

"Yes, Sire."

"First, take off your gear and help me to put it on."

"What?" Ahmad asked, not sure he'd heard Raz right.

"I'm going to joust in your place. It must be done, and I must do it."

"Are you certain, Raz? It is dangerous. Havrik is out for blood."

Prince Theiandar nodded, but his jaw set firm. "I am aware. Hurry. We are short of time."

Ahmad hesitated, but Raz already pulled the helmet away from him and unbuckled the straps before another protest escaped his mouth. It took several minutes to undo and remove the outer gear. He left on his chain mail and put on his scabbard belt, then assisted Raz in putting on another set of chain mail and Ahmad's armor. It didn't quite fit, but it came close enough that unless someone saw his face, no one would realize High Prince Theiandar wore the suit instead of Ahmad.

"Go," Raz said, a smile on his face. "Be the hero once again, my friend."

Surprised, Ahmad chuckled and shook his head again. "You are the real hero, Sire. Go with Almighty."

"And you as well."

They grasped arms and Ahmad dashed from the tent, out of the arena grounds, and toward the stables.

CHAPTER THIRTY-ONE
LIFE AND LOVE

ORN SAT IN THE STANDS, his son at his side exemplifying the exuberance of youth. He rubbed the stone resting on his chest and tried to block out the raucous noise of celebrating realmspeople. The dull ache in his head held on almost constantly now, but he attributed it to the stress of what he strived to accomplish here. In just a few short hours the high king would be dead, Prince Theiandar would be imprisoned, and as a close cousin to the high king, the Duodenocourt would make Orn proviso ruler of Twelve Realms until he was officially named as high king.

A warning forced itself tumbling through the pounding of his head, but no clear thought was forthcoming. Florian stood where he'd been most of the tourney, straight across from where Orn sat in the stands. Jeron sat near the king. Lady Idra's seat remained empty next to High Princess Caityn. The baby and his nursemaid were seated just behind her. High Prince

Theiandar had not arrived, and that might have been the instigator of the doubts now whirling through Orn's mind.

Where had the weakling prince got off to? He needed to be here for the plan to work. Had someone given away their strategies? Did a trap form even now? A deluge of uncertainties inundated his mind and brought him no end of aching thought. Many doubts had ravaged him over the months leading up to this event, but Nox had been quick to dispel each one. The little man wasn't here to remind him of his power or his place, and the doubts were heavy upon him as the moment drew near. But no, he would see this treason through to its success and make Twelve Realms the most powerful and feared nation in the world. He would sit upon the throne of this palace and bring the rulers of the world to their knees in fear and respect. Yes, today would be the beginning of his true life.

The giddiness of that thought brought him round to the present moment, where they sat in anticipation of the first of three jousts. Havrik would participate in at least one of them. Orn knew he would be in two, since the knight carried the reputation of being one of the best of the Realms. He reminded himself how important it would be to have Havrik by his side once the coup had been accomplished. He wholeheartedly believed no other knight lived displaying such loyalty.

It hadn't surprised Orn one bit that High King Dante had allowed Havrik to return for the jousts, though the knight found himself out of favor with the present high court. Dante's concern rested too heavily with keeping the nobles happy and the laymen from dissatisfaction. Though important to look strong in front of them, Orn knew the current high king did not rise to the occasion. In his weak-willed way, Dante would fall to this plan with little effort on Orn's part. The outcome would be extraordinary in some ways and perfectly ordinary in others.

Orn looked pointedly at Florian, who faced straight ahead. The changes in Florian made Orn extra confident the plan would work. Florian's will seemed to have melted away, and last they spoke he had been docile and malleable in his responses. Earlier that morning, Orn had met with him once more, his own heart racing at the prospects of what the day would bring.

Once this overthrow had been accomplished, it would be simple to finish off his wife, Queen Nikita—*oh, Niki, you foolish woman*—with the poison Jeron had prescribed and leave Orn free to take a new bride, a weak woman who would look beautiful upon his arm and give him even more power than he'd thought possible by joining Twelve Realms to the kingdom of Bensheerin in the Dark Lands. The allying would bring the most powerful nation from the north into alignment with Orn's plans for ultimate power. Niki must die for this to be possible, but he didn't feel distraught over the prospect, since she'd never loved him beyond doing her duty, instead reserving her affection for their only child, a son over whom Orn found himself torn in his regard. He believed Niki's influence on their son was significant, and Orn had to accept the possibility that the boy might not be willing to join him in his pursuits for a stronger, wealthier Twelve Realms.

Instead of letting the thought worry him, Orn focused his attention on Florian and rubbed the stone with more force. "You will kill King Dante. You will save your sister. What better way to prove your devotion to those you love most? Kill Dante and be a hero to your people."

"What did you say, Father?"

"Nothing, Son. I'm enthused for the upcoming jousts and the opportunity to see our own knight be victorious. Sir Havrik will not disappoint."

"He is the best knight I've ever seen," Orn's son said with the youthful awe of a ten-year-old, his face alight with excitement. "Someday, I wish to be as mighty and valiant."

"And someday you shall be," Orn said, a burst of pride welling up inside as he tousled the boy's shaggy hair. He shifted in his seat, the anticipation growing each second, consuming him.

* * *

To Idra, the sight of Solfen River seemed too good to be true, but there before them it raged in all its wild beauty. Sweeter still, stopping on the knoll, she spotted the bridge that crossed on the road to High Castle less than a mile away. Idra filled with a new wave of hope. In the woods, they'd lost their way, and she'd begun to doubt they'd ever make it back. Part of her even feared she'd not live that long. The pain in her leg had throbbed mercilessly and left her in tears on more than one occasion. The only thing keeping her from defeat had been Faye when she cried with her. The girl had moments of strength, but she needed Idra's to survive. She couldn't let her down.

They'd rested a handful of times, and Idra had stayed on her horse except when absolutely necessary to dismount. She'd been on the animal long enough during the last leg of their journey that now her lower body had gone numb, which actually worked in her favor since it dulled the throb in her bound thigh.

"Lead my horse, Faye. I must rest awhile," Idra said and laid her head upon her mount's neck. The horse seemed to sense her weakness and adjusted his head to make it easy for Idra to hold on. A soft neigh filled the still morning air. The only other sound to disturb the day came from the twittering of birds.

Faye took hold of Idra's reins and chirped to the horses, adding the tiniest kick to the ribs of her own mount. "Just hold on, my lady."

The meager confidence in Faye's voice did little to assure Idra, who hadn't fully recovered from the shock of her injury. She had to hold on. She had to warn them, to keep her king safe, and protect the ones she loved. Caityn had to be warned that Nox truly lived, that he had help to escape, and that Sabine's words had been truer than they imagined.

They snaked their way down the hill and to the bridge. With great caution, they approached, and both women knew that the location might be watched by Orn's men. If the ones they'd beaten back at the cave had escaped or anyone else had come, word would have traveled. It only made sense that they'd be headed back to High Castle, and in getting lost, they'd taken the long way to get here. Idra feared their meandering route along the creek had been a mistake. What if it had delayed them to the point that they'd set themselves up for ambush and failure? She wished they'd braved the trail near Solfen River where at least they never would have gotten lost and wasted precious time.

They stayed hidden in the tree line, listening, and stared into the open area around the bridge, but after two minutes squandered in this way, nothing seemed to stir outside the tender breeze shifting through the dead grass along the path.

"Enough of this. The way is clear. Come, Faye, we must go." Idra said the words with firmness, but inside she melted at the terrible thought that she wouldn't be able to make it. If she were not there with Faye, would they believe the girl? She had to hang on.

They crossed the river, but that old familiar sensation of being watched entered her mind, filling her chest with a tight, aching dread. Idra kept glancing over her shoulder but nothing stirred. Even without seeing anything out of the ordinary, she felt the urge to move faster and slapped her reins upon the horse's neck.

They were leaving the cover of forest for an open field where the trail widened when she chanced another peek behind, but this time her heart did a flip and her stomach twisted. A man, all in black, galloped toward them with his cape billowing out behind.

"Faye! Move! Now!" Idra screamed and slapped at her mount's neck again and again, urgent to get him to move faster, away from the threat looming behind. She held tight with her good arm and pressed on to the last sliver of strength.

Faye caught up and rode next to her. Idra did her best to ignore the concerned look on the young woman's face. Within a few brief minutes that felt like hours, they were in sight of the main road, where the path opened up wide enough for two carriages to pass each other without incident. Here Idra realized her first true, irresistible hope. Heading toward the castle, she saw a rider surrounded by six knights, but Idra would recognize the woman on horseback anywhere.

Lady Hilde.

She slowed her crazed gallop and looked back, but the man in black had disappeared.

* * *

He stood over the subdued traitor in the cottage, but Ahmad saw nothing except an image of Idra tied up in this dirty, forsaken little hutch of a place. Her red ribbon, the favor she'd bestowed on the first day of the tourney, had been tied to his sword hilt, and he stroked his fingers down it as his chest constricted with a sensation as if he'd heard her crying out to him. She called for him somewhere, and he hated himself for not running to her. It didn't matter an iota that he didn't know where to find her. What mattered was he knew her danger, and while she endured amid real threat, he existed here, safe, surrounded by thirty worthy knights of High Castle.

He resolved to stop this coup and be there to tell Idra how her bravery led to the downfall of a traitor. For him, this courageous and beautiful woman embodied an unseen force, bringing them all together in power against the evils infiltrating their kingdom. He sensed — maybe because he saw it — a peace that in whatever her circumstance, she would remain true to herself and be brave beyond reckoning. In one so fair and gentle there resided great command of will and courage. Oh, how he loved her . . ..

"I already told you, I can't tell you where they've gone," the man named Jass was saying.

Ahmad brought his thoughts into submission and focused again on the prisoner.

"They didn't show us where. I only know 'tis north. That Nox is who knew the place and shared it with King Orn."

Ahmad struggled to contain his anger. He'd let his frustrations control him too much of late, but especially when it came to Lady Idra and her safety. He trusted her strength and capability, and he had given her life over to Almighty to sustain. He needed to keep himself in check and find the peace that passes understanding if he were to come through this a worthy man, a man free to love Idra as she deserved.

"When do you expect this Merin to return?"

"He should have already come by now."

Ahmad watched Jass's lip quiver as an upset pout screwed up his face. He couldn't help but wonder what little it had taken to convince this weak man to serve the purposes of such treason with Orn. He came to wits' end with what to do about the situation, but aside from staying here and waiting, the only other option would be to ride out north and try to track the rushed route of Merin. Surely the traitor had left a goodly trail to follow.

Ahmad called to the captain, who stood outside the cottage. Saar stepped inside and waited for Ahmad to speak. "We will ride north and track Merin. Gather your men."

"Yes, sir," Saar replied and left the room without delay.

"You best be speaking the truth or you can be sure the Duodenocourt will not be kind to you."

He watched the man shiver in obvious fear. "I speak true! I swear. I speak Almighty's truth."

"Do not say such things. Even the truth you speak doesn't compare to that of Almighty. Your greed and selfishness taints your word." Ahmad strode from the cottage, wishing he'd kept his mouth shut but also feeling some liberation. If not for the love of Almighty, Ahmad would be a lost man.

They mounted up and Ahmad gave the remaining men orders to surround the cottage from the wood and keep watch for Merin. Then he and Saar, along with his unit, rode north on the winding path leading to Solfen River.

They'd gone nearly a mile before Ahmad stopped them and searched for signs of Merin's trek. Marks of the man's night dash were everywhere and kept them heading northwest. They stopped again, not more than a half mile farther along, and Ahmad ordered the unit to dismount and search for the trail which had disappeared into the brush. In the silence of their intense search, they heard the pounding of hooves from a distance, and Ahmad signaled the men to hide. He only heard one horse approaching, which disturbed him, especially since it could be anyone.

As the sound increased in volume, he calmed his erratic heartbeat by taking long breaths and listening. As soon as the horse and man rode within the confines of their trap, he hollered and the knights leapt from behind trees and bushes. The rider, taken by surprise, pulled back on the reins as the startled horses reared up on his hindquarters.

The man didn't lose his seat, but Ahmad rushed forward and grabbed his black cloak, yanking him hard to the ground. He landed in a muddle of grunts and heavy cloth, and Ahmad reached for his arm as he saw the rider go for a knife in his boot.

"Oh, no, you don't!" He grabbed the stranger's wrist and twisted it, causing a cry of pain to escape the man's lips. Ahmad suppressed the minor satisfaction he gained from the sound, thinking this man had to be one of those who'd abducted Idra, and if any harm had befallen her, the traitor would wish a twist of his arm were the worst he would get.

"Who are you?" Ahmad's low voice rumbled like thunder in his chest.

"No one," the man cried out and, to untangle himself, shoved the cape off his head with his free hand.

"Merin!" Ahmad recognized him from the night before. "Where are Ladies Idra and Faye? What have you done with them?" A terrible fear that he'd killed them both entered Ahmad's mind and squirmed around, causing a painful roiling down in his stomach. He twisted Merin's arm harder.

"Ow!"

"Where?" Ahmad said again, turning the man's wrist a fraction more.

"Ow! Ow! I don't know!"

He panted and Ahmad made as if to twist his wrist more, the knife Merin had reached for now in Ahmad's other hand.

"I swear! I don't know. They escaped. I had to kill the men left to guard them." Merin's dark hair fell over his eyes.

"I don't believe you," Ahmad ground out between clenched teeth. He reacted purely on instinct now and held the knife to the fallen man's throat. "What have you done with Lady Idra?"

Merin's eyes closed, and he looked as though he wanted to swallow but feared the blade pressed there would cut his throat at the slightest movement. In a half-whisper, his lips barely parting, he mumbled something.

"What?" Ahmad's patience had gone, and a fearsome urge to just kill the kidnapping, treasonous pig filled his gut.

Merin's eyes went wide, and he said a little louder, though still with teeth clenched tight, "High Castle. On their way to High Castle."

Ahmad, shocked, lowered the knife and released Merin's wrist. Two guardsmen immediately fell upon Merin, tying him up and throwing him on the back of a horse.

Ahmad rushed to his own mount. "You had better be telling the truth, or you and I will meet again and our blades will do the talking."

"I speak true," Merin said, something akin to anger mingling with fear in his voice.

Ahmad told Saar what he wanted him to do with the traitor and the one back at the cottage, then he galloped away toward High Castle and, hopefully, Idra. His mind reeled with the thought that she'd escaped and made her way home. He couldn't believe it, and yet he could. She had changed a great deal since having helped to save Princess Caityn from the clutches of the Beauty Thief. She was no coward or helpless maiden. He lifted a silent plea and pressed his horse to go faster.

CHAPTER THIRTY-TWO
CONFRONTING DOUBT AND FEAR

FLORIAN'S HEAD ACHED, A THROBBING pain either from staying up all night or from his encounter with King Orn that morning. It had been a mistake to agree to the last meeting. He knew it had, but something drew him to the Wyethian king like a fish ensnared in a net. He wanted to wiggle away, to free himself, but the pull held too great an influence and with each bout of resistance, the hook dug farther in.

The Fyll Blade rested against his ribs now. He shouldn't have brought it here, and yet he bore a compelling need beyond his own understanding to have it near his person. He didn't know why or how it would serve his purposes except as a sure weapon against anyone who stood in his way to rescuing Faye and Lady Idra. Somewhere in his mind he fought the silken voice whispering the fastest way to accomplish this would be to kill King Dante, but another soft, wavering voice lingered with a warning against it and against trusting Orn at his word.

No good would come from this plot, this plan, this treason, unless Faye was safe once and for all.

Horns blew, announcing the first of three jousts. Florian's attention flitted to the two knights who rode out on the field on their massive, prancing horses: Ahmad and Zaccur, another guardsman of unit Delphor. Zaccur would be a worthy opponent, but Ahmad's reputation in the jousts preceded him; Florian counted it unlikely that Zaccur would win.

After making a round of the tourney field, the two knights met at the midpoint of the joust fence and tapped their lance edges together in respect, which brought a rumbling cheer from the anticipatory crowd. But after that, the friendliness disappeared as they raced to their ends of the fence and took positions to face off. Florian kept his gaze on Ahmad; something about him seemed irregular. The steed stamped his hooves in impatience to begin while his rider did his best to hold the beast in check until the horn blew. When the trumpet blasted, both riders took off in a cloud of dust to the heady cheers of the boisterous crowd. Within seconds they lowered their lances, aimed, and both landed blows, though only Ahmad's lance broke, awarding him the most points for the round. Twice more they charged and their lances met, but Ahmad's broken lance from the first round won him a spot in the final joust. Something about the way he moved in the saddle unnerved Florian. Though his gait appeared familiar, Ahmad usually had a different posture when he rode.

Florian's hand itched to grab the Fyll Blade from beneath his tunic as King Dante stood to applaud the match while simultaneously glancing at his son's empty chair. The sudden urge to do the high king harm shocked Florian to where he stumbled backward, hitting his rear end against the cloth-covered railing. Florian's heart slammed in his chest, and he wrestled with deep dread as he watched King Dante return to his seat.

"Almighty! What is this madness?" he whispered to himself and clutched at his heart. A week ago he'd been sure he would never have seriously considered treason, but in that moment the desire to kill the high king had been near to overpowering.

The winner of the joust rode to the center of the arena and removed his helmet. Florian, as well as the audience, had expected to see Sir Ahmad beneath, but they were shocked speechless. The high king's angry yell echoed throughout the assemblage.

"What manner of trickery is this?"

Florian's hands dropped to his sides as he stared in wide-eyed shock at the prince in Ahmad's place. He couldn't miss Raz's stern and resolute posture as he trotted toward his father, the high king.

"My lord, I have done wrong by my guardsmen and my people by hiding the truth from them. I joust in place of Sir Ahmad in order that by his pursuit and my words we might strengthen the trust of our people and protect not only my family but the Realms from the deceit and treachery from within our own ranks."

"You cannot do this, Theiandar," his father said, his voice still angry but at a lower volume now.

"I can, Father, and I will. I will face Havrik. I will face the traitors and regain the honor I have left off by allowing fear to rule our decisions as high rulers of this kingdom."

"I will not allow this," the king said, vehement.

"I do not need your permission." Theiandar bowed his head and pulled the reins to direct the horse back to the center. "People of the Twelve Realms! Hear me now."

Florian watched him with a sense of alliance. He appreciated this man, the one who faced the people with courage, honor, and respect, and who would one day be their high king. But the dread that what Raz did right this second would forever seal the fate of his sister set his mind on edge. The whispering headache worked its way into the forefront of his skull, and he squeezed his eyes closed, but only after catching sight of Orn on his feet and rubbing the stone around his neck with such rapid strokes it seemed to glow with the touch.

"My people, you have been deceived. Among us is a man who would assume to take my father's throne by treacherous acts, acts that would inevitably cripple our great kingdom with division and distrust. I come before you now, as high prince and future king, to tell you that the powerful Nox who steals the beauty of innocents to sustain his life is alive and has turned our own people against us. He wishes to see our kingdom torn apart and has fed upon the greed of men to do his will. Even today, we are in the presence of these deceivers, and some of them sit among you."

A gasp reverberated through the assemblage. Florian opened his eyes long enough to see people looking at their neighbor with apprehension and fear. Who among them was an ally? Who had turned against the house of Dante in favor of a new ruler? This could go far beyond those of Wyeth and Emlyn.

"Enough of this," the high king bellowed. "The threat is to me and my family, not to the people. You go too far, Theiandar. You stir up fear and division with your words. Be silent."

The high prince ignored his father and said, "If you stand with the house of Dante, show us now. If you value the peace of our kingdom and wish to see them protected from the sickness that is the Beauty Thief, then show us now. Stand with me."

Florian had to witness what Orn might be thinking right then. He stared, wide-eyed, at the ruler whose anger seethed just below the surface while he stood by and watched the peoples of the Realms stand in solidarity with the prince. But soon Orn's attention shifted back to Florian. Their eyes met, and Orn rubbed the stone while his lips moved in a silent order that

Florian's mind heard as if the errant king whispered them directly in his ear.

"Kill Dante now!"

Of its own volition, Florian's hand reached into his tunic and pulled out the Fyll Blade, the shiny steel catching the rays of late morning sun as it beat down. The bright light in his eyes caused him to stumble, but not enough to stop him as he moved toward the king who stood with his back to Florian. He found himself losing the battle against the fear and doubt clouding his mind, while the still, small voice of reason and faith that they would overcome this evil seemed to be altogether snuffed out. He cried out, his arms aching with the internal battle as his muscles tensed to hold the blade at his side and his mind worked to force his hand up toward King Dante's back.

The king swung around at the same instant that the ladies screamed, the horrified shrieks filling Florian's ears as tears blurred his vision. Oh Almighty, was he so weak? He could see the king just standing there in surprise, not moving, not reaching for his own sword, and something inside him fought back, the shaking of his arms working into his fingers gripping the handle of the knife. Only a few seconds had passed, but in that span of time a thousand years flew by for Florian as he fought the splitting of his will. He looked at his knuckles, his mind and body racked by a battle of diverging will and honor, and pried his fingers loose of the blade, letting it fall to the floor at the same instant the royal guardsmen of High King Dante tackled him from the side.

The king, caught unawares, now faced Florian, looking down at him. Florian stared back, utter relief relaxing him in the knights' hold as he rejoiced in knowing he'd overcome whatever awful power had driven him mad. He felt lighter somehow. His only remaining doubt laid in his sister's welfare. But a movement behind the king from atop Orn's spectator box caught his attention. Everyone else looked at Florian. At first he couldn't tell what moved, but then a man stood up and the shadow of him morphed into an archer.

"King Dante! Look out!" Florian cried.

But not in time; never in time.

The arrow, released, hit its mark. As the words rattled from Florian's lips, so too did the life falter in King Dante's eyes. Though his arms were held fast, Florian reached for the king, whose chest displayed the pointed end and smooth shaft. Blood ran down the high king's doublet to match the ruby red of the arrow's head.

* * *

Orn pressed the heels of his hands to his temples and cried out as the pain of his last push on Florian's will drove him over the edge. Until that moment, he'd not realized the stone had caused this awful throbbing in his head. Nox hadn't told him this would happen when using it to control the will of others, the little mongrel of a thief.

He opened his eyes in time to see Florian move forward with the blade, but he couldn't let anything fall to chance. Florian had struggled against the power for too long, and he could sense it even now.

"Kelor, do it!" Orn yelled and waited only long enough to hear the snap of the bowstring and see Dante's body jerk from the impact of the arrow. He grabbed his son's hand and ran from the seating area. The thudding of Prince Theiandar's horse's hooves galloping toward his father almost matched the beat working to crumble the thoughts in Orn's brain as he fled the arena.

He'd lost, but he would not give up. He would escape and do what he'd promised Florian from the beginning. If the guardsman were to betray him, Faye would pay the price, but now it would not be Nox who would gain by her beauty. It would be Orn. He would demand it. The thief owed him. No, Nox would help him gain the kingdom. The little man had power beyond their wildest imaginings, and there must be another way for him to give Orn what he wanted.

* * *

The silence in Florian's ears deafened him as he stared at the king, who looked from him to the arrow in his chest and back before he dropped to his knees and Queen Zoe dropped to kneel next to him. Florian shook his head over and over, the word *no* running through his head without another thought present to stop it.

While staring hard, Dante's weak voice still carried command as he ordered his men to release Florian.

He fell back in shock at the king's commandment and watched as those same guardsmen rushed to their king and lifted him, four of them carrying him from the box and toward the keep. Others ran toward where the archer had shot his arrow. Florian struggled to his feet to see the chaos unfolding as people ran from the stands surrounding the field. Prince Theiandar jumped to the platform, his eyes speaking silent dread as he rushed toward his wife and child. Guardsmen circled around them, their swords drawn.

Florian hadn't expected this, and guilty sorrow crushed any relief. His heart broke to know that his weakness and choices made him culpable for this tragedy and pandemonium.

"Florian!"

Raz's cry gained his attention, but only just.

"Your Highness, I . . . I don't know what happened. I couldn't control it, but I didn't do it. I dropped the knife."

"I know, Florian. I saw. But you must go after Orn. He's escaped from the arena. Stop him."

"My liege," Florian said, his hand to his chest while he bowed and made as if to run from the stands. At the last second, he once again remembered the blade. He turned to look for it, but it was gone. His heart dropped into his stomach and a terrible fear crept over him. Florian frantically searched for a sight of his uncle, but Jeron had disappeared. What if he'd taken the blade?

He ran from the arena, looking every which direction in search of a sign of Jeron or Orn. Both men were a danger. If either of them ended up with that blade, Florian would never forgive himself. He caught sight of his uncle's balding head and rotund form as he jostled through the crowds toward the keep. In his hand, the Fyll Blade glinted in the midday sun.

In a split-second decision Florian chose his path, come what may. His uncle held something over which kingdoms would fall in the pursuit to gain its power, and as Lady Idra had told him, it must not fall into the wrong hands. Jeron had it because of him, and by Almighty, he would not lose himself to weakness and fear ever again. He pushed through the crowds, against the flow of frightened women and children, city folk and nobility alike. His uncle stayed far enough ahead that he could not reach him.

"Jeron!" he yelled over the heads of frightened citizens. "Stop!"

His uncle glanced over his shoulder, and Florian saw the look of utter fright pass over his face before he looked forward and pressed harder through the crowds. The man headed toward the keep. Why, in the name of all wisdom, would the man run farther into the city instead of escaping out of it? Didn't he realize he'd be trapped soon? There was no accounting for Jeron's path, but Florian kept sight of him and pursued with all haste through the busy streets.

He lost track just before reaching the open courtyard to the keep entrance, but once Florian cleared the street, the huge open space appeared almost uninhabited. His uncle's steps lagged, and Florian saw him up the stairway, breathing heavily, where he looked back and their eyes met again. Jeron let out a mad cry and dragged himself through the door, pushing a maid to the ground in his frenzied dash. In the same moment, Florian's jaw clenched, and he ran with renewed vigor toward the stairway and into the keep. The dramatic change in light caused him temporary blindness.

For all Jeron's heftiness, he proved himself rather agile, for as soon as Floria's vision cleared, he found his uncle had reached the top of the stairs.

"Look out!" he said in an urgent voice as he dodged around confused servants and courtesans.

Florian rushed toward Jeron's guest chamber and reached for the latch to throw it open, but he'd barred the door from the inside. Florian pounded his fist against the closed door. "Open this door, Uncle," he demanded, his lips near the wood surface.

From within, he made out the sounds of furniture slamming about and other shuffling noises, but Jeron made no response.

He drew in a breath and released it slowly. "Uncle, you will not escape this place. Think. If you stop now and turn yourself in, you'll live, but if you attempt to flee, you will die. Please. Don't do this."

The rustling from within died down, and on the other side of the door, Jeron spoke. "I will not let you stop me, Nephew. You stupid child."

With that, Jeron flung the bar and jerked the door open, the Fyll Blade held in his shaky grasp and pointed straight at Florian, who took two steps back at the sight of it. He looked from the knife to the insanity in his uncle's eyes and knew the man was not above using the enchanted weapon on him.

"Get out of my way, boy! I'll let you live," Jeron ground out between clenched teeth.

Florian had to stop him or terrible things would happen. That blade belonged to the Beauty Thief, and if he were to ever get it back, Twelve Realms would surely see the pain of its wickedness without mercy.

"No. I can't let you do this."

"You let me do nothing! I let you live those many years ago. Y-your mother's last gurgling breath held your name, an-and your father begged I spare you and your sister. I heard his last request! But I didn't have to do it! I could have killed you both after I killed him and your mother, but I let you live. I will not be taken. Get out of my way, I say!"

Florian's mind halted coherent thought as he absorbed the words his uncle had just spat in his face. "You? You killed them?"

"Yes, you stupid imbecile. Your father may have been firstborn, but I am meant to have my father's lands! Your father had been a sickly child, and our father promised me the world. But my brother grew strong by some villager woman's healing spells, and the world I stood to gain was ripped from me. Orn promised me those lands!"

In that moment, Florian couldn't begin to reconcile what he'd just heard with the stories he'd been told as a boy, stories of Crescent Cave people raiding and killing his parents.

"You killed my parents," he said again, his mind reeling and his flesh tingling as the truth sunk in. "Murderer!"

The cry burst from his lungs with such force that anyone listening might have thought Florian dragged and flung the detestable word out from the depths of the earth as the beast of lore does a man's heart. But the moment only lasted as long as the word, for as soon as he said it, Jeron jabbed the Fyll Blade forward, coming scant centimeters from Florian's chest. He looked from Jeron's cruel face to the blade and back to his dastardly uncle.

While the older man's own efforts distracted him, Florian saw an opportunity to rend the blade from his uncle's hand, but he didn't realize how tight upon the handle Jeron gripped. His hands shot out to tear at his uncle's over the hilt, but Florian couldn't pry it free.

Jeron let loose a cry like a banshee and rammed his heavy body into Florian who, seeing the new attack at the last second, gripped Jeron's hands on the blade handle with both of his own and pressed it upward, his shoulder barely missed by the swipe of the sharp blade as his back slammed into the wall opposite the chamber door. He grunted with the impact, and his heart flipped in his chest. It had been a close call. But his uncle refused to release his hold on the weapon.

Florian exerted as much force as he could gain against the weight of his uncle as the beefy man pressed into him. Jeron held a satchel in his other hand, but dropped it and reached up to pry Florian's fingers loose from the knife. Jeron's grunting, hot breath burned against Florian's neck and cheek as he looked up at their hands, but he refused to let go, and neither would his uncle. Desperate to get off the wall and wrest the blade away, Florian kneed his uncle in the groin, pulled one hand off the blade, and punched it into Jeron's round belly.

Jeron jerked back with a gasp and Florian almost lost his grip on his uncle's weapon hand. He took the opportunity to land another blow to his uncle's jaw, and Jeron stumbled back into the room with Florian in swift pursuit. He jumped, grabbing for Jeron's arms—the Fyll Blade always dangerously close to Florian's body.

During the struggle, he couldn't help thinking of Faye, and in an act that subtly became second nature to him, he lifted a prayer to Almighty that she be saved and protected no matter what fate Florian met this day. Nothing else of substance remained in the world for him but her.

"You were supposed to be easy to bend. Orn's necklace guaranteed your will to be bent," Jeron seethed as he ripped his hand free of Florian's hold.

The image of Orn rubbing the green stone around his neck popped into Florian's mind. He squinted in concentration as the truth dawned on him. Orn tried controlling him with some enchanted stone; Nox the thief had doubtless given over this trick. He shook his head and snarled low in his throat.

"You and that traitor king will not get away with this, and neither will Nox." Florian's voice raised a notch in intensity with each word until he yelled. "I will not fall prey to your evil purposes ever again! I vow to stop you!"

Jeron backed away and Florian witnessed a flash of genuine fear and cowardice blaze across his uncle's face. Jeron appeared to quickly shake off the reaction as he snarled like a dog and leaned forward. Florian knew what to expect in that split second, and both men ran at each other. *This will end now,* Florian thought as their bodies collided in a mishmash of aggression and hatred.

CHAPTER THIRTY-THREE
TRUE REWARD COMES BY HONOR

AS AHMAD NEARED THE CASTLE, he saw droves of people rushing out through the gates and guardsmen doing their best to stop anyone leaving, but unable to stem the tide. But amid the fray on the road, a group of six knights and what appeared to be three women galloped toward the castle. He recognized Lady Hilde and her father's knights, but even while squinting, he couldn't determine who else rode with her until he drew close.

"It couldn't be." He pulled back on the horse's reins and leaned forward in the saddle to stare hard at the one rider. She turned her face and before she laid her head upon the horse's neck, he saw the beauty of the woman he could never forget, so deeply had her presence been etched upon his heart. "Idra."

He lost all awareness of place and time when he recognized her and urged his horse to run, to fly toward her. "Idra!" he yelled. They didn't hear him over the noise of people leaving the city. He cried out again and again until Idra seemed to sense his presence. She sat up with a jerk and just as quickly hunched over again, almost toppling from her horse.

The group of knights and ladies halted, several hands reaching out toward Idra, but her presence stood out like a beacon amidst the escort.

Lady Hilde saw him first. "Tis Sir Ahmad! All of you," she ordered her knights, "clear the way!"

Ahmad watched them part like a heavy gate, as if they were once keeping him from the treasure he valued most. He pulled up hard on the reins and jumped from his steed, running the last ten feet to Idra's side. He took in her stooped posture and the myriad of dark blotches of blood staining every inch of her tattered skirt, and though pain marred her features, joy and waning strength reflected in her eyes even as they clouded with tears.

"Ahmad," she said in a soft voice, "I'm glad to see you." With that, her whole body relaxed, and she slipped from the horse's back, but Ahmad caught her limp form.

"Does she live, Sir Ahmad?" Lady Hilde asked, her voice fraught with trepidation.

His own heart had stopped beating for a second while he watched Idra's face. He lowered her to the ground and put his ear to her mouth. The soft feel of her breath against his skin sent relief flooding through him.

"She lives." There in the path's dirt, he pulled her close in his arms and stroked her hair. "What happened?"

"She would not say, Sir Ahmad," Lady Hilde replied, coming to stand by his side. "She was adamant we return to the castle with great haste."

"I . . . she rescued me from that cave, but those men who guarded us . . ."

Ahmad looked to the girl who'd spoken and saw the resemblance of Florian in her face and cropped hair. Her words had trailed off as a fit of crying overtook her.

"All will be well, Lady Faye. Lady Idra will be well, but I need you to tell me what happened," Ahmad said in as gentle a tone as possible in his panicked state.

She sniffed and nodded as she rubbed the tears from her face, then as quick as she could, told them what had happened: her remanding into the care of King Orn by her uncle; her introduction to a bent and shriveled old man; the journey to the cave; the men who guarded her; Idra's arrival and plan to escape.

"Are we too late?" Idra asked to Ahmad's surprise.

He hadn't realized she'd come to while Faye spoke, and his eyes traveled over her dirty, blood-smudged face. In his mind, he vowed to always protect her—even if she forsook his love.

"I cannot tell. There is a terrible commotion. Something must have caused this mass exodus of the castle. Can you stand?"

Idra frowned and shook her head, reaching for her leg with her unbound arm. Ahmad's eyes followed where her fingers went, and he finally saw what must be the cause of her stark paleness. She must have lost a good deal of blood by the looks of it, but the injury on her leg, though serious, would not kill her.

"I'll carry you with me on my horse."

Lady Hilde had already ordered one of her men to lift Idra from Ahmad's arms permitting him to stand and get on his horse to take her back, but before he even got his foot in the stirrup, Lady Faye gasped and cried out.

"There he is!"

Those who heard turned to see where she pointed, and Ahmad's eyes narrowed in anger. Orn and Havrik raced out on bareback horses from the castle. They came near to trampling citizens in their wake, and Ahmad's fierce anger welled up from the depths. He swung up onto his saddle and slammed his heels into the steed's sides to gallop straight at the two men.

They parted as if to let Ahmad pass between them, but he would have none of it. Ahmad veered toward King Orn with his sword drawn. Orn couldn't halt his momentum, and as Ahmad neared with the sword held forward to strike the traitor king, Orn leaned to the side. He went too far and tumbled from his horse.

Ahmad circled back around and jumped down. He strode over to King Orn, who worked to right himself, and pressed the blade of his sword just under the king's chin, who slowly stood tall. Orn put his hands out as if in surrender, but a flash of something sparked in his eyes. Ahmad noticed, and at the same moment, he heard the combined warning of Lady Hilde and her men.

He swung around just in time to block the thrust of Havrik's sword.

"It's time we finish what we started a few days ago," Havrik taunted.

Ahmad took a fighting stance, with sword in one hand and dagger in the other. "What you've begun can't be undone. You have killed Xavier, and I will not let you leave this place before you've seen the full power of the Duodenocourt's justice."

"I'd rather die," Havrik said, deadly calm, and attacked.

Ahmad blocked again and jabbed with his knife, but he couldn't reach the other man.

* * *

The knight who'd helped Idra up now stood next to her, supporting her to stand on one leg while they watched the battle between Ahmad and Havrik. She noticed Lady's Hilde's men form a circle of protection around them but wouldn't let anything distract her from watching Ahmad. He fought valiantly, his movements a measure of graceful strength and precision. But for every worthy action, Havrik presented an equally vehement reaction.

While they battled, people continued to flee into the countryside. Peasants, lords, ladies, servants. A mass flight of citizens raised the distraction of chaos, but Idra caught sight of something unallowable.

Hilde's knights focused on protecting them from unseen foes and didn't seem to notice as King Orn edged his way further from the two fighting men toward the horse Ahmad had been riding.

"Someone give me a knife," Idra said to the group surrounding them.

To her surprise, Hilde handed her one. Idra let go of the knight who'd been helping her to stand. She limped forward, pushing their protection aside, and cringed at the agony of pain ripping from her thigh up her spine and down to her toes. Idra gritted her teeth, took another step, and aimed the knife.

Orn looked over at her at that exact second, and she watched his eyes widen in shock just before he turned to run. She took one last breath and lobbed the blade at him, praying it would strike. The world around the knife and Orn blurred into nothingness as she watched it sail toward him and strike his shoulder. Upon impact, the world came back into focus, and she listened to him cry out in pain as he fell to his knees.

Hilde yelled for some of her men to stop him, which they did. Their appraising expressions of astonishment and respect when they looked back at Idra caught her by surprise and, for some reason, gave her a weary sense of accomplishment; she'd stopped Orn from escaping, and it satisfied knowing he'd see justice. But as the adrenaline of the moment subsided, she lost strength in her legs and tumbled to the dirt where Lady Hilde and Faye both hastened to kneel on either side of her, the remaining knights making a wall between them and the fighting.

Idra didn't acknowledge them, though she knew they were there for her. Instead, her eyes and mind . . . her heart . . . her soul, entirely focused on Ahmad. She stared at him on one knee, blade edge in one hand, hilt in the other, while he pushed back on Havrik's sword. A dizziness overtook her senses while her fingers dug into the tattered material of her skirt. Ahmad had lost his knife in the fray, but the determined look on his face did not waver, and that became her remaining comfort.

Havrik, though, grew angrier by the second. His swings were wild, and once his eyes darted to where Lady Hilde's knights held Orn, he seemed to lose all sense of control. He screeched and raised his sword high, and Idra's hand shot out as if of its own accord, as if she had the ability to stop the false knight from harming her love. And in that second, Ahmad got to his feet, the hilt of his sword in both hands, and lunged under Havrik's raised arms, where the blade of his arming sword pierced through the traitorous knight's exposed neck.

Havrik's arms instantly relaxed, and he dropped his sword, but Idra turned her face away and covered her mouth, unable to gaze upon the carnage left behind. Enervation overcame her like a wave as her muscles relaxed and Lady Hilde cradled her. *Thank Almighty*, she thought. Ahmad lived. She loathed to see any more death. Her memory seemed crushed under the weight of the violence she'd already experienced.

Within seconds, powerful arms scooped her up, and she cried out as jostling sent the pain of her arm and leg injuries shooting through her body once again.

"Almighty, Idra. I'm sorry," Ahmad said, short of breath.

Her eyes squeezed closed tighter, but she gave a short nod and leaned into him. He smelled of leather, the tang of metal, and the musk of sweat, but she reveled in the scent of him and the strength of his arms. Idra opened her eyes and peered into his, where the terrible longing she endured, one that consumed her waking and sleeping, reflected at her. She wrapped her fingers into his wild auburn hair and pulled his head down to meet hers, their lips pressed together in passionate, tender abandon. She held him there against her and let tears—both from joy and sorrow, pain and relief—slip from her eyes.

Ahmad pulled away first, his forehead pressed to hers. "Idra, I love you."

"And I you," she whispered, her lips a scant inch from his.

He kissed her this time, gentle and sure.

CHAPTER THIRTY-FOUR
WILL UNBROKEN

FLORIAN STARED DOWN, HIS JAW slack and hands shaking. Tears pooled in his eyes. He didn't know if he'd ever see Faye again. And one of the few people with the knowledge of how to rescue her, before the Beauty Thief ruined her, now lay dead at his feet. It had been an instant death as soon as Jeron had rolled over onto the blade held in Florian's hand. His own hand. He'd been the one to kill Jeron, and his feelings on the matter were in such a jumble he couldn't see straight.

On one part, he saw his uncle, his father's brother. On the other, he acknowledged the murderer of his parents and a traitor to not just him, but the entirety of Twelve Realms.

Florian lowered himself to the floor next to Jeron and rested his hand, still gripped on the Fyll Blade, on the hard surface beside him. Unwelcome tears dropped from his eyes. He wiped them away. In that moment of despair, a sound so familiar, and yet only a distant memory, filled his ears. Did he dream it?

"Florian!" the voice cried again, and the fog of nightmare seemed to lift little by little. He stared at the open doorway, unmoving as a rock, and willed it to be her.

Suddenly, Lady Hilde's swishing skirts and stern visage filled the doorway, and Florian's hope dwindled to almost nothing. His shoulders slumped.

"He's here!" Lady Hilde cried down the hall as she leaned forward with her hands on either side of the door frame, panting as if she'd been running.

Florian squinted and wondered to whom she spoke. He thought it must be someone come to drag him off to the dungeon, a fate he well deserved. He warranted nothing better. He hauled himself up and placed the Fyll Blade on the table behind him where he rested his fingertips on the jewels worked perfectly into the handle, and he imagined the color of Faye's hair, the sparkle in her eye. With his head bowed, the tears he'd been holding back slipped out, pelting the dainty lace cloth covering the table. He stared at the drop that hit the blade and wiped the remaining sadness from his eyes.

"Florian?" A questioning voice, a gentle and softly familiar tone, froze him in place. He had to dare the dream to be real.

He lifted his head, desperately seeking the face which had haunted his dreams these last weeks. There, behind the beaming Lady Hilde, stood his sister. Faye's eyes shimmered, and her chopped-off hair danced wildly around her shoulders. A mess of dirt and stains covered her dress, but her beauty shone through. Her youth. And that smile. She was set free.

His lips parted and he shook his head. The dream had become a hallucination. He didn't believe it. This nightmare might never end. He watched the apparition of his sister look upon their dead uncle and back up at him, her eyes compassionate and otherworldly. Seeing that look on her face shattered his heart into a thousand pieces as it pierced his soul.

"I-forgive me, Faye," he told his dream through the thickness of tears blocking his throat. "I'm sorry."

"Oh, Fidget," she said and stepped around the man, who, even in death, tried to come between them, 'tis not your fault. And for all you might have done, I forgive you. You are my brother and I love you."

He wanted this to be real, to not be imagining it, but the air felt too heavy, suffocating him. He thought he might have died until her hand reached up and cupped his cheek while she tilted her face in the same way their mother used to do when he had misbehaved; there encapsulated were love and disappointment and good humor.

"Almighty," he said. His lips parted, and he leaned forward an inch. "You're real."

Faye laughed, a tiny, soft giggle, but confusion drifted through her eyes. "Of course I'm real."

He didn't believe but he did. And suddenly he didn't care about reality anymore. This was his sister, safe and sound. She was away from Orn, away from their uncle, away from the grasping greed of the Beauty Thief. If this existed all as a dream, Florian yearned to embrace it. He grabbed her up in his arms and squeezed tight.

"By Almighty, you are safe! Thank you, Great One," he said and never meant it more than in that moment.

"Put me down. You're killing me," she said half out of breath, half full of unrepentant joy.

He put her down and touched her face, slid his hands down her arms, and looked for any sign of injury. Other than her hair and a few bruises, she looked well, and he almost couldn't reconcile the truth before him with the many horrible pictures he'd imagined.

"How are you here now?"

Her soft smile twisted his heart, repairing its brokenness. "Lady Idra saved me."

"Lady Idra . . . saved you?"

"You mustn't say it so, Fidget. Lady Idra took on the two guards in the cave and set us free. If not for her, I don't know what might have happened to me."

Lady Idra rescued his sister. Would wonders never cease? Not him, not anything he did or did not do saved her. The conflicted feelings of the truth of that statement were both a relief and a stabbing finger of guilt. He'd been at fault for Lady Idra being taken. He'd probably done more harm than good throughout the ordeal.

"Thank you for sending her to me," she said, her words breaking through his silent self-abasement.

"I didn't."

"But you did. She said so. She said Almighty's love had crossed your paths, and he sent her for me . . . or something of that nature."

He frowned at her. "Where is Lady Idra?" The sudden sense that she had not made it trampled over his peace at finding his sister well.

"Sir Ahmad has taken her to her chamber to be cared for. She was injured in the struggle. But she will be well," she added in haste.

He pulled her into the circle of his embrace. He had much to be thankful for, but he had to enjoy it now, in this moment, because soon he would see darkness and misery for the part he played in the treasonous attack on High King Dante, who Florian assumed even now fought for his life.

Florian had much to do to atone for his actions. Lady Idra rescued Faye. His uncle had met his demise, and the Fyll Blade would be safe from Nox. He held Faye at arm's length with a split-second decision half formed.

"Faye, I need you to trust me now. I know I don't deserve it, but can you?"

"Of course."

He looked to Lady Hilde, still standing just outside the room. "My lady, would you take charge of my sister and keep her safe?"

Lady Hilde's face showed her surprise, and she didn't bother hiding her pleased expression as she said, "Certainly, Sir Florian. It would honor me to shelter your sister. She will be safe with me. I swear."

Strange . . .. He'd never imagined Lady Hilde would need to make such little effort to be generous and kind. He stared at her determined face, but the twinkle of mischief hidden behind her long lashes drew him. "Thank you, my lady." He looked back at Faye. "Go with Lady Hilde and no one else. Do you understand?"

"Yes, Fidget, but can't I come with you?"

The look of fear and hurt she wore almost caused him to cave in and never let her leave his side, but where he needed to go, she could not. He had a duty to uphold. His fealty was sworn and he would stand by his word. "No, but do not fear. Lady Hilde and her knights are worthy and brave. You will be safe, and I will see you again. Soon."

He kissed the top of her head and walked out the door, but before he strode past Lady Hilde, she reached out and grabbed his arm. He looked at her pale fingers on the dark material of his tunic and then up into the entreaty of her eyes. He never realized how nearly purple they were.

"You are an honorable man, Sir Florian. The high king will not forget this."

His jaw clenched involuntarily at her soft-spoken confidence. Once he might have believed that of himself, but not today. Not after everything he'd done to hide what King Orn and his own uncle were planning and had almost succeeded at doing. She let go and he walked away, his shoulders erect though his spirit cowered within.

* * *

For the first time in three hundred years, the naming ceremony of a future high king of Twelve Realms was a closed affair, one where only the royal family and the members of the Duodenocourt were allowed attendance. Ahmad and the others of High Prince Theiandar's elite royal guardsmen were stationed about the family chapel, and he couldn't take his eyes off Raz. Prince Theiandar cradled his son and let the tears fall from his eyes without care to who might see. It brought the emotional turmoil of the circumstances to the surface of Ahmad's own heart and set him on edge.

Yes, they'd stopped Orn from escaping. Yes, Raz had possession of the Fyll Blade, safely stored in the king's vault. Yes, Idra lived, and so too, Florian's sister, Faye. But High King Dante, peaceful ruler of Twelve Realms, was dead.

The arrow shot from the stands had been drenched in poison and it pierced his lung. The damage of the arrow itself, paired with the poison, had pulled the king from their world into the next in a matter of hours. It had been a wonder to the physician that he'd lasted as long as he had.

Ahmad and Idra arrived at the king's chamber and were allowed entrance in time to witness his final words to his son, his wife, and his daughter. Ahmad had never seen Raz cry like that. The gut-wrenching agony of Queen Zoe's wailing still echoed through his memory as a sound he would not be like to ever forget.

High King Dante had charged his son to complete the ceremony and ensure his grandson's place as the next ruler. He spoke of forgiveness. He asked it of those he loved most in the world, and instructed them to serve justice upon Orn and his treason, but also to bring a stop to the Beauty Thief who plagued their kingdom. On his dying breath, he made Theiandar promise that once crowned high king he would pursue peace with Crescent Cave by any means necessary.

Raz only nodded then begged his father to live.

Almighty had other plans. High King Dante left them, as no one ever imagined. Raz had gone silent after that and had barely spoken two words together since yesterday. Princess Caityn had cried, holding her husband as he wept for his father, but it was she who'd taken charge of the naming ceremony, of cloistering it away in the chapel instead of the huge cathedral. She wrote the letters to be taken throughout the kingdom to announce the high king's death and her son's ceremony being complete.

Ahmad marveled at how strong Idra had become, how little she complained in the face of her injuries. He looked at her now, at the front of the chapel, sitting next to Princess Caityn and holding her hand. She'd refused to miss the ceremony and had to be carried in, but her fierce love for her family drove her to fight the misery. Idra embodied every bit of the honor Raz called for in his men.

Thinking about it reminded Ahmad of Raz's words to Florian earlier that morning. He pointed the duplicity and tragedy at Nox, who had worked his power, weaving it as a thread through the intricate tapestry of their lives with the intent to ruin. It had been quite the design he created, but his greed and revenge only went so far. Raz had pardoned Florian but said, *"Honor is what we make of our lives. It is who we are in our marrow, and who we will stay in the face of all uncertainty."*

Ahmad would cling to those words from this day forward. They would, each of them, always remember because Florian's pardon came as a call to a brotherhood stronger than flesh and blood. Honor held truth and trust in highest regard.

* * *

She leaned on the crutch she'd been provided the night before and watched as High Prince Theiandar, Caityn, and the officially named High Prince Bastien Dante led the Procession of Accord through the city streets. A herald strode before them, announcing the completion of the ceremony and the joy of the future high king.

The celebration mingled with a heavy sense of apprehension for the future, but Idra trusted Almighty's ways were not theirs, and his plan would be as it should be for the best. This did not mean they would stand by and let the cards fall where they may, but that their lives and choices and outcomes were part of something worthy and beautiful, in the perfect will of the creator of all.

In the stillness of her sorrow, Idra sensed something sinister still lurking in the shadows. She remembered the warning of Sabine's dreams—or her actual presence among them—was not to be taken lightly, and she shivered as the impression of being watched coursed through her veins. Nox was out there wating. Waiting for what? She could not say.

But even in the future's unknown, Idra vowed that the treason of yesterday would not mar the beauty of today. The past stood as a marker on time, but it did not dictate the future, and neither did the Beauty Thief. Not if she had any say in what lay ahead.

She reached out for Ahmad's hand as he stood silently beside her on the keep's stairs. The warmth of his fingers acted as a solace for her spirit. In the most precious ways, Ahmad was her steady rock; she trusted him. He'd proved time and again that his love and devotion went beyond gallantry to the depths of his soul, and hers answered back with a resounding yes.

CHAPTER THIRTY-FIVE
SEALED WITH A KISS

AHMAD SAT WITH FLORIAN IN the high king's strategy room and awaited the arrival of Raz. A servant announced the prince's presence at the door, and they both stood. Ahmad did not know what thoughts swirled through Florian's mind right then.

It had been two weeks since the tourney and the death of the high king. Raz carried with him a new solemnity, his once youthful edge all but eaten up in a terrible mourning that matched the dark band they each wore on their arms. Ahmad and the others were finding it difficult to grow accustomed to this change in him, this loss, which was made wholly apparent as Raz, the soon-to-be new high king, stepped into the room and waved them to sit again before taking a chair next to Ahmad.

"Thank you both for coming. In light of . . ." Raz cleared his throat in the heavy, uncomfortable silence lingering in the room. "Because of the consequences wrought by King Orn's treachery, I require your skills for a mission. I would do this myself, but I must remain here and bring to justice those who've participated in treason against the high crown."

"We are yours to command, Sire," Ahmad said, only hesitating as a thought of Idra forced its way to the forefront of his mind.

"I have considered long and hard the fate of Sabine of the Crescents, and I have concluded that she is integral to discovering a solution to counteract the Fyll Blade's curse, something she herself has confirmed might be possible. It is our duty to do everything in our power to see Sir Xavier healed."

"I was wrong in how I behaved toward Sir Xavier, Raz. I deeply regret it and want nothing more than to save him where I could not do so with his brother."

"I thought you might say that. Tis good and right. Now, as far as the young woman is concerned, she is essential in our fight to stop Nox once and for all."

"She's been a prisoner here long enough, Raz."

"She will remain as our guest, then."

"I promised her she could return home when this was all through. And beyond that, how can her terrifying dreams even begin to truly help us stop that man? He's more ancient than the crumbling castle ruins on the hill. For Almighty's sake, he's older than the Realms!"

Raz folded his hands on the table. The stern look he wore held a reminder of the countenance of the prince's father, one that took Ahmad by surprise; he'd never noticed the resemblance before.

"Ahmad, I realize you have taken a vested interest in her life, but she has information beyond her dreams. She knows these people, the Nokt, who seem to have an ancient knowledge of Nox, or Skotos, or whatever he is called. That very relationship will prove invaluable in learning his weaknesses. And before you protest again, Sabine has already agreed to take you to them."

"I can't leave," Ahmad said with finality, unwilling to acquiesce for several reasons beyond Sabine's welfare; one such being his unspoken vow to stay by Idra's side. How could he leave her again?

"You must and you will."

"But what of my sister?" Florian asked, his voice quiet and edged with trepidation, but successful in disrupting the intensity between Ahmad and Raz.

Raz turned his attention to Florian. "She will be safe and looked after. Princess Caityn insisted that if Faye was amenable, she wants her for lady-in-waiting. She would be here at the castle and protected as my wife is. Lady Faye would have a position of esteem and respect among the Realms."

Ahmad glanced at Florian, who looked like he had swallowed a fly and choked on it.

"My lord. Do not jest with me," Florian said after regaining his voice.

"No jesting, my friend. My wife sees in people their hidden potential, their worthiness veiled by life and circumstances. But unlike most, she will look beyond those things which mask the goodness in humanity.

"She believes you and your sister have been grievously mistreated from your youth, and she wishes to protect your sister and give her a new life with unimagined possibilities. Of course, Lady Faye must give up certain freedoms for this honor, privilege, and responsibility."

He paused and waited for their full attention. "The princess has already visited your sister at Hamlin House on several occasions the last two weeks and has not come to this decision lightly. And she reported to me that your sister has said yes on the condition that you agree. Judging by the look on your face, Florian, I would assume your sister has said nothing to you about Princess Caityn's visits."

Ahmad openly stared at Florian now, his face mirroring the shock on his fellow guardsman's. Florian shook his head, confirming what the prince had just relayed. Faye had kept it all a secret.

"Tis well, Florian. My wife asked that she speak of it to no one until a decision had been made."

"Yes, Sire," Florian finally said. "I don't know what to say, but thank you. Thank you on behalf of myself and my sister. After what my uncle did and what they attempted to make me do, I . . . I thought I would I hang. Though I never intended to go through with it, by that stone King Orn wore, Sire, I lost the will to fight in the fear of my sister's fate. I do not know who I became, but on the day your father . . . that day, I almost gave in to whatever force he wielded. It was my weakness, and I betrayed you in it. I deserve to hang."

"No, Florian. That is not true. You have already received an official pardon. I believe what you suffered under is real, as real as the curse upon Xavier and that which once stole my beloved," the prince said, interrupting Florian. "Please, say no more. My father's sternness verged on harsh at times, but he knew the risks and trusted you with his life, like I do. I am revealing this to you and you alone. You must not repeat this outside this room. He told me, the night before the final day of the tourney, after I'd explained everything to him, that he felt responsible for all of it, including what you suffered at the hands of these pernicious men. He didn't explain everything, but he said he'd known in his heart that Orn could not be trusted from the day he'd been crowned king of Wyeth at sixteen."

Ahmad saw the unmistakable sheen of tears glassing over Florian's eyes as his jaw clamped tight and he nodded. Both prince and guardsman had lost their fathers to violence and greed. No words need be spoken after that. Florian had been given full pardon in the misdeeds of King Orn. If Ahmad knew Florian as well as he thought he did, he was sure Florian would spend the rest of his life proving his loyalty to the prince . . .

soon-to-be high king . . . and would never again let his honor falter.

"Ahmad," Raz said and brought his attention back around.

"Yes, Sire."

Ahmad knew the prince was about to reiterate his plan for Ahmad and Florian to leave on this quest to find an answer to the curse of the Fyll Blade, but he couldn't get Idra's face out of his head.

"There is somewhere I think you must be before you leave on this journey. My wife tells me a certain lady is waiting and must wait no longer. It was rather cryptic, but she said you would understand."

"Sire?"

"Now is the time," Raz said, his simple statement like a key unlocking a forbidden door.

Ahmad never expected Princess Caityn to take on another lady-in-waiting; she'd had many young ladies offered up by hopeful nobles over the years, and she'd refused every one. And part of him feared that particular condition would come between him and Idra because she was Caityn's sole companion, but with Faye's presence that changed things. A slow grin spread across his face as the prince's implications dawned on him.

For the first time in weeks, a crack of a smile appeared on Raz's face. "Go to her."

Ahmad's skin tingled as he slowly pushed up from the chair. He looked between the other two men, who both nodded, and without a backward glance, strode from the room. He'd no idea where to find Idra, but find her he would.

An almost frantic search of the keep finally led him to Princess Caityn's salon where, with as much respect as he could muster, he knocked on the door and pushed it open. Inside sat Princess Caityn, Ladies Hilde and Faye, and his own Idra, her wide brown eyes alight with shocked confusion and a glint of pleasure. He reached for his tunic to pull it smooth and ran a hand through his unruly hair, taking a deep breath to quell the rush of emotion churning in his gut.

He was reluctant to look away from Idra's face, but the high princess deserved his respect, which he paid with a bow. The slight upturn of her lips displayed her amusement, and he returned the smile with a lopsided grin of his own.

"Your Highness."

"Sir Ahmad. To what do we owe this . . . pleasure?"

"Princess," he started and halted as what he'd come to say became more real to him than ever before. "I come to beg the Lady Idra of Tanfield of Taisce to be my wife."

"Oh. By all means, sir. I believe we are in one accord when I say we have been waiting for this moment for far too long."

Ahmad suppressed a grimace, but the cheerful, pleased look on the princess's face caused him to laugh. Ladies Hilde and Faye giggled as heat crept up his neck, and he found himself afraid to look Idra's way.

Princess Caityn stood, followed by the aforementioned ladies, who all filed from the room. He watched them go, unable to face the one person he wanted to see but with whom he also feared to speak. Once he secured her affection, he'd then have to dash both their hopes with the revelation of his duty to the high prince. How could he possibly ask this of her or even fathom leaving her again?

He squeezed his fist closed, trapping all his growing tension in it, and faced her, not willing to let the unknown of the future keep him from asking for the one thing he had wanted from the moment Idra had been captured with the princess by thugs in the woods of Nevin. He'd fallen in love with this brave, selfless woman then, and he loved her even more now.

But as he stared at her, every doubt and fear surfaced, choking back any words he might have come to say. She gazed back, her hands hidden deep in the folds of her skirt. She loosed them and wiped her palms along the material against her thighs, but her eyes stayed trained on Ahmad, who took in every detail of her presence.

He'd burst through the door only a minute before, but time slowed as he gazed into the deep well of her soul. How could he ask her for this, knowing he could be gone for months, possibly years?

He unwillingly succumbed to the traitorous rationality of his mind as he recognized the selfishness of expecting her to wait for his return from this quest. But he had to beg for the chance anyway. He swallowed his pride and spoke, his voice soft with overwhelming, unsearchable emotion.

"Before I trespass any further upon your heart, Idra, I must tell you I have been ordered to leave on a mission for the prince to take Sabine and gain answers from the Nokt. I don't know when I will return." His voice wavered like a candle in the breeze.

Just say it, you idiot!

How could he leave her? The crestfallen look on her face almost did him in. He contemplated refusing to obey the prince's orders.

"I don't want to leave you," he said quickly, speaking his strongest thought out loud.

In a sudden move, Ahmad crossed the room and dropped to his knee before her. His heart hammered and his hands shook, but he grabbed up both of hers and squeezed them while he bent forward and placed his forehead against her knuckles.

"Then it's settled. I'm coming with you. Surely Sabine will need a chaperone."

Her soft-spoken words held a finality. She pulled her fingers free of his grasp and placed them on either side of his head, lifting his reluctant gaze to meet hers. He truly hated to face her, but her words surprised him.

"No," he said, lacking any genuine conviction, while he greedily relished the warmth of her palms on his face. "It will be dangerous. Idra, don't you see? I need you safe, and . . . I cannot ask you to wait for me."

There. He'd said it, and the stab of the relinquishment twisted deeper into his heart than he ever imagined.

"I love you, Ahmad, but why must you be such a fool?"

Her question robbed him of speech, and the removal of her hands from his face did the same of every vestige of warmth from his body. He froze in a mixture of confusion, fear, and—dare he admit it?—hope. Dastardly hope that sent him spiraling through a myriad of emotions.

She stood to her feet and stepped around him, but he continued to stare at the place on the settee she'd just vacated. Her voice came from behind him.

"You think you have a choice as far as my going or staying is concerned? Hardly. Caity will see the wisdom of my going. And how dare you tell my princess that you come to ask for my hand in marriage and then say such a heartless, selfish thing to me."

Ahmad frowned, realizing that's exactly what he'd done. He rose to his feet and faced her, but what he saw made him want to fall to his knees again and beg her forgiveness. His words had obviously hurt her somehow. Her chest rose and fell in steady huffs of indignation that matched the beautiful fire lighting her eyes.

"Oh Almighty, how I love you, Idra." He didn't have any other words in the face of her heated, strangely alluring outrage.

He took a step toward her, but stopped. Idra's eyes shimmered and her lip quivered. It came near to breaking his heart.

"You say you love me, Ahmad, and when you have moved so close I can *feel* the breath of your soul, twice you hesitate behind your duty. Do you truly love me, or is it only the thought of me?"

He was pushing her away; by giving her this out, he'd thought he was being selfless, but she was right. It was selfish of him to force it upon her, especially when he'd made his feelings for her so plain. There was only one way to prove to her she was all he wanted, and that was to trust her implicitly, but especially with her own life.

"I am a fool. Every kind of fool. With you, I . . . well, I can't seem to think rationally. You, Idra. You rule this unworthy man I am the most selfish man alive because your well-being above anyone else's is all I care about for my own pleasure. But I am more selfish because I want to drag you with me, even to hell and back, just to have you by my side, to never have to say goodbye in this life."

He took a steadying breath, stepping closer to her when she remained silent, her face frozen in an unreadable mask.

"I love you, though I don't deserve you. And I will continue to be a fool, a selfish idiot, if you will promise to be my wife. Could live with that, with me, knowing what a stupid man I am?"

It was her turn to look surprised, and seeing her mouth drop open gave him the courage to continue in his stupidity. He closed the gap between them, leaving scant inches, and reached for her hands, wrapping his fingers between hers and holding them palm to palm.

"I love you, Idra. Will you be my wife? Can you risk your life, with me, for this kingdom?"

She stepped back and a surge of trepidation shot through him. She slid her fingers from between his, but her hands never left his as she pressed his palms out and up so that their fingertips faced the ceiling from between.

"Yes," she said.

Her answer had come with such simplicity that Ahmad doubted his ears. He searched her eyes, and finding what he wanted in the depths, a burst of pure joy shot from the deepest reaches of his soul. He ignored every doubt that surfaced in that second and leaned down, his arms encircling her now, and pressed his lips to hers.

She leaned back, breaking the kiss. "Marry me," she whispered, her expression earnest, "tonight. Under the light of the waxing moon, when the trees still carry leaves and their rustling speaks the promise of new life to come."

He studied her, at a loss for words. At first he only nodded, but as the image of their future together sunk in, a weight lifted from him he hadn't even realized he carried.

"I have agonized over you every time you have been out of my sight. I want you for my wife, Idra. I thought I could live without you, but I have loved you when hope seemed lost, and I have desired you in the quiet moments where distance has parted us." He brushed her hair from her forehead, the soft tendrils tickling the backs of his fingers. "I want that no more. I want you in my arms . . . and by my side. Always."

Idra bit her lip and blinked back tears threatening to spill. She nodded and whispered, "You are for me and I for you."

He lifted her feet from the ground, bringing her face level with his. His lips were scant inches from hers, but he hesitated amidst savoring her tantalizing nearness and rested his forehead on hers. She slipped her arms around his shoulders as he lowered her to stand.

They stayed like that for more time than Ahmad could count, he was so lost in the vision of reality.

* * *

The bright glow of the moon overhead, the soft rustle of leaves in the breeze, the soothing sound of flute and lyre playing from the base of the knoll, and the silhouette of two halves of one whole ensconced within the glittering night sky.

It would have been beautiful—the clandestine wedding of Sir Ahmad to Lady Idra—if not for the fact that Nox could not live with their happiness. Their lives were joined with that of his enemy, and he would see them suffer. All of them.

<<<<<< the end >>>>>>

. . . for now . . .

Love Never Fails.
1 Corinthians 13:8a

Main Characters:

Sir Ahmad – Prince Theiandar's 2nd, his most trusted guardsman. His loyalty to the Realms and his heartbreak from thinking Lady Idra loves another send him to the borders of Emlyn to protect the kingdom against invasion by Crescent Cave, but he returns home to some surprising changes when the child of the high prince is born.

Lady Idra – Princess Caityn's lady-in-waiting and cousin. She's used to blending into the background, but since Caityn's marriage to the high prince she has found herself in an unwelcome spotlight, which often puts her in the way of disreputable characters waiting for any opportunity to gain position or wealth. She loves Ahmad, but he didn't give her a chance to explain before he practically ran away.

Sir Florian – on of Prince Theiandar's twelve elite royal guardsman. His position puts him in a place to easily betray the high royals, especially when the life of his only sister is threatened. His parents were killed when he was a child before he and his sister, Faye, went to live with their Uncle Jeron near Wyeth Castle.

King Orn – Middle-aged king of Wyeth, a northern realm. He's a selfish, dissatisfied ruler who fell under the charm-ful (charming-harmful) deceit of Nox who his men discovered near-dead in the cave at Ophira's Peak. He and Jeron (Sir Florian's uncle), along with various other lower rulers in the kingdom have plotted to overthrow High King Dante with the help of some magical items from Nox's storerooms.

Other Characters:
Primaries –
Nox – The Beauty Thief. He didn't die in that fall, and that will
prove to be the undoing of the peace of Twelve Realms
Sir Xavier – Prince Theiandar's newest guardsman, taking the
place of his deceased brother Hanif from Parlan
Jeron – Sir Florian's uncle from Wyeth. He raised Florian and
his sister, Faye, after their parents were killed.
Sabine – A sixteen-year-old Crescent Cave girl. Thought to be a
spy, but she's so much more. Her life is irrevocably
intertwined with that of the Beauty Thief.
Faye – Sir Florian's younger sister, also sixteen years old. Faye
insisted her brother take the commission to become a
guardsman of the high prince even though she knew it
would take her brother far away from her and leave her in
the care of their less-than-kind uncle Jeron.
Secondaries –
Sir Havrik of Wyeth (King Orn's most trusted knight)
Lady Hilde of Hamlin (Friend to Idra & Ahmad)
High Prince Theiandar/Raz & High Princess Caityn
Sir Gavin & Sir Zaccur (more of Theiandar's guardsmen)
Other knights
Merin (King Orn's distant cousin who acts as a valet of
sorts)
Bit parts –
Kelor & Jass (Employees of Orn, low ranking soldiers)
High King Dante
Captain Jericho @ Emlyn border
Sir Drew @ Castle Emlyn
King Ekreton @ Castle Emlyn
Steward Wayne (steward of Castle Wyeth)
Noreeta (Idra's lady's maid)

ACKNOWLEDGMENTS

Dear reader, there are several people to whom I owe a debt I cannot pay, and so I will attempt to say a word of gratitude here. First off, I thank **you** kindly for spending your precious time with me and this story! We love you for it!

I'm sure it will fall terribly short, and I'll forget at least one important, beautiful person, but if that happens, I hope I won't alienate those who matter the most to me, you reader and you helper, who have supported and cared. Many thanks!

I've adored my editor, Susan Hughes, who has been fun, professional, and thoughtful during the years we've worked together. She continues to be one of my sweetest supporters.

Then there's that husband of mine, Karl, who continues to say, "You have to do it. You can do it." He's simply the best! My kids have made the occasional "Ugh, Mom's at it again," annoyed comment, but they always love on me and support this dream job of mine. Sometimes they're even excited about it. Then there are my parents (love you, Mom and Dad!), my in-laws, sisters-in-laws, aunts, uncles, cousins, nieces & nephews, church family, sweet friends. *gulps* The blubbering of thankfulness is about to commence. *deep breath* It's a lot to be thankful for.

I will happily mention, in deepest gratitude, all my dear beta readers and critique partners. These people make me so happy with their diligent efforts to read my manuscript, offer advice, and catch pesky typos. So, there's the girl that has been there from the beginning, my deary Sheila, who never fails to make me feel like I've accomplished the feat of climbing the steepest mountain with nothing but a pen and my wits with every manuscript. The super supporters are this varied lot, all of whom I adore: Kristi C, Stephanie K, J.A. Merkel, Niki Breeser

Tschirgi, Auntie Robbin, and Erin Wissing! I also want to thank this round of lovely-minded and gentle-hearted folks by the names of Catherine K, Colin G, S.T. Capps, and Kevin Cooper. Phew! I feel like I've run out of breath.

There are also my much-appreciated blogging buddies. I wish I could list them all here, but I have a feeling that would turn out something like another book. You know who you are! I love meeting new people and making friends. It's a huge blessing to be able to connect from a distance.

All cover art and design is mine. On the original cover, the sword is actually two different ones that both belong to my brother, Aaron, who so graciously let me take photographs of his equipment. Thank you for helping make the cover of *The Treasonous* a piece of art.

And lastly, but most importantly, I'm so thankful to God for giving me the opportunity to write and share stories. He's my hope in trials and my joy in all things. He has given me faith, hope and love. There is no one else who fulfills the deepest need of my soul and gives the beauty in life that sustains the days and holds the world together.

ABOUT THE AUTHOR

Rachael Ritchey is a writer of action-packed no-spice romance and adventure fantasy and science fiction and is a freelance book designer. As a creative jack of all trades, she loves inventive, useful work and learning new things.

She's the author of the adventurous fantasy series Chronicles of the Twelve Realms and published *The Crux Anthology* by sixteen international authors, several books of poetry by her amazing daughter, and takes on challenging projects as a book designer and graphic artist for other talented indie authors.

When she's not working on books, you can find Rachael homeschooling, dreaming up stories, keeping the laundry monster at bay, singing at the kitchen sink or in church, reading all the words, drinking coffee way too late into the day, and agonizing over what to make for dinner—Every. Single. Night. Rachael lives in the rural wilds of Florida's panhandle, avoiding fire ants and having a good laugh or two with her adorable, bearded husband and pretty amazing kids.

www.rachaelritchey.com
@RachaelRitchey on Instagram
@RachaelRitcheyAuthor on Facebook

www.ingramcontent.com/pod-product-compliance
Lightning Source LLC
Chambersburg PA
CBHW072202130726
47910CB00011B/1785